DEAD
BEAUTIFUL

DEAD BEAUTIFUL

YVONNE WOON

USBORNE

For Ted Malawer
and Nathaniel Greenberg,
without whom this book would not exist.

First published in the UK in 2011 by Usborne Publishing Ltd., Usborne House, 83-85 Saffron Hill, London EC1N 8RT, England. www.usborne.com

Copyright © 2010 by Yvonne Woon

Published by arrangement with Hyperion, an imprint of Disney Book Group, 114 Fifth Avenue, New York, NY 10011-5690, USA.

The right of Yvonne Woon to be identified as the author of this work has been asserted by her in accordance with the Copyright, Designs and Patents Act, 1988.

Cover photography: Girl by Elizabeth May/Trigger Image; Trees by Digital Vision.

The name Usborne and the devices ♀ 🎈 are Trade Marks of Usborne Publishing Ltd.

A CIP catalogue record for this book is available from the British Library.

ISBN 9781409530244

Just one *kiss*

will take your breath away...

CONTENTS

And when one of them meets with his other half...the pair are lost in an amazement of love and friendship and intimacy, and one will not be out of the other's sight...even for a moment: these are the people who pass their whole lives together, and yet they could not explain what they desire of one another. For the intense yearning which each of them has towards the other does not appear to be the desire of lover's intercourse, but of something else which the soul of either evidently desires and cannot tell, and of which she has only a dark and doubtful presentiment.

—Plato, *Symposium*

PROLOGUE

I DIDN'T KNOW ANYTHING ABOUT DEATH until I began studying philosophy. That was how I learned the truth about Descartes, about the ancient Greek and Roman civilizations, about my past. My mother used to tell me that matter was neither created nor destroyed, only transferred. She was filled with old theories that she would make me recite back to her, as if she were trying to tell me something about the world but couldn't find the right words. I never gave them much thought until she and my father were killed, but by then it was too late to ask what it had all meant. It wasn't until I enrolled at Gottfried

Academy that I began to make sense of who I was and what I was fated to become. But first, let me tell you about the peculiar circumstances surrounding the death of my parents. Because it was their deaths that set off the strange chain of events that led me to where I am now. And because if there's one thing I've learned from my first year at Gottfried, it's that sometimes you have to look back in order to understand the things that lie ahead.

CHAPTER 1

THE ENCOUNTER IN THE WOODS

MY PARENTS DIED ON a hot August evening. It was my sixteenth birthday, and my best friend, Annie, and I had snuck out to Santa Rosa for the day to celebrate. We took her car and spent the afternoon at Buzzard's Point Beach, tanning, flipping through magazines, and walking along the jetty. Around five o'clock, just as the tide began to come in, we packed up our towels and headed home so we'd be back before our parents returned from work.

Annie was driving, her long sandy hair fluttering out the open window as we sped down Prairie Creek Drive.

It was a scenic road that started at the coast and wound inland, meandering through the redwood forest. Annie didn't want to drive through the national park; the route was narrow and dark and gave her the creeps, but for some reason I felt that it was the right road to take. After ten minutes of convincing her that it was the fastest way back to Costa Rosa, she complied.

"So when are you seeing Wes again?" Annie asked me, adjusting her sunglasses.

Wes was a senior, tall and smart with perfect teeth, the captain of the soccer team, and the only guy in our high school worth dating. Unfortunately, all the other girls felt the same way. They followed him around in groups, giggling and trying to get his attention. I would never be caught dead doing that, partly because I thought it was pathetic, but mainly because I didn't have time. I had lacrosse practice, homework and a part-time job. And although I was decently popular, I had never been the outgoing type. I liked to pick my friends, opting for quality over quantity, and since I spent most of my time outside working or reading instead of socializing, I always assumed that Wes didn't even know my name. So when he asked me out, I was speechless.

"Saturday, supposedly. But he said he would call me this week and it's already Thursday... Maybe he changed his mind."

Annie rolled her eyes. "Don't be ridiculous. Of course he'll call."

I hoped she was right. I worked at a farmers' market on the weekends, manning a fruit stand. Wes had stopped by two weeks ago and asked me to help him pick out apples for his mom. He was completely lost when it came to fruit; there are so many different kinds of apples, he told me, running his hands nervously through his hair. Afterwards, he asked me to the movies, and I was so surprised that I dropped the bag of apples, letting them roll about our feet. Ever since our date I hadn't been able to think straight about anything except for the buttery kiss he had given me in the darkness of the theatre, his lips melting into mine with the taste of popcorn and salt.

I shook off the thought and shrugged. "I don't even know if he likes me that much," I said. I didn't want to get my hopes up.

"Well, I think you guys are perfect for each other," Annie said, leaning back in her seat.

I smiled. "Thanks, An," I said, and turned up the radio.

We'd both had a crush on Wes for ages, but Annie would never let it come between us. She was the beautiful one, modest and graceful with a gentle personality that was easy to love. I, on the other hand, was impulsive and skinny, and wished that I could be more like a character in a novel, so I would finally stop blurting out the wrong things at the wrong time. My brown hair was wavy and had a life of its own, with a sideswept fringe that had seemed like a good decision at the time, but never stayed in its proper place once I left the hairdresser. I preferred outdoors to indoors; running to walking. As a result, my knees were always covered with Band-Aids, and my cheeks were sun-kissed and sprinkled with freckles.

The road grew narrow, making sharp and unexpected twists and turns as we drove north into the redwood forest. My wet hair dangled around my shoulders, and I ran my hands through it while it dried in the warm California breeze. Ancient trees lined the kerb, and the sky began to turn an ominous shade of red. That summer, the weather had been strange and unpredictable, and after a day of blue skies, clouds were beginning to hover on the horizon.

Annie slowed down as we rounded a bend. The car smelled of sunscreen and aloe vera, and I was prodding my cheeks, inspecting my sunburn in the visor mirror, when I spotted the car. It was a rusty white jeep with a roof rack, parked on the shoulder of the road, by a cluster of trees.

I sat up in my seat. "Pull over," I said.

"What?"

"Pull over!" I repeated.

Annie pulled in next to the Jeep just as the remains of the California sun folded into the clouds. "Is that your dad's car?" she asked, taking the keys out of the ignition.

"Yeah," I said, confused, and opened the door.

"Why would it be here?" Annie asked, slamming the door.

I had no idea. He was supposed to be at work. He and my mother were both high school teachers in Costa Rosa, almost an hour away from here. Cupping my hands, I peered into the jeep. It was empty, with objects strewn across the seats, as if my father had left in a hurry. The giant trunks of the redwoods stood a mere three metres away, creating a boundary between the road and the forest beyond, which was quickly being swallowed by darkness. I reached into Annie's car for my jacket and pulled it on.

"What are you doing?" Annie asked apprehensively.

"He's got to be in there," I said, and made for the edge of the forest.

"What?"

I stopped. "Maybe he went...hiking. They do that kind of stuff sometimes on weekends." I tried to say it with conviction, but I didn't believe it. "I'm just going to check it out."

"Wait," Annie cried after me. "Renée! It's getting dark. Maybe we should just wait for him at home."

Without responding, I walked back to Annie's car and leaned through the passenger window. I fished around in the glove compartment until I found the flashlight that her parents kept for emergencies.

"Don't worry; I'll be back in few minutes. Stay here." And without saying another word, I turned and ran into the woods.

The redwood forest was cool and damp. My wet bathing suit soaked through my clothes as I darted between the trees, my sneakers sinking softly into the earth while the ferns and underbrush whipped my shins.

"Dad?" I shouted into the darkness, but my voice was overpowered by the wind rustling through the branches. "Dad, are you here?"

The beam of my flashlight bounced wildly about the trees as I ran, illuminating pockets of the forest in brief and sudden flashes. The giant redwoods loomed darkly around me, the tops of their trunks extending far above the fog, which had just begun to settle on the ground.

It felt like I had been running for ever when I stopped to catch my breath. Out of the corner of my eye I saw a glint of light reflecting off the ground. I slowed to a walk and edged towards it. My hand trembled as I guided the flashlight in its direction. It was a coin. I prodded it with the tip of my sneaker and walked forward cautiously. A long thin sheet of white cloth was embedded in the dirt next to it, and I followed it into the darkness.

As I stepped deeper into the forest, the air seemed to drop in temperature. I shuddered, pulling my jacket around me tightly, and scanned the ground with my flashlight. It was scattered with coins and pieces of white cloth. Curious, I bent over to get a closer look, when somewhere in the distance, the leaves began to shift. Then movement; the soft thump of footsteps against earth.

I raised my eyes to the shadowy thicket that surrounded me. It was still except for the wind rustling the branches above. Relieved, I took a step forward, when my foot hit something soft and large.

The muscles in my stomach tightened as I lowered my flashlight to the ground. And then I saw it. A hand, as pale as porcelain, its delicate fingers curled into the soil. I followed it to a wrist, an arm, a neck, a face streaked with dirt and shrouded with strands of long chestnut hair.

I gasped and looked away. The pungent smell of rotting leaves wafted through the air. Reluctantly, I looked back at the body.

"Mom," I whispered, barely audible.

She was lying on her back, her arms limp by her side. Her eyes were closed, and I might have thought she was sleeping if her skin hadn't been so pale. Her thin athletic legs, which I had inherited, were now cold and stiff, though they still retained the same girlish shape that she was so proud of.

I leaned over and placed my fingers below her jaw. Her skin was freezing. I don't know why, but I checked her pulse even though I knew she was already dead. Lifeless, she looked older than usual, as if she had aged ten years. Her cheeks were unusually sunken in, and her glasses were nowhere to be seen. Without them, the skin under her eyes looked raw and exposed, drooping down in circles like the rings of a tree.

My father was a couple of metres away, coins scattered around his body. The flashlight slipped from my fingers and landed softly in the dirt, rolling until its beam shone on my father's legs. As I stared at his boots, slumped unnaturally to either side, I felt my breath leave me. I wanted to look away, to run back to the road and call for help, but I couldn't bring myself to leave because I knew that these were the last moments I would ever have with my parents.

"Why?" I choked out. When I was growing up, my parents had always seemed to have an answer to even my hardest questions. But now, for the first time, they were silent. I wiped my eyes and touched my mother's lips. They were parted just enough for me to see a thin shred of cloth peeking out. Gently, I pulled it from between her lips and held it in front of the light. It was tattered around the edges and had the soft consistency of gauze. I turned it over in my hand and looked down at my mother. There were no signs of violence, no bruises or scratches on her body, no blood. But the gauze, the coins – this was the work of a person. The mere thought of it made my heart race. I turned and stared into the darkness, wondering if I was alone.

The woods seemed to be caving in on me, the tops of the trees circling and bending together. Images of my parents dying clouded my mind, and I felt dizzy and disoriented. Holding the cloth in my fist, I rested my head on my mother's chest and closed my eyes, listening to the creaking of the trees and hoping that when I opened them it would be morning and the woods would be empty and filled with sunlight, and everything would be clear. Around me the cool night air blew through the branches, and the shards of white cloth fluttered on the ground, like moths clinging blindly to a screen.

The day they buried my parents, I felt the first chilly breath from my past. I was lying on the floor of our living room, staring at the insects collecting on the edges of the windowpanes, when the doorbell rang. Annie's mom, Margerie, who was staying with me through the funeral, answered the door.

"Mr. Winters, I'm so glad you came," she said in a hushed voice.

I listened. The quiet murmur of voices, the sound of shoes scraping against the mat, and then a deep cough.

Footsteps.

"Renée," Margerie said gently.

I didn't move. Two feet stopped in front of me. I stared at the large brown shoes, the tassels, the creases embedded just before the toe.

"Renée, your grandfather is here."

I sat up. My hair was matted to the back of my head.

"Hello, Renée," my grandfather bellowed in a deep voice. He extended a large leathery hand to help me up. He had a professorial essence, with white hair, inordinately long earlobes, and a fleshy, oversized face that seemed stretched with gravity. The sweet aroma of pipe tobacco emanated from his clothes.

Ignoring his hand, I lay back down. Brownie Winters, my mother's father. It seemed odd that we shared the same last name, even though I hadn't seen him since I was seven. He had gotten into a loud argument with my parents, and then he was gone, the screen door slamming behind him. I hadn't heard from him since. Not even a card on birthdays.

"You missed the ceremony," I said coldly, staring at the folds of his neck.

He sighed. He had my mother's eyes, watery blue and somehow sad. "I didn't find out what had happened until this morning. I hope you can forgive my absence."

I said nothing. My mother used to tell me stories about the rigid rules he'd set while she was growing up in Massachusetts, about how he was only concerned with money and appearances and the family name, which was why he demanded that I have her name instead of my father's. My mother's childhood seemed so different from mine, growing up on a dreary estate in the woods. She'd always said it was lonely, that she had spent more time with her housekeeper than with her parents, which was probably why she and my father had moved to California. Our house was the kind where you could touch things, my mother used to say. It was modest but lived in, with stucco walls covered with photographs, and big glass windows that let in the morning light. The grass was never mowed on time, and the pool out back was littered with leaves and beetles that always got stuck in my hair; but on a hot summer day it all seemed perfect. I stared at my grandfather's shoes. They looked uncomfortable.

"I'm going to be staying with you for a while," he said, putting on his spectacles. "For a long while, I think. Your parents willed me as your legal guardian, which I'll admit came as a surprise, given the outcome of our last encounter. A pleasant surprise, of course, though I never would have wished it to happen under such tragic circumstances. I've always regretted not being a part of your life." He paused, and then spoke again, his voice gentler. "It sometimes helps to dwell on the good memories. They remind you that happiness does exist, though it may not seem that way now." When I didn't respond, he shifted his weight. "Well then, I suppose I'll look forward to seeing you at dinner, which will be served promptly at seven thirty."

I closed my eyes, willing myself not to cry. Even though he was my legal guardian, and almost the only family I had left, I didn't care if he stayed with me or if I never saw him again, and I definitely wasn't planning on eating dinner. I had lost my appetite completely since the night in the forest. I was alone, utterly alone, and I had no idea where my life would take me, or how I would live now that my parents were dead. People filed in and out of the house, but to me they passed in a haze, resembling shadowy figures more than actual humans.

My grandfather hovered above me, but I remained silent and waited until I heard him pat the pockets of his trousers and retreat to the kitchen. Overhead, the ceiling fan churned the air until it grazed my neck in thick, hot breaths.

The next week went by in a blur. I spent most of my time wandering around the house, trying to keep cool and avoid my grandfather, who seemed to always want to talk about my future, even though I was still stuck in the past. He was a professor – a retired professor now, ever since my grandmother passed away when I was a baby. Now that he was here, I was practically confined to the house. Almost overnight my life became a regimented routine. "Rules help us live our lives when we lose the will to do it on our own," he said. He'd brought his estate manager with him, a bald, saggy man named Dustin, who cooked, cleaned and chauffeured my grandfather around. Meals were served three times a day: breakfast at seven, lunch at one, and dinner at seven thirty. Sleeping through breakfast was prohibited, and I had to finish everything on my plate before I could leave the table. Normally that wouldn't have been a problem, but the food Dustin served wasn't the easiest to stomach: foie gras, escargot, beluga caviar, black pudding (which wasn't actually pudding), sweetbreads (which weren't sweet or made of bread) and spiny lettuce that looked more like a reptile than a vegetable.

My grandfather corrected my table manners at dinner, eyeing my ripped jeans and tank tops with distaste. My posture was terrible, he said, and I held my fork like a barbarian.

Tonight was no different. I scowled at him, wanting to fight back, but I had quickly learned to pick my battles and I didn't have time for an argument. I glanced at the clock. It was eight. I had to get out of the house. Everything – the plates, the silverware, the roll of paper towels hanging over the sink, the jar of coins sitting on the mantel –

reminded me of my parents, of the way they died. But if I wanted to leave, I had to do it soon, because for the first time in my life I actually had a curfew. Ten o'clock.

"I'm going out tonight," I mumbled.

Dustin stood in the corner of the room in an antiquated suit, his hands clasped behind his back as he gazed at the ceiling, pretending not to listen. I stared at him uncomfortably.

My grandfather put his fork down. "Please, try to enunciate."

I repeated myself, this time louder and more annoyed.

"Better," he said, and checked his watch. "It's getting late, though. You should stay in tonight."

Outside, the sun was setting over the houses that lined our street. "But it's still light out," I protested.

"I don't feel comfortable with you going out at night by yourself. It's not safe."

"I won't be alone. I'll be with…Annie," I said, improvising.

"I'd rather you not go," he said firmly.

"Then I should probably go upstairs, where I can sit alone in my room for the rest of my life, because that would be the safest thing to do." Picking up my plate, I stood.

Dustin moved to collect my setting, but my grandfather waved him away, and I felt slightly victorious as I turned my back to them and carried my dishes to the kitchen.

"Renée," he called out to me, "may I ask you a question?"

I ignored him and turned on the tap.

"How did you find your parents?"

It caught me off guard. The sponge slipped out of my hand and sank into the soapy water.

"I already told you."

"Yes," he said quietly, "you did. But I think there's more."

I didn't respond.

"I know we haven't talked about your parents; I wanted to let you mourn them in your own way, without my interference."

The kitchen was cramped – a tiny room of appliances just off the dining room – and I could feel my grandfather's eyes on me through the doorway.

"I haven't been present in your life up until now, but I know how difficult it is to lose someone you love. Your mother, Lydia, was my daughter. Her death was no accident. We both know that. After all, you were the one who found them." He paused. "Please, humour an old man."

For the first time since he'd moved in, his words seemed reasonable. I turned and raised my eyes to his. "We were driving back from the beach when I told Annie to take Prairie Creek Drive instead of U.S. 101."

"Why?"

"Because I thought it would be faster," I said, not revealing the true reason, which was that I'd felt inexplicably pulled in that direction.

"What happened next?"

"I saw their car on the side of the road. We pulled over and I went into the woods. Annie waited for me."

"And then what?"

Scenes of the redwood forest flashed through my mind. "I just kept running. I...I didn't know where I was going; I just knew I had to go deeper."

"And then?"

"And then I saw the coins."

The tap was still running. I watched the water cascade over the dishes.

My grandfather's voice broke the silence. "And then what happened?" he said gently.

I turned to him. "That's it. I found them. They were dead. Do you want me to relive the entire night? You know what happened. You read the police report. I told them everything I know."

I turned away and wiped my eyes over the sink.

"I'm sorry," he said softly. "I know it's difficult for you with your parents gone, and now with me here. It's strange and unexpected that the fates should bring us together again after all this time. But think. Does it not seem odd to you that you happened to stumble across your father's car on the side of the road, and that you were then able to locate the bodies of your parents, which were more than a kilometre north of their car? The redwood forest covers eight hundred square kilometres, yet you were able to find them within half an hour."

"Maybe it was a...a coincidence." That was what the police had called it.

He raised a white, bushy eyebrow. "Was it?"

"What are you implying?"

"I'm not implying anything," he assured me. "I'm just trying to understand."

"I don't know how I found them. I just did. I didn't even think about it; I just started running."

My grandfather looked like he was about to say something, but instead he leaned back in his chair and rested his chin on his fist. "You need new shoes. The ones you have on now are far too juvenile for a girl your age. We'll get you a pair next week."

Baffled, I looked down at my Converse sneakers. His remark shouldn't have made me angry, but it did. Here he was with his questions and rules and ten o'clock curfew, making me get rid of my favourite sneakers, forcing me to relive the one moment in my life I wanted to forget, and generally ruining my already ruined life.

"I don't want new shoes," I screamed. "I want my parents back." I ran upstairs, slammed the door to my room, and slid to the floor in an angry heap. Without thinking, I called Annie. She answered on the third ring.

"I have to get out of here," I told her. "Can you pick me up?"

"I'll be there in ten minutes."

We drove to the marina. I'd barely seen Annie since the day we'd gone to the beach. When I hadn't come out of the woods that night, she'd called the police, then went in to find me. After they discovered me with the bodies of my parents, and brought me home, she hadn't asked about what I'd seen or how I'd felt. I was relieved that she didn't know what to say, because I didn't either. How could I explain to her that I had died that day in the forest too, that nothing had meaning any more? The things I used to love – lacrosse, the beach, books, history, movies – they all seemed pointless now.

And then there were the people – the neighbours, the girls from the lacrosse team, the relatives, people from town – constantly stopping by the house, telling me about how they'd known my parents and how much they would miss them. For the first time in my life I was actually glad that my parents hadn't let me have a cellphone, because it was one less thing to answer. The police came. They had questions. Did I know why my parents were in the forest that day? Had they behaved unusually in the days prior? Did they have any enemies?

"No," I answered. "No."

But the hardest part was making sense of it all. The cause of each of their deaths was a heart attack, which could have been reasonable had it not been for the circumstances. It was too much of a coincidence that they'd both suffered from a heart attack at the exact same time. Yet the medical report confirmed that everything else inside their bodies was intact and healthy, and that there were no signs of violence, struggle, or anything out of the ordinary, with one exception: autopsies revealed that soil and ribbons of white fabric were found in the mouth of each of my parents. Was there anything strange about the fabric? "No. Just ordinary gauze you might find in any hospital," the police told me. But no one knew why it was there.

The police deemed that the heart failure had been brought on by a "hiking accident", but to me it was anything but resolved. "How could it be an accident?" I'd shouted at the police officers, the doctors, the nurses. "Do you actually expect me to believe that they both died of a heart attack at the *same exact moment*? That's impossible. They were healthy. They were supposed to be at work. They had *gauze* in their mouths! How is that natural?" They gave me sympathetic looks and told me I was going through a rough time and that they understood. They were going to keep the case open. But I knew there wasn't enough evidence to base a case on. Was it murder? I wasn't sure. Why would anyone want to kill my parents? And why the forest, the coins, the cloth? If someone had killed my parents, it was intentional, and that meant they were still out there. But then there was the way my mother had looked inexplicably older than she had the day before. How could that be? Maybe they *were* hiking and had heart attacks. Maybe it was suicide. Maybe I was losing my mind.

When Annie and I got to the marina, we took off our shoes and walked down to the rocky beach, beside the dock on the far side of the bay. The pier and the boats, which were so colourful by day, were now shadowed in shades of blue.

"Thanks for picking me up," I said, dipping my toes in the water.

"Any time." She sat down on the rocks. "So I ran into Wes the other day."

I looked up at her expectantly.

"He asked about you. He wanted to know how you were doing...with everything, you know. He said he's been calling but you haven't called him back."

"He called me?" I was surprised. I hadn't thought about

him at all in the past week, and it never crossed my mind that he could have been thinking about me. Since the night in the woods, it seemed like the phone had been constantly ringing – friends, neighbours, the police, insurance companies. Eventually I just stopped answering, letting my grandfather deal with it.

"He said he left messages on your answering machine. He was worried. He just wanted to make sure you're okay."

"It feels like years since I saw him," I said almost to myself, and smiled. For the first time since my parents died, I felt the inkling of something other than numbness. Thinking about Wes – about the stubble on his chin, his smooth, muscular arms, his curly brown hair, and the way he had run his hand down the back of my neck when he kissed me – it was almost as if nothing had happened and I could return to the life I'd had before. I hadn't felt anything since that night in the woods; I hadn't allowed myself to. Instead I'd spent the last week in a trance – my body wandering around the house as if it were alive, when inside my mind was with the dead.

All of a sudden I felt an incredible urge to feel something more: pain, happiness, it didn't matter. In front of me the water was tenuously still, as if the night air were weighing down on it with immense pressure.

I didn't have a bathing suit on, but it didn't matter.

The far side of the marina was always deserted at night. I tore off my clothes and jumped into the bay. My lungs constricted at the shock of the sudden cold, and the salt water stung my eyes.

When I surfaced, Annie was wading in, holding her hair above her head with one hand. I splashed her, and she let out a shriek. Diving underwater, I swam deeper. The boats around me bobbed idly in the water, their reflections stretching into the horizon. I looked to the shore. Annie was near the rocks, floating on her back and staring at the sky.

And then I saw something rise to the surface.

It was round and long, and had what looked like a train of tattered clothes hanging off it, lolling in the ripples of the water. Its surface was a sickly white.

I screamed and swam back to shore, my arms thrashing wildly in the water.

"What happened?" Annie said frantically.

I pointed to the bay. "There's someone floating out there."

Annie stood up and looked. "The buoy?" she said finally.

"I thought –" I said between breaths – "I thought it was a person."

Annie looked at me, worried. "It's just a buoy covered in seaweed."

Embarrassed, I blinked and forced myself to look at it.

Leaning over, I let out a sigh of relief. She was right. "I'm sorry. I must be losing my mind."

As if on cue, a light turned on and flashed into the water. "Who's there?" someone called from a boat harboured in the bay.

"Oh my God," I said, not wanting to be seen in my underwear. "Let's get out of here." And in the light of the moon we ran back up the beach.

After Annie dropped me off, I snuck through the back door, hoping that my grandfather had gone to bed. I'd just barely made it through the kitchen when a figure loomed in the doorway.

I froze.

"I see you've gone swimming," my grandfather said sternly. Even at this hour he was still wearing an expensive tweed suit and dinner jacket.

"I was feeling a little stuffy."

My sarcasm wasn't lost on him. "Do you think this is funny?" he said loudly.

I jumped at the sudden sharpness in his voice.

"You could have gotten killed. Do you think my rules are arbitrary? That I enforce them just to punish you?"

"Killed. Like my parents? Maybe that wouldn't be so bad if it meant I didn't have to live like this any more."

He studied me. I clutched my sweatshirt against my chest and waited for him to say something. It was so quiet I could hear the water dripping from my hair onto the linoleum floor.

"I'm sorry you feel that way," he said. "It wasn't my intention. Go dry off and get some sleep. We'll talk in the morning."

The next morning I woke up late and tiptoed downstairs. For the first time since he'd moved in, my grandfather had let me sleep through breakfast. It should have felt like a victory, but was so out of character that it made me suspicious. My grandfather was in the living room, sitting in my father's reading chair, a newspaper resting in his lap. Dustin was clearing a cup and saucer from the side table. I entered the room cautiously, trying not to draw too much attention to myself.

"Renée," he said, almost warmly, "come in." He motioned to the sofa across from him.

He was outfitted in trousers and a dinner jacket, with one of the French-cuffed shirts that Dustin starched and ironed every night. His thinning white hair, which was normally impeccably groomed, was tousled on the side, from leaning his head on his hand, I guessed. He took a sip of water, and I braced myself for punishment.

"Please sit," he said.

Dustin pulled out a chair for me and produced a napkin and place setting.

"I've been doing a lot of thinking about your situation," my grandfather continued.

I fidgeted with my shorts while he spoke, and studied his large, ruddy nose – a nose so massive that it seemed impossible for it to have ever existed on a younger person's face.

"And I have decided to send you to school."

I shook my head. "What? But I'm already in school."

"This is a boarding school. And an elite one at that."

I stood up in shock. My entire life was here: Annie, my friends, my teachers, the people I grew up with. They were all I had left. I was about to begin my sophomore year, and I had just made the school lacrosse team and gotten into Advanced History, which was normally closed off to sophomores. And of course there was Wes...

"But you can't!" I cried, though I wasn't so sure. How could he make me leave when my life was just beginning?

He clasped his hands over one knee. "It's high time you got an actual education. A classical education. I've seen how schools these days operate, letting young people choose what they want and don't want to study. It's an ineffective method that has been disproved over and over again. Gottfried Academy has been around for centuries.

I'm sure it will provide you with the same strong foundation that your mother had."

I meant to interrupt him, but when he mentioned my mother, I went quiet. I didn't know that she had gone to boarding school. She had told me stories about her childhood, about high school, and about how she met my dad, but she'd never told me that she went to boarding school, or that it was prestigious. My dad had to have gone there too, since they'd met in English class. Why would she omit those details?

"I'm not going," I said defiantly. "You can't make me."

He sighed and shook his head. "On the contrary, I can. Your parents entrusted me with your safety, as stipulated in their wills. As your primary guardian, it's my responsibility to do what I think is best for your future."

"But they hated you. Even when they were alive they wouldn't let you see me. So how can you possibly think you know what's best for me? You don't know *anything* about me."

"That may be the case," he said quietly, "yet the fact still remains that I am your grandfather, and you are a minor. I know more about you than you know about yourself. Now, sit down. Please."

I cringed and sank into my seat.

"Whether you like it or not, I am your legal guardian, and you're going to Gottfried. Now, I'm going to speak plainly and clearly. You are not safe here, Renée."

"What do you mean?"

"Your parents died. I don't know why or how or by whom, but it certainly was not by natural causes."

"But the police said—"

"The police believe that they both had some sort of heart attack. Do you think that's true?"

"No."

"Neither do I."

"So...so what, then? You think someone murdered them? That someone chased them into the woods and killed them?"

My grandfather shook his head, his jowls quivering. "I don't know, Renée. I only know that it wasn't an accident. Which is why we have to leave."

My mind raced through all of my options. I could run away, stay with Annie and her parents. Or I could just leave and never come back, live in a train like *The Boxcar Children* so my grandfather couldn't find me. I had to talk to Annie. Maybe she could help me convince her mom to adopt me.

My grandfather must have sensed my dissent. "We depart tomorrow morning. I will physically place you in the car if necessary."

"Tomorrow? I can't leave tomorrow. What about my friends?"

Suddenly I didn't care if there was some killer out there

who wanted to chop me to pieces. I was staying, and I was going to find out what happened to my parents. "I'll never go," I said defiantly. "Not with you or your stupid butler."

Dustin coughed in the corner of the room, but I didn't care.

"We don't have time for this," my grandfather said. "The semester begins in a week. You should be grateful that Gottfried is letting you enrol this late. If it weren't for my outstanding ties with the school, they probably wouldn't have even considered you."

"I don't understand," I said, angry tears stinging my eyes. "Why would I be safer in a different school? Why don't we just go to the police?"

"The police were here; do you remember how helpful they were? Gottfried Academy is the safest place you could be right now. I've left a suitcase in the hallway outside your bedroom. Pack lightly. You won't need much. The weather is different on the East Coast, and Gottfried enforces a strict dress code." He eyed my shorts and tank top. "I daresay your current wardrobe will not do. We'll find more appropriate attire when we land."

I thought I had misheard him. "The East Coast?"

"Gottfried is on the western edge of Maine."

I almost fell out of my chair. I expected Gottfried to be an hour, maybe two, away from Costa Rosa, but moving to Maine was different. I had never been to the East Coast before. The phrase alone conjured up images of stern, expressionless people dressed completely in black; of dark and unfathomably long winters. I couldn't even begin to imagine the degrees of unhappiness I would experience if I had to move there.

"I can't go!" I screamed. "I won't—"

But my grandfather cut me off. "Do you think your parents would want you to stay here, wallowing in self-pity as you've been doing for the past week?" He gave me a cold look and shook his head. "No, they would want you to move on with your life. Which is exactly what you're going to do."

The conversation was over, and I stormed out of the room. I went upstairs and sat by the window, tears blurring my vision as I watched the heat rise off the pavement in the morning sun. It was unreal how much my life had changed in just one week. Both of my parents were dead, and I had no idea what was going to happen next. But I wasn't scared. I was alive, and as I picked up the phone to dial Annie's number, I closed my eyes and made a promise to my parents that I would never take that for granted again.

Chapter 2

Gottfried Academy

When I told Annie about Gottfried Academy, she sounded more hysterical than I did. "But you can't move! Who will be my best friend? Who will be *your* best friend? You can move in with me; we'll be real sisters then, like we always wanted when we were little. You can move into the office." It was exactly what I wanted her to say, but hearing it from her made me realize how unrealistic it was. Annie already had two younger brothers and a sister that her parents had to worry about, which was why they didn't have any extra bedrooms or time. If my parents were alive, they would want me to be brave and independent.

Running away or going to Annie's house wouldn't solve my problems. Where would I go when the only place I wanted to be was back in time? So after Annie's monologue, I found myself in the unexpected position of reasoning with her.

"But where will your dad work?"

"In the kitchen. Or the living room. We'll find space."

I sighed. "I couldn't do that," I said. "And your mom is already so busy..."

"But what about school? And all of your friends? And Wes?"

I winced at the thought of leaving them all behind, but tried to convince myself that there was a reason why my parents had made my grandfather, instead of Annie's mother, my legal guardian. "Maybe Maine won't be that bad. If my parents went there it couldn't be too horrible. Besides, we'll talk every day, and I'll come back on holidays and in the summer." After a teary conversation, Annie and I made plans to meet one last time, that night at Baker's Field.

I spent my last day in California packing and wandering around the house trying to remember its every detail – the way it always smelled faintly of bread, the plush feeling of the carpet beneath my toes, the creaky fifth stair. Eventually I found my way to the office, where my father's papers were still scattered across his desk. Not ready to look at them, I pushed the documents aside and turned on the computer. First, I searched "heart attack", trying to figure out what could have possibly been the cause of my parents' deaths. When more than a million results popped up, I refined my search to "heart attack" and "gauze in mouth". That was more reasonable, but the results were all about wisdom teeth or complications with dental procedures. And after trying "heart attack, gauze", and "coins, double heart attack, gauze in mouth", which yielded nothing except the suggestion, "Did you mean *cost of double heath bar, gooey in mouth?*" I gave up. Frustrated, I typed in "Gottfried Academy".

There was only one listing for Gottfried on the internet. I clicked on it and was brought to an incredibly simple website with a blue-and-gold border, which I assumed were the school colours.

GOTTFRIED ACADEMY
VOX SAPIENTIAE CLAMANS EX INFERNO
A BOARDING SCHOOL DEDICATED TO STUDIES OF
AN EXISTENTIAL NATURE
CONTACT:
207 ATTICA CROSSING, MAILBOX 4
ATTICA FALLS, MAINE 04120

Beneath the inscription was a crest of arms and a very realistic pencil illustration of what I assumed was the school's campus. It was stone and gothic, with cathedral-like buildings surrounded by a giant wall that looked almost medieval. If there had been a pigpen and a watering trough in the picture, they wouldn't have looked out of place. Above the buildings, ominous dark clouds filled the sky. Out of curiosity I checked the weather forecast for Attica Falls, Maine. Sighing, I scanned the weekly prediction. Fifteen degrees and cloudy. Every single day.

What *was* an existential boarding school anyway? Opening a new window, I looked up the word "existential", which the *Oxford English Dictionary* defined as "of or pertaining to existence". How helpful, I thought, and went back to the Gottfried website. I clicked on the crest of arms, and then on "Contact", trying to go deeper into the site, but that was it. Frustrated, I closed the window. In addition to lacking pleasant weather, Gottfried also seemed to lack a proper internet presence. Great, I thought to myself. There probably wouldn't even be a wireless connection in the dorms.

Turning off the computer, I went into the hall. I had avoided my parents' room all week. Every so often I would tiptoe up to the door and graze my hand across the knob, trying to imagine them inside, sleeping. Now, with nothing left to do, I opened it.

The room was perfectly preserved: the bed made, the dresser cluttered with books, the closet door ajar, a few pieces of my mother's clothing still draped over the top. It was mid-afternoon and the branches of the trees brushed against the windows. That's when I saw the answering machine, blinking on their night table. The mailbox was full. There were a few messages from Annie, the girls from school, the insurance company, and other people I didn't know. I skipped ahead until I heard Wes's voice: "Renée," he said, "it's Wes. I heard about, well, you know... I just wanted to see how you were doing, and to say that I'm sorry. I'm so sorry." I skipped ahead to the next. "It's Wes again. You're probably busy with family, but I wanted to say hi. So...hi. Call me if you want to talk." I sat down on the bed, clutching a pillow to my chest. "Wes again; calling to check in. Thought you might need a friend. That's all, I guess." Rewinding the tape, I slipped under the covers, breathing in the smell of my parents on the sheets, and listened to Wes's voice until I fell asleep.

That night I snuck out. My bicycle was propped against the side of the house, where I'd left it two weeks ago. Quietly, I walked it to the end of the driveway. Somewhere in the distance, a dog barked. I jumped. "Hello?" I said, and then laughed at myself for being so easily frightened. After glancing back at my grandfather's window, I rode down to Baker's Field.

The football stadium was wide and flat, with the eerie stillness of a place trapped in time. The floodlights were off, letting the night sky spill onto the grass. It was empty, save for a dim glow off to the left, punctuated by laughter and the *tap click hiss* of beer cans being opened. Hopping off my bike, I walked towards the voices.

Annie was the first person I saw. She was there with some other girls from our class, and ran over when she spotted me. "Renée!" she said, giving me a hug. "You're here! I was starting to worry."

I gazed at all of the people on the turf. The girls from the lacrosse team were sitting on the grass, and a group of my friends from History class were standing around three coolers filled with beer. Behind them I recognized the boys from the soccer team, along with a few older guys, nursing drinks and holding cigarettes, the red ash of the butts flitting through the darkness. "What is all this?"

"It's your goodbye party, of course. You didn't think I'd let you leave without seeing everyone, did you?"

A goodbye party. It seemed so simple, so foreign. In the face of my parents' deaths, it was strange to think that things like parties were still taking place. I smiled and threw my arms around Annie again, speaking into her hair. "I'm going to miss you so much."

Behind her loomed a tall silhouette of someone I had barely allowed myself to think about. Wes. Annie gave me a coy look and turned to talk to some of our friends as he approached me.

"Surprise," he said softly.

He looked like he had just stepped out of a surfing catalogue, his frayed shorts and faded T-shirt blowing casually against his body in the breeze. Just the sight of him made me nervous. I swallowed and smoothed out my fringe, hoping I didn't look like I hadn't had a full night's sleep in a week, even though that was the truth.

"You look great," he said.

I blushed. "Thanks."

"I was worried about you."

"It was really" – I tried to find the right words – "busy. I didn't mean to—"

"Don't worry. You don't have to explain."

I let out a sigh of relief. Wes had an unbelievable way of making things easier.

"Take a walk with me?"

I nodded, and he slipped his hand in mine.

We wove through the crowd of people, saying hi to everyone as we passed. It was overwhelming to think that they had all come just to say goodbye to me. After walking across the field, we reached the bleachers and climbed up to the top row, the metal popping beneath our sneakers. Wes tried to talk about the summer, about soccer, about school, but I couldn't think of anything to say back to him. So I told him about Gottfried instead.

"So it's just a different school, right?" Wes said after an awkward silence. "We can still see each other."

"It's in Maine."

"Oh," he said, and went quiet. "Well, you'll be home for breaks. We'll talk. And before we know it, it'll be summer again."

Voices floated up from below on the night breeze. Those people were part of a world I could never go back to again. I couldn't talk to them about school and sports and classes any more; that place was gone for me, buried with my parents. I wanted to tell Wes that I missed my parents so much my insides ached; that I felt so alone I couldn't eat or sleep because I didn't see the point in it any more. I wanted to tell him about the way my parents had died and how scared I was that there was someone out there evil enough to have taken them away from me. I wanted him to say that I couldn't leave, that he would save me from my grandfather and we could run away together.

Wes asked me if I was cold, and wrapped his sweatshirt around me. We sat in silence, listening to our friends laughing, wishing it wasn't our last night together, both trying to convince ourselves that if we wanted it badly enough, we could will everything away. I was afraid to speak; afraid I would ruin the delicateness of the moment.

"I'll miss you," he said finally.

It wasn't an answer to all of my questions, but it was enough. "I'll miss you—" I started to say, but he placed a finger over my lips. His skin was warm, his upper lip beading with sweat. I gazed at him, curious, confused. He laced his fingers in mine, and before I could close my eyes, he leaned forward and kissed me. A cool, wet kiss that tasted of summer, of dew and freshly cut grass, of all the things that now seemed too simple to be real.

That was my last night in California.

We landed in Massachusetts, where Dustin was waiting for us. I squeezed into the backseat of my grandfather's custom-made Aston Martin, and Dustin drove us through the New England countryside, snaking over hills and ravines, through vast areas with nothing but trees for kilometres.

"This is western Massachusetts," my grandfather said. "The home of the Transcendental movement."

Transcendental? It sounded vaguely familiar from English class. Emerson, maybe, or Thoreau? I couldn't remember, and I didn't want to know badly enough to ask him. Instead, I opened the window, letting the wind blow my fringe around my eyes.

We crossed a bridge into a wooded area, past rocky streams and the occasional log cabin. My legs stuck to the leather seats as I gazed out the window. The thickets of trees, which normally would have looked pretty, now only seemed dark and forbidding.

Finally, the car slowed, turning up a long gravel driveway lined with lamp posts. At the end was a Victorian mansion surrounded by acres and acres of perfectly groomed lawns. We parked in front of a marble fountain. Off to the right, two men in green uniforms were crouched beneath a rosebush with spades and garden clippers.

Dustin opened the car door for me. "Miss Winters," he said with a nod.

I stepped outside, gazing at the mansion in awe. WINTERSHIRE HOUSE was engraved over the entrance. "What is this?"

"Thank you, Dustin," my grandfather said, hefting himself out of the car. "We're making a short stop."

The gardeners turned and stood up as my grandfather walked by.

"Is this your...your..." I paused, trying to think of the right word. "House?"

My grandfather smiled. "My home, yes. Transcendental, isn't it?"

Although I still couldn't recall what the word meant, this time it seemed like an appropriate adjective. I had only seen houses this big on television, which I assumed had been filmed somewhere in the French countryside or the English moors. Never had I believed that they existed in America, or even more incredibly, that my grandfather owned one.

The front door opened into a large hall with chequered floors and heavy light fixtures. Thick drapes framed the windows, letting hazy light fill the room. Two staircases broke off on either side of the hall and led up to the east and west wings, demarcated by a compass rose engraved in the wall between them. Beneath it was a tall grandfather clock, its brass pendulum swinging languidly. How appropriate, I thought.

"Dustin will give you the grand tour while I attend to a few matters that need to be resolved before we leave."

"We're not staying?"

My grandfather suppressed a smile. "Just for one night," he said, and handed me over to Dustin.

I followed him as we meandered through the mansion, stopping in every room, each with a name and a theme.

"May I present to you the Gingham Library," Dustin said as we entered an octagonal room with mahogany floors and shelves and shelves of leather-bound books. I touched a rolling ladder, which slid down the wall, just like in the movies.

We left and moved on to the Red Room, which was a velvet-lined sitting room, ostensibly for ladies. Dustin pushed open the door for me but waited outside. It had puffy ottomans and tiny side tables that were only large enough to hold a cup and saucer.

It was followed by the Parchment Room, a study

equipped with an old computer that looked like it hadn't been used in a decade. In front of it was a typewriter, a box of ink ribbons, a stack of cluttered papers, and a series of expensive-looking pens. We continued on through a maze of rooms, each more magnificent than the one before. I tried to keep them straight, but their names mingled together in my mind as Dustin announced them:

"The Game Parlour."

"The Hearst Drawing Room."

"The Hall of Marble and Glass."

"Verlaine Oil Gallery."

"Doldrums Wine Cellar."

"The August Smoking Parlour."

And finally, "The Second Living Room."

It was a normal sort of living room, only fancier, with an oriental carpet and a fireplace at each end. Victorian settees and divans sat in clusters around the room, along with a grand piano, a wall of bookshelves, and a chandelier made of antlers. Deer heads and portraits of distinguished-looking men hung on the walls.

"Wait," I said, just as Dustin was closing the French doors. "Where's the First Living Room?"

He gave me a blank look. "There isn't one."

My grandfather met us in the foyer just as we'd finished with the ground floor and the cellar. "Thank you, Dustin. I'll take it from here," he said, and he led me upstairs.

On the first floor, the halls were plastered in linen wallpaper and adorned with portraits. Every so often we would pass a sleeping chamber, as my grandfather called them, mostly for guests, though I could hardly imagine him entertaining.

At the end of the east wing, we entered a small spiral staircase that led up into the easternmost spire. At the top was a short, windowed hallway with only one door at the end. My grandfather opened it for me, and I walked inside.

It was a bedroom: the kind you only read about in fairy tales. It had tall curved windows and a conical ceiling. The walls were painted lilac and decorated with antique mirrors and paintings of pastoral landscapes. In the middle of the room was a giant canopy bed covered in silly little pillows that I had to resist the urge to jump into. I traced my finger along the monogrammed sheets. *L. C. W.* My mother's initials.

"This was her bedroom," my grandfather said, watching me explore the vestiges of her childhood. The yellowed papers on her desk, the tins of make-up and hairpins on the dresser. A box of stationery peeking out from beneath the bed. An antiquated bookcase stacked with creased novels and faded dust jackets. I could never imagine my mother inhabiting this room, let alone owning that many tiny pillows. She had always been pragmatic, inclined to hiking boots and machine-washable clothing, big comfortable couches, and decorations that wouldn't break if you dropped them. I had never seen her wear jewellery other than her wedding ring, and she rarely wore make-up. She had always encouraged me to do the same.

"If you'd like, you can stay in this room for the night. I thought it might be...comforting. Of course, I can have your things moved to one of the guest chambers if it doesn't suit you."

I spun around. "No, I want to stay here," I said quickly. My suitcase, which was virtually empty due to my lack of packing, was sitting in the corner of the room.

"Good. Good." My grandfather led me to a set of French doors in the corner of the room. "And this," he said, turning the knobs, "was her closet."

I stepped inside, the smell of potpourri tickling my nose, and pulled the string dangling from the bulb.

In the light, the closet was transformed from an old storage room into an enchanted boudoir filled with rows and rows of jewellery and shoes and clothes. Beautiful clothes, in styles I had never seen before. The mere sight of them filled me with an inexplicable childish excitement, and I ventured deeper, running my fingers along the racks, the hangers clinking together behind me. The fabrics melted beneath my fingertips – silk, crushed velvet, suede, taffeta, cashmere, fine cottons. I had to remind myself that I didn't like clothes like this. They were expensive, extravagant, snobby. My parents used to tell me I didn't need material things to define who I was, but now I couldn't help but want to put them on.

"These were your mother's when she was your age. I think she was about your size. Anyway, they're yours now. Everything in this closet adheres to Gottfried's dress code, so take whatever you think you'll need."

I glanced at the clothes, trying to imagine my mother at my age wearing the sweaters, the skirts, the dresses, the Mary Janes, the cloaks. I couldn't. I fingered the sleeve of a sweater. It was so soft.

"Well, I'll leave you to it. Lunch will be served at half past one."

I nodded and watched my grandfather's reflection in the mirror as he bowed out of the room.

I spent the next hour examining my mother's clothes. She had boxes full of hair clips and rings and headbands; drawers packed with silk pyjamas, scarves, earmuffs and lambswool mittens. I thought they might smell of her, but instead they just smelled like lavender, which made it easier to forget that they were hers, that she was gone. The only trace of her I could find was a single brown hair clinging to a cowl-neck sweater. I pulled it out and examined it in the light. The hair was longer than I had ever seen her wear it. I imagined her in one of the plaid jumpers in front of me, her long hair held back with a ribbon. "What am I going to do?" I asked her, my voice cracking. I thought of my father next to her, his hair short and parted on the side. He wore a shirt and tie, just like he did in the pictures of when they first got married. "Dad," I said into the empty closet, "what do I do now?" A row of extra hangers clinked together above me, mocking the silence. Suddenly I felt incredibly angry. It was unfair. Why did my parents have to die? Why did I have to find them? Now all of my memories of them were polluted by the image of them dead in the forest.

With a single movement, I knocked the hangers off the rack. They clattered to the ground, and I kept going, throwing her box of jewellery to the floor, her collection of headbands and hair clips, her scarves and mittens and hats, then sank into a sobbing heap, clutching my mother's clothes to my chest. What would my dad say if he were here? I thought back to when I hadn't made the lacrosse team last year. "Crying only makes your problems last longer," he had said. "Why don't you go practise? That way you'll make it next year." Wiping my tears on the bottom of one of my mother's dresses, I picked myself up and stood in front of the mirror. I wanted to see something of her in me, but all I saw was my plain, thick hair, the fringe that always got in my eyes, my freckled face, and my grey eyes, now swollen and red. Was I like her?

I searched through my mother's drawers until I found a

pair of scissors. Standing in front of the mirror, I took a lock of hair in my hand. I closed my eyes and cut it off. I continued until half of it was gone, and my hair fell just below my shoulders. Finally feeling free, I shook my head, the wisps fluttering to the ground and collecting on the floor like spaghetti. Satisfied, I took a dress off a hanger and tried it on, examining my reflection. To my relief, it fitted perfectly.

After packing three suitcases full of skirts, dresses, oxford shirts, cardigans, cable-knit tights and plush winter coats, I felt adequately prepared for whatever weather the New England winter had in store for me.

"You cut your hair," my grandfather said, aghast, when I walked downstairs for lunch.

I nodded. "I wanted a change."

"It looks very nice," he said.

"Thanks," I said, with a slight smile.

After a lunch of dainty sandwiches and cucumber salad, Dustin invited me to play a game of croquet. Manning a croquet mallet, I followed him to the back lawn. After only fifteen minutes he was already beating me by six swings. Frowning, I stepped up for my turn. I didn't like to lose. After a moment of deep concentration, I swung. It was a swift hit and I rested the croquet mallet over my shoulder while I watched the ball roll all the way to the other side of the lawn, in the complete opposite direction of the ring I should have been aiming for. Dustin chuckled, but I scowled and ran over to my ball. It was resting at the edge of the woods, where a thicket of birch trees shaded the grass. Dustin called out to me, but I ignored him and bent down. Just as my fingers grazed the ball, I jumped back.

A pulp of feathers and dried blood was resting in front of it, the bones jutting out at unnatural angles. Unable to control myself, I screamed.

Dustin ran over to me, surprisingly agile despite his age and the stuffy suit he was wearing. He summoned a garden worker as my grandfather approached and surveyed the scene. "Get rid of it, please," he said to one of the gardeners, patting me on the back. "Just a dead bird. Nothing to be frightened of."

"Right," I said, standing up, embarrassed that I had caused such a fuss. This had happened to me before. Even as a child, I seemed to find my way to dead things.

"Let's go inside."

Dusk settled over the mansion. My grandfather and I dined at one end of an exceedingly long table, and he attempted to make small talk about the subjects I was interested in at school. I told him I wasn't sure. I had always been good at History. Both of my parents had been high-school History teachers; my father had specialized in ancient

Greek civilizations, and my mother had taught on the Roman Empire. So when I did well in my History classes, they'd always encouraged me to read more on my own.

"But what are *you* interested in, regardless of what your parents wanted?" he pressed.

I hesitated. "I...I don't know. I like books and reading. And I like biology. Anatomy, dissection. It sounds kind of cool. But I've never really taken it, so who knows. I probably wouldn't even like it."

He gave me a troubled look. "Why do you say that?"

"Dad told me that science was a flawed field. Something about how it was just another form of prediction. It tries to explain the mysteries of life and death by using a very small vocabulary. That's what he said, at least."

My grandfather rubbed his chin. "I see. Well, perhaps you should give it a try, lest he was mistaken. At Gottfried."

I nodded. Was my grandfather actually being supportive of something I wanted to do? Maybe he wasn't so bad after all.

That night after my grandfather went to bed, I turned on the bedside light and explored my mother's room. It was like a museum, everything perfectly preserved, as if the sixteen-year-old version of my mother had just left for a date with my father, and would return any minute, sneaking in through the back door so my grandfather wouldn't catch her. I ran my hands just above her perfumes, her porcelain figurines, her pens and pencils, not wanting to touch them, to change anything about them. She had stacks of books, mostly paperback fantasy novels and children's tales, a pile of old notebooks scrawled with numbers and equations from Maths class, I assumed, and a binder full of notes from what seemed to be a literature class. In the margins, she had doodled my father's name over and over again. I traced my fingers around the letters. *Robert Redgrave.* I liked the idea that they had once been my age, passing notes and daydreaming about each other in class. With a yawn, I clutched the notebook to my chest and crawled into my mother's bed. Surrounded by her things, I finally felt safe, and fell into the first full night's sleep I'd had in weeks.

In the morning we set out. Dustin drove us through the grassy knolls of Vermont, the White Mountains of New Hampshire, and finally into western Maine. It was getting late in the afternoon, the sun beating a yellow orange on the horizon. In the distance an aeroplane left a trail of white steam heading towards the west, and I watched as it disappeared behind the mountains. We hadn't seen civilization in hours.

Up ahead, the darkened mouth of a tunnel was carved into the earth. Dustin locked the car doors. The radio became scratchy until it turned completely static.

When we emerged through the other end, we were in the mountains. The alpine passage had been carved into the granite. Giant peaks jutted out of the ground, framing the horizon like jaws. As we climbed higher into the mountains, the temperature dropped. Snowmelt trickled down from the peaks, soaking the road, and Dustin slowed as we turned a bend.

And then out of nowhere, we passed a house. It was half dilapidated, made of a dark wood that was rotting at the base. I was sure it was abandoned until I spotted a figure moving inside, behind the curtains of a cracked kitchen window.

I pressed my face against the glass to get a better look as we drove by. It was followed by another house, only this one was smaller and better kept, resting tenuously on a bed of granite. Slowly, we began to pass more houses until we reached an intersection with a general store, a gas station, and a diner with a faded sign that read *BEATRICE'S*.

"What is this place?" I asked.

"Attica Falls," said my grandfather.

A few cars were parked along the side of the road, and a man was pumping diesel into a rusty pickup truck at the gas station. A stray cat ran under a house porch. Otherwise, the town was empty. Dustin made a left at the intersection, then headed up a steep road that led us around the mountain. The town ended as suddenly as it began. I looked back to catch one last glimpse of it just as we hugged the bend. *Attica Falls.*

When I turned back around, we had come to a stop. Nestled into the forest were tall iron gates, spiralling together like the branches of a tree. Hanging at the centre was a brass plate engraved with GOTTFRIED ACADEMY. A crest of arms was inscribed below it, with the words VOX SAPIENTIAE CLAMANS EX INFERNO. A small man dressed in a guard's uniform approached the driver's side.

Dustin rolled down his window. "Mr. Brownell Winters," he said solemnly.

Surprised, the guard stepped back and stood up straight. "Sir," he said, giving our car a stiff nod and running to open the gates. As we drove past, he peered into the car curiously, but quickly looked away.

Inside the school grounds the terrain was much different than the rugged wilderness that surrounded it. The ground was flat and green, with sprawling quadrangles of grass and trees. The massive buildings that comprised the campus were made of dark brick that had been stained and faded by the elements until it had acquired a smoky hue. Ivy climbed up the walls, giving me the feeling that the buildings had not been built at all, but had grown naturally out of the earth.

We pulled into a half-crescent driveway and parked at

the foot of a staggeringly large stone building, with ARCHEBALD HALL engraved above the entrance. Dustin left the car running and took my suitcases out of the trunk.

"Oh, I can get that," I said, but he refused. With a bow, he carried them into the hall, leaving only my backpack at my feet.

"This is where we part ways," my grandfather said.

"You're leaving?" Suddenly I felt very alone.

"Would you have me stay?" He studied me pensively. "Edith Lumbar. She's a professor here and an old colleague of mine. Should you ever feel unsafe, go to her. She's very capable."

I nodded, fidgeting with the bottom of my cardigan.

"And you have my phone number. Don't be shy about calling."

"Okay."

"You remind me of your mother when she was your age. I should be happy if you turned out the same."

In a gesture intended to comfort me, he gave me a stiff hug. And with only one place to go, I walked up the steps to Archebald Hall.

I found myself standing in a giant hallway with a high-vaulted ceiling and mahogany-coloured walls that reminded me of the interior of a church. I ambled down the hall until I reached an open doorway on my right. I peeked in.

"Come in," said a friendly voice.

Startled, I stepped inside. A young woman wearing red lipstick and a secretary's skirt suit was seated behind a desk, sorting through a stack of files. She was simultaneously plain and glamorous, like a 1950s movie star. I half expected her to look up from a typewriter and pull out a long cigarette. She smiled when she saw me approach.

"Hi," I said. "I...I'm a new student."

She nodded. "What is your name?"

"Renée Winters."

She scanned the files with a long slender finger and handed me an envelope. I turned it over, not sure what to do. She seemed to know what I was thinking.

"Your schedule is inside." She motioned towards the envelope. "Everything you'll need is in your room, including your suitcases, which are being delivered as we speak. You're in 12E, in the girls' dormitory. Go straight out these doors and turn right. Follow the walkway past the green. When you get to the lake, you'll see it on your left."

I folded the envelope into my pocket. "Thanks."

I walked down a cobblestone path through the campus, which was lined with oak and maple trees and small leafy shrubs. There were students everywhere. Girls in pleated skirts and oxford shirts, boys in collared shirts and ties loosened around the neck. I looked down at my cardigan and collared shirt, which I'd patched together from my mother's closet, hoping my grandfather wouldn't notice when I paired them with my cut-off shorts. It was the last time I could wear them, and to my relief he hadn't said anything. But now I felt out of place. I picked up the pace, eager for the privacy of my own room.

As the path narrowed, I passed a large grassy area surrounded by trees, which I guessed was the green. Just past it was the lake, wide and still, expanding across the entire upper half of campus. The buildings reflected off the water, changing and distorting in its ripples. At the head of the lake stood a life-size statue of a bear on all fours, its face arched up towards the sky.

The girls' dormitory was made of a soft grey stone. Even from the outside it looked clean, as if it were made entirely of bars of soap. Across the lake stood an almost identical building that was made of a slightly darker stone. It was shaded by a collection of oak trees and seemed gloomier. A few boys were walking towards it.

Inside the girls' dormitory, the heat was on and everything had the calm colouring of warm milk. A wide stone staircase led upstairs, and I skimmed my fingers across the surface of the banister as I ascended.

My room was large and sunny with high ceilings and a fireplace. The walls were a welcoming yellow, and the sweet smell of yeast and baking bread filled the room, reminding me of home. On the far wall were two large windows overlooking the lake and the green. My suitcases rested beneath them. I bent down to begin unpacking when a cool gust of northern air blew in, followed by the sound of rustling paper.

On the desk was a large rectangular parcel wrapped in brown paper. *RENÉE WINTERS,* it said in bold letters. Resting on top of it was a manual with the Gottfried crest embossed on the cover. I opened it. *Gottfried Academy Code of Discipline.* It was 157 pages long. How could there possibly be that many rules? I set it aside and tore open the parcel.

Inside was a stack of books:

Latinvs, by Evangeline Rhine

Mythology and Rituals, by Gander McPherson

Lost Numbers, edited by J. L. Prouty & Linus Moss

Soil, by Brenda Hardiman

Origins of Existence, by Paul F. Dabney

Metaphysical Meditations, by René Descartes

The Republic, by Plato

Beneath them was a series of other books by Nietzsche, Aristophanes, Aristotle, and other names that I couldn't pronounce.

Confused, I pulled out the envelope from my pocket. Inside was a sheet of paper labelled: *Second-Year Schedule: WINTERS.*

Elementary Latin I
Ancient Civilizations
Imaginary Arithmetic
Horticulture
Philosophy
The Arts
Crude Sciences

Horticulture? Imaginary Arithmetic? In California we studied normal things like English, Algebra, Biology and languages that people actually spoke, like Spanish or French. What did Crude Sciences even mean?

I picked up *Mythology and Rituals,* which I assumed was my Ancient Civilizations textbook. Back in California, History had been my favourite subject. Out of my entire schedule, it was probably the only class I would really enjoy. But I guess I didn't have a choice, which seemed to be a recurring theme in my life over the past few weeks.

The sound of footsteps broke my train of thought. They stopped in front of my door. Startled, I stood up and watched the knob turn and the door creak open.

A girl walked in, lugging two overstuffed duffel bags behind her. A mess of wavy blonde hair was piled on top of her head, and her round cheeks were flushed from walking up the stairs. With a sigh, she let a bag drop from her shoulder. It fell to the ground with a thud.

"Who are you?" I asked, confused.

"Eleanor," she said, fanning her face with her hand. "Eleanor Bell."

She was carelessly pretty, with rosy skin and wisps of wind-blown hair framing her face in a way that made her look like she had just stepped off a private yacht in Nantucket.

"So why...what are you doing in my room?"

"What are you talking about?" she said, looking at me as if I were crazy. "I'm your room-mate."

"Oh." I felt my face turn red. In my hurry to open the package, I hadn't even noticed that there were two beds. I looked around the room more carefully and realized that it was true, there seemed to be two of everything: two desks, two chairs, two wardrobes, all divided by a fireplace. "They didn't tell me I had a room-mate."

"They almost didn't tell me either. My old room-mate left Gottfried at the last minute, and I was set to have a huge single all to myself...until a few days ago."

I shifted uncomfortably. "Sorry."

She shrugged. "It's okay. It'll be fun. Besides, living by yourself can get lonely." She looked at my legs and frowned. "You know you're not in dress code."

I glanced down at my shorts and then at her outfit.

She was wearing an impossibly short wool skirt, a perfectly pressed white collared shirt, and black knee-highs. I imagined that her parents were the sort of people who owned horses and played tennis on the weekend after hosting large brunches on their waterfront estate. "And you are?"

Eleanor ignored my comment. "No denim or clothes with writing on them," she recited. "Only skirts, collared shirts and stockings. And if you want to wear trousers, you have to wear a blazer."

I rolled my eyes. What was the point in getting so dressed up for school? "Well, I think I look fine."

Eleanor scoffed at me, sticking her button nose into the air. "You look fine for going to the beach. We're at Gottfried Academy! One of the oldest and most competitive schools in the country. Do you know how many people would die to be in your position?"

I had never heard of Gottfried until my grandfather told me about it, and I definitely didn't care how prestigious it was. I would have given anything to be back at my old school. "I guess it's just hard moving away from my friends." I unzipped one of the suitcases and then added, "I'm new here."

"I know." Eleanor hoisted one of her bags onto her bed. "That's the first thing you need to understand about Gottfried – it's small. Things have a way of being found out." She untied her hair, letting thick blonde locks fall around her shoulders. The smell of citrus and shampoo wafted through the room. "Which brings me to the second thing you need to know. The secrets that aren't found out are buried well. And probably for a reason."

I gave her a perfunctory nod, but thought she was being overly dramatic. I had been to high school; I knew how things worked, how people talked, how secrets were leaked.

Eleanor paused, and for a moment I thought she had finished and I could finally unpack in silence. But then she said, "For example, your name is Renée. You're one metre sixty, you got straight As at Costa Rosa High, you're a sophomore, like me, and you have an inclination for History and the social sciences. Your parents were teachers, but then they died and your grandfather sent you here. His name is" – she tried to remember – "Brownell Winters."

Surprised, I looked up at her. "How did you—?"

"And now you're here, probably thinking I'm some spoiled, self-centred trust-fund girl who's obsessed with make-up and name brands and only got into Gottfried because my family has legacy here."

"That is not true! That's just...it's not...I don't think that about you." The retort sounded cleverer in my head, but the worst part was that I probably would have thought all of those things if I'd had more time.

"It's all right. Everyone thinks it. And maybe they're not *totally* wrong. But I know that your family has legacy too. Which is why *you* got in. You didn't even have to take that ridiculous admissions test. And even though you couldn't have grown up rich – I mean, your parents were *teachers* – I know that you're an only child. Which probably makes you more spoiled than me, because I have an older brother, and everyone knows that only children don't know how to share."

I gaped at her, torn between anger and confusion. How did she know all this? I wanted to ask if it was her family's money that made her think she could talk to someone else that way, but all I managed to spit out was, "I know how to share."

"I told you," she said, reading my thoughts, "things have a way of being found out here. My parents are divorced, so I don't really see them. It happened a few years ago and was really messy. My mom got the house in Aspen, my dad got the house in Wyoming, and they're still fighting over the rest." She rolled her eyes. "Or their lawyers are. My parents can't even stand being in the same state. So of course they couldn't stop fighting about where we would live. Which is why my brother and I are here. That and the fact that practically our entire family has gone to Gottfried." She smiled. "And now you know everything about me, in case you were wondering." She looked into my open suitcase. "That's a really cute skirt."

I watched as she leaned over my personal belongings in all of her blonde, rosy glory, completely unapologetic for who she was and where she came from.

"Thanks," I said. "It was my mom's."

"She had great taste. Do you mind if I take a peek?" And without waiting for an answer, she bent down and sifted through the rest of the clothes in my suitcase. "You know, I've always had this fantasy of growing up in a normal family. A small, cosy house. My parents cooking pancakes for breakfast and borrowing eggs from the neighbours. Riding the bus to school. Oh, and of course I'd have to have a summer job. It's so romantic. I could work as a waitress and wear an apron and everything."

I gave her a confused look. "It's really not that romantic. The bus was crowded and there was always gum stuck to the seats. And I would have killed to not have a summer job. But then I would never have met the guy I was dating. He asked me out at the farmers' market where I worked."

She looked up at me in awe. "See! It *is* romantic! Tell me everything."

I couldn't help but laugh. I had never met anyone who fantasized about having a boring summer job or living in a small house.

"Let's start over," I said, and held out a hand. "My name is Renée."

Eleanor smiled. "It's nice to meet you." She held up a tan shirt with ruffles on the collar. "This is so vintage. Do you mind if I borrow it? It would look great with my new skirt."

I let out another laugh. "Sure. So how *did* you know all that stuff about me?"

"It wasn't hard. My brother, Brandon, is on the Board of Monitors. He's a senior, and practically the headmistress's pet. When I found out I had a room-mate, I asked him to look in your file and relay the details. He's not supposed to, but he'd do anything for me."

It didn't sound that easy. Actually, it sounded like a lot of work for information that she could have just found out by asking me. I watched her go through the clothes in my suitcase, holding them up to her body.

"Eleanor, how come your old room-mate didn't come back this year?"

She gave me a mischievous smile, as if she had been waiting for me to ask. "Now that's a question that's not so easy to answer."

CHAPTER 3

THE AWAKENING

HER NAME WAS CASSANDRA MILLET. That was all I was able to find out about Eleanor's old room-mate before we were interrupted by the chiming of church bells. Eleanor suddenly looked distraught.

"Is it six o'clock already? We have to go!"

"Go where?"

"Fall Awakening, of course. Come on, we're late."

"Wait, what's Fall Awakening?"

Instead of answering, Eleanor grabbed a cardigan. I did the same, and she took me by the elbow and rushed me out the door.

We walked briskly through campus, past Verning Theatre, a massive stone building with Greek columns lining the front; past Horace Hall, made of red brick, with tall darkened windows that gaped vacantly into the mountains. I could barely make out the engraving over its entrance: COGITO ERGO SUM. "That's where our classes are," Eleanor explained. Finally, we passed the Observatory, a stone tower in the middle of campus that doubled as an astronomy lookout and science laboratory. It was almost sunset when we reached the green. A low murmur of voices filled the air, and we walked towards them until we reached the clearing.

The trees grew thicker at the centre of campus, enclosing the lawn in a semicircle of oaks and evergreens. Above them, the darkening sky was scratched open, bleeding bright streaks of red and orange. In the distance was the chapel, its bells still swaying.

"This," Eleanor said, "is Fall Awakening."

The students were divided into four sections, one for each year, she explained. Everyone was already seated on long wooden benches that lined the outskirts of the lawn in the shape of a U. The first row of each section was empty. Eleanor was already squeezing her way onto a bench in the sophomore section. I followed her, but when she saw me take a seat beside her, she shook her head.

"It's supposed to be alphabetical," she explained.

"Which means you should be in the back with the rest of the Ws..."

We both turned to look at the back row. The only space left was on the far side, in between a scrawny blond boy with thick-rimmed glasses and a plump girl with frizzy brown hair who did not look very friendly.

"Oh...right. Okay." I hesitated before standing up, studying the blond boy in the back, who seemed to be counting something that no one else could see. "Who is that?"

Eleanor ignored my question. "But since the guy who sits next to me isn't here, I doubt anyone will notice if you stay," she said just as I was about to leave. "You're way better company. I've tried to make conversation, but he barely acknowledges me. Sometimes I think he doesn't even notice that I'm sitting next to him. He's like that with everyone. He even stopped hanging out with his friends, and now just does everything alone. He's sort of like this social outcast, except that everyone is secretly obsessed with him."

"Obsessed? What do you mean? I thought you said he didn't talk to anyone."

"He doesn't. The thing is...he's beautiful. He's this rugged, devastatingly gorgeous guy who has inexplicably chosen a life of solitude. And he's brilliant. Some Latin prodigy or something. Most people here can't decide if they love him, hate him, or are scared of him. For most people it's all three. Especially my brother. Brandon *hates* it when I talk about him, which is sort of weird because I don't think they've spoken even once."

"Who is he?"

Eleanor lowered her voice, the name rolling off her tongue like a dark secret. "Dante Berlin."

I laughed. "Dante? Like the Dante who wrote the *Inferno*? Did he pick that name just to help cultivate his 'dark and mysterious' persona?"

Eleanor shook her head in disapproval. "Just wait till you see him. You won't be laughing then."

I rolled my eyes. "I bet his real name is something boring like Eugene or Dwayne."

I expected Eleanor to laugh or say something in return, but instead she gave me a concerned look. I ignored it.

"He sounds like a snob to me. I bet he's one of those guys who know they're good-looking. He probably hasn't even read the *Inferno*. It's easy to pretend you're smart when you don't talk to anyone."

Eleanor still didn't respond. "Shh..." she muttered under her breath.

But before I could say "What?" I heard a cough behind me. Oh God, I thought to myself, and slowly turned around.

"Hi," he said with a half grin that seemed to be mocking me.

And that's how I met Dante Berlin.

So how do you describe someone who leaves you speechless?

He was beautiful. Not Monet beautiful or white sandy beach beautiful or even Grand Canyon beautiful. It was both more overwhelming and more delicate. Like gazing into the night sky and feeling incredibly small in comparison. Like holding a shell in your hand and wondering how nature was able to make something so complex yet so perfect: his eyes, dark and pensive; his messy brown hair tucked behind one ear; his arms, strong and lean beneath the cuffs of his collared shirt.

I wanted to say something witty or charming, but all I could muster up was a timid "Hi".

He studied me with what looked like a mix of disgust and curiosity.

"You must be Eugene," I said.

"I am." He smiled, then leaned in and added, "I hope I can trust you to keep my true identity a secret. A name like Eugene could do real damage to my mysterious persona."

I blushed at the sound of my words coming from his lips. He didn't seem anything like the person Eleanor had described.

"And you are—"

"Renée," I interjected.

"I was going to say 'in my seat', but Renée will do."

My face went red. "Oh, right. Sorry."

"Renée like the philosopher René Descartes? How esoteric of you. No wonder you think you know everything. You probably picked that name just to cultivate your overly analytical persona."

I glared at him. I knew he was just dishing back my own insults, but it still stung. "Well, it was nice meeting you," I said curtly, and pushed past him before he could respond, waving a quick goodbye to Eleanor, who looked too stunned to move.

I turned and walked to the last row, using all of my self-control to resist looking back.

"Sorry," I said as I squeezed through the row at the end of the alphabet, stepping over feet and pushing past knees. I stopped in front of the blond boy I'd seen from up front. He looked up at me through his glasses, then quickly averted his eyes, as if he had done something wrong.

"Is this *W*?" I asked.

It took a few seconds for him to realize I was speaking to him. Finally he nodded. "Welch, like the juice," he said, referring to himself, "and Wurst," he said, lowering his voice to a whisper as he pointed to the girl to his left, "like the sausage."

I let out a surprised laugh. "I'm Renée. Winters, like the season," I said, and sat down next to him.

He was a shrimp of a person, and blond all the way

down to his eyelashes. He had inordinately skinny arms and looked like he'd spent the majority of his life in his parents' basement playing video games. Yet still, there was something strangely interesting about him. I tried to place it. Was it the fact that he hadn't blinked since we'd started talking, or the way he leaned a little too close when he spoke? No, it was something more.

"I'm Nathaniel. I mean, that's my first name." He adjusted his glasses. His shaggy hair looked like it hadn't been washed or brushed in days, and his skin was as pasty as waxed paper, save for a collection of blemishes on his chin and forehead.

I smiled. "Got it."

"You're new here, right?"

I nodded.

"Me too. Well, I was last year. I'm not new any more."

A hush fell over the crowd. From the back, a line of people filed onto the lawn.

"Those are the professors," Nathaniel said.

They walked stiffly and all wore the same blue-and-gold scarf around their necks. The frayed ends dangled loosely above their waists as they took their seats in the front row.

At the centre of the lawn was an ancient oak tree. Its gnarled trunk was so thick that it looked as if three trees had twisted themselves into one. Draped over its branches were two flags. They were deep blue, and bore a constellation of a bear and the Gottfried crest of arms in yellow stitching. A small podium stood between them.

And then out of the darkness emerged the tallest woman I had ever seen, striding through the trees like the wisp of a ghost.

"That's the headmistress, Calysta Von Laark," said Nathaniel.

She couldn't have been far off two metres tall, with wavy white hair that was pinned loosely to the back of her head. She had blue eyes, large hands, and a slender figure that was slightly masculine in its proportions.

She walked to the podium and waited. The wind slowed, and everything was still.

"Students, faculty, welcome to another illustrious year at Gottfried Academy." Her voice was low and velvety as it echoed off the buildings surrounding the lawn.

"I hope that you all had an enlightening holiday and were able to use the time away from your studies to wade in the warm waters of everything that summer has to offer. To our new students, welcome. There is a complete list of school policies and procedures in the Gottfried *Code of Discipline,* which you received with your books and schedules. If you have any questions, I trust that our returning students will be able to aid you, as well as the dormitory parents, Mrs. Lynch and Professor Bliss."

A man and woman from the front row stood up and waved.

"Here at the Academy, we believe that limitations challenge the mind. Gottfried has a series of regulations that we hope all of our students will abide by during their stay here. While this is slightly out of procedure, I would like to use this time to reiterate a few that are especially critical after the events that occurred last spring."

A murmur floated over the benches. *What happened last spring?* I wondered, leaning over to ask Nathaniel.

"Someone died," he whispered. "A first year named Benjamin Gallow."

"What?" I asked. "How?"

But we were interrupted by the headmistress's booming voice, as she recounted the rules.

"First: boys are never permitted to be in the girls' dormitory, and vice versa. Second: leaving the school grounds is strictly prohibited and punishable by expulsion. And third" – the headmistress paused to brush a cluster of white hair away from her eyes – "under no exception is anyone allowed to enter into a romantic relationship of *any* nature at this academy."

What? I glanced around me, incredulous that they would even think of banning dating. But no one else seemed fazed. The sun was setting behind the library. Almost simultaneously the lights in every building on campus went out, leaving us to the purpling twilight.

"And, of course, let me emphasize that there shall be no use of artificial light after sunset, with the exception of candles. In this world, darkness is always looming on the horizon. At Gottfried, instead of avoiding the dark, we meet it head on. As headmistress, I urge you to do the same with your studies and with every obstacle you face in the future. Do not accept the confines of the world as you perceive it. Instead, look for what you cannot see. There are universes among us, within us. Our only way out of darkness is to learn how to see without light."

The crowd was silent. Crickets chirped lazily from the grass around us.

"And now, in the time-honoured tradition of the great thinkers who came before us, let us cast away everything we know and attempt to see the world as it really is."

The headmistress closed her eyes and bowed her head. Everyone followed, and I did the same. Then she began to speak in a language that was far different from anything I'd heard before. It started as a low murmur, and gradually grew into a chant. I opened an eye and tried to catch a glimpse of Dante, but all I could see was the back of his neck. It was a beautiful neck, smooth and lean beneath the collar of his shirt.

But my thoughts were interrupted by a voice tickling my ear. "Bring us death," said Nathaniel, barely audible.

I gasped. "What?"

"That's what she's saying: '*Bring us death so we can study it. To capture the mind of a child is to gain immortality.*'" His voice cracked, and he swallowed self-consciously. " '*So that when we die, our minds live for ever.*'"

I stared at the headmistress. It seemed a little morbid for a high school motto. In my old school, the principal didn't even give a welcome speech, let alone hold some bizarre night-time ritual.

"It's Latin," Nathaniel said, pretending to keep his eyes closed like everyone else. "She's saying that even though our bodies will die, our achievements will live on for ever."

"Shhh," hissed a voice from the section across from us. A prim and preppy girl glared at us, then shut her eyes.

"That's Genevieve Tart," he said quietly. "She's a junior. And she hates me."

"Why would she hate you?" I asked.

"My presence annoys her."

"Did she tell you that?"

"No, I can just tell. She barely speaks to me. And she thinks my name is Neil."

"That's ridiculous. How can you know she hates you if she doesn't speak to you?" I asked in a strained whisper.

"Shhh!" Genevieve said again, this time to me.

Nathaniel stared at his feet. "See?"

Before I could respond, a boy from the furthest section of the benches stood up. He was tall and athletic, with a face strikingly like Eleanor's. Her older brother, I realized.

He walked through the rows of his section with a military strut until he stopped behind a girl and tapped her on the shoulder. She was slender and rosy, with almond eyes and straight black hair.

Once tapped, she walked down the rows and tapped a short, bony boy, who made his way to the third-year benches and tapped a girl with freckles and red hair. She tapped a serious-looking boy who made his way to the back, directly towards me.

He stopped at our row, and I closed my eyes and waited. But the tap never came. Instead, he touched the girl across from us. Genevieve Tart rose and gracefully made her way down the aisle.

The six students lined up in front of the podium, their heads bowed and eyes closed.

"The tapping of the new Board of Monitors," Nathaniel explained. "Model students." His voice betrayed a hint of bitterness. "They make sure everyone keeps the rules."

"How are they chosen?"

"They're picked by the faculty. It's really difficult to get. There's this test you have to pass, but no one knows what it is, and the Monitors won't say. That's probably why they were chosen. They're suck-ups."

Headmistress Von Laark stopped chanting and left the podium. She approached the first boy from behind and tapped him on the shoulder. "Brandon Bell," she announced in a commanding voice.

She moved quickly down the line. "Ingrid Fromme.

"Schuyler Soverel.

"Laney Tannenbaum.

"Maxwell Platkin.

"Genevieve Tart."

Only juniors and seniors could be tapped, Nathaniel explained. Brandon, Ingrid and Schuyler were fourth years, and were on the Board last year. The third years were Laney, Maxwell and Genevieve. The headmistress pursed her lips, dark red and elegant. "Board of Monitors. Tonight I bind you to Gottfried Academy. From this moment on, the student body is your body. The student voice is your voice..."

The moon rose large behind the trees. Headmistress Von Laark lifted her head and gazed around the lawn.

"And now," she bellowed, "let us wake."

One by one the Board of Monitors opened their eyes and raised their heads. All of the students followed suit. The night sky was clear. The reflection of the moon rippled in the lake, and a cool breeze fluttered above, rustling the leaves.

The headmistress removed a small knife from the

podium and cut a deep slit into the bark of the tree. Thick red sap oozed out. She dipped her fingers into it and tapped each Monitor on the forehead, smearing a crimson streak just above their eyes.

Then she spoke in Latin, her voice booming across the green.

Nathaniel translated. *"'Blood from the oak tree, blood from our founders, resting in the roots beneath. May our minds be deciduous, constantly being reborn.'"*

The headmistress stopped speaking and turned to the new Board of Monitors. They looked frightening, almost biblical, with the sap dripping down their foreheads. I had never heard of a tree that bled red sap.

"Gottfried Academy, I present to you the Board of Monitors. In celebration, I would like to invite you all to join us in the Megaron for the first-of-the-year feast."

And with that, the headmistress walked past the Board, and one by one they filed off the green and back towards the dorms. The professors followed. No one clapped. No one spoke. The wind blew overhead, making the campus feel vacant.

Once they were gone, everyone stood up. I glanced back at the front row, but Dante wasn't there. Only Eleanor, talking to a group of girls. The rest of the students had already begun to head to the Megaron, which apparently meant *great hall* in Greek, for the feast.

Everyone except for Nathaniel, who was hanging around the benches, as if he were waiting for something.

"Are you going to the feast?" I said finally.

Looking slightly surprised, he straightened his posture. "Yeah." He fidgeted with the buttons on his shirt. Suddenly he slapped a mosquito off his arm.

"Do you want to sit with me?" I asked. He was a bit weird, but seemed nice and sort of funny, and since he hadn't left with friends, I was pretty sure he didn't have anyone to sit with.

He perked up and pushed his glasses closer to his face. "Really? I mean, yeah, sure."

We met up with Eleanor and her friends at a table in the Megaron. Eleanor's friends were just like her: pretty, rich and carefree. I wasn't sure who was more surprised – the girls upon seeing Nathaniel trailing behind me, or Nathaniel upon realizing that he was sitting with some of the most popular girls in our year. Even though I tried to pay attention while everyone was catching up, I couldn't help glancing around the dining hall, hoping to spot Dante beneath one of the iron chandeliers. But all I saw were the faces of strangers.

Then suddenly I heard his name. I turned back to the table, where all the girls and Nathaniel were staring at me, waiting for me to answer.

"Right, Renée?" Eleanor probed.

"What? Sorry. I was just looking at the, um, the Board of Monitors table."

"I was just telling them that you got Dante Berlin to talk. I think he even laughed."

I blushed. "Yeah, I mean, it wasn't a serious conversation or anything. He was actually sort of rude."

"Everything is serious with Dante. He *never* smiles or laughs," said Greta, an athletic redhead.

"He didn't seem *that* bad," I said, taking a bite of pasta. "He did have a sense of humour...kind of."

"He was different around you," Eleanor said. "Actually, I don't think I've ever seen him talk to anyone for as long as he did with you. Since last spring, that is."

"What do you mean 'last spring'? What happened?"

Rebecca, a lithe girl with short black hair, interjected. "No one really knows," she said, leaning on her elbows. "Just that Benjamin Gallow died. He disappeared, and then a few days later they found him in the woods. Dead."

Eleanor interrupted her. "You're telling it completely wrong." She waited until she had my full attention, and began. "So it was the middle of spring term, when one day Benjamin just didn't show up for classes. Benjamin was the kind of guy who had no idea how hot he really was. He was a straight-A student, the best épée fencer on campus, and was friendly to everyone, even the cook staff. Basically everyone liked Benjamin, and Benjamin liked everyone. So when he didn't show up for class, we all thought he was sick. Only he wasn't in the dorm that night.

"The school searched everywhere. They questioned his friends, his room-mate, his girlfriend, practically everyone who knew him, but nobody had any idea where he was. And then they finally found him."

Eleanor gazed around the table dramatically, her eyes glistening with excitement.

"He was in the forest. It was a Monday; I remember because I was wearing my pink-and-blue headband, the one I always wear on Mondays. We were outside in Earth Science when we saw them carrying Benjamin's body through the gates. Dead, of course. I remember they'd thrown his coat over him so none of us could see his face. All we could see was one of his arms swinging below him while Professor Bliss and Professor Starking carried him to the nurses' wing. It was so pale it was almost blue."

The table went uncomfortably silent, the din of silverware clinking against plates blurring into white noise around us as we all imagined Benjamin's arm dragging lifelessly across the green.

"But the strangest part was that nobody could understand what caused his death," Eleanor continued.

"He wasn't harmed in any way. No scratches or bruises or anything, so it was obvious that no one had attacked him or murdered him. And he didn't have anything with him, so it wasn't like he was trying to run away. When the nurses examined him, they said he died of a heart attack, and that there was no other possible cause of death."

I froze. "Wait," I said, my heart beginning to race. "He died of a heart attack?"

"Yeah. It did seem kind of bizarre at first. A fifteen-year-old dying of something like that. But that's what happened."

Images of my parents flooded my mind. The car, the woods, their lifeless bodies. "Did they find anything else? Like anything out of the ordinary? On his body, maybe?"

She gave me a confused look. "I don't think so..."

"They didn't find anything out of the ordinary but a dead kid," Rebecca added sarcastically, biting into a cherry tomato.

Eleanor rolled her eyes.

"So what does Dante have to do with it?" I interjected.

Eleanor gazed at me as if it were obvious. "Dante was the one who found him."

I stopped chewing.

"No one could understand how Dante discovered him. It was in such a remote location in the forest that the chances seemed nearly impossible."

I could feel myself begin to sweat.

"Afterwards, there were rumours that Dante had killed Benjamin. That's how he knew where he was."

"But why would Dante do that?" I said, trying to steady my voice.

"Well," Eleanor said, taking a sip of water, "Benjamin was dating my old room-mate, Cassandra Millet."

"Wait," I said. "I thought we weren't allowed to date." I paused. "Why aren't we allowed to date?"

Eleanor gave me a perplexed look. "Well of course we're not *allowed* to date. The school thinks it distracts from our academics. I guess that's the way they did it back then – brother and sister schools. Same with the dress code. No short skirts or bare shoulders. But that doesn't mean no one dates. You just have to be discreet about it. Anyway, Cassandra was adorable: creamy skin, these huge green eyes, flowing golden hair – a little Aphrodite walking around campus. Everyone loved her. Even Dante. They were best friends – both part of the same group. The Latin Club. People think Dante was in love with Cassandra and killed Benjamin to get to her."

"That seems a little extreme..." I said.

Eleanor shrugged. "It's just a rumour."

"So are they together now or something?"

"Cassandra dropped out," Rebecca said, shaking her head.

"Or transferred," Eleanor added. "Either way, she left the school."

"Maybe *Cassandra* killed Benjamin Gallow," a girl named Bonnie offered.

Eleanor shook the idea off. "Then they would have let the police deal with it. And I already said that the cause of death was a heart attack. How could a person have caused that?"

For the first time in a while, Nathaniel spoke up. "Maybe she tried to kiss him," he said in a small voice. "That would be enough to give me a heart attack."

Everyone at the table exchanged amused glances, and eventually the conversation drifted, leaving Benjamin and Cassandra's mystery unsolved.

After dinner we retreated to our dorm, where the girls dispersed to their rooms. Eleanor lit a candle and changed into a pair of pink pyjamas. I wanted to read, and already forgetting the rules, went to turn on the overhead light. But there was no switch. There really was no light after 9 p.m.

"I still don't see the point in all of these rules."

Eleanor shrugged. "The professors would probably say that it had something to do with our safety."

"But how do you do your homework without lights? How do you do anything?"

"Candles. Your eyes will adjust. Just do your work earlier. Besides, why would you want to do homework at night when you could be doing so many more interesting things?"

It was a nice idea, but I had a feeling that the headmistress would see to it that we wouldn't be doing anything more interesting than homework. No wonder my grandfather liked this place so much. His ten o'clock curfew seemed reasonable in comparison.

"Here," Eleanor said. "Use this." She opened her underwear drawer and searched through it until she found a half-burned candle. "You know, I always thought Nathaniel was sort of weird, like he gave me the creeps or something. But tonight he was really nice. And normal, in an abnormal way."

I nodded, but the boy I was thinking about wasn't Nathaniel.

"So Dante was...friends...with Cassandra?" I asked, trying to sound nonchalant as I ran a brush through my hair.

Eleanor looked up from her journal, her eyes wide with excitement, as if she had been hoping I'd ask. "They were both in the Latin Club. Well, that's what we called it because they were all in Advanced Latin. Anyway, it was Cassandra, two juniors named Gideon DuPont and Vivian Aletto, a sophomore named Yago Castilliar, and then

Dante. They're all really smart, and kind of elitist. They know everything about the classics, they're *fluent* in Latin, and they were always in the library together, whispering in it so no one could understand them."

Eleanor stood up to open the window, and then sat next to me on my bed. "Here, let me do that," she said, and began braiding my hair.

"After Benjamin died and Cassandra dropped out, the group fell apart. Well, not the entire group; just Dante. He had a huge argument with Gideon, Vivian and Yago on the green after curfew. I could hear the shouting from my room."

I hugged my knees. "What were they saying?"

Eleanor let out a laugh. "Who knows? It was all in Latin. The professors didn't get there till it was over. After that Dante basically removed himself from the school. He stopped talking to everyone and moved off campus. I think he's the only student at Gottfried who's allowed to live in Attica Falls."

"Maybe he knows something," I said, glancing out the window to the trees beyond the school wall.

"Something about what?" Eleanor asked, tugging at my braid. "And hold still."

"Benjamin's death. It's not normal, the way he died. And Dante found him." I turned to face Eleanor. "Maybe Dante found something on Benjamin's body and didn't

94

tell the school about it. Maybe that's what the fight was about."

Eleanor's forehead wrinkled in confusion. "Find what on his body? What are you talking about?"

"Like maybe a coin or something. Or cloth."

Eleanor gave me a strange look. "I mean, he was wearing clothes. And he probably had change in his pocket. Why does that matter? Benjamin died of natural causes. And who cares what they were fighting about? Their friend died, and Cassandra transferred. They were probably just upset."

I sighed. "I guess." Even though everything she said made sense, I didn't believe it.

"But if Dante *is* hiding something, maybe you can get it out of him," she said, wrapping an elastic around the bottom of my braid. "I think he likes you."

"He said three words to me, then told me I was in his seat. That hardly counts as liking."

"Okay, but you have to admit that he's gorgeous. Aren't you at least curious?"

I was, but not just because he was unreasonably good-looking. There was something about the way he'd looked at me that made me feel more alive than I'd felt since before my parents had died. Even though our interaction was brief, I couldn't get it out of my head. Why did he talk to me but not to anyone else? It seemed too coincidental that he had found Benjamin dead in the forest from a heart attack, just like I had found my parents. Yes, there was no *proof* he knew anything. He could have left his friends for any number of reasons. But what if there was more to it?

I was about to respond when someone knocked on the other side of the wall above Eleanor's bed. A mischievous smile spread across her face. She climbed onto her bed and knocked back three times, waited, and then knocked once more.

Tiptoeing next to the door, she pressed her ear against it to make sure no one was outside. "I'm going next door. Do you want to come?"

"What's next door?"

"Just the girls," she said, putting on her slippers. "Genevieve's going to be there, and I want to hear all the dirt on the Board of Monitors."

"Is there dirt? I thought they were model students or something."

"Oh come on, everyone has some terrible secret buried away." Raising an eyebrow, she teased, "Not just Dante."

"Isn't your brother on the Board of Monitors? Why don't you just ask him?"

She shook her head. "That's the only thing he won't tell me about. Obviously he doesn't understand reverse psychology. Keeping it a secret only makes me want to know more."

The invitation was tempting, but I was still trying to process all the things she'd told me about Benjamin Gallow. "Maybe some other night. I'm exhausted."

Eleanor shrugged. "Suit yourself."

She pulled on a sweater and slipped into the hall, where Rebecca and Bonnie were huddled outside. "Sweet dreams, Renée," she said, and closed the door.

Unsure of what to do with myself, I picked up our dorm phone and dialled Annie's number. Her mom answered.

"Hel... Hello?" my voice cracked. Even though I had only been gone for two days, it felt like ages. I had taken for granted what it was like to talk to someone familiar, and all at once my emotions about losing my parents and being ripped away from my friends and my life in California came bubbling to the surface.

"Renée, is that you?" Margerie's voice echoed from a world that I had almost forgotten.

I swallowed. "Yes," I said in a small voice. "Is Annie there?"

"Oh honey, she's out right now. Can I have her call you back?"

"Sure," I said, trying to hide my disappointment.

"Is everything all right?" she asked, after I had given her my dorm phone number.

"Yeah, it's great," I forced out. "Everything here is great."

There was a long silence on the other end, as if Margerie were weighing whether or not she believed me. "Okay. Well, call us if you need anything. And I'll make sure to tell Annie you called."

"Thanks," I said, and hung up.

I thought of all the places Annie could have been – the marina, the coffee shop, Lauren's house – all the places I used to go to, but would never see again. To take my mind off it, I rolled over and picked up the Gottfried *Code of Discipline* and opened to the table of contents. It had dozens of sections: Dress Code, Curfew, School Boundaries, Leisure Activities, Room and Board, and Attica Falls, among others. I flipped to the chapter on the history of Gottfried and began to read.

Gottfried Academy was originally founded as a children's hospital. The patients were housed in two buildings, one for boys and one for girls. Between the buildings was the only known salt lake on the East Coast. The founder and head doctor, Bertrand Gottfried, used the antibiotic qualities of the salt water to ward off disease, and the lake became a bathing area for patients. The infirmary grounds were built around it, including a wall that concealed the grounds behind four metres of stone, to protect the patients from the natural hazards of the White Mountains...

Although I was tired, something compelled me to continue reading. And that was how I ended my first day at Gottfried – thinking about rules and restrictions, about death and Benjamin Gallow and my parents, until I fell into a dreamless sleep.

CHAPTER 4

THE FIRST LAW OF ATTRACTION

THE FIRST WEEK OF SCHOOL only added to the strange events that had been occurring over the past few weeks. It started in Latin.

Horace Hall, where almost all of our classes were held, was the size of a small Victorian castle, with stone towers and large wooden doors hammered with iron. They were so heavy I could barely open them. Ivy climbed up the face of the building, meandering around the windows that looked out onto the green.

The doors opened into a foyer with red carpeting, stained wooden walls, and high ceilings supported by oak beams.

The windows were framed with heavy blue drapes, their folds gathering on the floor. Behind them, heaters hissed. In the middle of the foyer was a wide staircase with polished banisters that led to the outer wings of the building.

Our Latin class was somewhere inside. It was first period, and Eleanor was running late and had stopped by the dining hall to pick up breakfast before class, so I was left to find it by myself. A few minutes before the bell rang, I was still standing in the foyer, staring down at my schedule as students rushed past me.

Elementary Latin   M W F 8.00 a.m.

EW, II, VII, Horace Hall

I was pretty sure that meant east wing, first floor, seventh room. Or maybe it meant east wing, second room, seventh floor. Or maybe *EW* were the initials of my professor. I tried to ask for help, but everyone pushed past me in a rush to get to class, a swirling haze of pressed shirts, cufflinks, ties and penny loafers. This place couldn't be *that* hard to navigate; I just had to think. I had a gut feeling that it was on the seventh floor, so in a somewhat arbitrary decision, I made my way up the stairs to the east wing.

I found the room just as the bell rang. Breathless, I pushed open the door and flung myself inside, a flustered, sweaty mess. The entire class turned in my direction, and I knew I'd made a mistake. It was a small group; everyone was sitting around a single wooden table, hunched over their books when I interrupted. They all looked older and somewhat unwelcoming, particularly a brooding boy with short auburn hair that was neatly combed and parted down the side. He was wearing a black suit, far fancier than anyone else in the class, and tortoiseshell glasses. Next to him was a girl who could have been his sister. I couldn't decide who was more handsome. She was also wearing a man's suit, though hers was tailored to her slender frame. Her short black hair was parted and slicked back, as if she were a wealthy financier from the 1920s.

The professor was a robust young man with sandy hair that reminded me of a golden retriever. He was lecturing in a language I didn't understand. It was probably Latin, though I was sure this wasn't the class I was supposed to be in. The professor stopped speaking and gave me a questioning look. I could feel my face turn red.

"Is this Elementary Latin?" I asked stupidly.

The person in the seat closest to me turned around, and to my surprise, it was Dante. He raised an eyebrow, a beautiful eyebrow, and stared at me with amusement. Seeing him again, I felt embarrassed and excited all at once. He was leaning over the back of his seat, his collared shirt pulled tightly around his broad shoulders. His wavy brown hair was pulled back with an elastic band, a few stray locks dangling just below his chin. I imagined myself running my fingers through it.

We made eye contact, and I felt myself blushing.

"No," the professor said, taking off his glasses. Behind him, the board was covered in notes written in Latin. The only words I recognized were *Descartes* and *Romulus et Remus*. A simple six-sided figure was drawn over and over again in different iterations and dimensions. Confused, I looked at it again. It couldn't be anything other than the image that had been haunting me for the last two weeks: a coffin.

"I...I'm sorry," I murmured, and began to back out the door, when Dante stood up and walked towards me, his eyes never leaving mine. I fumbled with my things, and he reached behind me, his hand grazing my skirt as he opened the door. And giving me a barely discernible smile, he breathed, "First floor. Seventh room on the left."

I was late for Latin. When I walked into the classroom, it was the same thing all over again, all heads in my direction, and silence – a dead, pitying silence. Eleanor's eyes were wide and terrified for me. "What happened?" she mouthed, curling a ringlet of hair around her finger nervously. But I didn't dare respond. The professor stopped lecturing.

"I...I'm sorry I'm late. I got lost."

"I don't want you to speak; I want you to sit," she said, as if I should have known.

Trying to keep a low profile, I hugged my bag and made my way to the back of the room.

Our Latin professor was a fortress of a woman, wearing a wide, shapeless dress and a thick pair of glasses. *Professor Edith Lumbar* was written on the board in wobbly cursive.

Edith Lumbar. She was the woman my grandfather had told me to contact if I ever needed help. I closed my eyes and sighed, wishing I hadn't already gotten on her bad side.

"To continue where we left off, while you are in my classroom, there will be a number of rules. First, there shall be no slouching."

The sound of shuffling filled the room as people sat up straight.

"Practitioners of Latin must pay close attention to precision in all facets of life if they wish to master the subtle science of the language."

She began pacing about the room. "Second, you are not to speak unless you are called upon.

"And third, and this is by far the most important of all the rules, you are never, under any circumstance, to speak the language of Latin."

How could we learn a language that we were never allowed to speak? And what was the point of learning it in the first place?

"Why?" I blurted out before I could stop myself.

Professor Lumbar turned around and looked at me with surprise. "Were you not listening when I mentioned rule number two?" she asked, though it clearly wasn't a question. "What is your name?"

"Renée Winters," I said.

She gazed at me for a moment and then repeated, "Renée. *To be born again.* An old name, derivative of the Latinate and French verb *naître, to be born,* and shared by the great thinker René Descartes. While you clearly possess his proclivity for argumentation, it's evident from your rash behaviour that you lack his patience and wisdom to follow a logical progression through to its end."

I barely had time to process her diatribe before she continued.

"So, Renée, what is it that you don't understand?" Her tone was polite yet rife with sarcasm. The room was so silent I could hear my stomach growling.

I swallowed. "I was just...I was wondering why we can't speak a language that we're trying to learn."

"That's an interesting question. Does anyone want to answer her?"

A boy in the front row raised his hand.

"Yes," Professor Lumbar said. "What is your name?"

"Prem," he said.

"Prem, what do you think?"

"Is it because Latin is a dead language?"

"Latin has been considered 'dead' for centuries. Yet it is quite alive. Historically, Latin has been a language of the elite. Only select people were able to read it, write it, and most important, speak it. In this class we will study the legends surrounding the people Latin *chose* to speak through. Since this is an elementary class, it is obvious that no one in this room has been blessed with a Latinate tongue. To attempt to speak it out loud would thus be an act of hubris.

"However, if you choose to exercise your minds, I can teach you how to communicate the unspeakable. How do you describe the briefest sensation? A smell you haven't experienced since you were a child? The ecstasy of seeing an animal being born? The immeasurable grief we feel when faced with death? We can't even begin to communicate these complex emotions to each other. But Latin can illuminate sensations you never realized you had."

All eyes were glued to the professor. Suddenly, Latin became interesting. Even as a child I had felt isolated in my thoughts. I was sure that nobody knew the real me, the full me, even my parents. And now that they were dead, I was completely alone. How could I explain all the things I was feeling to another person? Maybe Latin was the answer.

Professor Lumbar picked up a piece of chalk and began to scrawl something on the board. *Latinum: lingua mortuorum.* I copied it in my notebook.

"Now, open your books to page twelve," she said, and proceeded to make us copy out verb conjugations until the period was over. Once out of class, I flipped through my dictionary to try and decipher what she had written. After writing out the translation, I looked around suspiciously.

Latin: The Language of the Dead.

The rest of the day went by in a blur. We were herded from one classroom to the next like cattle, lugging our books up and down the rickety old stairs of Horace Hall with just a short break for lunch. It had been so long since I had been at a new school that I had forgotten how difficult it was to be the new girl. I had no friends, and everyone at Gottfried acted like they'd stepped out of a polo match in the British countryside with the Prince of Wales. And considering that Gottfried actually had a polo team, and one of the senior students was distantly related to the Duchess of Kent, some of them probably had. Eleanor was clearly one of the most popular girls in our grade, and fluttered from group to group chatting about her summer. Because she was only in two of my classes and there was barely time to talk in between, we agreed to catch up at dinner.

Left to my thoughts, I wondered what my friends at home were doing. Annie would be in Biology, sitting in the back row, passing notes to Lauren while Mr. Murnane lectured about the body. And where would Wes be? In US History, or maybe English Lit. Daydreaming about Wes used to be something I looked forward to, but now it just made me sad. Was he still thinking about me, or had he already moved on? The thought of him with another girl was too unpleasant for me to bear, and I pushed it out of my head, resolving to focus on my classes. It was the only way I'd be able to get through the first day of school without losing my mind.

I was just about to head to Philosophy when I heard something drop. Behind me, a frail girl with stringy brown hair was kneeling on the ground, frantically trying to pick up the papers and pencils and books that had fallen from her bag.

Feeling her embarrassment, I set my bag down and approached her. She looked rumpled, with puffy eyes and a glazed-over gaze, as if she had just woken up.

"Do you want some help?"

She turned to me with gratitude and nodded. Her brown hair stood up in the back with static, and she had a run in her stockings that started at the heel and travelled all the way up to the hem of her skirt.

"I'm Renée," I said.

"Minnie," she said timidly.

Before I could respond, I felt a tap on my shoulder.

A woman with a metre stick was standing behind me.

She was short and squat, with thick calves and an oversized blazer with a peacock brooch on the left lapel. Her hair was a dull brown and was cut close to her head in a no-nonsense style.

Minnie's face contorted with fear and she stuffed the rest of her belongings into her bag and scurried away to the corner of the foyer, leaving a few stray pencils on the ground.

"Stand up," the woman said to me.

Upright, I towered over her, my eyes meeting the top of her head.

"What is your name?"

"Renée," I said, resentful of being ordered around and asked my name when all I'd been doing was helping a girl pick up her things. Professor Lumbar I could understand, since I had been late, but this was unnecessary. "What's yours?"

She stared at me, horrified at my impertinence. "The audacity—" she said, almost to herself. "My name is Mrs. Lynch. But don't busy yourself trying to remember it; in time it will ring familiar. An insubordinate child like you, I suspect, will be seeing a lot more of me in the future."

She took me by the elbow and led me to the foot of the stairs.

"What are you doing?"

"General procedure."

"But I haven't done anything wrong!"

"Kneel," she barked.

Startled by the abnormality of her command, I dropped to the ground in front of the staircase, trying to convince myself that teachers no longer beat students with rulers. Did they? Around us, a crowd of students had begun to gather. A group of girls pointed at me and whispered. I tried to ignore them, though I could feel my face growing red. The grainy wood floor was rough against my bare knees, and I shifted my weight uncomfortably.

Mrs. Lynch circled me, her brown clogs clicking against the floor like a timer. "No stockings," she murmured, dragging the end of the ruler across the back of my legs.

"Untucked shirt," she continued. She dropped the metre stick, its butt hitting the ground with a thud. A hush ran through the crowd of students. I winced, waiting for her to hit me, but instead she bent down and held the stick against my thigh. She looked at my skirt and frowned. "Five and a half centimetres above the knee. The dress code stipulates that skirts can be no more than five centimetres above the knee."

"But it's only half a centimetre!"

"Nevertheless, you are out of dress code," Mrs. Lynch sneered, showing a row of tiny yellowed teeth.

I glared at her and stood up, pulling at my skirt. How was this possibly punishable?

"You will go back to your room and change."

"But I have to go to Philosophy—"

She ignored me. "And on the way you'll pay a visit to the headmistress's office."

"I have class now!"

"You'll have to miss it," she said, and began to walk away.

"But it's the first day!"

She turned to me. "Young lady, you're lucky it's the first day. Otherwise your punishment would have been far more severe."

I was wiping off my knees when I heard a woman's voice behind me. "Excuse me," she said to Mrs. Lynch. Startled, she turned around.

The woman was thin and plain, with straight brown hair and a linen skirt. She was about the age of my mother, and had creases around her eyes from smiling. "This is one of my students. I'll deal with her."

I had never seen her in my life.

Mrs. Lynch gave her a suspicious look. So did I.

"I only mean to escort her," the woman said, studying me as if she had seen me before. "She's new."

Mrs. Lynch grunted in reply and went back to her office, her metre stick tapping as she walked. When she was gone, the woman turned to me. "Come."

The crowd in the foyer of Horace Hall parted, and I

111

held my head high as I walked, avoiding eye contact with anyone, to hide my mortification. Once we were outside, she stopped and glanced around us. "Go back to the dorm and change."

"What about the headmistress?"

"Do you really want to see her?"

I shook my head.

"That's what I thought."

I didn't know who she was or why she was helping me. "Why—" I started to say, but she interrupted me.

"Don't get caught out of dress code again."

With a nod, I ran back to the dormitory. I went through all of my mother's clothes until I finally found a more modest pleated skirt. I put it on, along with a pair of stockings. Then I tucked in my shirt, slipped on my cardigan, and stood in front of the mirror. I could barely recognize myself. If Annie saw me now she would have walked right by me. Yet for some reason the woman who had just saved me from the headmistress's office had looked at me as if she'd seen me before. Who was she? Sighing, I ran a hand through my hair and pinned it back with one of my mother's hair clips.

By the end of the day I had met up with Nathaniel, and together we walked over to our last class, Crude Sciences.

It was in the Observatory, a tall spindle of a building in the centre of campus. On the way, I told him about how I'd walked into the wrong class before Latin, and about Minnie and Mrs. Lynch and the mystery woman who had intervened.

"Yeah," Nathaniel said. His poorly knotted tie was too long, and swung against his chest as he struggled to hold his books and keep up with me. "Lynch loves watching people squirm. She's always on me for having too much facial hair." He fingered the three or four lone whiskers that had sprouted from his chin. "I don't even own a razor!" His voice cracked, and he blushed. "And next time don't worry about Minnie. She's always tripping over things and dropping stuff, which doesn't really help the fact that everyone here thinks she's crazy."

"Why do they think that?" I asked, gripping my book bag.

"She had this outburst last year in the dining hall. I don't really know what it was about. I wasn't there."

I shrugged. "Speaking of crazy, what *was* that class that I walked in on? There were all these morbid drawings on the board, and the teacher was speaking Latin, I think. And everyone looked miserable. Though I guess I would too if I had to stare at drawings like that all day."

Nathaniel wiped the sweat beading on his forehead with the end of his tie. "I don't know. It's not that weird.

113

It was probably one of the Advanced Latin classes."

"Okay. But what about the drawings on the board? And Dante was in it. He's in our year. Shouldn't he be in *my* Latin class?"

Nathaniel pushed up his glasses. "No. I'm in an Advanced Latin class too," he said proudly. "They group us based on ability instead of year, since there aren't that many of us. And as for the drawings, maybe they were just using them to learn vocabulary words."

I gave him a sceptical look. "A chapter on coffins? I highly doubt that."

The inside of the Observatory was much larger than its small frame suggested. The walls were white, and a single spiral staircase led up to the glass dome of the roof. When we made it to the top, we were in a laboratory with long concentric counters lined with beakers, scales and metal instruments. Bottles of brightly coloured liquids and vials of powder lined the walls. In the centre of the room, a giant telescope faced up into the sky.

Nathaniel and I sat at an empty bench in the back row. The professor was standing in the middle of the classroom, a position that emphasized his potbelly and disproportionately skinny legs. He wore spectacles and had the spacey look of a mad scientist who believed in conspiracy theories and aliens. Pens stuck out of his shirt pocket, and frizzy tufts of hair sprouted in a ring around the crown of his head. He glanced at his watch and flipped the lights on and off to signal the start of class.

I was about to ask Nathaniel more about his Latin class when I felt someone's eyes on me. I looked up and saw Dante. He was sitting on the far side of the classroom, the afternoon light bending around his silhouette. His dark hair was strewn carelessly about his face, making his skin look ashen and smooth in contrast.

Our eyes met, and I tried to smile, but Dante didn't waver. Instead he gave me a curious, almost troubled look. What was he thinking about?

The professor flipped the lights on and off one last time, making Dante's face disappear and then reappear like the flash of a ghost. When the lights came back on, he was still staring at me. A prickly feeling of anxiety crept up my spine. I shuddered and looked away.

"Professor Starking is my name, though this is but a formality. The details of our identities are quite insignificant in the complex system of forces that comprise our universe."

He patted the shaft of the telescope and glanced up through the glass ceiling. Clouds floated carelessly across the sky. A small flock of birds flew beneath them.

"But before we look into the outer realms of the cosmos, we must revisit *this* world. Thus we study the crude sciences. Biology, physics, chemistry – we will master these before we move on to the stars and planets."

Professor Starking tilted his head down and studied the class over the top of his glasses. "In our time together I will attempt to reshape your Galilean brains. You may experience discomfort. Expanding the mind can often be painful."

I glanced back at Dante, unable to help myself. Everything about him seemed irresistible – the waves of his hair, the stubble on his chin. I could look at him all day and still not have all of the contours of his face committed to memory.

"We've learned from history that we are more efficient when we work together," Professor Starking said. "Plato had Socrates, Galileo had Archimedes, Doctor Frankenstein had Igor." He let out a chuckle, which degenerated into a fit of coughing.

"So," he continued, clearing his throat, "everyone has been assigned a lab partner, who you'll be working with for the entire semester."

He began to read off names. Please, I thought, read my name with Dante's. Please.

"Nathaniel Welch and Morgan Leicester." Nathaniel shrugged and stood up.

"Greta Platt and Christian Treese. Paul McLadan and Maggie Hughes.

"Renée Winters and Dante Berlin."

Surprised, my body went rigid. In California, I always

seemed to be partners with Oily Jeremy, the boy with terrible body odour, or with Samantha Watson, who was only interested in talking about her nail polish. A chair scraped against the floor, and Dante walked across the room and took the empty seat next to me, his shoulder blades shifting underneath his shirt like tectonic plates as he leaned on the table.

After studying me for a few moments, he turned and faced the professor without even acknowledging me. Shocked by his rudeness and unsure of what to do, I turned my attention to the board and pretended to ignore him. We sat in silence until the professor finished calling off the names.

"The Laws of Attraction." He approached the board.

His voice was drowned out by the noise of rustling paper.

"The First Law of Attraction states that attraction and repulsion are two sides of the same force."

And as Professor Starking talked about physics and magnetism, I turned to Dante.

"Why do you keep staring at me?" I muttered under my breath.

He glanced around to make sure no one was listening and then leaned towards me. His voice was hushed. "You have pen on your face. Here," he said, touching the space by his nose.

"Oh." I felt my face go red as I wiped my cheek with my hand.

"That and you remind me of someone I know. Or once knew. But I can't place who it is."

"I thought you didn't have any friends," I challenged.

Dante smiled. "I don't. Only enemies. Which doesn't bode well for you, considering the fact that you must resemble one of them."

I raised an eyebrow. "You know, you're really good at compliments. Actually, it's surprising that a person with charm like yours has *any* enemies." The words came out before I could stop them. At this rate I would never be able to ask him about Benjamin Gallow, and it didn't help that every time he looked at me I wanted to melt.

"So you think I'm charming?" Dante countered, mocking me. "Is that why *you* keep staring at *me*?"

"Alarming, not charming. And no, I'm just curious."

"Curious?" Dante gave me a bemused look and leaned back, draping his arm over his chair. "About what?"

"Why don't you talk to anyone?"

"I thought that's what we were doing."

"To anyone else."

"Talking isn't the only way to communicate. I speak when I have something to say."

"Then you must be pretty boring, judging from what everyone says about you."

Dante let out a laugh. "And what are they saying?"

"That you won't talk to anyone at school because you think you're superior."

"And what if I am?"

I narrowed my eyes. "You're not. You just think you are."

Dante smiled and leaned towards me. "So now you can read my thoughts?"

I swallowed. "No. I can just tell."

"Really? What am I thinking now?" he said, lowering his eyes to mine.

It was difficult to act normal with him staring at me so closely, so intensely. My voice wavered. "You're...you're wondering where I'm from."

Dante's face softened. "That's exactly what I was thinking," he said, studying me. I wasn't sure if he was joking.

"Somewhere green, I'd guess," he continued. "With a lot of sun."

"How do you figure that?"

Without touching me, he traced his fingers through the air along the top of my cheeks. "Freckles."

I blushed. "California. And you...you're from—?"

"Here and there," he said, brushing off my question. "Nowhere, really."

I gave him a suspicious look. What did that even mean?

Though, admittedly, I couldn't imagine him being from anywhere. He was too handsome, too mysterious to come from a place.

Before I could ask him another question, Dante continued. "So why did you come here? You don't seem like the average Gottfried student."

"Why?" I said, taking offence. "Because I don't have a trust fund and a summer home?"

"Because you say what you think."

"Oh," I said, averting my eyes. "And people at Gottfried don't?"

"Not like you did to me at the Awakening. Or to Mrs. Lynch this morning."

I sighed. He saw that. "I'm not used to so many rules. My old school was more...laid-back."

"So your parents sent you here?"

I shook my head. "My grandfather..." My voice trailed off.

I felt Dante's eyes on me, examining my face.

"Do you have parents?" I asked, before realizing how stupid a question it was. Everyone had parents.

Dante hesitated. "No, not really."

"What do you mean *not really*?"

"Nothing," he said. "It's just...never mind."

I rested my chin in my hand, considering his aloofness. "What's the big secret?"

"No secret," he said with a smile. "Just nothing to tell."

I gave him a coy frown. "Or nothing you *want* to tell."

Around us, everyone was flipping through the pages in their textbooks as Professor Starking recited something about forces. I shuffled through the pages haphazardly, more aware of Dante's presence next to me than the vectors in the book.

He gave me the beginnings of a smile. "Look, I think we got off on the wrong foot. Can we start over?" He held his hand out beneath the desk. "I'm Dante," he said.

I studied the creases in his palms, the veins running up the contours of his arms, before responding. "Renée," I said quietly, slipping my hand into his.

His skin was cold to the touch, and I felt a tingling sensation in my fingers, as if they had just begun to go numb. Our eyes met, and my face became warm and flushed, my insides fluttering like a cage of small birds. It was alarming; nothing like this had ever happened before, and I didn't understand why I felt so strange. It wasn't just nerves or butterflies. I'd felt those with Wes; but this was different – frightening, almost supernatural. I opened my mouth to say something, but nothing came out.

He pulled his hand back quickly, and the sensation in my fingers slowly returned to normal, the warmth seeping through my skin like ink. I blinked once, and everything except for Dante seemed muted and distant. I stared at him – horrified, confused, excited – at his lips, parted and drawing breath into his body as he tried to understand what had just happened, and I knew that nothing would ever be the same.

CHAPTER 5

HORTICULTURE

DANTE WAS COMPLETELY WRONG for me. Unsociable. Severe. Intellectually condescending. Or at least that's what I told Annie. It was Thursday, and I was nearing the end of my first week of classes. I called her after lights-out. The gnarled cord of the phone was stretched across the room as I huddled beneath the covers and whispered into the receiver, trying to find some semblance of privacy.

"He's the exact opposite of Wes. And Wes is perfect, isn't he? So what does that say about Dante?" I asked her. All week I'd been trying to convince myself that I wasn't interested in Dante. I just wanted to get close enough so I could ask him about Benjamin. But the likelihood of that was slipping further and further away. After our hands touched in Crude Sciences, he'd stared at his and then at mine with a look of confusion mixed with disbelief. Lowering his hand beneath the desk, he opened and closed his fist, watching his knuckles turn white.

Turning to me, he asked, barely audible, "Did you...?"

But as he studied my face, his voice trailed off. Had he felt what I felt? I didn't have a chance to ask him, because without saying anything else, he stood up. The class turned to us as his chair scratched the floor. Professor Starking stopped lecturing.

"I have to go," Dante said, gathering his things and giving me one last glance, the door slamming behind him.

I had tried to talk to him the next time we had Crude Sciences, but he was too busy flipping through a Latin book under the desk and writing in a leather-bound journal to grace me with more than a one-word answer. As a matter of fact, he hadn't even looked at me, which made me even angrier.

"Could you pass me the—?" I'd asked during a lab about the physics of a butterfly, but instead of paying attention to the lab, Dante was reading. Before I could finish my sentence, he passed me the magnifying glass.

As he did, our hands brushed against each other. He pulled his hand back.

"Don't touch me," he said quickly, before averting his eyes.

His words stung as I stared at him, not knowing what to say. "What?"

"I'm sorry," he said, without looking at me. "I...I shouldn't have said that." He turned back to the book in his lap and flipped a page, tracing the lines with his finger until he found the sentence he was looking for. "It's a milkweed butterfly, by the way."

"How...how did you know that? You didn't even look..."

But he didn't respond. And after confirming that it was, in fact, a milkweed butterfly, I turned to him, frustrated. Holding the magnifying glass over my eye, I peeked over his shoulder, trying to see what he was reading. It was all in Latin.

"Is that for Latin class?" I asked, staring at his Roman profile, which was even more impressive when magnified.

Dante looked up, startled. "No," he said, shutting the book. "Grey," he remarked, staring at my eye through the glass. "Like the sky. Pretty."

So maybe he was strikingly handsome, and maybe his voice was deep and buttery. And maybe he did say brilliant things and always knew the right answer even though he had spent practically the entire class reading a mysterious book in Latin. I wouldn't let that distract me from the fact that he was exactly the person that Eleanor had described: evasive, arrogant and inexplicably distracted. But if all of that were true, I asked Annie, why couldn't I stop thinking about him?

"The weirdest part was when we shook hands. He touched my fingers and my hand got all prickly, like it was falling asleep. That's when he got up and left. He's pretty much ignored me since."

Annie laughed. "Oh, Renée. You're always so dramatic when it comes to guys."

"No, I'm being serious. I've never felt anything like it. It was like my skin was going numb."

I heard Margerie say something in the background. Annie covered the receiver, muffling her response. "Hold on, Mom, it's *Renée*," I made out before she returned to our conversation. "I don't get it. You lost circulation or something? Are you sure you weren't just nervous? Or maybe you were leaning on your funny bone."

I frowned. "No," I said. "I know it sounds crazy, but I felt it. It was real."

There was a long pause on the other side. "Don't worry," she said. "I believe you." But she wasn't very convincing. "So remind me again: if this guy is such a jerk, why are you so obsessed with him?"

126

"Because I think he knows something. And I'm not obsessed," I added, and told her about Benjamin Gallow and the incident last spring. When I mentioned the heart attack, Annie's end of the line went silent.

"Coincidental, right?" I said softly.

Annie hesitated. "It's different, Renée. Your parents... they were at an age when..."

"When what?"

"Nothing, it's just...I'm sure the doctors and police officers know more about that stuff than we do. No one suspects anything but you, right?"

I didn't respond.

"I bet that kind of thing happens more than we think."

I curled the cord around my fingers beneath the sheets. "Yeah, maybe..."

We talked for a few more minutes about California and my old school. Annie told me all of the gossip about what the new teachers were like, who was dating whom, which freshmen had made the lacrosse team. It should have been exciting, but for some reason I couldn't get into it. When she finally hung up, I threw my blankets off and stared at the ceiling. The receiver was resting on my chest, the dial tone dissipating into the darkness of the dorm room. What was wrong with me? Annie had been my best friend since we were kids; she was the only person left who knew everything about me. So why I did feel relieved when she said she had to go?

"I think it's perfectly normal."

Startled, I sat up. Eleanor was still sitting in bed, in silk pyjamas, holding a pink highlighter and a book called *Symposium,* by Plato. A half-burned candle flickered on the nightstand.

"What is?"

"Dante."

"You could hear me?"

"Of course I could. You were beneath a blanket. And you're not good at whispering. Anyway, I think what happened between you and Dante is romantic."

"Oh no, well, I don't think it's like that. I mean, I like someone else. Well, I did before I came here." Though I knew that reality was quickly fading away. Annie told me that Wes had been asking about me, but I hadn't heard anything from him since arriving at Gottfried. "I'm not going to get involved with Dante. He isn't right for me."

Eleanor raised a perfectly shaped eyebrow. "That's strange, considering you spent almost the entire conversation talking about him."

"It's also strange that you spent the entire time listening to my conversation when you were supposed to be reading," I challenged, giving her the beginnings of a smile.

"That's not strange, it's normal. What else was I supposed to do? Besides, if I hadn't listened, you wouldn't have anyone to talk about Dante with. So really, I'm doing you a favour. And if you want my opinion, I think it's obvious that he's into you. That hand thing. That means something."

I let out a sarcastic laugh. "Yeah, probably that I'm allergic to his cologne."

"Don't be ridiculous. I don't think it's *that* out of the ordinary."

I gave her a sceptical look. "Really? Has that ever happened to *you*?"

"Oh, no. Of course not. I've never heard of anything like it. But I think if something creepy like that *could* ever happen, it would be with Dante Berlin. Or maybe Gideon DuPont, though then you'd have to face the wrath of Vivian."

"They're Dante's friends, right?"

"They're Dante's old friends. The Latin scholars. Gideon's a senior. He always wears black suits and these old-man glasses, like he just stepped out of the Great Depression or something."

Immediately, I knew who he was. He was one of the people in the class I'd walked in on. Vivian must have been the girl beside him.

"And Vivian Aletto is his best 'friend'. Though everyone's

pretty sure there's something going on between them. They're always together and they're always arguing like they're brother and sister. But once I saw Gideon stroking the inside of her wrist. And Vivian sometimes wears his glasses. It's really bizarre."

"And they were friends with Dante and Cassandra Millet?"

Eleanor nodded. "And Yago Castilliar. You've probably seen him around; he wears a lot of pastels. Seersucker trousers that just barely make dress code; loafers with no socks. Always needs a haircut, but never seems to get in trouble for it. I think it's because he flirts with Mrs. Lynch."

I had seen him around. He was easy to spot, considering he was the only guy who was brave enough to wear a pink oxford shirt.

"Anyway, they were like a family. The oldest and most intimidating of the five were Gideon and Vivian, who were like the parents. Yago was the delinquent child, and Dante was the older brother, even though he's actually younger than Yago. And Cassandra was the baby, the darling."

"Don't they have real families?"

"Sort of. At least Yago does. His father is some Spanish baron, so he's always back and forth between Spain and New York. I think Gideon is from around here. New Hampshire maybe. And Vivian, who knows? I wouldn't be surprised if she killed her family and ate them.

"Cassandra lost her entire family in a skiing accident before she came to Gottfried, and inherited their fortune. I think technically her great-aunt is her legal guardian, but she always used to tag along with Yago's family on the holidays. Or with her boyfriend, Benjamin. Until he, well...you know. The heart attack." Eleanor closed her book and ran a finger back and forth through the flame of the candle, waiting for me to ask the question that we both knew came next.

"What about Dante?"

She sat up straight and narrowed her eyes dramatically. "He's the strangest one. Apparently he's an orphan. Or so he says. He never leaves Attica Falls on holidays; even over Christmas."

Attica Falls. The gas station, the general store, the diner. It was like an abandoned town. A stray cat and a rusty pickup truck were the only signs of life. "Where does he live?" I asked.

"In an old boarding house. I've only seen the outside, but it looks depressing."

"No wonder they were all so close," I murmured. "They didn't have anyone else." It was a situation I could relate to.

"I know. Can you imagine not having a family?"

"Yeah," I said quietly. "I can."

Eleanor went silent, and I immediately felt the

uneasiness that always followed when I brought up the death of my parents.

"Wait, how do you know all of this? Your brother?"

Eleanor shook her head. "Don't you remember? Cassie was my old room-mate."

Friday morning we woke up earlier than usual for our first Horticulture class. All of the other classes started at eight, but for some reason Horticulture was at six. Something to do with plants and the sun, I assumed. Eleanor was in the class too, and I glanced at my schedule while I waited for her to get ready.

Horticulture   F 6:00 a.m.   The Chapel

"Hey. Our class is in the chapel?"

"I guess so," Eleanor said, pulling on a wool skirt while simultaneously trying to pin back her hair. "Ironic, considering how ungodly it is to get up this early in the morning." She took one last look in the mirror and then grabbed her bag. "Okay, let's go."

It was a clear autumn day. The oak trees towered over us as we walked down the cobblestone path. The chapel was in the westernmost corner of campus. It was dreary looking, with gothic steeples that harkened back to the Dark Ages. All of the arches seemed to be slouching over, as if they had gotten tired of standing upright after three centuries. Statues of saints were carved into the façade, framing the door with blank, eyeless faces. Water stains ran down the stone figures, and a bird's nest was wedged between two of the apostles.

"It's been out of use for ages," Eleanor said. "I think like a hundred years ago Gottfried was a religious school, but then the chapel was abandoned. It's supposedly under renovations from some fire a while back, but I don't think I've ever seen anyone working on it."

We approached the tall riveted doors and attempted to open them, but they were locked. Eleanor and I looked at each other, confused. I jiggled the handles a few times and pounded on the door in frustration, but it was no use.

"I guess it's cancelled," Eleanor said happily. "We should probably go back to the dorm."

I was about to agree with her when we heard voices coming from behind the building. The entire class was standing in what looked like an overgrown graveyard. It was a small class: me, Eleanor, a pair of twins named April and Allison, who lived on our floor, a few guys I had never seen before, and a cute boy who looked uncannily similar to Wes. Eleanor and I joined them.

Professor Betty Mumm was a tiny birdlike woman. She had a weathered, wrinkled face from too many days in the sun, and short brown hair cut like a boy's. She stood in the grass in front of us, wearing tall rubber boots, gardening gloves, and a sun hat.

"Welcome to Horticulture," she said, and pulled out a bag of flower bulbs from a burlap sack on the ground. "Today we're going to be learning the basics of soil."

She passed out the bulbs, a set of trowels, boxes of matches and gardening gloves. She was surprisingly nimble considering she looked older than my grandfather.

"The first thing you need to know about horticulture is that without the appropriate bed for the appropriate plant, you will never succeed in growing anything. There are dozens of varieties of soil, each with its own unique characteristics. Fortunately for us, all of them can be found in this very garden, due to the fact that the ground in this particular area of campus has been dug up and replaced over the course of the last two centuries."

As Professor Mumm discussed the five most common kinds of soil, I glanced around the graveyard. The grass was speckled with wild flowers that grew up to the middle of my shins. They were moist with dew. Nestled beneath the weeds were barely visible fragments of chipped gravestones, centuries old. When I'd first seen Horticulture on my schedule, I hadn't known what to expect, and I would be lying if I said I'd been excited about the class. I'd assumed we'd be learning about plant biology, not digging around in an abandoned graveyard.

"Isn't this a little morbid?" I said to Eleanor, keeping my eyes on the professor, who was demonstrating how to hold a trowel correctly.

"What makes you say that?" a deep voice replied.

Startled, I turned around. Eleanor had moved closer to the chapel, and was now whispering to one of the twins. Standing in her place was the cute Wes impersonator.

"I'm Brett," he said with a grin.

Suddenly I felt very shy. "Renée."

Brett was tall and athletic, and looked like he had just come from playing rugby. His features seemed exaggerated, giving him a dashing and overly masculine look, which I had only attributed to characters in fairy tales.

"So who did you mean to talk to before I so rudely interrupted?"

"My friend Annie. I mean Eleanor. My room-mate Eleanor."

"Annie, Eleanor, which is it?"

"Eleanor. Eleanor Bell." I pointed to where she was standing. "Sorry, my friend Annie is from California. I mean...that's where I'm from too. I just moved here. I'm still trying to keep everything straight."

"A California girl. Aren't you supposed to be blonde?" He flipped a lock of my brown hair with his fingers.

I could feel myself starting to blush, and tucked my hair behind my ear. Brett seemed like the kind of guy who

135

could get any girl; who plays frisbee with his shirt off and his jeans rolled up at the ankle, whose sweat actually smells good; the kind of guy who I never imagined would talk to me. Just like Wes. Yet here he was, standing next to me, doing what I could only identify as flirting.

"Where are you from?" I asked.

"Maine."

"Aren't you supposed to be a bearded farmer?"

Brett laughed. "So that's what you thought it'd be like here? It must have been a huge disappointment."

"Devastating," I replied, and we both fixed our attention on Professor Mumm, who was motioning for us to follow her into the "garden".

"Each of you has a different kind of flower bulb – woodland, climbing, perennial, annual, or arboreal. Now, what I want you to do is find the most suitable soil for planting your particular bulb, and shovel it into one of these bags," she said, holding up a handful of cloth satchels.

One of the twins raised her hand. "But we don't know what kind of bulb we have. How are we supposed to know what kind of soil is best if we don't know what our bulb is?"

Professor Mumm gave her a wise smile. "Intuition. That is the first rule of horticulture. Intuition. Follow your gut!" she said, clicking her heels together. "And remember what we recited. H-E-R-B-S: Handle, Eat, Rub, Burn,

Smell. Now, don your gloves and man your trowels!"

Brett and I parted ways as everyone in the class started wandering aimlessly around the graveyard. Eleanor found her way to me and pinched my arm from behind. "Hey," she said, the twins beside her.

I jumped. "A graveyard is not the place to creep up on people!"

Eleanor laughed. "It's broad daylight! Besides, I wasn't the only one who crept up on you." She glanced at Brett.

April butted in. "He does that with all the girls," she said. Her sister Allison nodded in confirmation.

"That doesn't mean we can't look," Eleanor replied.

We all watched him bend over to pick up his trowel. As he stood up, he turned to us and smiled. Embarrassed, I looked away. Eleanor, on the other hand, responded by giving him a coy wave.

"I think I'm going to go 'test the soil' closer to Brett," she said. "I never get tired of his dimples."

I laughed as Eleanor skipped away, trying to inconspicuously follow Brett to the left side of the "garden". Around me, dozens of gravestones peeked out of the grass, their faces so faded that I couldn't read the inscriptions. My parents were like these people now, reduced to epitaphs, tombstones, coffins. Shaking the thought from my head, I picked up my bulb and turned it around in my palm. It was brown and bulbous like a ginger root. I held it up to my nose, but it just smelled like dry dirt. Intuition, I thought, and began to walk.

I didn't know where I was going, but I stepped forward, changing directions every few minutes as if I were being pulled by an invisible force. Every so often I bent over to sift through the soil. *H-E-R-B-S,* I repeated to myself. *H* for *Handle* as I felt its weight in my hand. *E* for *Eat* as I raised the soil to my mouth and tasted it. *R* for *Rub* as I pressed the soil into my palm, comparing its colour and texture to that of my bulb. *B* for *Burn,* though none of the soil was oily enough to ignite when I struck a match to it. And *S* for *Smell* – confusing smells of apple and grass and walnut, but none of them seemed right. Every batch of soil was either too dry or too gritty; smelled too much like pastrami or tasted too bitter.

Eventually I found myself a good distance away from the rest of the class, in a patchy area by a collection of trees. I bent over to pick up a handful of soil, which was cool and so moist it almost felt oily. I smelled it. Nothing. What had the professor said while I was talking to Brett? If the soil was grainy and smelled of smoked meat, it was best for woodland bulbs. If the soil was dry and tasted of salt, it was high in minerals and best for annuals. Or was that perennials? I couldn't remember.

Reluctantly, I pressed a finger into the soil and raised it to my mouth. At first it just tasted gritty. And then slowly,

138

it took on the faintest aftertaste of molasses. I examined my bulb, which was stringy and dry, and had the same brownish-red hue. For some reason, it felt right. Bending down, I shovelled a handful into my sack.

No one else seemed to have finished. Some were meandering through the weeds; others were crouched low to the ground, feeling around in the soil, dirt smeared on their cheeks. Professor Mumm was walking around examining our progress while offering tips about trowel technique. But instead of going back to the group, I walked on, inching closer to the forest. I didn't know why I was doing it, only that it felt as if I had just remembered something very important that I had forgotten to do, and that something was in the trees.

I pushed through the grass, which was wild and as tall as my knees. A lazy bee hovered over a bunch of wild flowers. Behind me, I heard Eleanor calling my name. "Renée! Where are you going? Did you figure out what bulb you have?" I glanced over my shoulder to see her running to catch up with me.

"No," I said. "Just looking around."

The morning sun was hot and beat down on the back of my neck. Ducking under the shade of a tree, I stopped. Was there something in the grass? Something brown that looked like a stick, but wasn't. Wiping the sweat from my forehead, I bent down. I heard Eleanor approach as I pushed the wild flowers aside with my trowel. And there it was, the thing that I now knew had been pulling me towards it. Behind me, Eleanor screamed.

It was a fawn, dead and curled up in the grass. Its limbs were contorted in unnatural angles. Flies buzzed around its head, its fur still a soft, spotted brown.

In seconds, the entire class had gathered around us, all staring at me and the fawn. Professor Mumm zigzagged through the group. When she reached me, she took off her hat and looked at the fawn and then at me.

"I...I just found it," I said. "I was looking for soil..." Even though that wasn't the truth.

Professor Mumm's face softened, and she took me by the shoulders. "Come away, dear," she said. "No use in looking at it. There's nothing we can do now."

She led us back to the chapel, where she collected our bulbs and bags of soil, murmuring comments as she sifted through each sack – none of which were the right match.

When it was my turn, she took my bag and shook it around. "An unorthodox pairing," she said, almost to herself. "Crocuses normally thrive on dry soil, cool and salty...though this might work. Yes...interesting. Very interesting. The mixture of the red clay and oil...that would definitely work."

Professor Mumm's eyes swept over me, curious. "Class dismissed."

As everyone dispersed, Eleanor ran up next to me. "What just happened?"

"I was just walking around when I found it," I said, knowing that even at Gottfried it wasn't normal to be pulled by an invisible force to a dead animal.

"Weird. It looked like you knew where you were going."

"Well, I didn't," I said quickly.

"How did you figure that out about your soil, by the way? That was pretty smart."

"I don't know. The soil that I picked just seemed to complement the bulb. They had the same colouring, and the bulb was dry and the soil was kind of greasy." I shrugged. "It seemed right."

"Intuition!" Eleanor said, mocking Professor Mumm's voice. "Your gut!"

I laughed. "She seemed pretty freaked out."

"She teaches *gardening*. She needs a little excitement in her life."

Just as we were about to head over to Philosophy, Brett ran over to us. "You're a natural," he said to me.

"Hi, Brett," Eleanor said with a smile, and leaned towards him to wipe the dirt from his face with her thumb.

"Now you really do look like a farmer," I said.

He laughed. "Is it that bad?"

Eleanor smiled. "A cute farmer." I rolled my eyes as Brett grinned. His resemblance to Wes wasn't just physical. He had the same easy-going walk, and spoke with the same flirty yet vacant banter; he even had the same teeth. That should have made me like him more, but instead it made him seem ordinary and unexciting.

"So, girls, what next?"

"Philosophy," I said, even though Horticulture started so early in the day that we had a short break before breakfast. But just as I spoke, Eleanor said, "Oh, nothing."

"Nothing?" Brett said. "Maybe we should make that a something. Breakfast?"

Unable to contain myself, I laughed, and then tried to cover it up with a cough when Eleanor gave me a threatening look. How many girls had he used that line on? Eleanor smiled. "That would be great. Renée was just saying how hungry she was," she said, elbowing me in the ribs.

"Um, yeah. Famished."

As we entered the Megaron, Brett talked about his classes and his family and his friends from home. At times I actually forgot that we were talking to Brett, and spoke to him as if he were Wes. So I wasn't surprised to discover that their lives were almost identical. He was the oldest of three and played on the rugby and soccer teams before coming to Gottfried, where he was disappointed that neither sport existed. Now he was the captain of the track-and-field team. He had a yellow Labrador, which he liked to play frisbee with in the summer; his favourite colour was blue; he liked any music except for country; and his favourite author was Hemingway (typical), or so he claimed, though I doubted he had read anything by him other than whatever was assigned at school. By the time breakfast was done and we were walking through the double iron doors of Horace Hall, Eleanor's eyes were glazed over with admiration.

"He's so dreamy," she said while we climbed the stairs to the second floor. "So manly. So American. So...tan."

"So rehearsed," I said, opening the door to Philosophy.

The classroom had high-beamed ceilings and two windows that overlooked the green. A few people were already sitting down, talking or shuffling through their papers. We took seats in the front, and I couldn't help but scan the room for Dante. He wasn't there.

Nathaniel scurried in behind me, his skinny frame hunched under the weight of his backpack, making him look like a turtle. He sat down in the desk next to mine just before the bell rang.

"Hi, Renée," he said, winded and sweating. He pushed his hair out of his face and adjusted his glasses. "Did you finish your essay? I stayed up almost all night doing it.

143

I had to rewrite it four times before I got it right."

A wave of queasiness passed over me. "Essay?" I looked to Eleanor, hoping it was news for her too, but she pulled hers out of her notebook.

"Yeah, about a myth that we want to believe in. You didn't do yours?"

"No, I had to miss class because Mrs. Lynch sent me home to change. Remember?"

"Oh, right..." Eleanor gave me an apologetic look. "Sorry. I thought you knew. You looked so busy during study hall that I figured you were working on it."

I sighed and tried to figure out what to do. "No, it's my fault. I should have asked."

"I have a couple of my drafts," Nathaniel said. "They're not that good, but you can use one if you want." He handed me a few crumpled sheets of paper.

It was a sweet gesture, but I wasn't keen on cheating. Plus, even though everyone knew Nathaniel was a maths prodigy, I wasn't so sure that his brilliance transferred to writing. "Oh no, that's okay. I'll just explain what happened to the professor."

But Nathaniel wouldn't let me refuse. "I really don't mind," he said earnestly, holding the essays in front of me. We both stared at them. With nothing else to do, I took them and began to read.

His handwriting was messy and there were smudges of

eraser marks all over the pages. The first one was titled, "I Want to Believe in Myself". I flipped to the next draft. "I Want to Believe that Calculators Can Replace the Human Brain". And "I Want to Believe in Imaginary Numbers". The last one was the most promising, though it looked more like a maths proof than an essay, and it didn't really fit the assignment.

I bit my lip. "These are really...good," I said, handing them back to him, "but I'd feel bad passing in your work. I'll just talk to the professor after class. Hopefully he'll understand."

Nathaniel shrugged and stuffed them back into his notebook. "It's a *she*."

As if to complete his sentence, a woman entered the room, carrying an armful of papers. She set them on the desk and walked to the front of the class, holding a book. I gazed at her in awe. It was the same woman who had saved me from going to the headmistress's office.

Annette LaBarge wasn't beautiful. In fact, she was quite plain. Her clothes were functional and basic, comprised mostly of earth tones: today a linen skirt that exposed her slender ankles and cork clogs. I pictured her in one of those women's catalogues, posing on a rocky beach while holding a long twig or a piece of driftwood.

"Fairy tales." Her voice carried like a wind chime. "What if they were true?"

She glanced around the room, her eyes wide with excitement. She was a small woman, thin and fragile looking, though her presence seemed to fill the room with energy. "What if the world once had giants and witches; animals that talked and monsters that threatened all that was good? These stories are the foundation of our society, and what most of Western philosophy is based on.

"I want you to think of the books we read this year not only as philosophical stories, but as realities."

She opened her book and flipped to the first page. "So let's go there, to that faraway land where 'Happily Ever After' still exists, and see where it takes us."

She began to read. "Once upon a time..."

And listening to the delicate sound of Miss LaBarge's voice, I was lulled into a daydream; a simpler place where people were either good or evil, and love lasted for ever, where problems could be solved just by believing, where fairies and fauns helped you find your way when you were lost.

After class, I waited until everyone filtered out, then approached the front of the room. Miss LaBarge was standing behind her desk, organizing some papers. I cleared my throat, and she looked up. "Oh hi, Renée." I was surprised that she remembered my name. It made me feel even more terrible about not doing my homework. "Professor, I—"

"You missed class earlier this week and didn't know there was an essay due. I know."

I looked at my feet. "I'm sorry."

"Just do it for next week," she said gently. "Write about something you don't believe in, but wish you did. And next time, just ask."

I nodded and hugged my books to my chest. I thought about my parents. About Benjamin Gallow. About the graveyard behind the chapel. What did I want to believe in? Life after death.

When I got to Crude Sciences at the end of the day, Dante was waiting for me at our table. This time, with no Latin book, no journal.

"Hello," he said, pulling my chair out for me.

Surprised, I sat down next to him, trying not to stare at his perfectly formed arms. "Hi," I said, with an attempt at nonchalance.

"How are you?" I could feel his eyes on me.

"Fine," I said carefully, as Professor Starking handed out our lab assignments.

Dante frowned. "Not very talkative today, I see."

I thrust a thermometer into the muddy water of the fish tank in front of us, which was supposed to represent an enclosed ecosystem. "So now you want to talk? Now

147

that you've finished your Latin homework?"

After a prolonged period of silence, he spoke. "It was research."

"Research on what?"

"It doesn't matter any more."

I threw him a suspicious look. "Why's that?"

"Because I realized I wasn't paying attention to the right thing."

"Which is?" I asked, looking back at the board as I smoothed out the hem of my skirt.

"You."

My lips trembled as the word left his mouth. "I'm not a specimen."

"I just want to know you."

I turned to him, wanting to ask him a million questions. I settled for one. "But I can't know anything about you?"

Dante leaned back in his chair. "My favourite author is Dante, obviously," he said, his tone mocking me. "Though I'm also partial to the Russians. I'm very fond of music. All kinds, really, though I especially enjoy Mussorgsky and Stravinsky or anything involving a violin. They're a bit dark, no? I used to like opera, but I've mostly grown out of it. I have a low tolerance for hot climates. I've never enjoyed dessert, though I once loved cherries. My favourite colour is red. I often take long walks in the woods to clear my head. As a result, I have a unique knowledge of the flora and fauna of North America. And," he said, his eyes burning through me as I pretended to focus on our lab, "I remember everything everyone has ever told me. I consider it a special talent."

Overwhelmed by the sudden influx of information, I sat there gaping, unsure of how to respond.

Dante frowned. "Did I leave something out?"

I thought about Benjamin, about my parents. This was my opportunity. "What about your friends?" I asked gently.

"I thought it was already decided that I didn't have any."

"And I thought it was already decided that there was more to you than you let on."

Dante gave me a pensive look. "Maybe I did have friends once."

"What happened?"

"They turned out to be different people than I thought they were."

"What do you mean *different*?"

"Capable of doing things I never thought they would do."

What was he talking about? "Like what?"

"Anything," he said. "That's the point."

"Does it...does it have anything to do with Benjamin Gallow?"

Dante stared at me, his eyes almost threatening. "Benjamin Gallow?" he said softly, so that only I could hear. "What do you know about Benjamin Gallow?"

"Nothing," I said quietly. "Just that he was dating your friend. And that he died. And that you found him."

"So that's why you wanted to talk to me. You wanted to gossip about a boy's death."

"No! I didn't mean to – I just – I don't think he died of a heart attack."

Dante began to respond, but held back, taking me in. "What do you think he died of, then?"

"I was hoping you'd know."

"And why are you so interested? So you can talk about it with your friends?"

His words hit me in the face like a slap. "My parents died three weeks ago. I was the one who found them. They both died of heart attacks. At the same time. In the woods. Just like Benjamin."

I could feel his eyes on me as I turned away from him and faced the board.

He didn't say anything for a long time. Finally he said stiffly, "I can't help you."

"Does that mean I'm right?"

Dante lowered his voice. "Maybe you're right," he said, almost mocking me. "Maybe it wasn't a heart attack. Maybe it was an attack of the heart."

* * *

It took me until Saturday to tell Eleanor about my suspicions about the connection between Benjamin's death and my parents. She thought I was losing it.

"You're losing it," she said, looking at me in the mirror while she did her hair. It was the start of the weekend and she was helping the Humanities department hold auditions for the school play.

I didn't respond.

"And aren't those the same things anyway? A heart attack and an attack of the heart?"

"Who knows. He was just making fun of me."

"What did you say after that?"

"Nothing. The bell rang. And then he was gone."

"Maybe *he's* losing it." She pinned her hair back with a clip. "See, you're perfect for each other."

I rolled my eyes. "It means he'd rather torture me with teasing than actually answer my questions."

"It means you're reading too much into it," she said, grabbing her bag. "Okay, I've gotta go."

Eleanor would be busy all day, so we agreed to meet for dinner in the dining hall.

"I would say you should try out," she said, "but only boys are allowed to act in plays. School policy."

I frowned. "Why?"

"Apparently Shakespeare did it."

"Isn't that illegal or something. Like sexist?" Even if it wasn't illegal, it was wrong.

Eleanor shrugged. "It's a private school. They can do whatever they want."

I normally would have been angry at such a ridiculous policy, though this one didn't seem much worse than Gottfried's other rules. But I was relieved to finally have time to myself. Or at least that's what I thought. I had so much homework that I spent virtually the entire day in my room, huddled over my books, leaving only for dinner. But Eleanor never showed up. I waited outside the Megaron, drawing circles in the dirt with my shoe as everyone but her filtered in. Finally I gave up and went inside by myself. Thankfully, I spotted Nathaniel sitting alone in a corner, surrounded by papers and glasses of milk. He was even more stressed about his homework than I was, and together we ate a quick meal before going back to the dorms.

When I got to my room, Eleanor still wasn't there. Maybe she was with the production crew. Alone at my desk, I didn't know what to do with myself. I tried to write my philosophy essay, but as I stared at the words I had written on the page, the letters blurred, rearranging themselves into shadowy silhouettes of my parents. And when I was able to push them out of my mind, they were only replaced with Annie, Dante, and a perturbing amalgam of Wes and Brett.

I glanced at the clock on the wall. It seemed that every time I looked at it, another hour had passed and I still hadn't gotten anything done. I needed to clear my head, but with Eleanor gone, I didn't have anyone to talk to. I could go next door and see if her friends were there, but the only thing we seemed to have in common was Eleanor. I checked the clock again. If it was eight o'clock here, then it would be five o'clock in California. I picked up the phone and called Annie, but no one answered. Slamming the phone down into the receiver harder than I had intended, I paced around the room. It was messy and cluttered with clothes. I picked them up and shoved them into my dresser, and continued cleaning until I found my way under the bed to get a sweater out of my suitcase. Dust bunnies were everywhere, and thin wisps of spiderwebs fluttered down from the bed frame. Yet as I reached for my suitcase, my hand was met with something soft. I pulled it back to find a collection of dead moths dangling in a dusty knot. I gasped and shook my hand, wiping it on the carpet until the moths were stuck to the floor. I grimaced at them. I had to get out of this room. Without thinking, I shoved my books into my bag and slipped out the door.

The hallway welcomed me with the tart aroma of femininity. Floral and citrus floated through cracked doors; hot bursts of steam wafted in from the bathroom showers; and the faintest trace of cloves seeped out from the fourth-year wing. The hallway was empty, yet muffled chatter hummed behind each door, giving the dormitory a feeling of enchantment, as if every room held its own enclosed universe.

Having only an hour until nine o'clock curfew, I scurried down the stairs and into the crisp night air. When I reached the fork in the path that led to the different corners of campus, I stopped. I didn't know where I was going or what I would do. In a split-second decision, I took a right and started to jog to the library.

Copleston Library was a massive Greek structure with thick Doric columns holding it up in the front. Above them, a triangular façade bore an ancient war scene. Engraved around the rim was another phrase in Latin: *HOMO NIHIL QUAM QUID SCIET EST*.

The giant iron doors creaked on their hinges when I opened them, and a warm burst of air escaped from inside. The librarian was a mole-like woman with bad posture, closely cropped grey hair, and a faint moustache. She stopped me at the entrance. "The library closes at nine o'clock," she cautioned. I jumped at the sound of her voice, which was far too loud to be appropriate in a library. "And no food or beverages. Or smoking. Or game playing. Or talking. Or whistling."

It seemed a little superfluous, but I nodded anyway. "Okay."

"Shhh!"

I rolled my eyes and stepped inside, trying to be as quiet as possible. The ceilings were unfathomably high, and rows of books lined the walls, reaching all the way to the top. I had known that this many books existed in the world, but never before had I seen them all in one room. As I walked deeper into the library, past study tables and card catalogues, the light grew dimmer and the musty smell of preserved leather and papyrus emanated from the walls, giving me the comfortable feeling of being in a museum.

I walked down the main corridor, trying to find a place to sit. Oil lamps lit the hallway in a flickering yellow light. The library was moderately crowded; every table was occupied by at least one student. The floors were covered in a plush red carpet, and other than the sound of pages turning, it was completely silent. I kept going, pulled in one direction by a force outside of me: up one flight of stairs, down an aisle and through a set of double doors that opened into the northern wing. I had no idea where I was going or what section I was in, though it was clearly one that wasn't frequented by many students, as most of the tables were empty. I walked to the back, passing enormous shelves of books, until I found a table overlooking the campus. I was about to sit down when I heard voices whispering from the other side of the bookcase. Gripping my papers to my chest, I tiptoed to the shelf and peered through the gap between the books.

"*Board of Monitors erat.*" Gideon DuPont's voice was deep and cold. He was wearing a black suit and tortoiseshell glasses, his auburn hair combed and parted to the left. He leaned back in his chair, crossing one leg over the other. He was sitting with Vivian and Yago. Stacks of books were piled on the table around them. I tried to read the titles, but they were too far away. I stepped closer, kneeling down to get a better look, when I saw a dead mouse curled up on the floor. I caught my gasp just before it escaped my mouth. But not quickly enough. Gideon, Vivian and Yago all turned in my direction. I covered my mouth with my hand to muffle my breathing. I was worried they might come over and find me crouching below the books with a dead mouse, but to my relief, they continued their conversation, this time softer. They must have assumed that no one could understand them anyway, considering they were speaking in Latin. And it was true – I had no idea what was going on, but judging from the way they'd reacted, I knew it was something secret.

"*Quis id fecit?*" Vivian asked, her voice full and commanding. She was wearing a tailored suit, with a ruffled white bow tied through her collar.

"*Non scio,*" Gideon replied.

Yago interrupted. "*Puto Headmistress Von Laark esse.*"

He was wearing a light blue oxford shirt and a white linen blazer. His tie was uneven and loose around his neck.

"*Erant alii*," Vivian interjected. She sounded vicious. "*Nonne quid illa puella adferret meministi?*"

"*Brandon erat. Brandon Bell,*" Gideon said. Vivian attempted to interrupt, but Gideon continued. "*Atque modus ad eum castigandum per Eleanorem sororem eius est.*"

I gasped at hearing what sounded like Eleanor's name. Thankfully, Yago coughed at the same time. What were they talking about? All I had been able to make out was *Board of Monitors, Headmistress Von Laark, Brandon Bell,* and probably *Eleanor.* Vowing to pay more attention in class, I glanced at the dead mouse. It was partially decayed and covered in dust. It must have been there for weeks.

Wiping the dust from my knees, I stood up with the resolve to finally begin studying. But when I turned around, I was face-to-face with Dante. Startled, I backed into the shelf, knocking off a book. With an almost inhuman agility, Dante caught it before it hit the floor. He put a finger to my lips. His skin was cold to the touch, a chill that seemed to seep into me. He quickly pulled away, and I shivered as my breath turned to fog. I looked up at him, wondering if he noticed it too.

"Renée." My name escaped his mouth almost soundlessly, as if it were a secret that he had slipped into my ear. Around us, books towered to the ceiling, and he lowered his head to mine, his dark hair falling across his face. I felt his eyes travel across me, reading each part like a word in a novel. No one had ever looked at me that way before. My chest grew hot and flushed with embarrassment, and I started to respond when I heard Gideon stop talking. He must have heard us, because it was followed by the sound of a chair creaking as someone stood up.

"*Let's go,*" Dante mouthed, and picked up my bag.

I tried to keep up with him as he wove through the maze of bookshelves. "Where are we going?" I whispered when we were out of earshot.

"Somewhere...less crowded," he said, even though the rest of the library was virtually empty.

We stopped in a dimly lit reading room, with doors on either end and stacks and stacks of books. We stood behind one, waiting in the shadows to make sure no one was coming.

"What happened back there? My lips, they were so cold all of a sudden."

He gave me a confused look. "They were?"

Maybe it was just in my head.

"What were you doing there?" I asked.

He looked down at me, considering how to answer. "Studying. What were you doing?"

"Studying," I said quickly.

"On the floor, in the dark?"

I bit my lip and reached for my bag, which he was still holding. But as I did, it dropped to the floor and all my papers scattered across the carpet.

"Oh God, sorry," I said, as we both bent over to pick them up. A few of my pencils had rolled across the aisle, and I went to collect them when I saw Dante looking through my papers. Blushing, I tried to grab them from him, but he waved them out of my reach.

"'Life After Death'," he said, reading the title of my essay. "Of all of the myths, that's the one you'd want to believe in?"

"Don't read that!" I said, grabbing at it.

He looked at me with curiosity. "You don't believe in an afterlife?"

"I don't mean in the religious sense."

He gazed at me. "You mean in the literal sense," he murmured pensively. "People coming back to life."

I looked at my feet. I knew it was juvenile, but that was exactly what I wanted to believe in. "I miss my parents," I said quietly. It was a slightly pathetic disclosure, but it was the truth.

Dante's face softened. "I bet we have more in common than you think," he said, handing me the stack of papers.

I took them and shoved them into my bag. What did that mean? That he missed his parents? Or that he wanted to believe in an afterlife, too? At least he didn't think I was ridiculous or stupid, which he would have if he had seen my Latin homework, which had a giant C+ scrawled over it in red.

"Oh, and about your Latin homework."

My face dropped. "You saw it?" I wanted to die.

"You know, I'm pretty good at Latin. I could help you." He leaned against the bookshelf, his sleeves rolled up, revealing veins that outlined the muscles on his forearms and disappeared underneath the cuffs of his shirt.

"How am I supposed to know you're good at it? What if you're just trying to sabotage my grade?" I said, with a hint of sarcasm.

He laughed. "There isn't much to sabotage. But you did walk in on my class, Advanced Latin. Isn't that enough to convince you?"

"Prove it," I said before I could stop myself.

Dante gave me an amused look. "What do you want me to do?"

"What were they saying? Gideon and Vivian and Yago."

Dante studied me, half of his face obscured in the shadows. "I don't know."

I narrowed my eyes. "Yes you do."

"They were talking about the Board of Monitors. Something about who did what. I couldn't hear anything else."

I wasn't sure if he was telling the truth or just trying to placate me. "I don't believe you."

He leaned in until his face was centimetres away from mine, so close I could feel his loose hair brushing against my cheeks. He stared at me with an intensity that could only have been born from extreme desire or hatred, but for a moment I didn't care. I closed my eyes and waited for what would come next.

"You don't trust me," he whispered into my ear, his breath surprisingly cold.

I shuddered. "No." Around us, the oil lamps flickered and dimmed, signalling that the library was closing.

"But you are talking to me. Does that mean we're on for Latin?"

I meant to say no, but for some reason the word "Okay" came out of my mouth.

Neither of us said anything for a long time; instead we stood there uncomfortably, each considering what we had agreed to do.

Finally Dante spoke. "Meet me in the foyer of Horace Hall next Friday."

I nodded, and without saying anything else, we snuck down the corridor and stairs and out into the cool Maine air.

When I got back to the dorm, Eleanor was sitting on her bed, combing her hair in the candlelight, a textbook open on her lap. When she saw me, she put down her brush.

"Where were you?" she demanded, a worried look on her face.

"Where were *you*?" I asked, angry with her for deserting me at dinner.

"Auditions lasted longer than I thought. I couldn't leave. I figured you'd understand."

I dropped my bag on the floor and collapsed on my bed. "I do. What are you studying?"

"Um, maths," she said, as if it should have been obvious. "We have our first quiz on Monday, remember?"

"Oh, right," I said. I had forgotten about that.

"What were *you* studying?"

"I wasn't," I said with a sigh. "I saw Dante in the library. And Gideon."

Eleanor's face brightened with curiosity. "Tell me everything."

She curled up across from me on my bed, and I told her about Gideon and Vivian and Yago; about Dante and my essay and Latin.

"And they mentioned your brother's name too."

Eleanor sat up with surprise. "What? Why would they be talking about Brandon?"

I shook my head. "I don't know...but there's more." I hesitated, unsure of whether or not I should tell her since

I wasn't exactly sure if I had heard correctly. "They also mentioned you."

"Me? I don't even know them. It's probably because Brandon hates them. And they hate Brandon and the Board of Monitors. It's a known fact."

I bit my lip. I thought Eleanor would be disturbed upon finding out that they were talking about her and her brother, but she didn't seem fazed. "I don't know. They definitely seemed like they were up to something. And Dante seemed to be spying on them too. But why?" I said, almost to myself. "I have to find a way to get it out of him. It's not like I can ask Gideon."

Eleanor gave me an incredulous look and shook her head. "I cannot believe you're obsessing over Gideon when Dante Berlin just asked if he could tutor you in Latin."

I shook my head, smiling. "So I take it you don't think they're up to anything..."

"They probably are. They're always up to something. They wear three-piece suits to school and only speak in Latin and lurk around the darkest parts of campus. But what could they *really* be up to? And more important, who cares? Dante Berlin asked you out. This is epic. Epic!"

"But there's more..."

Eleanor shook her head. "What? He asked you to run away with him to Transylvania or wherever he's actually from?"

I laughed. "No. When he brushed against me, his fingers were freezing, and when he put them to my lips, my breath went completely cold." I looked at her nervously, hoping she wouldn't think I was going insane, which I already knew was what Annie would think. And for good reason, too. It was unreal.

"What do you mean 'cold'? Like you were inhaling cold air?"

I nodded.

"That is weird. I don't know. Maybe you were just nervous being that close to him – I mean, anyone would be – and thought your breath went cold, when it was probably just a draught or something."

The library *was* kind of cold. And Dante said he didn't feel it. It must have been my mind playing tricks on me.

We heard Mrs. Lynch walking past our door, her metre stick clicking behind her. Even though we were allowed to talk after curfew, there were no locks on the doors, and it was better not to give Lynch an excuse to punish us. Eleanor squeezed my ankle and hopped off the bed. While she pulled her class notes out of her bag, I slipped under the covers with my maths book. But when I opened the pages, the words and numbers blurred until all I saw was Dante. So I lay there, imagining him in front of me so that I could study the contours of his face, the texture of his smell, the fluctuations of his voice, until all I would remember for my maths quiz was the way I felt when he whispered my name.

CHAPTER 6
THE FORGOTTEN HISTORY

LATIN WASN'T SO BAD WHEN you were learning it from the most beautiful boy in school. The next Friday I met Dante in the foyer of Horace Hall for our first tutoring session. He was sitting on a radiator, which was on even though it was still September. It was Maine, after all. His hands were shoved in his pockets as he leaned against the thick blue drapes behind him, gallant in his solitude. My insides fluttered. After running a hand through my hair and adjusting my skirt, I approached him.

"Aren't you hot?"

He looked confused and then saw me staring at the

heater below him. "Oh. No, I didn't even notice it." He smiled and raised an eyebrow. "I guess I'm cold-blooded."

I laughed, and he took my bag and carried it while we walked. I figured we would study in the library, but the librarian was so strict about noise that it would have been impossible to actually talk. So instead Dante suggested we use an empty classroom in Horace Hall. "Are we allowed to do that?" I asked.

He smiled. "As long as we're quiet."

Dante led me to the classroom in which I had Latin. Before entering, he cracked open the door and looked inside. The room smelled faintly of Mrs. Lumbar's perfume. "Come on," he said, and we slipped inside.

"It's the declensions you're having problems with," Dante said, flipping through my notebook. "The amazing thing about declensions is that they give each word a personality. Depending on the other words it's paired with, each noun or object takes on a different form and different sound."

A lock of hair fell in front of his face, and he pushed it behind his ear and looked at me. "So a word that might sound ugly could actually be beautiful when coupled with the right pronoun. It's sort of like when two people bring out the best qualities in each other."

I blushed. He was talkative around me, even sweet at times. And even though I didn't want to admit it, the only

167

time I got close to forgetting about my parents' deaths was when he was around.

"Sorry," he said, noticing that he'd made me blush, and handed my notebook back. "I'm not very good with words."

"That's not true. I really liked your explanation. I think I understand a little more now."

"You understand more about me, or about Latin?"

"Latin. Other than the music you like and the books you read, I hardly know anything about you. Your past."

Dante leaned closer, looking at my blue pleated skirt, my black stockings, my turtleneck. "What do you want to know?"

"Where are you from?"

He hesitated. "I'm from the West. The Northwest. British Columbia, mostly. We moved around a lot."

"You mean your family?"

Dante nodded. "Me and my sister. My younger sister. That was a long time ago, though. She passed away in an accident. My parents, too."

"What kind of accident?"

"Plane," he said quickly.

"What was her name?"

He leaned back in his chair, giving me a level look. "Cecelia."

I tried to think of something to say. "I'm sorry," I said.

Dante studied me. "It's in the past."

"So then you came here?"

"No, first I was moved to a foster home. I hated it; I knew I had to get out. And then I found Gottfried."

"Do you miss them? Your family, I mean."

"I honestly can't think of a single real memory of them. It happened so long ago that they've faded away. I miss missing them."

He smiled, his face transforming into something soft.

"Tell me about your parents," he said gently.

"They were teachers." I stopped and pictured them – my mother and my father together in our house. Even though I missed them every day, I hadn't actually thought about the way they were, about the way *we* were as a family, for weeks.

"What else?" Dante said.

I told him about the kind of people they were, about the way we lived in California, the way I was before their deaths. Dante didn't take his eyes off me when I explained how they'd died, how I found them, how I came to Gottfried. And then suddenly we were back in the present.

There was a long pause, then Dante leaned over and wrote a phrase in Latin on my notebook. *Mortui in nobis vivunt.*

"What does it mean?"

"*The dead live within us.*"

I waited for him to say more, but instead we sat in an awkward silence.

Finally he spoke. "Conversation isn't easy for me. There aren't many people I like talking to, so I don't get much practice. But I like you. Listening to you, I mean. You see things differently than other people."

I blushed. I'd never been good at taking compliments. "How are you so good at Latin?"

"I never used to be. I guess you could say I just woke up one morning and it clicked. You know how that happens?"

I nodded as he flipped through my papers. We spent the next half hour going over the mistakes I'd made on last week's homework. And then something inexplicable happened. As Dante turned a page, the corner cut into his thumb, slicing the skin. He pulled his hand away.

I sat up in my seat. "Are you okay?"

"What are you talking about? I'm fine," he said, his thumb hidden within his fist by his side.

I gazed at him and then at his arm. "Let me see your hand."

Dante gave me a bemused look, but didn't move.

"Let me see it," I repeated, taking his arm. It was ice cold. Startled, I let go.

Dante studied me, waiting to see how I would react.

"Open your fist," I said softly. "Please."

One by one, he lifted his fingers until his palm was resting on the desk. I looked at his thumb, but there was nothing. No cut, no blood, not even a trace of a cut. Baffled, I picked up his hand. My fingers began to tingle, but I didn't care. I held his thumb to the light, examining every angle. There was nothing.

I gaped at him. "You just cut yourself and it's not there any more."

"I told you," he said with a confused smile, "nothing happened."

"But why did you pull away like that? Your skin, it...it started to bleed...I saw it."

"Maybe the pen leaked."

I picked up the pen and shook it. "It didn't."

Dante looked into my eyes. "Renée, you're imagining things. How could my skin have healed that quickly? I'd have to be some sort of monster."

Bewildered, I shook my head. That wasn't what I meant at all. "I don't think you're a monster."

"What do you think I am, then?"

That he was brilliant. That he was dangerous, but still made me feel safe. That he was different from everyone else I had ever met.

"Strangely perfect," I said, before I could stop myself.

Dante looked at me with surprise as the words left my

mouth. He didn't reply for what seemed like ages, and I looked away in embarrassment, staring at my Mary Janes. "You must have a backward view of perfection, if that's what you think." He closed my notebook and handed it to me. "See you next week? Same time, same place."

Mortified at my admission, I looked at him and then at his thumb. Had I had actually seen what I thought I had, or was Dante right?

"No one's perfect, Renée."

I nodded, but as I watched him stand up, I realized that everything that was wrong with him was right. His solitude, his callous reticence, his unpredictability – it only drew me closer – his flaws making him all the more real.

"I always knew there was something different about him," Eleanor said, half joking, when I told her what happened. I tried talking to Annie about it, but she literally thought I was losing my mind. Was I feeling okay? Maybe I should see a counsellor at school. She meant well, but it only frustrated me more. I saw what I saw, and Annie was treating me like a child. Eleanor, on the other hand, was exactly the opposite.

"I can't believe I told him I thought he was perfect," I said, lowering my fork. We were in the Megaron, eating dinner. "It just came out."

"Well I guess he is sort of perfect, in a brooding, self-important kind of way. Which really makes him imperfect."

"Or more perfect," I said, just as Nathaniel walked up with his tray.

"Can I sit with you guys?" he asked.

I smiled. "Of course."

Eleanor pushed her tray over to make room, and then continued. "Maybe he's superhuman. A demigod. After all, he is an Adonis."

I shook my head. "He's too dark to be a superhero."

"That must make him the villain, then," Eleanor said with a mischievous smile. "Even better."

Nathaniel pushed his glasses up. "What are you guys talking about?"

Eleanor looked at me for permission to divulge, and I shrugged.

"Can you keep a secret?" Eleanor asked him, lowering her voice seductively.

Nathaniel glanced nervously at Eleanor and then at me. "Of course I can. Who am I going to tell, anyway?"

"We're talking about Dante Berlin."

"Oh," he said, not seeming very excited. "What about him?"

Keeping my voice low, I told him what had happened when he'd cut his finger. "Have you ever heard of that before?" If anyone would know, it was Nathaniel. He knew everything about science and maths.

Nathaniel stared at me, his eyes magnified through his glasses. "I...I don't know, Renée. Maybe you were seeing things."

I shrugged. I probably was. So why did I want to believe so badly that I wasn't?

Nathaniel picked at his tuna. "What's so great about him, anyway? So he doesn't have any friends. Lots of people don't have friends. Why does that make him interesting?"

"Oh, come on. Haven't you seen him?" Eleanor exclaimed.

"It's because he's tall, isn't it? Tall and the long hair."

Even Nathaniel's crude description made me want to see Dante again. Unfortunately, he never came to dinner, probably because he lived off campus.

"He's really smart," I murmured.

"And confident," Eleanor added.

"It's like he's older than everyone else," I said. "Like he knows what he wants and isn't afraid of taking it."

"What she's saying is that he's manly." Eleanor grinned. "Though I think you meant *colder*, not older."

I laughed, but Nathaniel wasn't amused. "There is one explanation," he said.

Eleanor and I went quiet, waiting for him to continue.

174

"Cold skin, older than everyone else, withdrawn from society? The only humans who have those characteristics are dead."

There was a long silence. Nathaniel was right, but Dante was a living, breathing, moving person. I laughed. "Are you implying that Dante Berlin is dead?"

Nathaniel blushed and looked at his plate, from which he had barely eaten anything. "I...I don't know. It was just an observation."

Eleanor smiled, twirling a ringlet of hair around her finger. "Dead beautiful."

By the middle of October, the last of the trees had changed colours and the entire campus was blushing red and orange leaves. Every morning while I walked to class, the breeze would pluck them from their branches and carry them around campus, making them swirl around my feet like a flutter of monarch butterflies. After a month at Gottfried, things were getting better. My grandfather called to check in on me every so often, but our conversations were brief. I told him about my classes. Horticulture was quickly becoming my favourite. Surprisingly, it wasn't about plants at all; and while we did spend some time learning the different species of flora and their climates, we spent most of our classes learning about soil, root and irrigation systems, and how to plant things. I was usually the best in the class, and I loved it.

I had made friends with several people, including some of the girls on our floor, who I got dinner with when Eleanor was busy. Brett and I were also becoming friends. I kept bumping into him outside the girls' dorm or outside the lunchroom when Eleanor and I were leaving, as if he were waiting for someone; but he always walked with us. Although our discourse primarily consisted of light, insubstantial banter, it was okay; it reminded me of the way things had been with me and Wes, who I still hadn't heard from. Annie, I had. We tried to talk on the phone every week, but the pauses in our conversations were growing longer and longer as we became more involved in our separate worlds. And my world was quickly beginning to revolve around Dante.

We kept meeting after the paper-cut incident, though he still wouldn't admit that anything weird had happened. After only two weeks, I was getting As on all of my assignments, and finally felt like Professor Lumbar was warming up to me. I should have been ecstatic, but when I saw a big *A* scrawled on top of my latest exam, all I could think of was losing Dante. I clearly didn't need tutoring any more, and Dante would know that when he saw my grades. The problem was that I liked having an excuse to be around him. Friday had become my favourite day of the week because of our private sessions. Every time I looked at him, I discovered something new. A freckle on his neck or the white vestiges of a scar next to his left ear. And I couldn't deny the bond I felt in knowing that he too had lost his parents. He was the only one I could talk to about it – he always knew exactly what to say and what to ask to make me feel better, and he knew so much about dealing with death that I was becoming almost dependent on his advice. It seemed like I had no other choice. So I began to purposely write down the wrong conjugations; I made grammatical errors and mixed up vocabulary words, and to my relief, my grades began to drop. Dante glanced suspiciously over my marked-up exam, bleeding with red ink, and suggested we start meeting twice a week. I happily obliged.

I still wanted to ask him about Benjamin Gallow, about Gideon and his old friends and what had happened last spring, but that hadn't gone over so well last time. So I settled on something easier.

"What was growing up in Canada like?" We were sitting in the Latin classroom, the candlelight casting shadows across the beamed ceilings.

"Cold," Dante said, leaning towards me, his dark eyes glimmering. "And wild."

"What do you mean *wild*?"

"My parents were ranchers. My father hunted wild

game and sold the meat and pelts to traders, and my mother was a taxidermist. We lived in a farmhouse that was so far north there were more trees than people. The house was full of dead animals, but outside was even worse because there the bears and wild boars were alive. It would snow for weeks in the winter – big sheets of it piling up past the windows; wind so cold you'd freeze to death if you sprained an ankle while you were hunting or gathering wood. In a place like that, you're constantly reminded of your own mortality; of the strength of nature, of how unforgiving it can be. It was humbling."

I let my eyes fall across his body, envisioning him trekking through the wilderness, an axe in one hand, a shotgun in the other, a dead deer slung around his shoulders. What I would have given to be snowed in with Dante.

"Maine must seem tropical to you," I joked lamely.

Dante laughed. "Not exactly."

"Do you like it here?"

He thought about it. "I think it's good for me."

His answer was slightly disappointing. What I wanted him to say was something along the lines of, "I was miserable here until I met you." Or, "You are the only thing worth studying at Gottfried." Or, "Renée, you are the love of my life. I will follow you to the ends of the earth, carrying a deer on my shoulders that I killed with my bare hands just to prove my devotion." Or, "I want to

178

take you right now with my strong, inexplicably cold hands, and whisper sweet Latinate words in your ear."

"And I think you're good for me," Dante said.

I blinked. Did he actually say that or was I merely fantasizing about him saying that? He leaned towards me, waiting for me to respond.

"What?" I said softly.

Dante rubbed the side of his neck. "I mean, I think this is good for me. Talking to you. I'd almost forgotten what it was like to have friends."

Friends, I thought, my heart dropping. Right. "What exactly happened with them?" I asked gently. "You never told me."

Dante scrutinized my face. "We just grew apart. Benjamin died and then Cassie...transferred. After that I realized I had different priorities from the rest of them."

"What do you mean?" Annie and I were growing apart because we *were* apart, not because I chose to push her away.

"We all met in a Latin translation class. Back then we were attracted to the same ideas, about myth and lore, about morality, about how to be good people and make the right decisions. I'm still fascinated by all that, but I can't say the same for the others."

"But it didn't have anything to do with Benjamin's death?"

Dante considered how to respond. "No. Just a coincidence."

Coincidences. There seemed to be a lot of those going on recently. "And I'm guessing it was also a coincidence that you found Benjamin in the woods?" Just like I had found my parents in the woods, I thought.

Dante crossed his arms. "Yes," he said, as if it were obvious.

"It's just too weird that he died of a heart attack in the woods just like my parents. Out of the blue." I gave him a sidelong glance, hoping he would tell me something about Benjamin's death that he hadn't told the school.

"If you're looking for incriminating information, I don't have any. He was dead. In the woods. A heart attack, like they said."

I studied him, trying to figure out if he was telling the truth.

"So why were you spying on Gideon that night in the library?"

"I wasn't spying; I was studying."

"In that exact spot in the library?"

Dante straightened out his tie. "As I recall, you were there too."

He was right. How had I happened to find them? It was a little coincidental. So fine, maybe he had a point. But there were other things that I still had questions about.

"They mentioned Eleanor and her brother. I heard that Brandon doesn't like you, or Gideon. Why?"

"I don't know. Maybe out of a personal distaste? Do you know why people dislike you?"

"Who dislikes me?" I said forcefully. I was a nice, considerate person. Why would anyone dislike me?

Dante grinned. "It was hypothetical."

I blushed. "Oh. Well, how come you never talk to Eleanor, even though you sit next to her in assembly?"

"She never talks to me."

Frowning, I leaned forward. Was he mocking me? He had legitimate answers to all of my questions; questions that I was sure would force him to reveal the truth about Benjamin and his old friends. But what kind of admission was I expecting?

"Why do you live off campus?"

"I don't like shared bathrooms."

"Why are your hands so cold?"

"Poor circulation."

Sighing, I pushed my hair out of my face and collapsed back in my chair.

Tapping his fingers on the desk, Dante gave me a pensive look. "There's something else, isn't there?"

"Why am I the only one you talk to?" I asked softly.

Dante hesitated. "Because you're impulsive. And stubborn. And too quick to judge. You question everything

181

and you can't keep your thoughts to yourself, even when you're wrong..."

Incredulous, I gaped at him and was about to interrupt, when he cut me off.

"And you're sincere. And searching. And challenging. Even when you're angry, you're so full of life that it spills out of you. You think that nobody understands you," he said gently. "But it's not true."

My lips trembled, and I was unsure of whether I wanted to laugh or cry. "You didn't answer my question," I said, trying to hide the quiver in my voice.

Dante smiled. "I talk to you because you make me laugh."

I told Eleanor everything. Which was that I had found out nothing. And upon her advice I put my investigation on hold. The only thing I didn't tell her about was the last bit, partly because I wanted to keep it for myself, and partly because she wouldn't let me get a word in edgewise. Eleanor had a crush on our History professor, Mr. Bliss, and couldn't stop talking about him. So maybe he was young and sort of good-looking for a teacher, but in reality, he was closer to our parents' age than he was to ours, and he smoked out the window before class, and he ate a weird sandwich every day for lunch that made him smell like onions.

"But it's not just the way he looks," Eleanor said, licking the oatmeal off her spoon. "It's what he says. He's brilliant."

I rolled my eyes. We were in the dining hall, eating breakfast before class.

"Like that thing he said the other week. What was it?"

I shrugged and played with the crusts of my toast.

"Oh right, I remember," Eleanor exclaimed. "He said, 'The truth is generally seen but rarely heard.' Isn't that just so true?"

A few months ago I would have agreed with it, but now I wasn't so sure. Nothing that I had seen in the past month had seemed like the truth. How had my parents died? How had Benjamin died? I was beginning to doubt that the truth even existed. "Ironic that he said it out loud," I muttered.

"You're just in a bad mood because of your Latin test."

She was partially right. I did get a C on my exam, but that was intentional and I wasn't about to admit it to Eleanor. Regardless of Latin, I was still convinced that most of the things Professor Bliss taught us were made up. "Okay, so what about that time he told us that Napoleon was actually a little boy? Or his theory that ghosts actually exist?"

"He's just a spiritual person," Eleanor said. "And how do *you* know who Napoleon really was? You weren't alive back then."

I sighed. Thankfully, it was time for class. And lucky for Eleanor, we had History.

Professor Lesley Bliss was in his late thirties. "Call me Mr. B.," he had said on the first day. To my surprise, he was the same professor who I had walked in on teaching Advanced Latin on my first day of school. As a result, I thought he would be cold and brooding like the students he taught, when in fact he was exactly the opposite.

He was a grown-up boy, with a goofy smile and free-flowing hair that flopped in front of his eyes while he lectured. He always wore hiking clothes to class – zip-off combats and khaki shirts rolled up at the sleeves – which made him look like he had just come from digging in some exotic location.

"Burials," he began, and approached the board, drawing several images in chalk. The first was a pyramid, the second was a funeral pyre, and the third was a coffin, just like the one I had seen on the board in Advanced Latin. I looked at it again. In Horticulture, we were also studying burials, though of course there we were using bulbs.

"Why do we bury our dead?" His nose was dented in at the bridge like a sphinx; the cause of which I could only imagine had been a freak archaeological accident.

I thought about my parents. They had requested in their will that they be buried side by side in a tiny cemetery a few kilometres from our house. "Because it's respectful?"

He shook his head. "That's true, but that's not the reason we do it."

But that *was* the reason we buried people, wasn't it? After gazing at him in confusion, I raised my hand, determined to get the right answer. "Because leaving people out in the open is unsanitary."

Mr. B. shook his head and scratched the stubble on his neck.

I glared at him, annoyed at his ignorance and certain that my responses were correct. "Because it's the best way to dispose of a body?"

Mr. B. laughed. "Oh, but that's not true. Think of all the creative ways mass murderers have dealt with body disposal. Surely eating someone would be more practical than the coffin, the ceremony, the tombstone."

Eleanor grimaced at the morbid image, and the mention of mass murderers seemed to wake the rest of the class up. Still, no one had an answer. I'd heard Mr. B. was a quack, but this was just insulting. How dare he presume that I didn't know what burials meant? I'd watched them bury my parents, hadn't I? "Because that's just what we do," I blurted out. "We bury people when they die. Why does there have to be a reason for everything?"

"Exactly!" Mr. B. grabbed the pencil from behind his ear and began gesticulating with it. "We've *forgotten* why we bury people.

"Imagine you're living in ancient times. Your father dies. Would you randomly decide to put him inside a six-sided wooden box, nail it shut, then bury it two metres — that's six feet — below the earth? These decisions aren't arbitrary, people. Why a six-sided box? And why six feet below the earth? And why a box in the first place? And why did *every society* throughout history create a specific, ritualistic way of disposing of their dead?"

No one answered.

But just as Mr. B. was about to continue, there was a knock on the door. Everyone turned to see Mrs. Lynch poke her head in. "Professor Bliss, the headmistress would like to see Brett Steyers in her office. As a matter of urgency."

Professor Bliss nodded, and Brett grabbed his bag and stood up, his chair scraping against the floor as he left.

After the door closed, Mr. B. drew a terrible picture of a mummy on the board, which looked more like a hairy stick figure. "The Egyptians used to remove the brains of their dead before mummification. Now, why on earth would they do that?"

There was a vacant silence.

"Think, people! There must be a reason. Why the brain? What were they trying to preserve?"

When no one responded, he answered his own question.

"The mind!" he said, exasperated. "The soul!"

As much as I had planned on paying attention and participating in class, I spent the majority of the period passing notes with Eleanor. For all of his enthusiasm, Professor Bliss was repetitive and obsessed with death and immortality. When he faced the board to draw the hieroglyphic symbol for *Ra,* I read the note Eleanor had written me.

Who is cuter?

A. Professor Bliss

B. Brett Steyers

C. Dante Berlin

D. The mummy

I laughed. My hand wavered between *B* and *C* for the briefest moment. I wasn't sure if you could really call Dante cute. Devastatingly handsome and mysterious would be the more appropriate description. Instead I circled option *D.* Next to it, I wrote *Obviously!* and tossed it onto her desk when no one was looking. Eleanor rolled her eyes, wrote something below it, and tossed it back to me.

Has he kissed you yet?

I wrote a one-word response and passed it back.

No!

She slid it back with a reply. I unfolded it in my lap.

What's taking him so long? Maybe he doesn't know how, and that's what he's so pensive about.

I smiled and scrawled back a response. I was wondering the same thing.

Maybe he doesn't like me like that. I mean, I don't even know that much about him. He deflects all of my questions. And he called me a "friend".

Eleanor looked puzzled when she read my note. Out of the corner of my eye I watched her crush it in her fist and drop it into her backpack. Then she mouthed "Later" to me and focused on the board.

Just as Mr. B. turned to write something on the board again, a folded piece of pink paper hit my arm and dropped to the floor. I picked it up and flattened it out. In a loopy blue cursive, which didn't look like Eleanor's handwriting, it read:

When darkness falls and eyes stay shut
A chain of voices opens up.
Let wax not wane give breath to death.
Room 21F, Friday, October 31, 11 p.m.
PS Shhh

I glanced suspiciously around the room to see who had thrown it, but everyone was focused on the board. "Did you write me that note?" I whispered to Eleanor.

"What note?" she mouthed with a grin, and held up an identical piece of pink paper with what looked like the same words on it. Putting a finger to her lips, she bent over her notebook and started copying the terms on the board.

While Mr. B. talked about cremation, my mind drifted from death and burials to the cryptic note and what it meant. Absent-mindedly, I started doodling in the margins of my paper.

Renée, I wrote in cursive, and then again in bubble letters and then in the loopy handwriting of the mystery note. I drew a tiny picture of the moon above a lake. And then stick figures of people swimming in it. And then for some reason, I wrote *Dante.* First in print, and then in large, wavy letters, and then in all caps. *Dante. Dante. DANTE.* I had just finished writing, when I heard someone say my name.

"Renée?"

I shook myself out of my daze to discover that Mr. B. and the entire class were staring at me.

"Earth to Renée. The most primitive tombs. What were they called?" he repeated.

I glanced at my notes for the answer, but they were covered in doodles.

"Dante," I blurted out, reading the first word I saw. Immediately my face went red. "No, sorry, I meant...I meant dolmen."

I winced, hoping I was right so that I would be saved from further embarrassment. Thankfully, Dante wasn't in my class.

Mr. B. smiled. "Correct," he said, returning to the board. He drew a diagram of a stonelike lean-to, which I recognized from the reading. I took notes and kept my head down for the rest of class.

After the bell rang, Eleanor and I walked back to the dorm. But when we climbed the stairs to our room, the door was ajar. We exchanged surprised glances and pushed it open. At first it seemed like nothing was different. But the papers in my desk drawer were out of order, my bookshelf was rearranged, and my dresser drawer was pulled slightly out. The same was true for Eleanor's.

"Someone was definitely here," Eleanor said, looking through her closet, which she claimed was messier than it had been; though I doubted it could get any worse than it was before.

There were no locks on any of our doors, but it was an unspoken rule that you never entered someone else's room without permission. "Who do you think it was? Should we report it? Maybe it was Lynch. You know she doesn't like me," I said.

Suddenly Eleanor ran to her underwear drawer, as if remembering something important. She rifled through it, throwing its contents on the floor, and then sighed. "No. We shouldn't report it," she said, her back to me. "If Lynch wasn't the one who took it, I definitely don't want her trying to get it back, because then she'd read it."

"What are you talking about? What's missing?"

She turned to me. "My diary."

Chapter 7

Twisted Whispers

According to Professor Bliss, some cultures think that Fridays are unlucky, especially when they fall on Halloween, but what happened that Friday had nothing to do with luck. I've never been a superstitious person. I'm not scared of graveyards or curses. In fact, ever since my parents died, it seemed like I was drawn to death. Every word my professors uttered seemed morbid and ominous, and everywhere I looked things were dying: moths dangling in spiderwebs under the radiator, bees curled up on the windowsill, and the oak trees, now thin and naked, their leaves crunching under my shoes like beetles. But I wasn't afraid. I didn't believe in life after death, and I definitely didn't believe in ghosts.

That Friday was windy and overcast. The clouds hung heavy in the sky, their bellies black and swollen with rain. Gottfried didn't do anything to celebrate Halloween. In fact, I think the school intentionally ignored it, which I found strange, though acceptable. The day had been eerie enough already. I had spent most of it indoors, waiting out the storm. Eleanor told her brother Brandon about the stolen diary, but there wasn't much he could do except keep an eye out. The one thing he did know was that Mrs. Lynch hadn't taken it. If she had, word would have gotten to him, since he was on the Board of Monitors.

"What did you write in it that's so bad?" I asked Eleanor.

"Everything," she said. When I pressed her for specifics, she evaded my questions. "I just hope that whoever has it keeps it to themselves. If the stuff I wrote in there got around, I would kill myself."

I still didn't know who had passed me the note in History class, but something about the way Eleanor refused to talk about it made me sure she knew what the rhyme meant. All I knew was that 21F was Genevieve Tart's room, though why we would go there was a mystery to me. Up until that point, I thought I was more or less a patient person, but

Eleanor was testing my limits. "Does it have something to do with Halloween?" I asked, but she wouldn't answer. "Come on, it's Friday night, we're supposed to do whatever it is the note meant any minute now. Why can't you just tell me? I mean, what's the big secret?"

"Why can't you just wait and see?" Eleanor said, sitting on her bed in her school clothes with a book in her lap. A single candle illuminated the room. "Besides, if I tell you, I know you won't come. And if you don't come, we won't have enough people. Plus, I think you'll like it."

"That doesn't make any sense. If you think I'll like it, then why wouldn't I come?"

"Because you'll think it's stupid. And you *never* like things at first.'"

"What do you mean?" I said, taking offence. "Of course I do."

Eleanor rolled her eyes. "You didn't like me. And you didn't like Dante. And you didn't like Gottfried."

I sighed, but before I could respond, there was a tap on the wall over Eleanor's bed. It was 10.45 p.m. We both froze and listened. There was another tap, then two more.

Eleanor's face perked up. "It's time."

She opened her dresser and pulled out two candles. "Are you ready to go?"

Room 21F was on the fourth floor. We were on the second.

193

I gave her a sceptical look.

"Fine," she said. "I'll give you one hint, but you have to promise you'll come."

I nodded.

"Suffice it to say, it has to do with Genevieve Tart and some of the other girls. They have these secret gatherings that no one gets invited to except for the girls that Genevieve thinks have potential. Whatever that means."

"What do they do?"

"Each gathering is different. And sometimes people aren't invited back. So don't say anything ridiculous before you give it a chance."

Defensive, I put a hand on my hip. "Why would I say something ridiculous? Do I say ridiculous things? And what if I don't want to be invited back?"

Eleanor shook her head and pulled her hair back into a loose ponytail. "See, this is exactly what I'm talking about."

"Fine. I won't say anything impolite or rude. In fact, I'll try not to speak at all. Now, how do we get past Lynch?"

Eleanor smiled. "You'll see," she said, and unbuttoned her skirt.

I looked at her blankly. "What are you doing?"

"I don't want to get my clothes dirty," she said, peeling her stockings off. "You should probably take yours off too if you don't want to ruin them. It's dusty in there."

I raised an eyebrow. "In where?"

I thought the fireplace in our room was merely decorative, but as it turned out, it wasn't. Eleanor threw the candles into a bag that she hung around her wrist. On the side of the mantel was an iron knob. Eleanor pushed it to the left, and the flue creaked open. A mixture of cold air and dirt gusted into the room. I waved it away with my hand, then peered up into the shaft. A sprinkling of soot fell on my face.

"Have you done this before?"

"All the time."

I was sceptical. She hadn't done it all this year.

"It's the only way," she added, as if reading my thoughts. Then, wearing just a tank top and a pair of pink underwear, she stepped into the fireplace and hoisted herself up. I watched as her torso, then her legs, and finally her feet disappeared into the chimney.

I stripped down and changed into my pyjamas – a pair of shorts and an old T-shirt – then followed her. The chute was sooty and so narrow I barely fitted inside. Metal rungs were nailed to one side, creating a makeshift ladder.

"Don't fall," Eleanor teased, her voice echoing against the brick walls.

I looked down. The shaft of the chimney ran all the way from the basement to the roof, connecting our room to the rooms above and below it. I let out a nervous laugh and tightened my grip on the rungs. Wisps of broken spiderwebs floated around the edges of the passage, getting caught in my hair. My knees scraped against the brick as I inched up.

We emerged on the roof. Dozens of other chimney stacks poked out around us.

"The ladders were for the chimney sweeps," Eleanor explained, counting three stacks to the right, and then two down. "This one," she said before climbing inside.

Descending was faster than going up. Eleanor counted to herself as she stepped tenuously down the rungs – fifteen, fourteen, thirteen, twelve – and then stopped.

"I thought Genevieve Tart was on the Board of Monitors," I said. "Aren't they supposed to follow the rules?"

Eleanor glanced up at me. A finger of soot was smudged across the right side of her forehead. "Exactly. Lynch would never suspect Genevieve." Eleanor tapped the flue twice with her foot. After a moment, it creaked open. "And besides," she said just before squeezing her body through the narrow hole leading to the fireplace, "this was her idea."

Genevieve's room was lit by candlelight. Seven candles were positioned in a broken circle on the floor, and seven girls were lounging about the room. I knew some of them from my classes; a few others were friends of Eleanor's. The rest were juniors who I had seen around campus but never met before. There were legs everywhere – Maggie's thin calves draped over a bed frame as she talked to Katherine; Greta's athletic thighs crossed on the carpet, cradling a magazine; Charlotte's pale knees, which she hugged while Rebecca braided her hair; Bonnie's ankles, just visible beneath her nightgown as she opened the windows; and Genevieve's long, tan legs, which stemmed from a pair of blue shorts.

"Finally," Greta said, closing her magazine.

Eleanor wiped her hands on her thighs. "Are we the last ones?" she asked, lighting our candles and placing them on the floor with the others.

Charlotte nodded. Charlotte was Genevieve's room-mate. She had large eyes and banana curls that bounced when she walked. The walls above her bed were plastered with posters of actors and musicians, the most prominent being David Bowie, whose hollowed face stared back at me over the foot of her bed.

In contrast, Genevieve's side of the room was pink and neat and bespoke an obsessive attention to order. Everything was placed in a careful arrangement: the make-up on her dresser in perfect symmetry, the notebooks and folders on her desk all organized by colour, the photographs on the wall framed and centred.

Eleanor nestled herself between the girls and introduced

me. "Everyone not in the know, this is Renée. She's my room-mate."

Genevieve gave me a fake smile. "We know who she is. Why do you think she was invited?" Then she looked at me. "The headmistress is always talking about you. She says you're one of the best students in your year in Horticulture."

I gave her a confused look. I hadn't met the headmistress. How could she be talking about me? But Eleanor cut me off before I could say anything.

"And she's dating Dante Berlin." She smiled, her blue eyes growing wide as everyone in the room looked at me with new interest.

Genevieve cocked her head. "Really?"

I blushed. "We're not dating. We're just friends."

Eleanor rolled her eyes. "She's being modest. Dante is practically obsessed with her. He's even tutoring her in Latin."

"That's not true. I mean, he is tutoring me, but it's just because I'm terrible at it. And the headmistress couldn't have said that about me. I've never even met her."

This didn't seem to bother Eleanor. "Professors talk. Maybe Professor Mumm told her about you."

"And you shouldn't be so sure that you and Dante are just friends," Charlotte said, tossing her curly hair over her shoulder. "Latin is a Romance language, isn't it?"

"Don't be stupid, Charlotte," Genevieve snorted. "It's a Latinate language."

Charlotte looked stung by her remark. "But aren't the Romance languages based on Latin?" she asked.

"The language is dead," Genevieve said with a hand on her hip. "Just like the people who spoke it."

A rigid silence fell over the room, and Genevieve stood up and cleared her throat. "Okay, is everyone ready?"

She opened a leather-bound book titled *Talking to the Dead* and began to call out instructions. "Sit in a circular formation. Position a candle in front of each person, thus forming two concentric circles."

It took me a few seconds to realize what we were doing, but when I did, I had to suppress a groan. "*A séance? Really?*" I mouthed to Eleanor after we sat down. She was right; I did think it was stupid. Nonetheless, I couldn't leave now. We sat in a circle around the candles. Eleanor was to my right, Genevieve to my left. Our shadows flickered across the walls.

"The sacrificial flesh, when burned, should form a triangle," Genevieve read.

I pinched Eleanor.

"Ow!" she squealed. Genevieve squinted at her.

She passed around a pair of metal scissors, and we each snipped off a lock of hair and held it over the flame of our candle until it ignited. Instantly, the room was filled with the stench of burning hair. Eleanor winced. I coughed and wafted the smoke from away from my face, but Genevieve didn't flinch. Without asking, she took the top sheet from Charlotte's bed and laid it on the floor. After all the hair had burned out of her candle, she took it and dripped wax across the sheet so that it formed a large triangle within the circle of candles.

Charlotte gasped.

"Relax," Genevieve scolded. "It's just wax; it'll come off. Now, we all have to concentrate on our 'object', or, in other words, the dead person, which Charlotte and I have decided will be the first headmaster of Gottfried Academy, Bertrand Gottfried."

Before she continued, Eleanor interrupted. "Why do you get to decide?"

"Because I organized it. And we have to see if it will even work."

"But I don't want to talk to him."

"Do you have a better suggestion?"

Eleanor went silent. "What about a celebrity or something." She winked at me. "Or how about Benjamin Gallow?" Now I understood why Eleanor made sure I came. I gave her the beginnings of a smile.

Genevieve rolled her eyes. "What, so you can ask him how he died? We all know how it happened, Eleanor. He had a heart attack."

There was a long silence as everyone tried to pretend they weren't paying attention.

"You know, I don't really want to talk to the headmaster either," I said. "Can't we all just pick our own objects?" I gazed around the circle for approval, but everyone avoided eye contact.

Genevieve sighed. "Fine." Raising the book again, she said, "We each have to think of someone who died. Once you choose the person, you have to concentrate on them as hard as you can. The book says, 'The object that you choose should be someone you were intimately acquainted with or know a great deal about. In order to conjure it from the dead, you must visualize your object in its entirety. Repeat its name in your head, and then once you hear its voice in your ear, silently speak your question.'"

Genevieve lowered the book and gave us a sombre look. "Does everyone understand?"

"What if we can't hear its voice? How will we know when to ask?" Eleanor said.

"If you do it right, it'll work," Genevieve said, dismissing her question. "Okay, now close your eyes and visualize your object."

I closed my eyes and thought about my parents while Genevieve began to chant in Latin. I tried to imagine my mother sitting in the sunroom with a book in her lap, and my father eating toast while doing a crossword puzzle. But their images kept fading away from me. Sitting in Genevieve's dorm room surrounded by candles and girls I barely knew, I felt so far away from my parents that it was hard to conjure any sort of tangible memory. It was as if they had ceased to exist in my mind as real people, and instead had become nothing more than the blurry idea of two people I had once met in a dream.

I opened my eyes and looked around the circle. Everyone else had their eyes shut, concentrating on their objects. I shut my eyes again and tried to focus, but the images of my parents kept darkening, becoming overshadowed by the one person who I couldn't get out of my head since coming to Gottfried Academy. Dante.

I pictured him in the library, the way he'd pulled me through the stacks of books, his legs brushing against mine as we'd waited, hushed, in the dark. I blushed just thinking about it. Where was he right now? Probably in his room in Attica Falls, sleeping, or maybe reading. I wondered if he was thinking of me too.

Then a gust of wind blew through the open windows, rattling the shutters and rustling the papers on Genevieve's desk. The candles flickered.

A whisper blew around us like an autumn breeze. The low murmur of voices filled the air, though none of us were speaking. My body acted without me, and I leaned towards Genevieve and cupped my hands around her ear as if I were about to tell her a secret. Then my mouth began to move against my own volition, the words coming out jumbled and strange. They were more sounds than words, eerie utterances that spilled out of me faster than I could process them. Even my voice was different – it was deeper, the pitches varying quickly and capriciously, as if coming from a different body. I tried to make it stop, to stop speaking, but I couldn't control my lips or my tongue.

One by one, each of us leaned towards the girl to our left, perched against her ear like we were playing a game of telephone.

And then I felt something tickle my ear. Before I could turn to see what it was, a voice began whispering to me. It was Eleanor, but it wasn't. Her voice was low and deep and sounded like it belonged to a man. My dad. I was so shocked that I completely forgot I was simultaneously whispering to Genevieve. The only thing I wanted to do was listen. All at once, a million questions crowded my head. I chose the most important one and concentrated on it.

How did you die?

The voices stopped. All I could hear was Eleanor's breath, deep and husky, on the back of my neck. And then a sound rolled off her tongue, which turned into another sound that folded into another. The words spilled into my ear like a flood. They were nothing but strange sounds that started as words but transformed into an echo of a place, a smell, a feeling, a taste that I once knew.

The ocean. I felt its sticky air clinging to my skin. I smelled the rain as it pounded against the asphalt and evaporated into steam. I heard the seagulls crying as they circled above the marina, the tide lapping to shore, and then a splash.

The image of a person thrashing in the ocean appeared in my mind. He was in the deeper side of the marina, past where the boats were docked. He was being pulled under by something, and was reaching out into the air, grabbing at nothing while the waves pushed him under. I thought it was my dad, but I couldn't understand why he was drowning and where my mother was. But just as quickly as the image had entered my head, it vanished.

My mind was racing. *Where are you?*

All of a sudden an image flashed through my mind. It was of an ancient tree with long sweeping branches. It seemed familiar. I focused on the image, trying to place where I had seen it. Somewhere in California, maybe, in the redwood forest, or at a friend's house. For the first time in months I thought about places that I had taught myself to forget, but none of them matched the tree in the image.

Finally, Eleanor stopped talking.

At the same time, my mouth slowed until the sounds

stopped. I regained control over my hands and prised them free from Genevieve's ear. I tried to move my tongue, and to my relief I could move that too. Once separated, the other girls seemed to be experiencing the same disbelief I was. For a moment none of us moved as we pondered what had just happened.

Slowly, everyone began talking.

Bonnie heard from her grandmother, who had died four years ago. Charlotte had spoken to Kurt Cobain, and looked like she was about to faint from the shock of it. Greta was visited by her old tennis coach, and Maggie by Audrey Hepburn. I wanted to ask them questions, but I was still in shock over the fact that I had actually conjured my father from the dead. A few of them asked about my encounter, but I barely answered. I was still trying to figure out what had happened and what it meant – the marina, the drowning, the tree.

Lost in my thoughts, I gazed out the window. It looked out on the lake, which was surrounded by giant oak and spruce trees. And then it clicked. Amazed at how obvious it was, I stood up.

Eleanor approached me just as I was about to leave, and pulled me aside. "We have to talk," she said in a tone that was so serious I couldn't believe it was Eleanor.

I pushed my hair out of my face. "Can it wait till later?"

"Not really," she said, studying me. "What's wrong?"

"How can I get outside?" I asked, my knees brushing against each other as I shifted my weight and scoped out the room.

She gave me a strange look. "You climb down the chimney to the basement," she said slowly. "Why?"

"It...it worked. It actually worked. I talked to my father. And I...well, I just have to go. I'll explain it all later."

"Do you know how to get back? Want me to go with you?"

"Don't worry, I'll figure it out. I'll meet you back in the room. Okay?" I bit my lip.

"Sure," she said, though I knew she was sceptical. "If you walk past the furnace, there's a fire escape. It leads to the back of the dorm. The alarm won't sound; it stopped working years ago."

I smiled in gratitude. "Thanks."

"Are you sure you don't want me to go with you?"

I nodded and grabbed my things. "I'll see you later."

I shimmied down the chimney chute until I got to the basement. Squeezing my way through the fireplace, I lowered my feet to the ground. Steam hissed from the pipes lining the ceiling, filling the room with the soggy smell of laundry and mildew. I hid behind a large beam and surveyed the room to make sure Mrs. Lynch wasn't lurking in the hall. To my left was the furnace room, to my right the laundry machines. In front of me was a long cement corridor. Everything seemed to be made of corrugated metal. There were rusty pipes everywhere, leaking a viscous liquid that left yellow stains on the floor. Otherwise the room was empty. I counted to three and ran down the hall, dodging the drips until I spotted an eroded metal staircase that led to a fire escape.

In the cold night air, my body tightened. Goose bumps prickled across my skin, and I remembered that I was barely wearing any clothes. Immediately, I felt self-conscious, even though I knew no one was there to see me. Stupid Renée. Now I might freeze to death before I even made it to the green, and if Eleanor ever conjured me up in a séance, all she would see was me tiptoeing around campus like an idiot in my shorts.

But what else could I do? If my father was out there, I had to find him. I walked across campus, past the lake and through the trees, until I was standing in eyesight of the great oak. Its gnarled trunk looked thicker without its normal shroud of leaves, and its bare branches extended over the lawn like a system of roots. It was the exact same tree as the one that had flashed through my mind during the séance.

And then in the distance, two figures materialized out of the darkness by the Ursa Major statue. I squinted. It looked like a man and woman. It had to be my parents. Without thinking, I ran towards them. They seemed to be heading in the direction of the girls' dorm. Maybe they were coming to meet me. A gust of wind carried the sound of the voices across the path, and I wrapped my arms around myself in the cold.

"Mom?" I called out as I approached. "Dad?"

At the sound of my voice they froze, then spun around. I realized, to my horror, that they weren't my parents at all. Instead, I was face-to-face with Gideon and Vivian. "I... I'm sorry," I said, and backed away. "I thought you were someone else."

Vivian looked wildly around her, as if caught in the midst of a crime. When she was sure I was alone, she whispered something to Gideon, and they both looked at me. Why were they out here at night in their antique suits, and what were they talking about, and why did they always look so angry?

It's okay, I told myself. They're just students. What could they do to me?

Gideon said something to Vivian in Latin, and she nodded and approached me. The sky rumbled with thunder, and I began to back away from them, when I felt someone directly behind me. A hand clamped over my wrist and pulled me aside. I recognized his touch immediately.

"Dante." My voice was barely audible in the night wind.

"Stay behind me," he said, stepping in front of me, his voice low and authoritative.

"Friends," he said, looking between Gideon and Vivian, "what are you doing out past curfew on a night like tonight?"

Vivian narrowed her eyes. "I could ask you the same." It was the first time I had heard her speak English; it sounded clumsy and unpleasant.

Gideon came up behind her, his hand on the small of her back, and said something to Dante in Latin. Dante paused and then responded.

What had he said? Even though my eyes were trained on Gideon and Vivian, the only person I was aware of was Dante. He loomed in front of me, gripping my wrist as he spoke, my arm tingling as it grew cold, now a familiar sensation, and one that I was slowly growing fond of. It was uncomfortable, inexplicable, unsettling. The woodsy smell of his body tickled my nose, his shirt brushing against my back with every breath that he took. I shifted my weight until our legs were almost touching.

Suddenly he turned to me. "Let's go," he said, giving a sidelong glance to his old friends, who were walking away.

"What did you say to them?" I asked as we headed towards the girls' dorm.

"Nothing. Just that you were here to meet me."

But I wasn't. "Why are *you* here?"

But Dante's eyes were focused on something in the distance. "Someone's coming."

The front door to the girls' dorm opened, and Mrs. Lynch stepped outside. She must have heard us talking, because she peered into the darkness.

We backed away to the safety of the trees, but a burst of lightning illuminated the campus. In a flash, Mrs. Lynch's eyes met mine in a furious, gleaming glare.

"She saw me," I whispered.

Thunder shook the ground below us, the sky cracked open, and it began to rain.

"Come on," Dante said. I trembled as he took my hand, my fingers chilling as they curled around his.

We ran across the green, the rain pouring down on us as we splashed through mud and puddles until we reached Horace Hall. The double doors were locked, and as Dante bent over them, I squinted into the rain, waiting for Mrs. Lynch's stocky figure to appear. "She's probably on her way. What do we do?" I said, water dripping down my nose. But just as I finished speaking, the doors clicked and Dante pushed them open.

"After you," he said, and we slipped inside, the doors locking behind us.

Horace Hall was different at night. Without students,

it was so quiet I could hear the water dripping from my hair as Dante led me upstairs and into the darkened classroom where I normally had Latin.

"What just happened?" I asked, my lips quivering. "And why were you out there tonight?"

"I was following them."

Dante glanced out the window to make sure Mrs. Lynch wasn't coming, then turned to me. I must have looked surprised at finally getting a real answer from him, because he smiled.

"I figured you wouldn't stop asking until I told you, so there it is. I was following them. And you," he said. "Once I realized you were there."

"Why?"

"I think they're up to something. And no, I don't know what. I'm just getting used to your questioning routine, so please take it easy on me."

He was still wearing his clothes from school, his blue oxford shirt now soaked through and matted against his chest. He ran a hand through his hair, shaking the water from it.

His eyes travelled across my body, and a slow smile spread across his face, reminding me that I was in my pyjamas. I pulled at my T-shirt, which was now transparent and clinging to my body.

"What?" I asked, trying to sound nonchalant.

He let out a laugh. "Nothing," he said, shaking his head. "You seem to be out of dress code."

"I didn't realize we were going to class."

"Well, as your teacher, I should make you write lines."

I gave him a challenging look. "What do you want me to write?"

He took a step towards me. "*Cupido,*" he uttered. His voice was full and rich, as if he weren't uttering just a word, but a command.

I picked up a piece of chalk. "How do you spell it?" I asked, my voice shaking.

Dante wrapped his fingers around mine, guiding my hand. A prickling sensation climbed up my arm, and I shivered. "What does it mean?"

When he spoke, he was right behind me.

"The thing about Latin is that you can say so much more than in any other language. The words, the tenses. They're different, they evolve – it makes it easier to explain what you're thinking. Do you ever feel like you want to say something, but you don't know how to say it?"

I nodded. Mostly when I was with him.

"Can I try something?" he whispered.

He turned me towards him, brushing his hand across my cheek, and played with the loose wisps of hair around my neck. His fingers tickled my skin, and suddenly I lost all of my words. I swallowed and nodded.

My heart began to beat faster, and everything inside of me began to tremble like the leaves of a tree rustled by an autumn breeze.

My legs moved without me, and I stepped closer to him until our legs were tangled. He grazed his fingers down my thigh, and with a sudden, almost uncontrollable force, pressed me against the blackboard, the slate cool against my skin. Lacing his fingers through mine, he pulled me towards him until our lips were barely touching. His eyes were ravenous as they crawled over me; something about him felt raw and dangerous; even if I'd wanted to push him away, I knew I couldn't. I closed my eyes, waiting for the kiss, but it never came. His grip softened, and he ran his hand gently through my hair as he kissed my neck, my shoulders, my arms. I closed my eyes, my breath growing shallow as I felt his mouth against my skin, his hand on the small of my back, sending shivers up my spine.

"Renée," he sounded out, as if he were learning my name for the first time.

I wanted to say something back, but I didn't have the words to describe what I was feeling. I thought I knew what it meant to kiss, to touch, to embrace, but this was something that I'd never felt before.

I closed my eyes and raised my hand to his face, passing it over his nose, his eyes, his lips, memorizing the way they felt. He pulled me towards him, and without thinking, I leaned into his kiss.

But just before our lips met, he turned his head. "Not on the lips."

Suddenly, everything inside me began to deflate. "What?"

"Do you feel different when you're around me?" he asked.

I nodded.

"How?"

"My skin tingles and everything goes numb, like my body is starting to freeze. Do you feel it too?"

He took my hand and traced it down his arm. He closed his eyes. "Desire," he breathed. "That's what it means. And yes, I feel it too."

I leaned against the blackboard, my chest warm and flushed. "Why...why won't you kiss me?"

He let his hand slide down my leg, and I felt my insides melt. "I want to. I've always wanted to. But please, just trust me."

"Why do I feel so strange whenever I'm near you?"

He leaned his forehead against mine, his hair brushing against my cheeks. "I don't know."

Outside, the rain had let up. "Come on," he said. "Let's get you home."

Our fingerprints and chalky silhouettes were imprinted

on the blackboard, smudging the Latin scrawled across it. Dante slipped his hand into mine, and together we escaped from the building, into the night. We didn't speak. We didn't have to. We both knew that some things couldn't be translated into words.

"Where were you?" Eleanor asked. She'd been pacing around the room when I climbed in through the chimney. "You're soaking wet!"

"I was outside. And then in Horace."

"Horace Hall? What were you doing there? And why did you run off like that?"

While wiping my face with a towel, I told her about my father, about Vivian and Gideon, about Dante and their conversation in Latin, about Mrs. Lynch, and finally about our time in the classroom.

"Whoa, whoa, whoa, back up. You made out with Dante Berlin in Horace Hall?"

"Sort of..."

She gave me an expectant look, waiting for me to continue. "Well, was it good?"

I considered all of the events that led up to the moment in the Latin classroom. Why wasn't my father by the tree, like I'd seen during the séance? And what had happened between Dante and his old friends? Why wouldn't Dante kiss me? It was confusing and frightening and inexplicable and surprising. And strangely wonderful. It didn't even matter any more if I liked it or if I didn't like it. I felt something...something too delicate and ephemeral for words. "It was unreal."

"So you thought you were going to see your parents, but instead you found Dante and Vivian and Gideon?"

I nodded. "I don't know why my dad wasn't there, though."

"Maybe you got the location wrong. Or maybe it wasn't your dad that you saw."

"It was definitely him. I mean, who else could it be?"

Eleanor shrugged. "I don't know."

I thought Eleanor would offer some absurd suggestions or ask me to recount every detail like she normally did, but instead she sat at her desk and looked out the window.

I wiped my cheeks with my hands and began to wring out my hair, when I noticed her standing in front of my bed. "What?"

"Now you're supposed to ask me about my night."

A wave of guilt passed over me. I had been talking about myself and my problems all week. All month, in fact, never once asking Eleanor about how she was. "Right. Sorry. I'm terrible. What happened?"

Eleanor sat cross-legged on my bed. "I summoned Benjamin Gallow."

I was pulling a sweatshirt over my head when her words registered, and I froze. "And?" I asked, my voice muffled through the cotton.

"And there are complications."

"What do you mean?" I asked, fumbling with the arm and head holes until I finally forced my shirt on.

"Well...I don't think I did it right, exactly. First I was thinking of him, but then I was thinking of him and Cassandra, and then I was thinking of Cassandra even though she wasn't dead, and then I sort of summoned both of them."

"But that's impossible. Cassandra isn't dead; she transferred."

"Not according to her."

CHAPTER 8

THE GOTTFRIED CURSE

MONDAY MORNING, MY ALARM CLOCK woke me from the best dream I'd had in months. The autumn sunlight streamed through the windows, and I stretched beneath the sheets, smiling to myself as Dante kissed my wrists, my arms, my shoulders, my neck. "I love you," he said, running his fingers through my hair.

He leaned in, and all at once I opened my eyes.

Outside it was grey and drizzling, and the dream dissipated into the November mist. Across from me, Eleanor was still asleep, shifting beneath the blankets, her blonde hair spilling over her pillow like corn silk. Everything that had happened now seemed like a dream.

Eleanor and I had spent the entire weekend trying to piece together what had happened to Benjamin and Cassandra, but with no luck. Maybe today would be different, I thought as I got dressed and headed to class. But by second period we were just as confused.

"The last thing Benjamin remembered doing was kissing Cassandra. After that, everything was blurry," Eleanor was explaining to Nathaniel. We were sitting in the back of class before the start of Philosophy. "So romantic," she added.

Nathaniel groaned.

"Anyway," I said, interrupting her, "since Eleanor had envisioned both of them at the beginning of the séance, she summoned Cassandra too."

"Which means she's dead!" Eleanor added loudly.

"Shhh!" I cautioned, glancing around to make sure no one heard. "Which *might* mean she's dead," I corrected. I still couldn't figure out what had happened at the séance. I had definitely summoned someone – a man who I had assumed was my father. But then why hadn't he been at the great oak like he'd shown me? Something about it didn't seem right. "The séance didn't exactly work for me, so we don't actually know if it worked for you either."

Eleanor ignored me. "But the craziest part is *how* she died," she continued excitedly. "She was buried alive."

Both Eleanor and I watched for Nathaniel's reaction, but he didn't seem as shocked by it as we were.

"Who did it?" he asked, biting his fingernails.

"She didn't know. She had some sort of bag over her head when they did it," Eleanor explained. "I wonder if it happened at school or somewhere else. The last thing she remembered was being brought to the headmistress's office. After that it went black, until suddenly she was being carried somewhere outside. She was put into a wooden box that was then nailed shut. And then she heard the sound of dirt pounding on top of her until everything faded into nothing. But even if that was her last memory, it doesn't mean that's what did her in. I mean, Benjamin's last memory was kissing Cassandra, and that had nothing to do with his death."

"Did he say how he died?" Nathaniel asked.

"No. Every time I asked, he kept showing me the same scene of him kissing Cassandra. It was kind of romantic. That's how I started thinking about her in the first place, and then suddenly I heard her voice in my ear."

"But if she died, why would the school lie and say that she transferred?" I countered.

"Maybe they didn't know," Eleanor said. "Maybe she died after she transferred. Maybe she was summoned to the headmistress's office just before she left, for transcripts or whatever. And then it happened."

We both turned to Nathaniel. "What do you think?" we said, almost simultaneously.

Nathaniel pulled at his tie, trying to loosen it. "Why are you telling *me* all of this?"

"Because we're not sure if we should believe it or not," I said. "And you're the smartest person we know." Well, that wasn't exactly true. Dante was the smartest person I knew. Nathaniel was really just nerdy.

"And because we know you won't tell anyone," Eleanor added in a low voice. "You won't tell anyone, right?"

"I won't tell anyone."

Eleanor and I exchanged glances and smiled.

"Why don't you just do another séance and try her again?" Nathaniel suggested.

Eleanor shook her head. "Proper séances only work on Halloween."

"Either way, the séance sounds iffy," Nathaniel said to Eleanor. "If it didn't work the right way for Renée, you can't trust what you heard either. But if I were you, I'd talk to Minnie Roberts."

Our smiles quickly faded. What was he talking about? Minnie Roberts? The mousy girl who had dropped her bag in Horace Hall on the first day of classes? I turned to ask Eleanor, who put a hand to her forehead. "Oh my God. Why didn't I think of that?!"

"Think of *what*?" I said.

Eleanor turned to me as if just remembering I was there. "Last spring Minnie exploded in the dining hall."

"I...I remember hearing about that. You mentioned it," I said to Nathaniel.

"It was the night before finals," Eleanor continued, running through the history quickly. "After Ben died, after Cassie left. Everyone was in the Megaron when Minnie burst in and started screaming about how Cassandra Millet was murdered by the headmistress and the Board of Monitors. She claimed that she saw them burying Cassandra just outside of campus by the woods. She'd been trying to tell the professors, but no one would listen to her."

"What?" I said, incredulous. "The Board of Monitors?"

"Everyone in the dining hall went nuts, and the professors ended up carrying Minnie out and bringing her to the nurses' wing."

"That's why everyone thinks Minnie Roberts is insane," Nathaniel added.

"She still might be," Eleanor murmured. "Rumour has it that her parents sent her to the loony bin last summer."

"Why would she come back?" I asked.

"Her parents are big-time donors," Eleanor said. "They probably wouldn't let her leave. I know mine wouldn't." She looked at Nathaniel.

"So you think she was telling the truth?" I asked.

Eleanor snorted. "No. Not the whole truth, at least. Why would the Board of Monitors and the headmistress bury Cassandra Millet alive? My brother would never kill anyone...let alone Cassie. Why would *anyone* kill her?" Her voice trailed off. After the séance, after Eleanor had finished telling me everything she'd seen, I questioned her for hours about her former room-mate. Did she have any enemies? Was there anything out of the ordinary about her behaviour? The same questions the police had asked me about my parents. And just like me, Eleanor had nothing new to add. Cassandra was beautiful, a straight-A student, no enemies, and no strange behaviour; kind and generous to everyone she met. The least likely person to be murdered. Just like my parents, I thought.

"She might not even be dead," Nathaniel reminded us.

"He's right," I said. "I summoned someone, but I don't think it was my father."

"Either way, we need to ask Minnie," Eleanor concluded.

When the bell rang, Miss LaBarge stood up and began talking about Plato and something about the soul and a cave, though I was barely paying attention. Halfway through class, her lecture was interrupted by two raps on the door. Without waiting, Mrs. Lynch flung herself inside, wearing a grey frock and loud square shoes.

"The headmistress wishes to see Renée Winters."

Miss LaBarge put down her lecture notes and looked at me. "I suppose you have no choice."

I gathered my things and followed Mrs. Lynch into the hall, glancing back at Nathaniel and Eleanor, who were giving me questioning looks.

"Out of your room after curfew," Mrs. Lynch barked as she held me by the elbow. "With a boy. Outside without a pass. Running from a teacher."

"You're not a teacher," I muttered, but if she heard me she didn't let on.

"Better start packing your things," she said with a sneer. "The headmistress has an extremely low tolerance for blatant disobedience."

The list of rules I'd broken was longer than I thought. Suddenly, the possibility of expulsion became frighteningly real. When I had first arrived at Gottfried, being expelled might have been the answer to all my problems. But now the thought was unimaginable, and not only because I didn't have a home to go to. I loved my classes; I was leagues ahead of everyone in Horticulture, and I found Philosophy to be far more interesting than any of the classes I'd taken in California. For the first time in my life I was actually learning things that correlated to my interests. To my surprise, the classical subjects that Gottfried offered were far from outdated; in fact, I had a feeling they would be useful in the future, though I wasn't sure how. Not to mention meeting Dante and Eleanor, and even Nathaniel. Yes, the only thing we shared was Gottfried, but now that my parents were gone, that was all I had.

The headmistress's office was in the northern wing of Archebald Hall. Calysta Von Laark was standing by a tall stained-glass window, petting a Siamese cat on the sill. A second Siamese twined between her ankles. Her wintery hair was parted to the right and pinned up with a silver comb, a frizzy wave of short white tresses falling across her left eye.

When she saw us enter, she left the window and took a seat in a plum velvet chair behind her desk. Soundlessly, the cat jumped off the windowsill and followed her, leaping into her lap.

Spanning the wall was a giant mural of *The Last Judgment* by Michelangelo. The mere sight of the painting was frightening. Crowning the ceiling were angels sitting atop a bed of clouds, the paint peeling off their chubby faces in rosy flakes. Below them, throngs of men, women and children clutched each other, covering their eyes and hiding their half-naked bodies, their faces contorted in pain while they waited for the final fall. Demons carrying clubs and pitchforks pulled them towards the abyss by their ankles while they thrashed about in the air, trying to grasp anything that would keep them in the blue world behind them.

The floor was made of a dark marble. Words, engraved into the floor in Latin, circled the edge of the room and spiralled down to its centre. I translated it roughly with the Latin I had learned from Dante. *To capture the mind of a child is to gain immortality.* It was the same phrase that the headmistress had recited at the Fall Awakening when she had tapped the Board of Monitors.

"Renée," the headmistress said, stroking the Siamese. A heavy sapphire ring rested around her slender middle finger. "Welcome." Her tone was surprisingly gentle. Behind her, a wood and glass hutch filled with what looked like golden walking sticks was partially obscured by her desk. Above each stick was a plaque with a nameplate and a set of dates. Could this woman have buried Cassandra alive? Now that I was sitting across from her, watching her pet her cat, the idea seemed preposterous.

Mrs. Lynch spoke up immediately. "She was outside past curfew with that boy Dante Berlin. And when I told them to stop, they ran away from me. And the girl is out of dress code."

"She didn't tell us to stop," I blurted out, before realizing that I had admitted I was guilty. Sighing, I looked down to inspect my skirt. It wasn't out of dress code.

"Untucked shirt," Mrs. Lynch said. "And a run in the stockings."

I twisted around to look at the back of my legs, only to

see a long run inching up my left heel. "That's not my fault!" I protested.

"Thank you, Lynette," the headmistress said soothingly. "Would you give us a moment alone?"

Mrs. Lynch gave a stiff nod and stepped outside.

"Please," said Headmistress Von Laark, "have a seat."

I sat in an upright leather chair across from her, staring at her brooch, which looked something like a bear. On top of her desk sat an hourglass filled with white sand, a globe, a stack of papers and a small pile of books. Behind the desk, a narrow spiral staircase was carved into a stone wall, probably leading down into the bowels of the building.

Headmistress Von Laark smiled. "So, you snuck out after hours to meet a boy?"

I swallowed and nodded. "Just a friend."

"How did you get out?"

I couldn't tell her about the chimneys, or they'd block them off for good. "I waited until Mrs. Lynch was on a different floor."

The headmistress gave me a curious look. "I see. And you ran away when she saw you?"

I nodded. "But I didn't mean to. I wasn't thinking. It was dark and rainy. I couldn't really see her." I paused. "Please don't expel me," I said softly.

The headmistress laughed. "I would have done the same thing." The second Siamese cat leaped onto her desk.

"Have you met my darlings?"

"No, I don't think so."

"This is Romulus." The cat sauntered across her desk, meowed, and curled around the hourglass. "And this is Remus," she said, stroking the cat in her lap. "Aren't they handsome?"

I nodded. "Very."

The headmistress leaned back in her chair. "So, tell me about this Dante Berlin."

I must have looked puzzled, because she continued, "You two are dating, no?"

"No. We're just friends."

Von Laark put a finger to her lips. "Hmm," she murmured. "Are you sure?"

I swallowed. Even if the headmistress had somehow found out about us, the best I could do was deny it. "Yes."

She gazed at me pensively, her blue eyes fixed on mine. "Professor Mumm tells me you're excelling in Horticulture. She says you're the best student she's had in at least a decade."

I blushed. "It doesn't feel that way. There's still so much to learn."

She clasped her hands on her desk. "You're just like your mother. Very modest."

"You knew my mother?"

The headmistress nodded. "I was a professor of Philosophy here when your mother was a student."

Questions flooded my head. What was my mother like? What were her friends like? What did she look like? And had the headmistress also had my father as a student?

"Incredibly sharp, your mother. Your father too. And ambitious. You never would have guessed they were from wealthy backgrounds. Always so humble."

"My father was wealthy?" I didn't know. His parents had died when I was a baby, and I had only met my four aunts, who were each fussy, overweight, inclined to hats, and generally auntlike.

"Why, of course. You weren't aware? The Redgrave fortune. Redgrave Architects? They specialized in custom-made foundations, cellars, enclaves, wells, and so on. Quite artful, actually. Tragic that it's a dying form."

"I...I didn't know. He never told me."

"Robert was a private boy," she murmured. "Clearly you take after him. Professor Mumm told me that just last week you identified the only form of shrivel root in the field, and were also able to identify the appropriate soil and plot for it to be planted in."

It was true.

"Very impressive for someone your age," remarked the headmistress.

"Thanks."

"Well, I suppose if you have nothing else that you want to tell me, we have nothing more to discuss today."

She waited a moment, but when I said nothing, she smiled. "Go then, and enjoy your youth."

Grateful for the reprieve, I stood up. Something about her demeanour was unsettling. Maybe it was her cats.

"Oh and, Renée, tell me, when is your birthday?"

I turned just as the headmistress put on a pair of reading glasses.

"August twentieth. Why?"

"A Leo," she said, smiling. "How fitting."

Just before I turned, a file on her desk caught my eye. It was a manila folder partially covered in papers. It was labelled *Dante Berlin*. I thought back to the day I'd met Eleanor, when she'd told me she'd asked her brother Brandon to check my file in the headmistress's office. Quickly, I glanced around the room, looking for a filing cabinet. I didn't see one, though I knew it had to be there somewhere.

"Is there something wrong, Renée?" the headmistress probed.

"No," I said quickly. "Nothing." And I stepped into the hall.

To my surprise, Dante was sitting outside on a bench, in a collared shirt, his blue tie loose around his neck. I wanted to stop and talk to him, but knew I couldn't in front of the headmistress. We made eye contact as I passed, and Dante gave the beginnings of a smile when the headmistress poked her head out the door.

"I'm ready for you," she said in a firm voice.

I walked by slowly, and as Dante stood up, our hands brushed against each other, his skin cold against mine. The door shut behind him, and I was left alone in the hallway. There was a folded piece of paper on the bench where Dante had been sitting. I flattened it out to find the following words written in Dante's neat handwriting:

Meet me in front of the library at 7 p.m.

Folding the note into my pocket, I left for class.

"I talked to Minnie," Eleanor said as she closed the door. I was sitting at my desk, trying to read the footnotes of *The Iliad* in the dim light of my candle.

I sat up straight. "And?"

She hefted her bag onto the desk. "Disaster."

"What happened?"

"I cornered her in Art. We were working on portraits. I made sure to sit next to her so we would be partners. While I was sketching, I asked her about what happened last spring with Cassandra. That was my first mistake. She got all weird and hunched over, and her face wouldn't stay still... It ruined my portrait."

"What did you say to her, exactly?"

"I just asked her, 'So what really happened last spring with Cassandra?'"

"A little more tact, Eleanor!"

"Well, I wanted to cut to the chase. She's not exactly easy to talk to. And besides, I thought she *wanted* to talk about it."

"Not to us. She probably thought you were making fun of her."

"Well, I wasn't, obviously. But now what do we do? There's no way I can ask her again. She practically ran away when the bell rang. She didn't even show me the portrait she drew."

I thought for a moment. "I saw Dante's file when I was in the headmistress's office. It was on her desk. She didn't give me a detention, but she suspects that we're a couple."

Exasperated, Eleanor collapsed onto her bed. "Can you please prise your mind away from Dante for just a minute and focus on the problem at hand?"

Ignoring her, I continued. "Do you think everyone has a personal file?"

"I know they do," she said, staring at the ceiling. "My brother told me."

I looked behind me to make sure Lynch's feet weren't outside the door. "Even dead people?"

Eleanor gazed at me with wonder. "Ingenious! They wouldn't just throw them away."

Even though the validity of the séance was suspect, looking up Benjamin's and Cassandra's folders couldn't hurt. "I didn't see a filing cabinet, but it's got to be there. We just need to get into the office."

Checking the clock, I put on my jacket and grabbed my bag.

"Where are you going?"

"The library," I said, omitting the fact that I was meeting Dante there.

When I got to Copleston Library, Dante was waiting for me by the entrance, leaning against a stone pillar. A book bag was slung over his shoulder.

"Fancy meeting you here," I said. He smiled and took my bag, and together we went inside. He led me upstairs to the second floor, which was relatively empty, and set our bags down on a wooden table by the window. I told him about the headmistress and how she had asked me about him.

"The headmistress didn't mention you at all," he murmured, gazing at me pensively. "She asked me about how I was feeling and about how my classes were going, then let me go."

I thought fast. Should I tell him about the séance, about how Cassandra might actually be dead? What if I was wrong? Unlike Eleanor, I decided to go for the tactful route.

"Do you still talk to Cassandra?"

Dante paused and then bent over to open his bag. "Not much," he said, his back to me.

"But you've talked to her since she left?"

He straightened. "Why do you ask?"

"I thought you were friends with her."

"I was."

"So you still talk to her?"

He hesitated. "No, not really."

"Not really, or no?" I asked, growing frustrated.

"No," he finally conceded. "I told you, things sort of fell apart last spring. None of us keep in touch any more. Would it be a problem if I did? You seem disturbed by the idea."

"I'm not jealous," I said defensively. "If that's what you're implying."

"Right," he said.

There was a long silence. Was he being intentionally vague, or did he actually not know? Judging by the way he treated his ex-friends here, it didn't seem out of the ordinary for him to cut off Cassandra too.

"So what do we do now?" I asked, assuming his invitation to the library had some sort of mysterious ulterior motive.

Dante gave me a confused smile. "Study, of course. What else does a person do in a library?"

I blushed. "Oh, I...I don't know," I said, fumbling my words in embarrassment. I pulled a book out of my bag and opened it in front of me.

"It's upside down," Dante said with a smile, as he tilted back in his chair and tapped my book with his pencil.

"Right," I said, even more mortified as I flipped it around. And in the light of the oil lamps, we studied together until curfew.

What did it feel like to be dating Dante Berlin? Every time he looked at me, it was like he was seeing me for the first time. Every time I got close to him, he inhaled deeply, as if he were trying to absorb as much of me as possible... Everyone stared when we were together on campus, pointing when our hands grazed against each other's in class. "They're looking at us," I muttered to Dante as we walked through the library together, trying to block my face with my hair. "I don't blame them," he said, pushing the hair away from my face. I blushed. I was as much in awe of us as everyone else was. Every night Dante waited for me during study hall outside the dorm, and every night I met him. He always took me somewhere different – a walk around campus, the library, Horace Hall, the lake.

And every night I sat by the window, thinking he wouldn't come, but then there he was, his tall figure like a pale ray of light in the darkness. Every time I saw his face, it seemed even more beautiful and complex than the day before. Every time he touched me, I shuddered and felt all of my warmth, all of my sensation being pulled towards him. It no longer mattered that I didn't understand the way I felt around him, or the way he felt around me. One touch from him and everything inside of me blossomed with emotion: excitement, nervousness, anxiety, desire. I had never been in love before. Was this what it felt like?

But Dante wasn't the only thing on my mind. By the second week of November, almost all of the leaves from the maples and oaks around us had dropped off and were now floating on the surface of the lake like a carpet. Eleanor and I were still trying to find a way to get into the headmistress's office to get Benjamin's and Cassandra's files. The possibility of Cassandra being dead too only made me more suspicious about Benjamin's "heart attack", and those files were the only chance I had to figure out how he really died. The only problem was that the headmistress's office was impossible to break into, and if I got caught, I would most definitely be expelled. Usually when I didn't know how to solve a problem, I asked my parents, but they were dead. So instead I called Annie.

"Remember what I told you about Cassandra and Benjamin?"

"The two kids from last year?" she asked, her tone sceptical. "The one who died of a heart attack?"

"Yeah. Well, supposedly a heart attack."

Annie didn't respond.

"There's a possibility that Cassandra might be dead too."

There was a pause at the end of the line. Finally, Annie said, "How do you know?"

"Well, I don't know for sure, but we did this séance a couple of weeks ago, and I tried to contact my parents, and I ended up meeting Dante, but that's an entirely different story. The point is that Eleanor tried to contact Benjamin, but actually ended up contacting Cassandra."

I waited for her excited response, but it never came. "So...?"

"So that means if the séance was right, Cassandra might be dead too," I said, exasperated. "And that the school is purposely covering up her death by telling everyone that she transferred. I mean, why would they do that?"

"Maybe they're not doing it. Renée, it's a séance. I mean, everyone knows they don't work. It didn't even work for you."

"I guess, but I summoned someone that night. Or at least I heard someone. And so did Eleanor. It couldn't hurt to check, right?"

237

"Are you listening to yourself? *Summoning?* What happened to the sarcastic, sceptical Renée that I knew?"

I stared at the receiver in frustration.

"Is this about you missing your parents?"

"What? No. Well, yes. But it's not only about them. If Cassandra is dead, that probably means that there's more to Benjamin's death too. It couldn't be a coincidence that they died so close together."

"Just like your parents."

I gripped the receiver harder, trying to restrain myself. "It's not just about my parents. It's about people dying. It's about uncovering the truth."

"Renée, it's okay that you miss your parents and are confused about their deaths. I mean, it's hard—"

"No, it's not okay. Like I said, it's not *only* about my parents. Why does everything have to be about my parents?"

I could hear Annie's breathing on the other end of the line. "Because they died. And it's not fair, I know. I miss them too; we all—"

"No," I said, interrupting her. "You don't know." And I hung up the phone.

What do you call a secret society that's not a secret? In Rome they were called the Illuminati. In Greece they were called the Pythagoreans. And at Gottfried they were called the Board of Monitors.

According to the *Code of Discipline*, their official duty was to "represent the voice of the student body to the faculty". As Gottfried's version of a student government, they were supposed to "keep the order and preserve peace among the student body". But the most we'd ever seen of them had been at the Fall Awakening, when they were tapped. They didn't monitor the halls or discuss school decisions with us. In fact, they never seemed to do much of anything at all.

Yet I always saw them together, whispering as they passed each other in the dining hall, or walking in a group across campus at night because they were the only students allowed out after curfew. But if they weren't performing their appointed duties, then what were they doing? Everyone knew that they held private meetings, but no one knew where or what for. Charlotte told us that Genevieve would disappear for hours at a time without an explanation. "Terrible things might happen if I tell you," she said. We all assumed she was joking, but she never smiled when she said it.

Grub Day was the only real day that the Board of Monitors had a defined responsibility, which was to escort everyone down on our first trip of the year to Attica Falls. It was also the only day of the semester that we could wear clothes out of dress code, which would have been more exciting if I hadn't had to wear three layers to combat the sub-zero November temperature.

Dante had called me the night before. "Meet me at 46 Attica Passing at 5 p.m." He wouldn't say why. I wanted to ask why so late, but didn't, for fear of sounding too nosy. So I wrote down the address and went to sleep.

The next morning I woke up to frost on the windowpanes. It was early and Eleanor was still sleeping when I pulled my suitcase out from beneath my bed and unfolded my old pair of jeans. I hadn't looked at them in months, and when I put them on, their worn fabric flooded my mind with memories of California. But when Eleanor woke up, she pulled on nylons and a skirt, then piled her books into her backpack.

"What are you doing?"

"Going to the library," she said with a sigh.

"But it's Grub Day!"

"Oh," she said. "I totally forgot about that."

"How could you forget?"

"Other things on my mind, I guess." She pulled her hair into a ponytail, fluffing it in front of the mirror nervously, and shoved all of her books in her bag, trying not to make eye contact with me. Finally she looked up. There were circles under her eyes. "Look, I'm basically failing Maths and History. I've been going to see the professors for extra help, but I'm not getting better."

"Can't you take a break? Just for one day?"

She shook her head. "If I want to do anything after I leave this place, I have to get my grades up," she said, slinging her bag over her shoulder. "Eat a pancake at the diner for me," she said, trying to smile.

"Okay. I guess I'll see you at dinner. Or are you going to skip that too?" It was meant to be a joke, but it came out a little harsher than I intended.

She shot me a guilty look. "I'll try to make it."

Outside, the sky was grey and overcast. Everyone was lined up at the front gate. The Monitors were positioned around the periphery, herding us down the winding road that led to Attica Falls. I wedged myself in until I found Nathaniel. He was standing behind a few girls from my floor: Bonnie, Maggie, Rebecca, Greta, and the twins, April and Allison, who wore matching corduroy trousers, sweatshirts and pompom hats, a Gottfried scarf tucked under each of their coats.

"You were great in Horticulture the other day," Allison said to me as we walked. "I don't know how you manage to identify the different kinds of soils. They all look the same to me."

"Oh, it's easy," I said. "You just have to smell it. The soil with the most minerals smells kind of like metal."

"You guys are in Horticulture?" Bonnie asked. "I've

241

always wanted to take that class, but it's so hard to get into. I love flowers, though."

"Really? I didn't even have to apply," I said pensively. "We've only learned a little about flowers. So far it's been more about soil biology. A lot of stuff about root systems."

"What do you do if you don't learn about plants?" Rebecca asked.

"We learn how to plant things, not about the plants themselves." I tried to explain, but they didn't seem to understand. "The other day we did learn about the soil that produces medicinal plants," I offered.

Save for the twins, all of the girls gave me confused looks. I guess it did sound kind of silly when I put it that way, but they didn't know what it felt like to bury something where you knew only you could find it. They didn't know what it felt like to know exactly which location had the best soil for a certain flower, which minerals rendered weeds edible, which rock deposits gave moss antibiotic properties. I shrugged and kept walking.

Attica Falls was the only town within walking distance from Gottfried. It lay just beyond the campus and was comprised of one main street, Attica Passing, that branched off into side alleys lined with grungy stores, dilapidated houses, and barns. There was a general store, which sold groceries, hunting and camping equipment, and small

242

gifts like balsam fir, locally made maple syrup, and fruit preserves. Across the street was a gas station that only dispensed diesel, and was used primarily for purchasing cigarettes, lottery tickets and bags of ice. And then there was Beatrice's, a diner.

Once we got to Attica Passing, everyone dispersed, and Nathaniel and I loitered around the street, deciding where to go first. That's when I spotted Eleanor's brother, Brandon, walking into Beatrice's. Without thinking, I pulled Nathaniel into the restaurant.

Beatrice's was a dingy old diner that served pancakes all day. They also served other things – eggs, corned-beef hash, meat loaf and a variety of dishes made with canned tuna fish. Our waitress was in her early forties. She had bottle-dyed red hair sculpted around the top of her head in a way that defied all laws of physics and probably required half a bottle of hair spray. A plastic name tag that read *Cindy* was pinned to her left breast pocket.

She looked us up and down and then walked us to a table at the other end of the restaurant.

"Actually," I said, "can we sit over there?" I pointed to the booth on the other side of the wood panelling from Brandon Bell, who was sitting with the rest of the Board of Monitors.

"Fine," the waitress said with a sigh. She tossed our menus on the table and read out the daily specials in a monotone that was too fast for us to understand, then disappeared behind the double doors of the kitchen.

"What are you doing?!" hissed Nathaniel. "Stalking the Board of Monitors?"

"If Cassandra is dead—"

"Which she might not be," Nathaniel added.

"—and if the school knows, and is covering it up by saying she transferred, then the Board of Monitors might know."

"And you think they're going to talk about it out of nowhere, right here at Beatrice's?"

"Well, we're not going to hear anything by sitting on the other side of the room."

The booth was sticky with syrup and grease, its upholstery cracked down the middle, revealing a spongy yellow interior. I took off my jacket and mittens, and sat down. A wood panel was the only thing that stood between our table and the Monitors'.

Their voices were muffled through the wood. I leaned over and pressed my ear against it. Nathaniel did the same, but to no avail.

"I can't hear anything," he mumbled. "What are they saying?"

I put a finger to my lips. Nathaniel gulped down his water, held the empty glass against the panel, and listened through it. "I don't know," he said. "I can't make it out."

"Oh, give it to me," I said, grabbing the glass from him.

A junior named Max Platkin was talking. "I would kill," he said, "to get out of that class. It's so boring. The prof is practically dead anyway. She can barely sit up straight."

The table laughed. I gave Nathaniel a shocked look, until I processed the rest of his sentence, and then rolled my eyes.

"Well, next year you'll be a senior and you can finally opt out of Latin," Ingrid said. I imagined her tossing her silky black hair over one shoulder.

"Yeah, plus, the headmistress wouldn't like that," Schuyler joked. "Killing professors isn't exactly on the menu." But just as Schuyler finished his sentence, our waitress approached and pulled a skinny green pad out of her apron. We sat up straight and looked at our menus.

"What do you want?" she said, chewing a piece of gum and not seeming to notice or care that we were eavesdropping on the booth next to us.

I scanned the menu, eager for her to leave. "I'll have an omelette with sausage and cheese. And an orange juice."

She scribbled down my order and looked at Nathaniel.

"Just water. And granola."

"No granola," she said. "Just pancakes, eggs, hash, or tuna." She waited with her hand on her hip while Nathaniel flipped through the menu.

245

"White toast?"

Cindy nodded. After she left, we resumed our positions by the wood panelling.

"She keeps talking about Renée Winters," Genevieve said, with a hint of disgust. "Asking me to keep an eye on her and her boyfriend."

I almost gasped when I heard my name. Nathaniel gave me a questioning look, but I ignored it. "Who is she?" asked Schuyler.

"She's a sophomore," Genevieve continued. "Apparently she's the best in her Horticulture class."

"She's my sister's room-mate," Brandon added.

"I spent some time with her in October. She seems nice, but forgettable," Genevieve said. I glared at her through the wall. "Other than that she's *close* with Dante Berlin. The headmistress is highly interested in them."

Brandon interjected. "Well, obviously. He was friends with Vivian, Gideon and Yago. He was probably in love with Cassandra too, just like Benjamin."

"*Was* friends with," Schuyler emphasized.

"It doesn't matter," said Brandon, cutting him off. "My point is that we don't know what he's capable of. Just like Cassie. Just like the rest of them. If Renée were smart, she'd stay away from him."

Genevieve laughed. "That's the problem. When it comes to Dante, no one can think straight. Don't worry, though. If the headmistress is right about her skills, I'm sure Renée can take care of herself."

The waitress came with our food. She slid our plates across the table and left us with a handful of mini-jams and a bottle of ketchup, but I wasn't hungry any more. Why was the headmistress asking about me and Dante, and what did Genevieve mean by my "skills"? She must have meant in Horticulture, because it was the only class that everyone seemed to compliment me on.

Brandon stood up. The rest of them followed. As he walked by our booth to the door, he gave me a sidewards glance. I quickly stuffed a piece of omelette into my mouth.

"What just happened?" Nathaniel asked, tucking his napkin into the top of his shirt like a bib, and I remembered that he hadn't heard any of it. When I was sure no one was listening, I recounted everything.

"What did they mean about Cassandra and the rest of them?" I asked. "And why should I stay away from Dante? What is he capable of?"

Nathaniel looked troubled, though admittedly he almost always looked troubled. "I don't know," he said. "And neither do they. That's the point."

I rolled my eyes. "You're a genius. Have I ever told you that?"

"No, really," he said. "If they don't know what Dante is

capable of, it means he hasn't done anything yet. And neither have the rest of them. It's Cassandra that's the problem, because clearly she did *something*."

"But what?"

He shrugged. We finished eating, and the waitress came back with our bill. I watched her impatiently as she counted out the change. "Thanks," I said when she was done, and grabbed Nathaniel by the arm. "Come on. We've got to find them."

But when we got outside, the Board of Monitors had disappeared. "Why is the headmistress interested in *me*?" I said. "And Dante?"

Nathaniel said nothing. "Maybe," I said while we walked, "the headmistress also thinks something weird happened to Benjamin and Cassandra. She probably thinks Dante knows something since he used to be friends with them and was the one who found Ben. And she's interested in *me* because she thinks we're dating." I had to be more careful, I told myself.

"Are you dating him? Like, it's official?" Nathaniel asked, staring at me, his blue eyes magnified through his thick glasses.

"I...well, we haven't really talked about it. But I think so. I mean, we spend a lot of time together."

"Why isn't he here today? Doesn't he live here?" Nathaniel asked earnestly.

I didn't know why we weren't meeting until five. "Oh, he has studying to do," I said quickly.

We walked down the street, towards a small row of stores, when I bumped directly into Brandon Bell.

"Renée," he said.

I looked up at him, his sandy hair a short, military version of Eleanor's. "Oh, hi."

"Have you seen my sister?" he asked. Eleanor had introduced us a few times, but the encounters had been brief and unpleasant. Brandon had a way of making every conversation sound like an interrogation.

"I...uh...no, she went to the library instead."

He gave me a suspicious look. "Is everything okay?"

"Yeah...sorry, I'm just...well, I have to...*we* have to go," I said. "See you later!" Grabbing Nathaniel by the shirt, I pulled him into the alley. A rickety wooden sign with chipped blue paint bore the name *LAZARUS BOOKS*. I pushed open the door, and we both stumbled inside.

"Well, that went well," Nathaniel said. "Not conspicuous at all."

The bell over the door chimed as it slammed shut, and an old man emerged from a room behind the counter. He had a round face with a ruddy nose and a salt-and-pepper beard. He propped his elbows up on the counter. "School books are in the back."

"That's Conrad Porley," Nathaniel told me as we walked

249

to the back of the store. "People say that he won't sell a book to you if you rub him the wrong way. And I don't know about your theory that the headmistress and Board of Monitors are hiding something about Cassandra or Benjamin," Nathaniel added. "Why would the school cover up a death? They didn't cover up Ben's death."

"But what about what Minnie Roberts said?"

Nathaniel stopped walking. "She said that the headmistress and the Board of Monitors killed Cassandra. Come on, even you have to admit it's a crazy idea."

"Do you have a better one?"

"Benjamin died of a heart attack, Cassandra transferred, and Minnie Roberts is crazy."

"What fifteen-year-old dies of a heart attack in the woods? And what about what Eleanor saw in the séance?"

Nathaniel shook his head. "I thought we already went over this."

I sighed. I guessed he had a point. "But that still doesn't explain why the headmistress is so interested in me and Dante."

"Well, you did get into some trouble, didn't you?"

"Just once," I said, thinking of getting caught with Dante after the séance. And then I remembered the dress-code incident on the first day of class. "Okay, twice. Maybe you're right," I conceded, and turned to check out the store.

Unlike normal bookstores, each section was categorized not only by genre, but by subject matter. One shelf read *Puberty.* The one across from it read *Pet Saves Owner and Dies,* and beside that were sections titled: *Superhero Origin Stories, Babies, Death in the Family* and *Girlfriend in the Refrigerator.*

I scanned the walls and walked towards Nathaniel. He was a few rows away, looking at a book in the section on *Vampires and Zombies.* But before I got to him, a section title caught my eye. *Boarding School.* I crouched down to read the titles. There were a lot of novels and a few non-fiction books on prestigious prep schools, but there wasn't anything on Gottfried Academy.

I approached Nathaniel, who was flipping through a teenage romance about vampires. I wasn't really interested in zombies or vampires, but with nothing else to do, I knelt beside him and looked at the titles, pulling one out every so often. Most of them were horror stories with fangs and gravestones and bandaged, faceless monsters on the cover. I was growing bored, my eyes going in and out of focus, when I spotted a book that stood out from the rest. It had a plain ivory binding, with letters so faded they were barely legible.

I pulled it out and cradled it in my lap. It was thick and dusty. The cover read: *Attica Falls.* I opened it, my excitement mounting as I flipped through the pages. It had a full chapter on Gottfried Academy, which was more information than I had ever seen on the school, and it had pictures. It must have been shelved in the wrong section accidentally. Satisfied, I tucked it under my arm and brought it to the register.

Mr. Porley coughed into his arm. "Interesting choice," he said in a gruff smoker's voice.

"I'm new to the East Coast."

"Up at the Academy, I'm guessing?" he asked, taking me in. He had large hairy hands and wore braces, as if he had been either a fisherman or lumberjack in some former life.

I nodded.

He opened the book cover and charged me ten dollars, half of the price asked. "Seems you have some luck about you. This one's out of print," he said, before putting it in a paper bag.

I thanked him and left with Nathaniel at my heels.

With nothing better to do, we walked to the end of the street until we reached an abandoned house. It was white and crooked, with a wrap-around porch and pillars that looked half eaten by termites. I tested the steps with my foot to make sure they wouldn't collapse before Nathaniel and I sat down. A few groups of students ambled past us, chatting and sipping cups of something hot and steaming. Down the street, Professor Bliss was smoking a cigarette outside the general store. I opened the book and flipped through it, skipping over the chapters on the history of Maine, the founding of Attica Falls, and the natural wonders of the White Mountains, until I found what I was looking for. Chapter 7: Gottfried Academy.

I began to read while Nathaniel looked over my shoulder. Some of it I already knew – the Academy's role in the Revolutionary War, its transformation from a religious to a secular school...but just when I was beginning to accept that there was nothing more to Gottfried than a superficial history, one page caught my eye. On the bottom right was a photograph, a normal black-and-white image of Gottfried Academy, and one that I normally wouldn't have glanced at twice if it hadn't been for the familiar face staring back at me.

"That's...that's my grandfather," I said in awe.

Nathaniel pushed his glasses closer to his face and squinted. "Which one?"

I pointed to a tall broad-faced man in a suit and waistcoat. His hair was darker then, his glasses thinner. He was standing in front of the Gottfried gates with a school scarf draped around his neck, smiling and looking almost nothing like the dry curmudgeon I'd encountered last summer. The caption read: *Headmaster Brownell Winters, 1974.* Below it was a newspaper article, reprinted in the book from *The Portland Herald.*

The Gottfried Curse
July 7, 1989
By Jacqueline Brookmeyer

After nearly two hundred calamity-free years, a fire ravaged the forest surrounding Gottfried Academy, the preparatory school located near Attica Falls. The school is known not only for its stringent classical academics, but for its proclivity for disaster. Since its founding in 1735, Gottfried Academy has been plagued by a horrific and inexplicable chain of tragedies, including disease, natural catastrophe, and a string of accidents of the most perverse and bizarre nature. These recurring events have brought attention to Gottfried Academy, attracting a series of enigmatologists who have attempted to understand the causes and patterns behind the disasters. All of them died under suspicious circumstances, until 1789, when the disasters stopped. But has this phenomenon, coined locally as "the Gottfried Curse", truly been buried?

It began in 1736 with an outbreak of the measles and mumps. The school was originally founded as a children's hospital by Doctor Bertrand Gottfried, who attempted to ward off the epidemic. Despite his efforts, more than one hundred children perished. Rumour has it that the doctor built catacombs beneath the hospital grounds to bury the children and contain the infection. Three years later, Bertrand Gottfried mysteriously died. His body was found in the lake by a groundskeeper, his death apparently caused by heart failure.

I paused and stared at the words. *Heart failure.* "It can't be," I murmured.

"What?" Nathaniel asked over my shoulder.

"Bertrand Gottfried died of a heart attack. Just like my parents."

"He was old," Nathaniel said. "It's not the most bizarre way to die."

"It is if they find you in a lake."

"Maybe he was swimming when he had the heart attack," Nathaniel offered.

"Or maybe it wasn't a heart attack."

"Turn the page."

Though none of the catacombs were ever discovered, they are purported to have been the beginnings of the subterranean tunnels that still run beneath the premises. All previous headmasters, including the newly incumbent Headmistress Calysta Von Laark, have refused to comment on this matter.

After the death of Bertrand Gottfried, the hospital

stopped accepting new patients and closed its doors to the outside world. For a decade, no one came in or out, save for a weekly groundskeeper, who delivered groceries and supplies from the local general store. Yet, just as suddenly as the hospital closed, it reopened. This time, as a school. The head nurse at the time, Ophelia Hart, ascended as the first headmistress. She named it "Gottfried Academy", after its founder.

Over time, the infirmary's tragic history was forgotten, and students began to filter in. The disasters continued like clockwork. The unexpected collapse of the building that is now the theatre, in 1751; the nor'easter of 1754; the tuberculosis epidemic of 1759; and the food-poisoning incident in 1767. Ten years later, the school was partially destroyed during the Revolutionary War, which was followed by a series of disasters culminating in the chemistry lab accident of 1789.

But what was the origin of the curse, and is it really over? Some believe that it's the area itself. Others believe it was Bertrand Gottfried. "Everything started to happen after he died," local Esther Bancroft said. "He wasn't a doctor, he was a sinner. Lord knows what he did to those children. And then they killed him, and his soul is trying to tell people to stay away. Stay away." But others blame the curse on Gottfried's first headmistress.

"It was that woman," local Hazel Bamberger, 84, claims. "That nurse that started the whole goddamn school. Ophelia. She was with that Doctor Bertrand, not like normal doctors and nurses are, but closer. After he died, she became the first headmistress, and that's when everything started. That's why it's always couples that die. She's seeking her revenge on people in love."

Although some might not believe Bamberger's theory, there is one more disturbing coincidence that even the townspeople aren't aware of, and that is the manner in which many of the people died. According to confidential police files, which were leaked by an ex-Gottfried professor who wishes to remain anonymous, more than half of the deaths at Gottfried were deemed heart attacks.

I put the book down and turned to Nathaniel. "This is it," I said, gripping the page because I didn't know what else to do with it. "This is the proof that connects my parents to Gottfried. To Benjamin. To everything."

Nathaniel said nothing, allowing me my moment.

"But why?" I said almost to myself. I had to tell Eleanor. And Dante.

"I don't know," Nathaniel said.

"What time is it?"

"Four thirty."

Half an hour till I met Dante. It seemed like ages from now. I turned the page.

So how was it that so many students died of heart attacks at such a young age? And was the school covering up the deaths with claims of disease, war and natural disaster? To this, many people have answers – conspiracy theories, stories bordering on the supernatural – yet even the most fervent believers are unable to explain why the curse unexpectedly stopped.

The Second Autumn Fire, which occurred this May, was the first unexplained tragedy since 1789. Even Headmaster Brownell Winters, who has held the post for nearly seventeen years, was left speechless, as he refused to comment on the fire's origins or circumstances. It consumed the entirety of the north forest, now known as the "Dead Forest", turning the treetops completely orange – hence the name, the Second Autumn Fire. It then spread across the wall, ravaging the Gottfried Library. "A real tragedy," local bookstore owner, Conrad Porley, said. "All those books gone for ever." The books destroyed included the few written about Gottfried and its history.

To the surprise of the members of the Gottfried community, Headmaster Brownell Winters has not participated in the investigation, nor has he attempted to rebuild the library. In early June, just weeks after the fire, he stepped down from his position as headmaster and left the school. When asked about the Gottfried Curse, his only response was, "There are no such things as curses; only people and their decisions." As for what he meant, that, along with the cause of the fire, remains a mystery.

I turned the page to read more, but there were only illustrations and photographs. The first was a drawing of men plunging children into the lake, the same lake that was still in the centre of campus. The caption read: *Doctors cleanse infected students, 1736 outbreak of measles and mumps.*

Below it was a photograph of my grandfather. He was standing in front of Archebald Hall, a forced smile on his face. Two women were standing on either side of him, their hands clasped behind their backs in stiff poses. They were younger than my grandfather. The first woman I didn't recognize, but the second I did. She was tall, with a narrow face, sharp eyebrows and greying hair. She was wearing a housedress. The caption read, *From left to right: Professor Cordelia Milk, Headmaster Brownell Winters, Professor Calysta Von Laark, 1988.*

The picture had been taken one year before the fire. I stared at my grandfather's face, trying to comprehend the idea that he had once been the headmaster of Gottfried.

I stared at the pages, the words blurring into grey. What had been the cause of the heart attacks at Gottfried Academy, and what did it all have to do with my parents, who had been five thousand kilometres away when they died? I flipped through the rest of the chapter, looking for more information, but there was nothing else of any interest. I stared at the book, frustrated that it didn't have more answers. The rest of the chapters were about Attica Falls – the weather, the town's setting, the demographics of the inhabitants. No wonder the book was out of print.

"Do you think there really is a Gottfried Curse that's causing the heart attacks?" I asked Nathaniel. If there was, why would my grandfather send me here?

Nathaniel shook his head. "It's probably just a story made up to sell newspapers. And even if it's true, nothing's happened in twenty years. Everyone knows Gottfried is the safest school ever. I mean, we're surrounded by a four-metre wall, and we have more rules than the military. It's like your grandfather said: curses aren't real. Science is real. People are real. Statistics are real."

"What about the heart attacks? You can't tell me you still believe it's a coincidence. My parents, Benjamin, and now this…"

Nathaniel gave me an apologetic shrug. "I don't know."

Students were gathering at the end of the street, getting ready for the walk back. "Better go," Nathaniel said as he stood up and brushed off his trousers. I didn't move. Instead, I stared into the book, at my grandfather's photograph.

"Are you coming?"

I hesitated, not wanting to tell Nathaniel that I was meeting Dante. I didn't want to draw any more attention to us. "I just…need a minute. To think."

"I'll wait."

"No, go ahead. I'll catch up."

"There's no curse, Renée," Nathaniel said as he picked up his things. "It's just – life."

The sun began to set, splitting on the horizon like a yolk. Tucking the book under my arm, I walked down the street until I reached number 46. It was a dilapidated building that looked like a hotel from the 1800s. Dante was waiting for me, leaning against a porch pillar.

"You look worried," he said, taking my bag.

"Take this instead," I said, handing him the book as I sat down. "Turn to chapter seven."

When he finished reading the article he was silent for a long time.

"Did you know about this?" I demanded.

"About the Gottfried Curse? No."

I searched his face. "You know something," I said, my hair blowing around my face, tangling with my scarf. "You knew that there was something off about Benjamin's death and you wouldn't admit it. Here's proof. My parents and Benjamin and all those other people who died of heart attacks at Gottfried. It's all the same."

Dante took my hand. "Come with me."

The inside of 46 Attica Passing was dimly lit by wall sconces and had patchy red carpeting on a staircase that zigzagged up the building.

"What is this place?" I asked, running my hand up the banister.

"A boarding house."

I glanced up at the numbers on the doors, and then at Dante.

The stairs creaked under his feet. "I live here."

We walked up three flights of stairs and then turned down a hallway. It was narrow, with floorboards that were warped and uneven. Dim lamps hung from the ceiling, filling the hall with hazy yellow light. His room was towards the end. There were doors on either side of his, but it looked like no one had lived there for decades.

He fished around in his pocket for a key.

His room was freezing. Both of his windows were wide open, letting in the thin November air. He turned on a small desk lamp.

"When I found Benjamin Gallow, he had already been dead for days," Dante said. "His face looked older, like he had aged ten years. His tie was balled up and shoved in his mouth. That's all I know."

"His tie was in his mouth?" Just like my parents and the gauze. Sort of.

Dante nodded.

"Like a gag?"

Dante said nothing.

"Who do you think did it?"

"I don't know. He might have done it to himself. People do odd things when they're afraid."

"What do you think scared him?"

"Death," he said quietly. "Isn't that what scares everyone?"

I glanced around his room. It would have been cosy if it hadn't been so cold. It was clean but cluttered, with stacks of novels and stationery and encyclopedias colouring the walls. Piles of piano music sat on a side table by the window: Schubert, Rachmaninoff, Chopin, Satie and dozens of others I had never heard of.

Beneath the window was a modest bed, with one pillow

but no sheets or blankets. Across from it was a wooden desk, upon which lay an open book with a pencil lying in its crease. Next to it was a box of salt, three cinnamon sticks, and a handful of shells and rocks. Dante didn't protest when I picked them up, turning them over in my palm. "Were there coins around his body?" I asked as I wandered through his room.

"No," he said, watching me examine his belongings. He seemed surprised at my interest in such small, mundane objects. Of course they were only interesting to me because they were his.

A small collection of cologne and deodorants were gathered on his dresser. And at the end of the room was a bookcase. I tilted my head to read their titles. *Rituals, Spells, and the Occult*; *Arabic Number Theory*; *The Metaphysical Meditations*; *The Republic*. Some were in English, but most were in Latin.

"When I found my parents, they were surrounded by coins," I said softly, tracing my fingers across the worn spines. "And there was gauze in their mouths. The police said it was a hiking accident. That they died naturally. But I just don't see how that could be."

"Renée," Dante said softly. He was standing behind me, his voice filled with yearning. He took a step towards me until he was so close I could feel his knees graze the back of my legs. "I believe you. And if I knew how to help you,

I would. That's why I brought you here. So you would know me. Trust me."

"Why?" I said, blinking back memories of my parents dead in the woods. "Why me?"

"When I'm around you, I feel things..." His hair tickled my collarbone. "Things that I haven't felt in so long."

Every muscle in my body tightened.

"Like what?" I whispered.

He ran his fingers through my hair. "Warmth," he said. I could hear him breathing.

My voiced trembled. "What else?"

He reached his arms around me and slipped my coat off. It dropped to the floor, and he laughed when he realized that I had worn two cardigans beneath it. Slowly, he unbuttoned them. He inched closer and leaned in. "Smells," he uttered into my ear and buried his face in my hair. A draught blew through the open window, and I shivered. I felt his hand on my shoulder as he brushed the hair away from my neck.

"Tastes," he said, and kissed my neck so gently that I could barely feel it.

A prickling sensation budded underneath my skin and began to travel down my body. I leaned into him, and he let his hand slide down my arm. His fingers were cold, and my skin quivered under his touch, cooling and then warming, as if an ice cube were being rubbed across my body. He slipped his palm into mine, entwining our fingers together. I turned to him. "What else?"

He gazed at me with a yearning look that almost seemed sad. "Pain."

Raising my hand to his face, I touched his lips. As he kissed each of my fingers, I closed my eyes, feeling his hand on the small of my back.

"Desire." He tightened his grip around me and kissed my collarbone. I ran my hands through his hair, pulling him closer, and raised my lips to his. But he turned his head and pulled away before we kissed. Surprised, I shrank back from him.

Then he pressed his body against mine, pushing me against the bookcase. It banged against the wall. The books on the top shelf clattered to the floor. His hands roamed across my body, tangling my tank top.

My body felt soft and watery, like my insides were melting. "Dante." I hardly noticed his name escape my mouth. "Dante."

The entire room blurred around us until the only thing I could see was Dante. Suddenly I felt weak. I couldn't see, I couldn't feel, I couldn't smell. Everything tangible seemed to be slipping away from me.

"Stop," I said softly. "Please stop."

He let go of me, and I folded onto the ground. "What's

wrong?" he asked, kneeling beside me. Fallen books surrounded us, their pages open and fluttering in the draught.

I searched for the words but I couldn't find them. How could I possibly explain the dozens of contradicting ways he made me feel? "It's too much," I whispered. "My legs... I can't hold myself up."

Dante went rigid as he stared at me with alarm, but his face softened when he realized he was frightening me.

"I...I don't know what's happening to me," I said, my voice cracking. "What's happening to me?"

He pressed his forehead to mine. "Please, don't leave yet. Just lie with me for a little while."

He led me to his bed, pulling a coat over me, and I curled up beside him.

"You make me feel alive," he breathed.

And we lay there together until the sun rose, Dante resting his head on my chest, listening to my heart beat.

Chapter 9

The Flood

I woke up the next morning to a different world. Outside, everything was dusted in white. It was the first snowfall of the season; the unexpected kind of snow that drapes itself over the ground like a blanket, covering street signs and burying cars. I blinked. Last night couldn't have been real. But it must have been, because there was Dante, lying beside me. His eyes were closed. Asleep, he looked statuesque, as though his features had been carved out of stone. I held out my hand, my fingers quivering as they grazed his cheek. Suddenly, his eyes opened. I gasped and pulled back my hand.

He smiled. "Did you sleep?"

I nodded and stretched my legs like a cat. "Did you?"

He propped himself up on an elbow and played with a lock of my hair. "I never sleep."

I rolled my eyes. "You must've slept at least a little."

He traced his finger around my elbow. "Let's get you back to campus before they realize you're gone."

Instead of going through the main gate, Dante walked me to a street on the edge of town. Because he was a day student, he was allowed to go on and off campus as he pleased. I, on the other hand, had to be more careful.

"How do I get back?"

"There are two ways. You can try to sneak past the guards at the gate, but they practically sleep with their eyes open, and there's a good chance you'll get caught."

"What's the other option?"

Dante hesitated. "It isn't pleasant."

I looked up at him expectantly. "That's okay."

Dante didn't look particularly excited about it, but he nodded and took my hand.

We stopped in front of a run-down house with a dirt driveway lined with overgrown shrubs, now covered in snow. We kept to the edge of the yard, crouching low behind the bushes. Behind the house, the yard expanded into a white field surrounded by a circle of naked trees.

"Where are we going?"

But just as the words left my mouth, we stopped. In front of us, shrouded by a crab apple tree, was a stone well. Its narrow mouth was covered by a wooden board. Dante wiped off the snow and tossed the board on the ground.

"Remember those tunnels from the article?" he asked.

I nodded, my cheeks growing red from the cold.

"This is one of them. It leads to campus, beneath the pulpit of the chapel. I found it by accident when I was wandering around out here last summer. Supposedly there are dozens of others, but this is the only one I know of."

I peered into the well. The hole was dark and narrow, just large enough for a body to fit through. A warm draught emanated from somewhere inside its recesses. I couldn't see to the bottom. "Is there still water in it?"

"It was never a well," he said, wiping his hands together. "It doesn't even run deep. You just have to climb a couple of metres down and then it curves and opens into a tunnel."

It looked like it could crumble at any minute, and the fact that it had been built in the 1700s merely affirmed my doubts. I kicked the ground with my shoe until I found a pebble beneath the snow. Picking it up, I threw it into the well. It didn't make any sound.

Frowning, Dante gazed at me, deep in thought. "You'd better climb in or you'll be late for class."

I looked up at him with surprise. "You're not coming?"

Dante shook his head. "I don't go underground."

I gave him a strange look. "What do you mean?"

"It's a childhood thing. Bad experience."

I hesitated, wanting specifics, but then nodded. After all, it was just a tunnel, right?

Dante rummaged around in his bag. "Take this." He handed me a candle and a box of matches. "You might need it. When you're down there, just walk straight. Don't take any turns."

I pushed a lock of hair behind my ear. "I'll see you in class, then?"

"Yeah. But in case we don't get a chance to talk, meet me in front of the chapel tonight? Eleven o'clock?"

"Why wouldn't we have a chance to talk?" I asked, trying to hide my bewilderment.

"Just meet me in front of the chapel. I have something to tell you."

I nodded, and Dante helped me into the well.

A makeshift ladder was made out of bits of stone sticking out of the well's interior. "Bye," I said, and began climbing down. With a worried look, he watched until I disappeared into the darkness.

The well was murky and constricting. I couldn't see anything, and I barely had enough space to bend my knees. I climbed slowly, unsure of what would meet me at the bottom. A few rungs down, my foot hit dirt. I struck a match.

In front of me was a cavernous tunnel, big enough to stand in. The walls were made of caked dirt, which crumbled off under my fingers like chalk. It smelled faintly of mulch. Feeling around in the darkness, I struck another match and lit the candle. Every so often I felt a cool breeze coming from the opposite wall, where the tunnel forked off to the left. I pressed myself closer to the wall, trying not to think about what would happen if I got lost. Finally, it sloped upwards, and I came to a dead end. Blowing out the candle, I pulled myself into the damp air of the chapel.

I emerged below the pulpit, through a corrugated grate. The chapel groaned and wheezed as the winter wind blew around its steeples, and I could hear bats chirping from the stairwell. Light filtered through the stained-glass windows, casting red shadows across the floor. Not wanting to linger any longer than necessary, I snuck through the pews, my footsteps echoing off the vaulted ceilings as I unlocked the deadbolts and stepped out into the November morning.

In the snow, the Gottfried campus was transformed into a sprawling, pristine landscape. Each tree, each cobblestone, each blade of grass was frosted in a delicate layer of white. A group of boys passed me on the way to the dining hall, and I checked my watch. It was almost 8 a.m., and I still had to shower and get through all of my classes before I could see Dante again. Buttoning my coat,

I ran across campus, replaying the events of last night over and over in my head.

When I got to the dorm, I opened the door only to step into a big puddle of water. Startled, I jumped back to discover that the entire ground-floor foyer was flooded. I ran upstairs, where I found girls crowding the hallways. Everyone looked sleepy and irritated, the freshmen complaining about the wet carpets in their rooms. I wandered through the crowd, looking for Eleanor, pushing past throngs of girls wearing robes and slippers, nightgowns, flip-flops and oversized T-shirts. Finally I spotted Rebecca. She was standing in the corner with Charlotte, Greta, Maggie and Bonnie.

"What's going on?"

"There's no running water," Rebecca said.

"What happened? The entire ground floor is flooded!"

"We don't know," said Maggie. "Lynch is on her way up now to tell us, I think."

"Have you seen Eleanor?"

Maggie shook her head. She hadn't put her contacts in yet, and seemed self-conscious in her glasses. "We figured she was with you."

"Oh," I said nonchalantly, not wanting to let on that I wasn't in my room last night. "Maybe she's still in the room."

"Or maybe she's with Genevieve," Charlotte said. Her

hair was pinned around her head in rollers. She was clutching a loofah and shower caddy with dozens of shampoo and cosmetic bottles inside. "She wasn't in our room this morning when I woke up."

"She probably had an early Board of Monitors meeting," said Maggie, almost bitterly. "She's never around any more."

Charlotte shrugged and started talking about her plans for winter break, when the door to the hallway swung open. Mrs. Lynch bounded down the hall, her heels clicking on the wood floors.

"Girls," she shouted.

Everyone quieted down.

"It seems there's been a plumbing malfunction in the bathroom. It's likely that one of the pipes froze overnight and burst. Maintenance should be here within the hour to fix it and drain the water from the ground floor. In the meantime, Professor Bliss has generously offered us the bathroom in the boys' dormitory. He's in the process of evacuating them as we speak." Professor Bliss was their dorm parent.

A murmur ran through hall.

"So get dressed and gather your toiletries. We're heading over in fifteen minutes."

Stepping into the boys' dorm was like walking into a parallel universe. The layout of the building was exactly the same, but the walls were painted a deep shade of maroon, and the sunlight seemed to dodge the windows, creating a shadowy atmosphere that would have been more fitting in a cigar shop. Everything smelled faintly of leather. A pair of dirty gym shorts dangled over the banister.

The boys' bathroom was in the western wing of the first floor, just like our dorm. The door to the showers was propped open, and steam billowed into the hallway. Eleanor hadn't been in our room when I'd gone back to get my towel and soap. Her bed was completely undisturbed, the pillows puffed and the covers folded and tucked. So where was she? I walked through the rows of showers, listening for her, but all of the voices belonged to other people: first years, second years, third years, but no Eleanor.

After I showered and got changed, I dawdled outside the bathroom door, waiting to see if she'd come out, but after the last girl left, I gave up and went downstairs, out into the white, wintery morning.

When I got back to the girls' dorm, Mrs. Lynch was standing on the stoop with four maintenance workers. They all towered over her, and were dressed in overalls that were soaked from the waist down.

I slowed as I passed them.

"Something went really wrong with the pipes down there," one of the men said in a gruff voice, wiping the sweat off his temples. Grey stubble climbed up his neck, and a grease-stained rag hung out of his pocket. "It's impossible to tell where the leak is coming from. We'll have to shut off the water in the building and drain it. In the meantime, you'll have to make do with space heaters and the fireplaces. We'll work on getting enough wood."

I lingered on the top step to wait for Lynch's reply, but she must have noticed I was listening, because she glanced up at me and glared. Not wanting to get into any more trouble, I hurried through the doors and went back to my room, unable to shake the three words that kept running through my mind: The Gottfried Curse.

I didn't tell anyone else about the curse or my night with Dante. I would have told Eleanor, but she never showed up for Latin. Or Philosophy. In fact, she didn't go to any classes at all. I sat taking notes while Miss LaBarge scribbled something about Descartes on the board. Every so often I forgot that Eleanor wasn't there, and leaned over to whisper to her, only to be met with an empty chair. But I didn't think much of it. Finals were coming up in a few weeks, and Eleanor's grades were terrible. She'd been skipping meals all semester to go to the library.

Without her, classes dragged by, and I grew frustrated with her for being gone when I had so many important things to talk to her about. Eleanor would surely have a theory about the heart attacks. "Radiation below the school grounds," she might say. "Or a mass murderer equipped with a new kind of weapon that induces heart failure." And the cloth in both my parents' mouths and Benjamin's were used as gags. Maybe they were electrocuted. Maybe someone was out to get Gottfried students. But why them in particular? Nathaniel was right: there was no such thing as curses. Only people and science. So that's what I focused on, watching the clock, counting down the minutes until the last period, when I would see Dante in Crude Sciences. Last night seemed like a dream, except I could remember every detail – the way my stomach fluttered when he kissed my neck; the way the books fell at our feet, making us stumble around them; the way our bodies left a crescent-shaped crease on his bed. I unwrapped each memory like a gift, letting Dante's velvety voice envelop me while I drifted off in class or waited in line in the dining hall. It didn't matter that Professor Lumbar was in a particularly bad mood or that Professor Chortle made us solve proofs for an hour and a half.

When fifth period rolled around, I walked to class anxiously, inspecting my reflection in the windows before opening the door to the Observatory.

Professor Starking bustled in behind me just as the bell rang, carrying a box of films and a messy pile of papers.

Dante was already sitting at our bench, his tie crisp around his neck and his blazer slung around the back of his chair. I approached slowly, watching him from a distance. A lock of hair dangled in front of his face as he wrote something in his notebook.

I walked up the side of the aisle until I was just behind him, and looked over his shoulder. He was writing notes in Latin. Suddenly I felt nervous, as if everything I'd ever wanted in my life was on the verge of happening and I only had to reach out and take it. But just as I lifted my hand, Dante grabbed it without looking away from his notes. I gasped. He turned to me, and with the beginnings of a smile, he brought my palm to his lips and almost imperceptibly kissed it.

We barely spoke during class. The sky was overcast, and Professor Starking switched off the lights and turned on a projector. Suddenly an image appeared on the wall. It was a photograph of outer space, of a rust-coloured cloud of dust cresting upwards like fingers.

"The Pillars of Creation," Professor Starking said. "This is what stars look like before they're formed. They're called celestial nebulas."

He flipped to the next slide, and then the next – each of different nebulas, their otherworldly forms projecting onto the darkened wall of the Observatory.

"What did you want to tell me?" I whispered to Dante.

"I can't tell you here," he replied, studying the images. "It's too important." In the blue light of the projector, his face emerged out of the darkness like a ghost. I tried to imagine what it was he wanted to say to me. He'd profess his undying love. *Renée,* he would say, *I love you. Run away with me. We'll go north into the wilderness and live desperately, dangerously.* And I would say yes. Or maybe that's not what he had planned at all. If it was, why couldn't he just say it here, in the darkness of the Observatory? Things said in private were usually bad things: things that were too shameful, too embarrassing to declare in the light of day, in front of other people. If he loved me, wouldn't he want to tell me as quickly as possible? I self-consciously adjusted my skirt. Maybe he'd changed his mind. It had been dark in his room last night; maybe now he could see flaws he hadn't noticed before – blemishes, the scar under my chin, the way my ears always seemed too large.

Professor Starking stepped back to admire the nebula projected on the wall. "At first glance, they may seem strange and alien," he said. "But all of us are made of the elements you see here. Their beauty lies in confusion. It gives them a kind of energy that fully formed stars don't have."

While the slides were shifting, Dante inched closer to me and slipped his hand into mine. I trembled at his touch, his palms cool and dry.

Neither of us dared to look at the other. Instead, we remained stoic, keeping our eyes trained on the pictures. I shifted closer to him, pressing my leg against his. To the rest of the class we looked like a boy and girl sitting side by side. But beneath the surface, everything within me was trying to burst out into a swirling cloud of particles, ephemeral and constantly changing, like stardust.

By curfew Eleanor still wasn't back. It was unusual: she always came back before lights-out, but I was too excited about meeting Dante to dwell on her absence. She was probably in the library, asleep in one of her books, or out working on the school play for the Humanities department. I would see her when I got back tonight, and then I could tell her everything.

I sat on my bed, hovering over my books but not looking at them. Instead, I was gazing impatiently at the clock, counting down the minutes until I would see Dante. When the hands finally reached 10:45, I opened the flue, pulled myself into the chimney, and began to climb down to the basement. I was still wearing my school clothes – a herringbone skirt, black tights and an oxford shirt with an overcoat on top to keep me from getting sooty.

The climb didn't seem so bad now that I had something to look forward to at the end. I was so anxious to see Dante that I barely noticed the cobwebs and dust and crumbling brick. But when I reached the bottom of the chute, something wasn't right.

The flue was only partially open, just enough for me to squeeze my body through. Instead of the normal hissing sounds that the furnace gave off, it was completely silent. In the distance, I could hear water trickling. And then drips, like a tap leaking into a bathtub full of water.

I climbed down a rung, and then another, until I was almost completely out of the chimney. But as I lowered my foot to the last rung, my leg became submerged in water. I pulled it back and leaned out the bottom of the chute to see what was going on.

The entire basement was flooded with water, which had risen to just a little way below the ceiling. I sighed, only now remembering what the maintenance workers had said to Mrs. Lynch outside the girls' dormitory. The water was dark and placid, barely rippling from the disturbance of my foot. The hanging lights reflected dim yellow orbs in its surface, like beams of flashlights shining up from beneath.

For some reason I felt pulled to the room, as though an invisible force were towing me down. I scanned the basement, searching for some way to get outside, but it was useless. Reluctantly, I climbed back into the chimney. My left shoe was soaked, and squeaked as I ascended, each step taking me further and further away from Dante. When I got back to my room I called his landline, but the phone rang and rang and rang, and I went to bed imagining him waiting for me in front of the chapel, leaning against the stone beneath the gargoyles, his face slipping into the shadows.

It took ten days to drain all of the water from the basement. The Maine winter crept up on us early, preserving the entire campus in a thin layer of ice. It was early December and the ground outside was hard and impenetrable, so they pumped the excess water into the lake, using long floppy hoses that trailed across the pathways like the arms of a jellyfish. Every morning I stepped over them as I walked to class, unaware that the water inside was freezing, preventing them from emptying the basement sooner. If it had been eight days, or even nine, things might have turned out differently. But numbers are strange and uncontrollable; they operate under their own set of rules. And as I would soon discover, ten was an entire rule unto itself.

In the meantime, we used the boys' bathroom every morning at 8 a.m., and every evening at 8 p.m. But the problem in the basement was more than just an inconvenience. It meant that I could only see Dante in class. The basement was the only way out of the dorms at night, or at least the only way that I knew of.

But let me start from the beginning. On the night that I discovered the flood, I had trouble getting to sleep. I paced around my room, staring at the fireplace, waiting for Eleanor to climb through it, but she never did. Eventually I gave up and collapsed in my bed. Pulling the covers over my head, I fell asleep, dreaming about Dante and our night together, and hoping that he was dreaming of me too.

But the flood was just the beginning of a strange chain of events that was taking place at Gottfried.

Eleanor didn't come back the next morning. I woke up from a dream only to be sobered by the sight of her unruffled bed. I immediately went next door to Maggie and Greta's room. Maggie opened the door with a yawn. She hadn't seen Eleanor since Grub Day, which was already two days ago. I went to see Bonnie and then Rebecca, and finally Genevieve. They hadn't seen her either.

The last door I went to was on the ground floor of the girls' dorm. It was my last resort, and I lingered in front of it for a moment before building up the gumption to knock. But just as I raised my fist, the door swung open. I gasped and jumped back.

Mrs. Lynch's squat figure greeted me, her short hair making her look more like a man than a dorm mother. She looked me up and down. I checked my outfit, making sure all of my buttons were buttoned and buckles snapped, worried she was going to reprimand me for being out of dress code.

"Yes?" she said, eyeing me with a quiet distaste.

In a low murmur, I informed her of Eleanor's disappearance.

"What do you mean she's missing?" she said sharply when I was finished.

"She wasn't here last night or this morning."

Upon hearing this news, Mrs. Lynch threw on a scarf and coat. "Why didn't you report it sooner?"

"I...I thought she was at the library." Which was the truth.

Mrs. Lynch slammed the door. "Come," she said, already four steps ahead of me.

I trailed behind her as she walked to Archebald Hall, asking me questions the entire way. When was she last seen? Did she have any reason to run away?

I didn't know. Maybe yesterday? And as for running away, she hadn't packed up any of her things, and even if she had tried to leave, there was nothing beyond Attica Falls for kilometres.

Our destination was the headmistress's office, but she was exiting the building just as we were entering. The headmistress was dressed in a long luxurious coat, plush and blue with a deep hood. Her snowy hair fluttered in the wind, making her look like an aged nymph. "Headmistress Von Laark," Mrs. Lynch called out. "This young lady has something to tell you."

After I finished, the headmistress addressed Mrs. Lynch. "Inform her parents immediately, and make a call to the ranger's office. In the meantime, I'll dispatch a search party."

The headmistress then inspected me, her blue eyes icy and unreadable.

"I can help," I said, verging on pleading. I couldn't shake the feeling that Eleanor's disappearance was somehow my fault. If I hadn't stayed with Dante, if I had gone home that night or reported her missing earlier, maybe it would have been different. "I want to join the search."

"Certainly not. You are to go to class and focus on your studies."

"But she's my room-ma—" I tried to protest before the headmistress cut me off.

"You are dismissed."

"Where were you?" said Dante, appearing out of nowhere in the hallway and pulling me beneath the stairwell. "I waited."

"I tried calling but you didn't pick up," I said softly. "The basement in the girls' dorm is flooded. There's no other way out after curfew."

Dante frowned. "I was worried something had happened. When you didn't show up I waited outside the dorm trying to find your window, but they were all dark. By the time I got back to my room, it was so late that I didn't want to call, in case Mrs. Lynch heard."

I meant to apologize to him, to explain how I had tried to meet him last night, but instead I blurted out, "Eleanor's gone."

"What do you mean?" Dante asked, leaning over me against the brick, his brow furrowed in confusion.

"She never came back last night. I don't think she was there the night before, either. I...I don't know if she ran away or if she was kidnapped, or I don't know what. I mean, where could she go?"

"You'd be surprised. There are a lot of places to go in this school if you don't want to be found."

"But what if she does want to be found?" The thought made me feel sick.

"Then she'll be found," he said pensively, though his mind was clearly somewhere else. "When was the last time you saw her?"

"Just before Grub Day. She said she was going to skip it and go to the library to study."

Dante raised his eyes to mine as he pulled his bag over his shoulder. "I have to go."

"What? Where? Do you know something? Do you know where she is?"

Dante shook his head. "If I did, I would find her for you."

"I know," I said softly.

"When can I see you again?"

"We have class together in three periods," I said, confused.

"Alone, I mean."

I bit my lip. "With the basement off-limits, meeting after curfew is basically impossible. Maybe during study hall? I can meet you outside the Megaron after dinner." His tie dangled in front of me, and I twirled it around my fingers.

The bell rang, signalling the start of class, and the sound of footsteps pounded on the stairway above us. "I'll be waiting," Dante said, and smiled.

During lunch, Mrs. Lynch and Professor Lumbar searched our room. When they found nothing, they searched it again. It felt odd watching them going through my underwear drawer, tossing around Eleanor's things. They even confiscated Eleanor's notebooks, though after reading them they found nothing of interest except illegible scribbles and pages and pages of love notes written to Professor Bliss.

Mrs. Lynch confronted him about it just before fourth

period. I was walking down the hall when I saw them in his classroom through the window in the door. I crouched outside and watched as Mrs. Lynch handed him Eleanor's History notebook and crossed her arms.

Mr. B. flipped through it, reading the notes slowly. Suddenly he dropped the notebook and stood up, gesticulating wildly with his hands. They got into an argument. I pressed my ear against the door and listened.

"If you have an explanation, now's the time," Mrs. Lynch threatened.

Professor Bliss claimed he had no idea the love notes existed. "Eleanor was my student. Nothing more. It isn't abnormal for a teenage girl to have a crush on her teacher. These things happen all the time. It doesn't mean I abducted her."

Unexpectedly, the knob on the door turned and the door swung open. I threw myself out of the way just before Mrs. Lynch stormed into the hallway with so much force that she didn't even notice me pressed against the wall behind her.

I met up with Nathaniel and told him about Eleanor and what I saw as we walked to Philosophy.

"So the last time you saw her was after Grub Day?" he asked.

I hesitated. I had lied to everyone in order to hide the fact that I'd spent the night at Dante's. But someone had to know the truth. I needed Nathaniel's help. "No. It was actually the morning of Grub Day."

Nathaniel looked confused. "What? But why did you tell everyone that—"

I cut him off. "I spent the night with Dante," I said quickly. "Please don't tell anyone."

Nathaniel went silent. "So you don't know when she disappeared?"

I shook my head.

"This is bad, Renée. Really bad."

I swallowed. "I know."

"Well, if we assume that whatever happened to her happened on Grub Day, then it couldn't have been Professor Bliss. I even saw him later that night patrolling the boys' dorms, so either way, he's safe."

"Why do you think it happened on Grub Day?"

"I mean, think about it. It's perfect. Everyone is in town, including most of the professors and the Board of Monitors. So the real question is, who wasn't in Attica Falls that day?" But the question was impossible to answer. There were far too many people, and besides, we hadn't been keeping track.

"Do you think it could be..." My voice trailed off.

"The Gottfried Curse?" Nathaniel said, finishing my sentence. "Maybe."

When we walked into class, Annette LaBarge was

sitting on her desk, her legs dangling freely like a child on a swing. A glass of water sat by her side. Unlike my other professors, she taught everything as if it were a story.

"A long time ago, we used to believe that people were made of two things – the body and the soul. When the body died, the soul lived on and was cleansed and reborn into someone new. The idea was explored by many, though namely in Western culture by Plato, and then René Descartes.

"Descartes was a famous philosopher in his time. He was obsessed with death – he wrote about it incessantly. He even claimed to have discovered the path to immortality. He was going to reveal his secret in an essay he claimed would be his lifetime achievement, and which he worked on up until his death. He called it his *Seventh Meditation*. When he died, people believed that his death was a hoax, an experiment. They thought he had found a way to cheat death and become reborn.

"That, of course, was never proven, and Descartes was never heard from again. All that remained were his papers. People combed through them, searching for the *Seventh Meditation*, but they only found six, none of which contained anything about the key to immortality.

"After everyone had given up hope, rumours began to surface that they had found something buried beneath the foundation of his house. Descartes' *Seventh Meditation*.

But the book was banned just before it was released. According to rumour, all copies were immediately burned, as were the men who had printed it. And before it could even be read, the book was gone, along with all of its secrets."

While she spoke, I looked out the window, and watched the branches of the trees sway in the wind. A boy ran into Horace Hall holding a messy stack of papers, clearly late for class. A maintenance worker shovelled snow along the edge of the green. The flood, followed by Eleanor's disappearance, seemed to fit with all of the other "accidents" that had been reported on in the article from *The Portland Herald*. And if Eleanor's disappearance was related to Benjamin's, then there was a good chance she would soon be found dead of a heart attack.

"We do, however, have glimpses into what his final work contained, facts that scholars have gleaned from other books published back then. In the *Seventh Meditation*, Descartes stated that children couldn't die. He said that, unlike adults, the bodies of children only appear to be dead. After ten days, they wake up and live again, soulless. According to Descartes, children stop rising from the dead at the age of twenty-one. Some philosophers speculate that this is why the age of twenty-one now embodies the idea of adulthood."

If I had only found a way to get to those files in the

headmistress's office, I might have found some piece of information that would have helped prevent whatever had happened to Eleanor. Quietly, I tore out a piece of paper from my notebook.

We have to find a way into the headmistress's office.

I folded the note, and when Miss LaBarge wasn't watching, I passed it to Nathaniel. He gave me a cautionary look, as if he knew what I was planning to do and didn't approve. Nonetheless, he scribbled down a response and passed it back to me.

I don't think you need my help doing that.

I immediately felt stupid. Why hadn't I thought of it before? I didn't have to break into the headmistress's office; I just had to get into trouble and be sent there. I had no idea how I would get to the files once I was inside, but I would deal with that later. Satisfied, I crumpled up the note and slipped it into my pocket.

After classes, the investigation for Eleanor began. One by one, we were called in for questioning. Solemnly, we watched each girl walk downstairs to Mrs. Lynch's quarters. A door slammed. After fifteen minutes it reopened. And then the next name was called. No one spoke after their interview. With Eleanor missing and Mrs. Lynch arousing suspicions among the student body, the atmosphere in the dorm was grim.

Finally it was my turn.

"Winters!" Mrs. Lynch's voice echoed from downstairs. On the way down I passed Minnie Roberts, who had gone in before me. I tried to say hello, but she kept her head bowed.

Mrs. Lynch's quarters were strategically positioned right next to the entrance so she could hear anyone sneaking in or out. When I got there, the door was slightly ajar. I knocked. When no one answered, I pushed it open.

Mrs. Lynch was sitting in an overstuffed plaid armchair, her stubby feet resting on a matching ottoman. She was scribbling notes on a yellow legal pad.

"Shut the door," she said without looking up.

The room looked like something a grandmother might live in. It had a low ceiling, dingy floral curtains and a shag carpet. It smelled like potpourri and mothballs. The walls were decorated with pictures of lighthouses, which, upon closer examination, were not paintings, but needlepoint.

Finally Mrs. Lynch stopped writing and looked at me. "Miss Winters."

There was nowhere to sit, so I stood in the middle of the room.

"Eleanor Bell has been missing for what seems to be two days now. You are her room-mate, correct?"

I nodded.

"Eleanor never went to Attica Falls on Grub Day."

"She said she was going to the library."

"And did she return to the room that night?"

"No," I said. "Wait, yes. Yes she did."

Mrs. Lynch gave me a suspicious look. "In your short time here at the Academy, you have garnered quite the reputation for troublemaking."

I gave her a confused look. "What?"

"Called to the headmistress's office three times."

"But the first time I hadn't done anything—" I tried to say, but she continued.

"Caught severely out of dress code; breaking curfew with a boy; blatantly disobeying the authority of professors..."

"But that was all really just one time—"

"Talking out of line," she said with contempt. "Where were you on Grub Day?"

"I was in Attica Falls. People saw me there; you can ask Nathaniel Welch. I was with him."

"Where were you that evening?"

I hesitated. "I was in my dorm room, studying."

"And what were you studying?"

"Latin," I said quickly.

"And Eleanor was there that night?"

"Yes," I lied.

"And you can produce no other witnesses of your whereabouts that night?"

"It was after curfew. We were alone in our room."

She put down her pencil and clasped her hands together on her lap.

"Miss Winters, where is Eleanor Bell?"

"I...I don't know."

She sighed and then jotted something down on her pad. "I think you do."

"But I don—" But she cut me off before I had a chance to respond.

"And you said that she wasn't –" she picked up her pad, referring to her notes – "no, forgive me, that she *was* in your room that night?"

I swallowed and nodded.

"Yet conveniently, no one else saw her. Or you."

I shifted uncomfortably, staring at a Persian cat that had sauntered into the room and was glaring at me from the windowsill.

"So really you have no alibi for the night after Grub Day."

"I do, but—"

"And you didn't report her disappearance until today because you weren't sure she was gone."

"I would have, but—"

She jotted down one last note and shut her pad. "That will be all."

* * *

By twilight, the search parties came. Professors and school administrators flocked to the green with flashlights and flares. They looked odd outside the context of class. Their casual clothes, boots and raincoats made them look puttering and old, exposing the fact that they were vastly outnumbered by a campus full of teenagers.

The Board of Monitors was supposed to regulate the students, watching the dorms and making sure that everyone was in by curfew, but did so half-heartedly. After dinner, I lingered outside the dining hall until everyone else filed outside. When the path was clear, I started to walk back to the girls' dorm, but then quickly changed routes and jogged towards the green.

Students weren't allowed to participate in the search. "Too dangerous," Professor Lumbar had said. They didn't care that Eleanor was our friend, and that we cared about finding her just as much as they did. It seemed like everyone was gathering on the lawn except for the people who were closest to her. Even a few people from town had been recruited for the search. I crouched behind a tree and watched. Together they huddled beneath the evergreens as the sun set on Gottfried Academy, until all that could be seen of them were the yellow beams of their flashlights reflecting off the fog rising from the lake.

The search was led by the headmistress herself. She

wore a long overcoat and carried a lantern, a two-way radio and a bag of flares.

"Friends," she bellowed. The crowd grew silent.

"Thank you for leaving your families to help us here tonight. It's a tragic day for everyone when a child goes missing, especially when it's a member of our own small community. If anyone hears any information regarding Eleanor Bell's whereabouts or the manner of her disappearance, please alert me or one of the professors immediately.

"To make the most of our time, we will break into groups. Each group will search a different area. Miriam, Edith and Annette will take Horace Hall. Lesley and I will search Archebald. William, Marcus and Conrad will search the edge of the forest..."

As she called out the names, each party broke off and began to comb the campus grounds looking for Eleanor. When the lawn had emptied out, I slunk out from behind the tree and jogged towards the lake. Dante was exactly where he said he'd be, leaning against one of the spruces, his hands in his pockets. He was perfectly preppy, crisp yet rough around the edges in a shirt and tie, a Gottfried scarf draped over his blazer, and his hair pulled into a messy knot.

We sat by the lake, against the back of a large rock. I hugged my knees. The calm water reflected the night clouds.

"What do you do when you don't know what to do?" I asked, staring into the darkness.

Dante followed my eyes to the outskirts of school, where we could see dim flashes of light bouncing off the trees and buildings. "I follow my instincts," he said, touching my shoulder.

I tossed a pebble in and watched the ripples dilate until they reached the shore. What were my instincts telling me? "I think Benjamin and my parents were murdered. I think Cassandra was too." I said it quickly, in case it sounded ridiculous. I told Dante about the séance, about how I had tried to summon my parents but only found him, Gideon and Vivian on the lawn; about how Eleanor had tried to summon Benjamin but got Cassandra, too. "And I think the same person got to Eleanor. I don't know why or how, and I don't have any reason to think any of these things other than a feeling. A really bad feeling."

Looking at my feet, I waited for him to react, but instead he stretched out his legs and leaned back on his elbows. "Do you really believe in that stuff? Séances?"

I looked up at him, my eyes watering in the wind. "I want to."

"You want to believe in ghosts? In monsters?"

"I want to believe that things don't have to end," I said, looking away, but Dante didn't let me.

"I want to believe that too," he said.

"Do you think Cassandra is dead?"

Dante hesitated. "Yes."

His frank answer somehow disturbed me, and a series of questions escaped my mouth before I could process them. "What? How? Why? Who do you think—?"

"Slow down," he said. "One at a time."

I paused to compose myself. "Do you think Benjamin was murdered?"

"Killed, yes."

"Do you think it's related to my parents and the deaths in the article?"

He thought about it. "Yes."

I hadn't expected so many affirmatives, and was at a loss for what to say. "So you believe me? Why didn't you tell me earlier? After the séance?"

"I didn't know you were looking for your parents when I ran into you that night," he said, almost to himself. "You were in your pyjamas, which caught me off guard. And you looked so surprised to see me; I couldn't tell if you were happy or upset. I remember holding your hand and running through the rain; the way the water collected in droplets on your eyelashes. I couldn't believe you were real. I still can't."

"You remember that?" I whispered.

"I remember everything."

I looked up at him, and he moved closer. I shivered.

299

Raising my hand to Dante's face, I coiled my fingers around the back of his neck and pulled him towards me.

We met halfway, my neck arching up to meet his. But just as our lips were about to touch, he pulled away and kissed me on the cheek.

His face was centimetres from mine. "Why won't you kiss me?" I asked, my voice betraying more despair than I intended.

When he finally spoke, his words came out slowly. "Because I'm afraid of what might happen."

"What could happen?"

"That's what I'm worried about – I don't know."

Not knowing what I was doing, I let my hand fall down his cheek. Dante pressed his finger to my lips, as if to stop me, but instead let his hand pass over them and roam down to my collarbone, guiding me towards him. His touch tickled my skin, like dozens of snowflakes falling and melting. His eyes were trained on mine.

"Renée, wait, there's something you need to—"

Everything happened at once. I closed my eyes, feeling his breath dance around my lips. Then voices emerged from the distance, floating towards us, followed by the sound of footsteps thumping against the frozen earth. And then light.

I pulled away from Dante and froze. A flashlight shone on us.

"Stand."

I shielded my eyes and squinted into the glare. It was Miss LaBarge, her cheeks rosy from the cold. She shone the light in my face, and then in Dante's.

"What was about to happen just now?" she asked him, her voice sharper than I had ever heard it.

"Nothing," he said. "Nothing."

She shone the light in his face for a few more seconds before turning it off.

"You shouldn't be out here tonight. Or any night, for that matter. No students are allowed outside during the search, only professors. You know that."

I stepped forward to explain, but Dante gripped my hand, holding me back.

"I'm sorry, Professor, it was my fault. I asked her to meet me here."

Miss LaBarge gazed at him. "Fault is a slippery thing."

Dante nodded, and I sat very still. I could hear the footsteps of the rest of her party walking in our direction. Miss LaBarge glanced around. "I'm going to pretend I didn't see you. Get back inside. And don't let me catch you again."

Dante reached for my hand, but I stopped him, remembering the note Nathaniel had written to me earlier. There was only one way to get into the headmistress's office to find those files. I couldn't sneak in, I had to be sent there. And what better time than now, when the headmistress was clearly distracted?

"Wait, no," I said. "I don't want you to pretend you didn't see us."

Both Miss LaBarge and Dante gave me confused looks.

"Send us to the headmistress's office."

"Renée," Miss LaBarge said, "you don't want this."

"Yes I do."

Miss LaBarge looked behind her shoulder. "You realize you could be expelled."

At that point I didn't care. What I cared about was Eleanor. My parents. The Gottfried Curse.

"Go," Miss LaBarge ordered, pushing us away from her.

Dante tried to pull me with him. "Renée, what are you doing?"

"Getting us information," I said, and coughed.

From the bushes, I heard people fumbling around. "What was that?" Professor Lumbar said loudly as she pushed through the brush and ran towards us. Miss LaBarge shined her flashlight on us just as the professors emerged through the trees, their faces shrouded in darkness, their eyes gleaming at us through the glare. Mrs. Lynch stepped forward. "Good work, Annette," she said while staring at me with a pleased grin. "Got you."

* * *

"We have to distract her," I said to Dante as Mrs. Lynch dragged us to the headmistress's office. "I need to get to the filing cabinet."

Dante studied me, then nodded. "I'll try."

The headmistress met us outside her office, emerging out of the shadows in the hall.

"Renée, Dante," she said. "Come."

Once inside, she walked past the wall of bookshelves, running her fingers along the bindings as she sat in the leather chair behind her desk. She didn't speak for a long time. Dante and I stood in front of her, trying to think of a plan. Finally she spoke, her tone firm and rather agitated.

"Be seated," she said, picking up a Siamese and dropping it into her lap. She rapped her fingers on the desk. "You look cold. Would you like a cup of tea?"

"Yes, please," Dante and I said at the same time, almost too quickly.

Headmistress Von Laark glanced between the two of us, and smiled as she unlocked the china hutch on the far wall. "If my memory serves me correctly, this is the second time you've both been here this semester," she said, her back to us as she poured our tea. "Sugar?"

"No thanks," Dante and I said simultaneously.

Just before the headmistress closed the doors of the hutch, I noticed two filing drawers at the bottom. I

303

watched them disappear behind lock and key. In order to get into the files I had to get her out of the office, a task that seemed more and more impossible the longer I thought about it. It would only take an emergency for her to leave us here unsupervised, and considering that we were already in the middle of an emergency, our chances were slim.

One of the cats emerged from behind her desk and walked towards Dante. Curling around his legs, it began to meow and paw at his trousers. As he tried to shoo it away, the other Siamese leaped down from where it was sitting on the bookshelf, and after sniffing around Dante's chair, also began to claw at his trousers.

"Romulus! Remus! Behave yourselves," Headmistress Von Laark barked, and reluctantly the cats retreated behind her desk. I gave Dante a questioning look, but he avoided my gaze.

"Miss Winters and Mr. Berlin, found together outside, after dark by the lake. How very romantic," she said with no hint of a smile. "What do you have to say for yourselves?"

"It was my fault," Dante and I blurted out at the exact same time.

"I asked him to meet me so we could try to find Eleanor," I said, just as Dante said, "I asked her to meet me so we could join the search."

The headmistress pondered our situation for a moment. "Since it seems I cannot deem who is more in the wrong, and since I can't have you wandering the school grounds any more tonight while the search is going on, and since I don't want to let you out of my sight while I get my work done, I'm going to have you alphabetize my library." She turned over the hourglass on her desk. "Now."

There must have been hundreds of books, all out of order, some so old and tattered that it was difficult to read the words on the binding. "I'll find all of the A's," Dante said. "You work on the B's." I nodded, and we set off while the headmistress sat behind her desk, glancing up at us every so often as we worked. The hutch with the filing cabinet was just a few steps away; the two cats walked around it, backs arched, as if reading my thoughts.

I could go to the bathroom, I thought. I could cause a commotion, which would draw the headmistress out. Then I could return and check the files. It was a flawed plan, but it was a plan nonetheless.

Trying to be as inconspicuous as possible, I walked past Dante. "Find the key while I'm gone."

He grabbed my elbow. "What are you doing?" Ignoring his question, I turned to the headmistress, but before I could speak, there was a knock on the door.

"Enter," the headmistress commanded.

The door swung open, and Mrs. Lynch stepped inside,

pulling Gideon DuPont by the arm. "I found him trying to sneak into the girls' dormitory. Meeting a girl," Mrs. Lynch added.

Gideon gave her a cold, heartless glare filled with spite, which transformed into amusement when he rested his eyes on Dante. How could Dante ever have been friends with such a hateful person? I wondered.

The two cats sauntered towards Gideon and clawed at his trousers. Gideon didn't seem to notice; his eyes were trained on Dante.

"Have him wait outside," the headmistress said. "And watch him." Mrs. Lynch nodded, while Gideon kicked Romulus and Remus off his legs as he backed out the door. The headmistress tsk-tsked, but the cats didn't respond. Frustrated, she stood up and made the sound again, but they were intent on Gideon. "Close the door behind you, please," she called out to him, betraying the slightest hint of anxiety. "Don't let them out." Gideon looked up and smiled. With deliberation, he slipped out of the room, leaving the door ajar, and the cats followed, their tails disappearing into the hallway.

Trying to hide her anger, the headmistress threw open her desk drawer and pulled out a string and two tiny muzzles. Turning to us, she said, "Keep working. I'll return shortly." And with that she was gone.

Without hesitating, I ran to her desk and grabbed her

keys, trying each until I found the one that fit the hutch. Throwing the drawers open, I flipped through the files. I checked under *M* for *Millet,* but Cassandra's file wasn't there. I checked again, and then under *C,* but it wasn't there either. Confused, I tried *G* for *Gallow* and then *B* for *Benjamin,* but his file was missing too.

Frantically, I went through the rest of the files, looking for anything. Minnie Roberts's file was gone too, as was Dante's and Eleanor's. And to my surprise, so was my own. From the door, Dante coughed loudly, looking at me and then the door. Swiftly, I closed the file cabinet and locked it, returning the key to the desk. Nothing. There was nothing.

CHAPTER 10

THE STOLEN FILES

THE SEARCH FOR ELEANOR CONTINUED for a week, but they found nothing. Her bag, her books and all of her things were in our dorm room. The beams of their flashlights occasionally flickered through my window, and I watched them dance across the walls as if they were looking for Eleanor in her bed. It was coincidental that the flood in the basement had occurred around the same time as her disappearance, though no one thought the two events were related, since I had told everyone that Eleanor had been safely in our room that night. Besides, the water level was still too high for anyone to access the basement.

So instead they taped up posters around campus and Attica Falls, plastering the entire area with Eleanor's face. Underneath it read one word: *MISSING*.

Her parents flew in separately, her mother a tall, elegant blonde in riding boots and a slim black jacket; her father a suited corporate lawyer who talked to everyone as if he were interrogating them. They bickered like children, blaming each other for Eleanor's disappearance; though they were surprisingly kind to me. "Eleanor spoke highly of you," Mr. Bell said. "She said you were one of her closest friends. Am I correct to believe that you helped her with her grades in Horticulture?"

I gazed at him, confused. "I, um...no, I only gave her a few pointers. She didn't need much help."

"Modest, too," he said, looking me up and down. "If you were leading the search, where would you look?"

"The basement," I blurted out.

He didn't speak for a long time, until he put his hat back on and buttoned his coat. "They said she couldn't be in the basement."

I shrugged. "It's just a hunch."

"Eleanor was right about you."

I gave him a questioning look.

"You speak your mind."

But I seemed to be one of the few people he didn't despise. He marched around campus, his son, Brandon, beside him, his ex-wife, Cindy, and his two assistants trailing behind, ordering the rangers, the townspeople, the professors, even the headmistress around, all of whom he accused of being incompetent and lazy. Yet even with more people, the search yielded nothing. Slowly the parties disbanded.

Campus affairs seemed to go back to normal, or as normal as they could have been with a sixteen-year-old girl missing. Everyone was scared, and even though there was no proof, it was hard not to project Benjamin's fate onto Eleanor. Mrs. Lynch seemed almost excited. She patrolled the halls and conducted random room searches with the kind of enthusiasm born from years of putting up with children who deserved to be disciplined, but rarely were. A scandal like this would merit a punishment she could only have dreamed of.

I sat through my classes, hardly paying attention as I tried to smother my imagination. Somewhere out there, Eleanor was in trouble. I felt useless, and Professor Lumbar's lecture about ancient forms of declensions was hardly enthralling enough to take my mind off it.

"What can Latin tell us about ourselves?" she asked, her giant body housed beneath a tent dress. She wrote a word on the board in large, slanted cursive: *Vivus eram.*

"There is a form of ancient Latin called *Latinum Mortuorum,* which can only be spoken in the past tense. It doesn't have any other tenses. You couldn't say, 'I am alive'; only 'I *was* alive'. It was spoken by children, often orphans. For them, the present, the future – these realms of time didn't exist. Instead they spent their lives looking backwards. In essence, living in the past."

I stared at the board, copying down the phrase. It was difficult to leave the past behind. First the death of my parents, and now Eleanor's disappearance. Maybe it was my way of trying to relieve the guilt I felt about my parents, that finding Eleanor would somehow make them come back. How could I not be haunted by the past when death was looming so close to me? I *was* alive.

That night I called Annie, and told her about Eleanor.

"Why don't you go to the police?" she asked.

"They were here. Plus, what would I say? That someone is killing people by giving them heart attacks, and that Eleanor was probably the next victim?"

"It does sound pretty ridiculous."

"I know. And I have no proof."

"Have you told anyone?"

"Just Nathaniel and Dante."

"You're still talking to that guy?" she said.

"Dante? Of course I am," I said defensively. "Why wouldn't I be talking to him?"

"The last time we talked you thought he was some sort of mutant."

"Oh, right..." Thinking back to our previous phone conversation, I was almost embarrassed at how angry I had gotten at Annie. "I'm sorry, An," I said. "All these things were happening that I didn't understand, and nothing seemed fair."

"And now everything makes sense?" She sounded sceptical.

I laughed. "Definitely not. I think I just changed. I like Dante. I like him a lot." I wanted to tell her everything about him; I wanted to describe the way he looked at me, the way his voice sounded when he spoke in class, each word like a tiny piece of a sprawling love letter written only for me. But I knew she wouldn't understand.

After we hung up, I sat in my room and listened to the muffled sound of girls laughing through the walls. How could they laugh when one of their friends was missing? With nothing else to do, I decided to clean my room. The recesses beneath my bed were treacherous at best. Large stacks of papers and books crowded the floor, surrounded by dust bunnies. I began to sift through them, when I saw the book I'd bought from Lazarus Books. It was lying on its side beneath a pile of notebooks and folders. I wedged it out and wiped off its cover. *Attica Falls.* Its woven ivory binding was slowly unravelling along the edges. *The Gottfried Curse*, I thought. I had spent so much time worrying about how the curse related to my parents and

Benjamin and Eleanor, that I had totally forgotten about the only part of the article that related to *me*. Literally. I stood up and paced the room until I found myself picking up the phone and dialling my grandfather's number. Dustin answered.

"Winters residence," he said stoutly.

"Hi, Dustin," I said softly, feeling suddenly very much like a little girl. "Is my—"

Upon hearing my voice, Dustin interrupted me. "Miss Winters?" he exclaimed warmly. "I've been wondering when we were going to hear from you. Calling about your winter travel arrangements?"

"Um, no, I actually wanted to talk to my grandfather. Is he there?"

"I'm afraid he's away," Dustin said. I imagined his forehead wrinkling as he said it. "Until next week, I'm afraid. Is it an emergency? Maybe I can be of service."

I hesitated. "No, it's fine – it can wait. Thanks, though."

"But we'll see you for the holidays, yes?"

I nodded. "Yeah."

"Excellent. I'll be picking you up next Friday. And you can talk to Mr. Winters when you get home. He wouldn't want me saying it, but he's very much looking forward to seeing you again. As am I, of course. It will be such a joy to have a young person around the estate again. I fear we have all become statues."

I laughed. "Okay," I said slowly, not sure how to respond. "See you next Friday, then."

I was about to blow out the candle and go to sleep, when I heard something hit my window. I got out of bed and looked outside, only to find Dante standing on the path below. I opened the window and leaned out.

"What are you doing here?" I asked.

"Come down," he said.

I looked behind me again. "I can't! I'll get caught."

"Mrs. Lynch is gone. I saw her leave for the headmistress's office ten minutes ago."

I threw on a pleated skirt and sweater, and checked my appearance in the mirror, clipping my hair to the side.

Dante was waiting for me by the path in just a shirt and tie, no jacket. He was leaning on a lamp post, his hair swept back from his face, save for a few loose strands that blew in the wind. Without saying a word, he wrapped his hand around mine and led me through the green. The night was grey and foggy, the moon barely visible beneath the clouds.

"Where are we going?" I asked, trying to keep up with his long stride.

Slowing down, he looked at me and smiled. "Trust me."

We stopped in front of the chapel, its massive stone buttresses leaning beneath the weight of the steeples. I let my hand slip from his as he walked ahead of me. Along the archway over the door, dozens of white flowers were blooming from gnarled vines. I gazed at them in awe. I had never seen them during the day.

"Moonflowers," I said, remembering them from the night-blooming plants class in Horticulture.

Dante smiled and held open the riveted doors, which, surprisingly, were unlocked. With delicate footsteps, I stepped inside.

The chapel was lit by dozens of candles all arranged in a line between the two aisles of pews. I picked one up and cradled it in my palm, glancing back at Dante with a surprised smile. He nudged me forward, and I followed the candlelit path into the belly of the chapel.

It was dark and shadowy, with the faint smell of musk and rosewater. The candlelight reflected off the stained-glass windows, covering the floor in a dark mosaic of blue and purple light. The ceilings were vaulted and covered in peeling frescoes of clouds and angels and beautiful women with long, flowing hair.

The candles led to the back of the chapel, behind the altar, and up into a narrow spiral staircase. The wind rattled the windows, and I looked back at Dante, who was just steps behind me. His fingers grazed the ends of my hair as I climbed, watching our shadows dance across the stone.

We emerged at the top of the steeple, where a ring of candles wrapped around a giant bell in the middle. I stepped outside, the cold air refreshing on my cheeks. In front of me was the entire campus, now small, and behind it the forest and the rocky peaks of the White Mountains disappearing into the clouds.

"It's beautiful," I uttered, though it hardly described what I felt.

"You like it?"

I turned to face him. "I love it."

Dante studied me, his face almost sad as he gently ran his fingers down my arm. "Renée, I—"

I looked up at him expectantly, curling my hands into the sleeves of my coat.

Dante's eyes searched mine. "I can't lose you."

My voice trembled as I stepped closer to him. "Why would you lose me?" I said with a faint smile.

He raised my hand to his lips and kissed it. We sank to the ground, surrounded by candles, and listened to the wind.

"If you could have anything you wanted, what would it be?" Dante asked as I rested my head against his chest.

"To have my parents back."

"If I could give that to you, I would," Dante said, kissing the inside of my arm, making it feel like dozens of white flowers were blooming across it.

I turned to him. "Then a kiss. A real kiss."

Dante ran a melancholy hand down my cheek. "I can't."

"Why?" I asked, my face centimetres from his as I drew him closer. He leaned in, unable to help himself. I felt his hand on the back of my neck, pulling me towards him until our lips were nearly touching. The air fluttered in my lungs, and I closed my eyes, letting my body go soft in his arms. I couldn't think or feel anything except his arms knotting themselves in my hair, grasping at my neck as if it were clay. And then suddenly he pulled away. "I can't—" he said. "I can't trust myself around you. I can't help myself."

"I trust you," I said softly.

"Renée, what if I hurt you? I would never forgive myself."

"You won't hurt me, I know you won't," I said, raising my hand to his face. He pressed it against his cheek.

"You don't understand. You don't know what I'm capable of. I'm afraid to touch you, in case I break you; I'm afraid to talk to you, afraid you'll realize that I'm a monster. But every day you're still here." He gazed at me. "I can barely control myself when I'm around you. I have to have you. I have to keep you."

"You do have me."

He spoke slowly. "Renée, I need to tell you—"

But before he could finish his sentence, I saw a person

walking down the pathway towards the chapel below us, carrying a lantern.

"Mrs. Lynch," I said frantically. We ran downstairs and snuck out the back entrance into the cemetery. With barely enough time to say goodbye, I ran to the dormitory.

By the next morning, the magic of the night in the chapel seemed like nothing more than a dream, and the reality of Eleanor having been gone for over a week made me so nauseated that I barely had an appetite. I was stuffing books into my bag after Philosophy when Miss LaBarge approached me. "How do you feel about tea?" she asked.

I hesitated. Mrs. Lynch had already questioned me three times about Eleanor, and I wasn't up for it any more. "I...I—"

"That's what I thought," she said with a smile, and held the door for me as we walked to her office. It was on the second floor of Horace, in the east wing. I wiped my feet on a mat outside of her door that read, WELCOME, FRIENDS, and entered. The room was covered in books. They were stacked on shelves, lying in piles on the floor, propped up against the windowsill, tucked behind the door. I sat in a Victorian armchair as Miss LaBarge busied herself over a platter with dishes, cups, saucers and a teapot.

"I don't know where she is," I blurted out before she could say anything.

"Madeleine?" she said, her back to me.

I stared at her, confused. "No. Eleanor. She's in our class..."

Miss LaBarge turned around and smiled, holding out a plate of biscuits. "Of course she is. Madeleine, as in the cookie."

"Oh...right. Thanks," I said, turning red.

She held up a jug. "Milk?"

I nodded, and she poured it in my cup and sat in the armchair across from me.

"Sorry," I said. "It seems like every time someone talks to me these days, all they ask about is Eleanor."

She frowned. "I'm not interested in your involvement with Eleanor's disappearance, which I assume you had nothing to do with," she said, sipping her tea, "but in your involvement with a certain someone else, who also has a proclivity for making himself scarce."

She had a confusing way of speaking, and it took me a few seconds to figure out what she was asking me. "Who?" I asked, confused.

"The boy from the lake."

I stopped chewing. "Oh...he's just a friend."

She picked up her saucer. "Ah, boys. Always problematic."

"There's no problem," I said quickly. "There's nothing going on."

"It didn't seem that way," she said, clasping her hands over her knee. "But you needn't tell me that. I am a professor, you are a student, and I understand that we have to operate under the contrivance that nothing romantic is going on with you and this boy, as the *Code of Discipline* decrees it."

I swallowed.

"However, if there *were* something going on, say, as more than friends, I want you to feel comfortable coming to me if there are any...complications."

Was Miss LaBarge telling me that if I wanted to talk about Dante with her, I could? "There aren't any complications," I said. "With our...friendship."

Miss LaBarge gave me an earnest look. "Good," she said. "Good. Just making sure." She nibbled on a cookie. "So tell me what it is that you wanted to talk to me about."

I wanted to remind her that *she* was the one who had brought *me* here, not the other way around, but instead I blurted out "The Gottfried Curse" before I realized the words were leaving my mouth.

Miss LaBarge coughed and set down her cup of tea, the china clattering against the saucer. "Sorry," she said, wiping at her blouse with a handkerchief. "You caught me off guard."

"So you know about it?"

"The deaths, yes."

"The heart attacks, you mean."

Miss LaBarge narrowed her eyes. "I presume you're implying that they were somehow unnatural and that Eleanor is part of the pattern."

I gazed at her in awe. "Yes."

"Renée, I know it's a comforting idea to think that when someone dies, it's for a reason, or that someone is responsible, but sometimes these things just happen. After all, we are just humans. We can't control life and death."

It was supposed to make me feel better, but even the thought of Eleanor being dead made me feel queasy.

"However," she said as I looked away, "we can control the way we react."

I gave her a confused look.

"Descartes once said that instinct trumps all. Follow yours," she said, and winked.

I set down my tea. She was right.

The next morning in the boys' dorm, I lingered in the shower, letting the water pound against my back as I tried to figure out what I should do. Instinct, I repeated to myself. What did my instinct tell me to do? But I couldn't think of anything that might help me find Eleanor or figure out what was behind the heart attacks. By the time I turned off the water, all of the girls had cleared out. Clutching my towel and shower caddy, I stepped into the hall.

The boys' dormitory was eerily still. I glanced down the stairway. There was no one there. Without thinking, I ventured into the hallway. It was lined with doors, all wooden and perforated with slanted shingles, like in a psychiatric hospital. I walked past, running my fingers along them until I found myself standing in front of one door in particular. It looked the same as the rest: no one else would have been able to perceive its irregularity, yet for some reason I couldn't walk past it.

66F.

I glanced around me. If the boys' dorm was the same as the girls', there wouldn't be any locks. I knocked lightly, and when no one answered, I turned the knob.

The room was immaculate, the kind of clean you only find in an expensive hotel room. Or at least one side was. The bed was tucked and made, with no creases or lumps; the books in the shelf were arranged in alphabetical order, and when I opened the closet, it was full of suits. Antique suits, all hung, starched and colour coded in varying shades of grey, black and brown. Gideon DuPont. I poked one, as if to make sure he wasn't hiding inside, then jumped back when the hangers jangled on the bar. There were no photographs, no paintings or prints, no mirrors. The room had four windows, two overlooking the lake, two overlooking Horace Hall. Light streamed in, casting hazy beams across the wooden floor like invisible dividers, cutting the room in half. The other side of the room was the complete opposite of Gideon's. I didn't know who his room-mate was, but I imagined that they didn't get along. Dirty clothes were piled in wrinkled clumps; ties hung on the bedposts, crumpled papers surrounded the base of the trash bin. I approached Gideon's desk.

I didn't know what I was looking for when I opened the drawer, but I assumed I would know when I found it. I went through everything: his books, his notebooks, even his *Code of Discipline*. If there was anything that implicated him in Eleanor's disappearance, I couldn't find it, because all of his class notes were written in long, sweeping Latin. After I went through all the drawers in his desk, shuffled through all of the books on his shelf, and crawled under his bed, which was strangely free of dust or bugs, I gave up. All the girls had probably left by now, which meant that the boys would be returning to the dorm soon.

I quickly tried to rearrange his things, hoping he wouldn't realize anyone had tampered with them, when I accidentally knocked over the bottles of fancy colognes that sat on his dresser. Getting down on all fours, I started picking them up, smelling each as I went. They were strong and pungent, and I winced and held the bottles away from my face. Why did he have so much cologne anyway? I bent down to pick up the last of them when I saw something brown sticking out from Gideon's pillowcase.

Forgetting about the cologne, I pulled it out, only to discover that it was a file folder. And not just any file folder. On the cover it said: *Eleanor Bell.*

I blinked, unable to believe what I was seeing, but when I opened my eyes it was still there. I opened the folder and flipped through. It was her personal file. I glanced back at the door. I could hear voices floating up from the open window. The boys were coming back. Without wasting any time, I reached into Gideon's pillowcase to see if anything else was inside, and to my surprise, there were two more files, both brown, both with names printed on the front:

Benjamin Gallow

Cassandra Millet

I stuffed them into the bundle of my wet towel and replaced the pillow and the last of the cologne. Shutting the door behind me, I scurried downstairs, trying as best as I could to conceal the folders.

The boys were pouring into the foyer as I left. They stared at me and whistled while I pushed through them, my wet hair dripping onto my collared shirt. Yet just when

I thought I had made it out without getting caught, I bumped directly into Gideon as we walked through the double doors. I froze, clutching my towel and the folders to my chest. Gideon glared at me and brushed off his shoulder where my hair had left a wet mark. The doors swung together, bumping me out and him in. Thankful for the act of fate, I ran back to my room to dry my hair before class.

When I got back, I slammed the door and sank to the ground. Unable to contain my curiosity, I dumped out the contents of each file and flipped through the pages, skimming for anything of interest. Each file was embossed with a giant Gottfried crest in blue and gold ink, and began the same way:

ELEANOR BELL

Height:	165 cm
Weight:	52 kg
Hair Colour:	Blonde
Date of Birth:	June 5, 1994
Origin:	Maryland
Parents:	Cindy Louise Bell, no occupation;
	Gareth Aaron Bell, lawyer;
	DIVORCED
Siblings:	Brandon Bell, Monitor
Status:	MONITOR

Attached were Eleanor's transcripts, letters of recommendation, records of detention and work details, and her admissions application package, which included a personal statement about her parents' divorce and some sort of scorecard, which I assumed was from an admissions test. Nothing seemed out of the ordinary except for her status, which read "Monitor". It must have been a typo; Eleanor wasn't on the Board of Monitors. Otherwise, there were no notes on the margins, no plans hatched on the back in Gideon's handwriting. Disappointed, I flipped through the rest of the files.

Cassandra's was much thicker than Eleanor's, stuffed with documents regarding the death of her family in an avalanche. I skimmed through them until I found her official Gottfried records.

CASSANDRA MILLET

Height:	162 cm
Weight:	50 kg
Hair Colour:	Blonde
Date of Birth:	November 21, 1990
Origin:	Colorado
Parents:	Colette Millet, ballet teacher;
	Bernard Millet, hotelier;
	DECEASED

Siblings:	George Millet, Pauline Millet; DECEASED
Status:	*NON MORTUUS*, DECEASED
Primary Date of Death:	February 14, 2005
Secondary Date of Death:	May 15, 2009
Primary Cause of Death:	Skiing accident
Secondary Cause of Death:	*Sepultura*

I read her status again, my mind racing. *NON MORTUUS*, DECEASED. What did it mean? *Non Mortuus* translated as "Not Dead". But if she wasn't dead, why would they list it, and why would she have two causes of death, the second of which translated as "Burial", each on different dates and in different years?

I turned the page. Suddenly I was face-to-face with Headmistress Von Laark. It was a drawing sketched in charcoal, and showed her standing in the woods, at the head of a deep hole. The Board of Monitors stood solemnly beside her, all staring at Brandon Bell, who was holding the limp body of Cassandra Millet in his arms as he lowered her into the pit. The edges were darkened with the night sky. In the corner, the sketch was signed: *Minnie Roberts*. I shuddered. Even in pencil, the scene was haunting.

Finally I opened Benjamin's folder.

BENJAMIN GALLOW

Height:	180 cm
Weight:	75 kg
Hair Colour:	Brown
Date of Birth:	September 18, 1994
Origin:	Pennsylvania
Parents:	Karen Gallow, school teacher;
	Bruce Gallow, dentist; MARRIED
Siblings:	None
Status:	PLEBEIAN, DECEASED
Date of Death:	May 12, 2009
Cause of Death:	*Basium Mortis*

I had to read the last line once, twice, before I could figure out what it said. *Basium Mortis.* I let the words roll off my tongue like a curse. "Death Kiss," I translated from the Latin. Or maybe it was "Kiss of Death". My mind raced with possible explanations as to why such a cryptic phrase was on an official school document, but none made sense. I must have translated it wrong: maybe it was a medical phrase like *rigor mortis.* I shuffled through the pages that followed: his transcripts, information about his parents and friends, until finally I found the hospital's death certificate. It was dated May 12, 2009. *Approximate Time of Death: 7.12 p.m. Cause of Death: Heart Attack.* Which was definitely not the same as *Basium Mortis.*

Behind it was an envelope marked *GALLOW*, held closed with a paper clip. My heart beat faster as I opened it.

Inside was a collection of photographs, all taken at different angles of the same subject. Benjamin Gallow's body, dead and pale, splayed out in the woods. The first was a distant shot, the lighting so dark I could barely see anything except for the startling whiteness of his skin and the yellow caution tape wrapped around the trees in the background. I flipped to the next, and then the next, each closer and more detailed than the one before, until I could finally see his body in detail.

My heart beat faster as I stared down at a surprisingly familiar scene. Benjamin was still in dress code, his red tie unknotted, one end hanging loose across his shoulder, the other stuffed violently in his mouth. I knew where I had seen this before. His skin looked old and somehow ravaged; not at all the bright, knavish face that everyone had described to me. His brown hair was unexpectedly speckled with grey along the temples. His eyes were closed, purpling bags hanging beneath. The more I looked at it, the more the image blurred until I was looking at my parents, dead in the woods, white cloth stuffed in their mouths.

CHAPTER 11

THE INCIDENT LAST SPRING

IT'S FUNNY HOW THE THINGS you want sometimes turn out to be things you wish you had never laid eyes on. I had barely managed to push the gruesome details of my parents' deaths out of my mind before Benjamin's files plunged me back into that hot summer night. I sat on the floor, hugging my knees and willing myself not to cry, before I was able to compose myself enough to go to class. I walked briskly to Horace Hall, stopping by the library on the way, where I hid the files between two oversized books on the third floor, glad to be rid of them for the moment. If the files proved anything, it was this: both Benjamin and

Cassandra had been murdered, and their deaths were somehow connected to the murders of my parents. But who was behind it? I thought back to what Eleanor had said about Gottfried the first day we met. *The secrets that aren't found out are buried well. And probably for a reason.* The only problem was that this secret now had to do with me.

Plus, I had to worry about Mrs. Lynch. I didn't dare risk keeping the files in my room – not with the possibility of her searching it. That would only give Lynch further evidence that I was to blame for Eleanor's disappearance. After jotting down the titles *Toads of New England* and *Amphibious Past Lives,* along with their Dewey decimal numbers, I set off for class.

"Gideon has something to do with it," I told Nathaniel, pulling him aside before lunch.

"And what drew you to this conclusion? Wait, let me guess: you snuck into his room and found Eleanor's body."

"Actually, that's not far off. Come with me."

I dragged him to the library, which was now crowded with students studying frantically for finals. I led Nathaniel up three flights of stairs and through the maze of bookshelves until I found the oversized book section, which, to my relief, was empty, probably because it was dark and musty, which wasn't the best condition for studying.

"I found these files shoved in his pillowcase," I said, relaying all the details of my trip to Gideon's room.

"What do you think *Non Mortuus* means?" I said, flipping through Cassandra's file. "Or *Basium Mortis*? The tie. It has something to do with the tie."

But Nathaniel ignored my questions. "You actually went through his stuff?" he said in disbelief.

I blinked. Had he not heard me? "Benjamin was murdered," I said quietly. "And Cassandra is dead. I don't know how, but she's definitely dead and the school is covering it up. And now Eleanor's gone. She could be dead too. Does that mean nothing to you?"

Nathaniel shrank back in his seat. "Of course it does. But how exactly do you think Gideon is involved? Do you think *he* killed Eleanor?"

"I don't know. Why else would he steal her file? And I did see him lurking around the girls' dorm."

"Lots of people hang out outside the dorms. That doesn't mean he killed someone."

I sighed. "I know... And he never would have killed Cassandra. They were friends. Or Benjamin. I mean, why would he do that? And there's definitely no connection between him and my parents..." It was hopeless.

"Maybe he has the files for the same reason you wanted them. To know."

He had a point.

"So what are you going to do?" Nathaniel probed when I didn't respond.

"I have to tell someone," I said, gathering the papers and stuffing them back in the files. "I have to tell Mrs. Lynch. Or a professor. Or someone."

"Renée," Nathaniel said, pulling me back. "You can't. First of all, why do you think Mrs. Lynch would believe that you didn't steal these files yourself?"

"Because I didn't. I found them in Gideon's room."

"I know," Nathaniel said. "But it doesn't look good. What are you going to tell her, that you snuck into Gideon's room, went through his things, and found these hidden in his pillowcase? She's going to think you're lying. And even if she does believe you, you'll still be in trouble."

My shoulders dropped. He was right. Minnie's drawing of Cassandra's burial flashed through my mind. What had actually happened the night Cassandra died? If we couldn't hold another séance, there was only one other person I could go to.

"Renée? Hello? Earth to Renée."

I shook myself out of my thoughts and looked at Nathaniel. Shoving the files back between the two books, I grabbed my bag. "I have to go."

That evening after dinner, I lingered around the showers in the boys' dorm until almost everyone had cleared out of

333

the bathrooms. I brushed my teeth slowly, waiting for Minnie Roberts to show up; I knew from the state of her hair that she took showers at night. The bathroom was filled with steam, which fogged up the mirrors around the edges and condensed into droplets on the taps and door handles. A few remaining girls came and went like ghosts, their presence heard but not seen – the toilet flushing, the tap running, the stall door creaking on its hinges. But Minnie never showed. Giving up, I hopped into a shower stall and turned on the water.

I was just about to rinse the bubbles from my hair when I heard the sound of a showerhead turn on across from me. The swish of a curtain. And then a voice, talking to no one.

I peeked out, my head lathered in shampoo. The curtain across from me was only half closed, and a skinny silhouette hovered behind it. I leaned out to get a better look.

Minnie Roberts was standing under the shower in her bathing suit. If it were anyone else, the bathing suit would have been weird, but Minnie was already so eccentric that I wasn't surprised. Everyone said she was a hypochondriac and a germophobe. The water beat down on her, pushing her hair across her face. Every so often her body pulsed forward with the change in water pressure.

Stepping out of the shower, I dried off and waited until

I heard her turn the water off, followed by the sound of her feet padding against the tile floor. "Wait," I said.

Minnie gave me a frightened look, her eyes darting around the room to make sure no one was watching, as if she didn't want to be seen talking to me. She was wrapped in a towel, her skin red from the hot water.

"Can I ask you something?"

Minnie seemed caught off guard by my request. "I...um...I don't know. I don't think so," she said, turning away.

"I don't think you're crazy," I called after her. That made her stop.

"Well thanks," she said, almost sarcastically.

"I also don't think you were lying last year."

She hesitated, and without warning, gathered her things and was about to leave the bathroom when I called out to her.

"What do you know about Cassandra Millet?"

She froze. "I don't know anything," she said quickly, her back to me. "I should go."

"No, wait!"

Minnie didn't move.

"I need to find Eleanor. She's still out there somewhere. Please, help me."

She turned and stared at me with a mixture of disbelief and fear. "Why are you asking me?"

"Because I think Eleanor's disappearance has something to do with Cassandra Millet. With her death."

"Her death?" she said slowly, trying to figure out if I was mocking her.

I looked her in the eyes. They were dull and haunted, with the steady gaze of a person on the brink of madness. "I believe you," I said.

Her lip quivered, and I thought she might cry. Hugging her clothes tightly to her body, she let out a sigh of relief. "Come with me."

Minnie's room was at the opposite end of our floor, and was, to my surprise, exceedingly normal. It felt like a cosy country bedroom, with a quilted comforter, a leafy plant hanging by the window, and prints of Renoir's ballerinas on the wall. Minnie hung up her towel and sat on the edge of her bed. A row of satin ballet flats lay at the foot of her fireplace.

"Do you dance?" I asked. She was so clumsy at school, always dropping her tray in the lunchroom or tripping up the stairs in Horace, that I could hardly picture her balancing on one toe.

Minnie laughed nervously. "No, I...I just draw them."

The other side of the room was empty, the desk barren, the mattress naked.

"No one wanted to live with me," Minnie said.

Minnie kept a cautious eye on me as I surveyed her room. Spread across the floor and the empty mattress were dozens of loose sketches, all black-and-white. The lines were sparse and drawn bluntly in charcoal, yet somehow the images were even more stunning than the subjects were in real life. In addition to the drawings of ballet slippers, there were also landscapes of Gottfried's campus, and portraits – beautiful portraits – of an old woman, a young girl, an old man, and one of Minnie herself.

"Did you draw these?" I asked.

Minnie nodded.

"They're beautiful."

"Thanks," she said softly. "When everyone tells you you're crazy, after a while you start to believe it too. Drawing helps me...remember...that I'm not."

"I know the feeling." Was I crazy to think that my parents' death was a murder? That there was more to Dante than he was letting on? I didn't have anything like drawing to remind me that I was sane.

"You got into Horticulture, right?"

I nodded.

"What's it like? My dad wanted me to get into that class, but I didn't pass the test. He was so angry when he saw my schedule; I thought he was going to break something. I'm not even old enough to be tapped, but I

337

guess he could tell from my classes that I wouldn't be. Our family has been at Gottfried for centuries, and we've always been on the Board of Monitors. Whatever gene that was, I definitely didn't inherit it."

I didn't understand why Horticulture had anything to do with the Board of Monitors, or why her father would be so upset that she didn't get into the class. "It's okay," I said, trying to play it down. "We learn a lot about ecosystems and soil and burying things and stuff. Otherwise, nothing too interesting."

When I mentioned burials, Minnie tensed up. "Burying things?"

"Just bulbs, flowers, you know. But now we're learning more about the different species of plants."

Minnie gazed at her drawings. "I was sketching when I saw them," she said, wringing out her wet hair. "It was at night. There are moonflowers that climb up the gates of the chapel, and I wanted to draw them while they were in bloom. So after dinner I walked over to the chapel with my sketchbook and pencils. On my way I saw Brandon Bell bringing Cassandra Millet to the headmistress's office in Archebald Hall. Benjamin had just died from the heart attack, and I figured the headmistress just wanted to check up on her or ask her questions.

"When I got to the chapel, I sat on the grass and waited for the moonflowers to open. And they did. They were beautiful." Minnie gazed at her feet and continued.

"Halfway through my drawing, I heard a noise. I hid behind a tree and waited. At first I thought it was an animal, but it turned out to be the Board of Monitors. There were five of them, each carrying shovels; the only person missing was Brandon Bell. They walked to the chapel and went inside. Normally I wouldn't have followed them, but my dad always talked so much about the Board of Monitors, and I wanted to be one so badly. I thought maybe if I listened in on one of their meetings, I could figure out what it took to get nominated. So I followed them.

"I waited until they had all gone inside, then took off my shoes and snuck in before the doors closed. They were almost out of sight when I made it to the pews, and I just barely saw Ingrid Fromme, another junior Monitor, crawl through the hole behind a grate near the pulpit."

"Wait," I said. "They all climbed into a hole in the back of the church?"

Minnie nodded.

"I didn't want to go in it at first, but then I figured if the Board of Monitors was using it, it must be okay. So I followed them. The opening was about half a metre wide and tall, and it had a little stepladder going down. It was dark and dusty and I couldn't see anything. After only a couple of metres I hit the ground, and it was sort of like a tunnel or a passageway or something. I didn't bring my candle so I just ran my hands along the wall and walked towards their voices.

"I walked for ever. They took a bunch of turns until I had no idea which direction they were headed. Finally, it emptied out on the other side of the wall, right on the edge of the woods. When their voices were far enough away, I climbed out and followed them. They were going to the Dead Forest.

"The headmistress and Brandon Bell came from the opposite direction. Brandon was holding someone. A scarf was wrapped around her face, but I recognized Cassandra's hair. She was shaking; otherwise I would have thought she was dead. A handmade coffin was next to them." Minnie swallowed. "And then they started digging while the headmistress gave them instructions."

"Headmistress Von Laark? Are you sure?"

"I'm positive. After they were finished, Brandon picked Cassandra up and put her in the box. Then he did the weirdest thing. He put a coin on each of her eyes."

"Coins?" Suddenly, all I could think of were my parents, and how their bodies were surrounded by coins.

Minnie nodded. "I could hear her whimpering when he covered the coffin with a plank of wood, but she didn't move. Brandon hammered it shut with his spade, and they all lifted it and set it in the hole. They covered it with dirt, and that was the end of it."

"Brandon? Brandon Bell as in Eleanor's older brother? As in the top Monitor? You're saying he buried Cassandra Millet alive?"

"Not just him. All of them. And the headmistress. I tried to dig her up after they left, but it started to rain, and the soil was packed so tightly. I marked the area with a stick so I could find it again, but when I brought Professor Lumbar back, it had been washed away."

"But why? Why would they do it?"

"I don't know. I'm sure you heard about the day in the dining hall when I told everyone."

I nodded.

"After that, I was called to the headmistress's office. I was so scared; I thought she was going to kill me too. I called my parents, but they thought I was making it up, just like everyone else. I even wrote a will." She went to her desk and pulled out a slip of paper from the back of the drawer. "See, I still have it."

The Final Will and Testament of Minnie Roberts, Age 14

Bequests
1. *I leave my Japanese fighting fish to my cousin Jenny.*
2. *I leave my sketches to my parents.*
3. *I leave my clothes to my cousin Jenny.*
4. *I leave my ballet slippers to the Bethleson*

Children's Hospital.
5. I leave my books to the Gottfried Copleston Library.

Final wishes
1. If you're reading this, I will probably already be buried in the Dead Forest. Please find me.
Thank you for a beautiful life.

I blushed as I read it, feeling like I was violating her most private moments. "It's perfect," I said.

"Thanks," she said, folding it into the drawer. "I also left a note explaining what I had seen that night, along with a sketch of the scene, which I drew afterwards. Those were confiscated by the school.

"Anyway, when I went to the headmistress's office, I thought I was going to die. But instead, she just told me that I was wrong. She hadn't even been at Gottfried that night, and had witnesses to prove that she was actually in Europe. And then she gave me a week of detention for sneaking off campus after hours. Everyone said the same thing. That I made it up, that I was crazy. My parents sent me to a psychiatric ward for the summer." Minnie gazed at her sketches. "The thing is, I spend most of my time watching things. I know what I saw. I'm not lying."

She stared at me, her eyes watery and searching. I could tell that by now she wished she was wrong because the

342

reality was even more disturbing to accept. "I believe you," I said.

A symposium dinner was held at the end of the fall semester to celebrate the beginning of winter. In the tradition of Plato, it was a themed dinner designed to encourage discussion on various philosophical subjects. But the only thing people were interested in talking about was Eleanor.

The dining hall was filled with long rectangular tables, each covered in royal blue tablecloths that collected in folds on the ground. The feast was elaborate and distinctively New England, with buttered corn, poached gourds and candied yams, venison, quail, wild turkey and Cornish hen, all roasted to a golden brown, along with blueberry cobbler, sugared fruits and an elaborate array of desserts made from maple syrup. The professors were sitting at tables that lined the edges of the hall, forming a U around us. In the middle were the student tables, one for each grade, girls on one half, boys on the other. I was sandwiched between Emily Wurst and Amelia Song, a quiet girl who played the harp in the orchestra and kept to herself. Minnie Roberts was actually one of the few people I wanted to talk to, but it was impossible to ask her more about Cassandra in the dining hall, so I spent most of the dinner watching her push the food around on her plate.

I tried to pretend I couldn't see people staring at me, whispering my name and then Eleanor's. Every so often I glanced around the room, hoping to see Dante, who told me he'd be there, but was only met with Nathaniel, who looked just as bored as I did on the other side of the table.

I pushed my fork off the table with my elbow. Trying not to draw attention to myself, I crouched down to pick it up and crawled under the table, letting the tablecloth fall behind me like a curtain.

Beneath it, the din of the dining hall was muted, and everything was dark and calm. I sat there for a few minutes, staring at the line of feet on either side of me, and then began to crawl to the door.

When I finally made it outside, I let out a sigh. The only thing I was sure of was that both Cassandra and Benjamin were dead, and that the school knew about Cassandra. That much I knew from the files. But was Minnie right? No, I thought. Impossible. Rubbing my temples, I turned to make my way back to the dormitory, when I saw one of the maintenance workers run up the path and into the dining hall.

Moments later, the door to the dining hall burst open and Headmistress Von Laark strode outside, her ivory cloak billowing behind her. I ducked behind a bush. Professor Bliss and Professor Starking pushed out of the dining hall on the heels of the headmistress, all staring out towards the dormitories.

In the distance I could barely make out a person carrying something down the pathway. I watched him through the leaves as he approached, until he was close enough for me to see his face.

Dante emerged from the night fog, cradling a body in his arms. I clasped my hand over my mouth to muffle the gasp that involuntarily escaped. It was Eleanor.

Her blonde hair dangled just above the ground, blowing in the winter wind. She was unconscious and wrapped in a thick wool blanket, her body convulsing in sudden, violent jerks. I could see the quiet rise and fall of Dante's breathing as he handed her to Professor Bliss and Professor Starking, who carried her to the nurses' wing, her limp silhouette swaying back and forth like a hammock.

Dante glanced through the bushes in my direction, as if he knew I was there, and then turned his attention to Headmistress Von Laark, who was questioning him. He looked exhausted. Just behind him, a pair of maintenance workers approached.

"This young man has been lurking around here all week, trying to find the girl," the older man said, wiping sweat from his forehead. "We had been trying to get into the basement for days, but the pipes kept freezing," he continued, "so we couldn't drain it. And then all of a sudden this young man emerged from the front of the girls' dormitory, carrying the girl in his arms."

The headmistress looked from the man to Dante. "Is this true?"

"I was walking past the dormitory when I saw her stumble out the front door. She could barely walk. I caught her just before she fell," Dante said calmly.

"It's been a week and a half, and we still haven't been able to drain that place," the maintenance worker said with exasperation. "The water is still almost up to the ceiling. Who knows how she managed to find a crevice to breathe in. How she even survived is beyond me."

The headmistress narrowed her eyes, which were darkened with eyeliner. "Curious," she said, her lips red and pursed. She turned to Dante. "Why were you outside the girls' dormitory?"

"I told you. I was just walking past on my way to the dining hall," he said. "Right place, right time."

The headmistress didn't look like she believed him, but gave up questioning for the moment. "See me in my office tomorrow morning," she said, dismissing him.

"And do we know how Eleanor Bell ended up in the basement?" she asked the maintenance workers.

They both shook their heads. "We just work the plumbing," the older one said. "The flood was caused by a series of broken pipes on the ground floor. They were clean breaks, though, not made from freezing or bursting. Broken on purpose, if you ask me."

Headmistress Von Laark flinched.

"Disgusting business, whatever happened down there," the man said, spitting a wad of chewing tobacco on the ground. "But I guess there's only one thing that matters."

The headmistress had started to walk away, but stopped on his words. "Which is?"

"She's alive."

The headmistress frowned. "Let us hope."

CHAPTER 12

THE FIRST LIVING ROOM

ELEANOR SURVIVED. SHE SPENT a week in the nurses' wing before being transferred to a hospital in Portland, Maine, and then home over winter break to recover. Between the panic that ensued after her discovery and final exams, I barely saw her before she left. Nathaniel and I visited her every afternoon, but most of the time she was delirious. The nurses said that she was technically fine; they couldn't determine if anything traumatic had happened to her other than malnutrition and a slight case of pneumonia from being in cold water for such a long time. But there were a few complications. Her skin was freezing yet she refused to use any blankets or sheets; she was hungry but turned away all of the food given to her; she was tired but she never slept. Eleanor didn't know what had happened either. She told Mrs. Lynch that the only thing she remembered was going to the library to study. After that, everything was blurry.

The news only made people more uncomfortable. Had she been attacked? Was it an accident? I obviously thought the former, though the fact that she wasn't afflicted with any sort of heart failure did disturb my theory. And even though I was happy she was safe, I was also more confused. Mrs. Lynch reopened the investigation, looking for new leads, new evidence. But just when they were ready to begin, winter came in full force, burying the campus – and all of its secrets – beneath a metre of snow.

But let me rewind. After Dante carried Eleanor out of the girls' dormitory, he came and found me in the bushes. "This is a nice spot," he said over my shoulder into the evergreen shrubs. I all but screamed at the shock of him suddenly behind me.

"How did you find her?" I asked him.

"You said you thought she was in the basement. So I've been going to the dorm every day to check."

I gave him a curious look. "I didn't tell you that I thought she was in the basement," I said. "I told Eleanor's father that."

Dante stared at me. "You didn't?"

I shook my head. "No."

Dante looked troubled, but I didn't care.

"Cassandra is dead," I said bluntly, because how else can you say something like that? "I saw her file. Which I found in Gideon's room, by the way."

"How did you get into Gideon's..." But his words trailed off. "Wait, her file? You have it?"

"Yes, but—"

Suddenly he stood up. "Show me."

I led him to the third floor of the library. On the way I told him about the rest of the files and their contents, and the real reason why I'd wanted to find them. But when we got to the oversized book section, the files were gone. I double-checked the decimal numbers, even took half the books off the shelves and shook them by their spines, but the files were unmistakably missing.

"They were here," I said. "I put them back the other day."

"Did you show them to anyone else?"

"Only Nathaniel, but he wouldn't have taken them."

"Could anyone else have known that you took them?"

I shook my head, until I remembered running into Gideon as I was leaving the boys' dormitory. By now he must have realized that someone had been in his room and that the files were gone, but could he have known it was me, and followed me to the library? I swallowed. "Yes."

* * *

Finals came and went. I studied for them in a blur, meeting up with Nathaniel during study hall, where we talked briefly about Minnie's story. Nathaniel brushed it off. "Everyone knows she's crazy," he said, looking up from his geometric proof. And somewhere between exams and my study dates with Dante, I tried to do research, starting with the cryptic phrases on the school files, because it was the only evidence I had. This time Dante helped me, though by help, I mean sat next to me in the library scouring Latin books without telling me how they were relevant to figuring out why Gideon had had the files and what the files actually meant. But all of my work yielded nothing. When I asked Dante if *Non Mortuus* meant anything to him, he replied, "*Not Dead.*"

"I translated that too," I said over my book. "But does it have any significance to you?"

Dante shook his head. "No."

"What about *Undead*?"

He laughed. "Like revenants and zombies?"

I sighed. "That's all I could come up with too."

There were virtually no books or documents on Gottfried Academy, just like the article had said, and no matter how many times I searched "Undead" in the library catalogue or online, I couldn't find a single legitimate piece of information other than the expected websites about the general category of vampires and ghouls and zombies. I tried "*Non Mortuus,* Gottfried", and then "*Sepultura,* Attica Falls", and then various iterations of "Cassandra Millet", "*Non Mortuus*", "Two Deaths", "Benjamin Gallow", and "Deceased", before I gave up.

By the Friday before Christmas, everyone had already started to leave campus. Cars lined the half-crescent driveway in front of Archebald Hall; chauffeurs were packing luggage in trunks while everyone said goodbye for the winter holidays.

Dustin came, just like he said he would, in my grandfather's Aston Martin. I was standing with Dante beneath the lamp post in front of the building, my luggage resting at my feet as large flakes of snow floated down on us. When I saw Dustin pull up the path, I threw my arms around Dante, breathing in the woodsy smell of his skin for the last time before break.

"I don't want to go," I said. "I want to stay here with you."

"It's only a few weeks," he said, checking his watch. "See, we're already five minutes closer to seeing each other again."

"Come with me," I said. "It'll be so much fun. We'll explore the mansion, play croquet in the snow, sneak into my grandfather's cigar parlour..."

Dante shook his head and laughed. "As tempting as that

sounds, I'm not sure your grandfather would like me."

I sighed. "Okay, fine. How about this: on Christmas Eve, I'll sneak into my grandfather's library, and you sneak into Copleston Library, and it will almost be like we're together."

Dante raised an eyebrow. "And on the night in question, what kind of book should I be reading?"

"A love story. And not a tragic one. I hate those."

"It's a date."

I heard the engine turn off and the car door open. "Miss Winters," Dustin said with a smile, stepping out of the car in a three-piece suit. Against my protests that I could do it myself, Dante carried my luggage and packed it in the trunk, while Dustin held the door for me.

"Bye," I whispered through the window as we backed down the path, my breath leaving a foggy imprint on the glass where Dante's face had been.

After a long snowy drive through evergreen forests and quaint New England towns, we arrived at the Wintershire House. Its sprawling lawn was now covered in snow, the trees naked and glazed in a glassy sheen of ice. As we meandered up the driveway, the black lamp posts turned on, one by one, until we reached the crescent entry of the mansion.

Dustin opened the car door for me, and I stepped into the greying December dusk. The windows of the mansion glowed warmly, and I walked inside, past the frozen fountain and the topiaries, which lined the front of the yard like faceless statues.

"Your grandfather will be arriving for dinner shortly. In the meantime, I'll take the liberty of bringing your luggage upstairs to Miss Lydia's old room."

Dinner was served promptly at seven o'clock. I barely had time to unpack my bags when the grandfather clock downstairs chimed. Minutes later, Dustin knocked on my door, wearing a dinner suit and bow tie. He led me down through the foyer, where two men were standing on ladders, stringing lights around a six-metre-tall Christmas tree.

My grandfather was already seated at one end of an excessively long table in the main dining room, which was decorated almost as lavishly as Gottfried's Megaron. He smiled and stood up as I entered. "Renée," he said warmly, giving me a stiff hug before unbuttoning his dinner jacket. His face was pink and weathered from the cold, his nose and ears even larger and droopier than they were in summer. A heavy chandelier hung over the middle of the room, and candles decorated the centre of the table. Dustin bowed as he pulled out my chair for me, and after a flurry of swift swoops, I was suddenly sitting down, my chair pushed into the table, a napkin draped over my lap, a bowl of salmon-coloured soup in front of me.

"Thanks," I said, trying to decide which spoon to use.

Dustin made a modest bow and retreated to the kitchen to bring out our meals. My grandfather smiled from the seat beside me at the head of the table. He had a moustache now, bushy and white like a mop, and I watched it expectantly as he took a mouthful of soup. Our places were set with an elaborate array of cutlery that included far too many forks and spoons. I chose the smallest one and dipped it in my bowl. All at once, the flavours and textures unfolded in my mouth: salty turning to bitter, and then tart and sweet.

"It's cold," I blurted out. "And bitter. But also kind of fruity."

"It's supposed to be cold, my dear. And that's the goat cheese you're tasting. *Potage effrayant de figue, tomate et fromage de chèvre.* And quite delicious," my grandfather said, raising a glass of Scotch to Dustin. "Thank you."

I managed a smile as Dustin replaced my soup with the second course, a delicate arrangement of asparagus, stuffed figs and duck confit. We ate in silence.

"I was informed about your room-mate," my grandfather said, working at his duck with a fork and knife. "I'm glad she has recovered. I'm told she's doing well?"

"She was trapped in a flooded basement for over a week," I said.

He stopped chewing. "Yes, I was aware. I've already

spoken to my contacts at the school." His knife scraped the plate. "So how are you finding your classes? Stimulating?"

I put down my fork. A giant moose head stared at me from over the mantel. "I know what you were," I said, watching him eat.

My grandfather coughed, choking on a fig. After pounding his chest with his fist twice, he composed himself. "What's that, you said?"

"I know what you were."

My grandfather exchanged a glance with Dustin, who was standing in the corner of the room with a napkin draped over his forearm. My grandfather put his fork down and let out a sigh of relief. "You must have questions. I knew you would come to it on your own once you started at Gottfried. Though I did not think it would be this quickly. Your mother didn't figure it out until she was elected to the Board of Monitors in her third year. That's how she met your father."

I sat back in my chair. My parents were Monitors? "What do you mean she didn't figure it out until her third year? Wasn't it obvious when she saw you around campus?"

"Surely you must have realized it when you began Horticulture?"

I shook my head, confused. "Horticulture? What does that have to do with you being headmaster?"

My grandfather considered my words. "My being headmaster? This is the matter that you wished to discuss?"

"Why didn't you tell me?"

Picking up his glass of Scotch, he sat back in his chair, the ice cubes clinking as he took a sip. "I am sorry," he said slowly. "It must have slipped my mind."

"Really?" I said sceptically. "Because it seems kind of convenient that you would remember to tell me that my parents went to Gottfried, but forget to mention that you were the headmaster for over thirty years and that my parents were Monitors."

The candlelight flickered. "I'm glad to see you're getting a good education," my grandfather said, finishing his drink in one gulp. "Dustin, could you fetch me another Scotch?"

"What caused the heart attacks?"

My grandfather narrowed his eyes. "Heart attacks?"

"I know you know what I'm talking about. The Gottfried Curse."

"Legend and lore created by idle townspeople and failing journalists."

"But last year two students were murdered."

"Just one. Benjamin Gallow," he said. I gazed at my grandfather in astonishment. "Yes, I was made aware of his death and Cassandra's...disappearance."

I blinked, baffled that he wasn't more disturbed by this information. "Why did you send me there if you knew it wasn't safe? Even if the Gottfried Curse is a legend, you knew about it."

"Your parents died; you were far less safe in California."

"Why not send me to a different school?"

"Our family has been attending Gottfried for centuries," my grandfather said loudly. "There *are* no other schools."

Infuriated, I stood up. Dustin rushed over to my seat to pull my chair back for me. "My room-mate is in the hospital and my parents are dead. Cassandra Millet is dead too. I read it in her file, her official Gottfried file, which means the school is covering it up. Minnie Roberts claims that the headmistress and the Board of Monitors are behind it."

My grandfather set his fork down on his plate. "That is preposterous," he said quietly. "You trust the words of a girl you barely know, without any other proof, and against the words of the headmistress and the Board of Monitors, at an institution in which your parents placed their utmost trust. And here I thought you were intelligent."

I went silent.

"You're here, and you're safe. Or as safe as one can be in this world. Now, I want you to listen to me very carefully. Education is safety. Knowing what's out there is safety.

Knowing how to fight and protect yourself is safety. So sit down. We still have one more course."

With no better option, I obliged. Dustin pushed in my chair for me. "Thanks," I mumbled over my shoulder as he retreated to the kitchen to bring out dessert.

"I was the headmaster at Gottfried Academy for thirty-two years, during which time your mother and father attended the school. That is where they met, as you already know. The Gottfried Curse is a legend, nothing more. While I was the headmaster, there were no accidents, no deaths. I became familiar with many of the faculty members that teach at Gottfried today. Professor Lumbar was a colleague; as were Professors Starking, Mumm and Chortle. Annette LaBarge was a classmate of your mother's, and a good friend of both your parents. And while Headmistress Von Laark was a new hire when I was reaching the end of my last term, I have reason to believe that you are in the best of hands at Gottfried."

"But they're just...they're just teachers. What could they do? They obviously couldn't protect Eleanor."

"Some things in this world, as you know, are unpreventable. It is my belief that if it were not for the current professors, the students at Gottfried would be far less safe. As is the case with most other schools."

That evening, while I was looking through my mother's papers, trying to find out more about who she and my father were when they were at Gottfried, Dustin knocked on my door. He was holding a tray with a note on top. "A phone call for Miss Renée," he said properly, with the twinge of a smile. I picked up the note and unfolded it. *Mr. Dante Berlin.*

"He's on the phone? Right now?"

Dustin made a little bow in reply. Unable to contain my excitement, I ran downstairs to the sitting room.

"Hello?" I said, barely believing that he was on the end of the line.

Dante's voice reverberated gently through the phone. "I had to hear your voice."

I coiled the cord around my fingers. "So I guess that means you miss me already."

I expected him to laugh, but to my surprise, he was serious. "I do. Very much. I don't like being away from you."

Smiling into the receiver, I sat on the chaise longue, cradling the phone. "Well, hi," I said softly.

I imagined his dark, pensive eyes staring into mine. "Hi," he said in a hushed tone. "So tell me what I missed."

I told him about my grandfather, about our conversation over dinner and how my parents were Monitors, about the long table and the moose head and the cold soup, which I still wasn't certain I liked yet.

Dante laughed. "No cold soup, no goat cheese. I'll make a mental note. And no Gottfried Curse."

"And for you it's no food at all. No sleep. And no tunnels."

"I'm low maintenance."

"Is that what you are? Because I've been trying to figure it out all semester."

"And what have you concluded?"

"A mutant. A rare disease. A creature from the inferno. *Dante*."

"And what if you found out you were right?" he asked. "What if it meant that I could hurt you?"

"I would say that I'm not scared. Everyone has the ability to hurt. It's the choice that matters."

We talked every night. My grandfather was in and out of the house for business meetings, funding numerous ventures, charitable foundations, et cetera, et cetera. So I spent most of my days alone, exploring the house and the estate grounds. After going through his entire library looking for information on Gottfried, my grandfather, or the curse, I found nothing, and resorted to trudging through the snowy Massachusetts woods in tall boots, imagining my mother doing the same thing when she was my age, her cheeks flushed and rosy, her lips chapped, her nose dripping from the cold.

And even though every morning I prepared myself for the inevitable night when Dante didn't call, he always did. We talked for hours; our voices travelling to each other in waves and currents; the distance somehow pulling us closer together.

After talking to Dante, I looked through my mother's belongings over and over again, picking things up and putting them back delicately, afraid to hold anything for too long. I found dozens of books about cats, a sewing machine and a box of bobbins, a photograph of my mother and father from when they first met. They looked only a little bit older than me and were sitting on the grass beneath a giant tree, staring at each other and smiling. It was my first Christmas without my parents, and I missed them so much it was unbearable.

"Nothing's the same," I told Dante. "I miss cutting down the tree with my dad and trying to fit it into the station wagon. Drinking hot chocolate and listening to cheesy Christmas songs while we decorated the tree together. How my dad always left cookies and milk by the fireplace, even when I was a teenager. The tree here is too perfect. It's not even crooked or anything. It's unnatural."

"Unnatural?" Dante said softly.

"I don't even think its needles fall off. What kind of tree is that?"

"Evergreens aren't supposed to die."

"Everything dies." Immediately I thought of my parents. "Sometimes too soon."

There was a long silence. Finally Dante said, "It will get better, Renée. Don't wish your life away just because your parents lost theirs."

I sighed. "It would be better if you were here."

"I'll get to see you every day for the rest of the school year," he said. "It's only fair that I let your grandfather have a week or two."

"Don't I get a say in this?"

"That's what I worry about. That one morning you'll come to your senses and realize that a girl like you would never want to be with someone like me."

I shook my head, confused. "I would never think that. You helped me pass Latin. You stood up for me in front of Gideon and Vivian and the headmistress. And you found Eleanor. You're like no one I've ever met. What kind of girl do you think I am that I wouldn't want to be with you?"

"Unreal."

On Christmas Eve there was a blizzard. Snow piled up to the windows, burying the lamp posts, the statues, the fountain. I sat through a stiff holiday dinner with my grandfather, Dustin standing in the corner while I picked at my ham. Midway through, I turned to him.

"Why don't you join us?"

Dustin, surprised at being addressed, didn't know how to respond. "I...um...thank you, Miss Winters, but I've already eaten."

"Well, that can't be true. I saw you just before dinner, polishing the silver and setting the table."

Dustin looked embarrassed.

"Thank you, Miss Winters, but I'm quite all right here."

I rolled my eyes. "You don't look all right. You look uncomfortable. Who can stand for that long?"

Dustin's eyes travelled to my grandfather, who coughed and stopped chewing.

"Why yes," my grandfather said with a jolt. "How silly of me. Dustin, please do sit. We have more than enough for three."

I gazed at the heaped platter of ham and cured meats and yams in front of us, and stood up to pull out the chair next to me for Dustin. "You can use one of my forks. I have too many anyway."

So Dustin sat down at the table, probably for the first time.

After dinner I helped him clear the table. Then we did the dishes together and left a glass of milk and two cookies beneath the tree. My grandfather retired to the Smoking Parlour. "Merry Christmas, Renée," he said, squeezing my shoulder. He put on his glasses. "If you need anything, I'll be downstairs."

Just before midnight I crept downstairs in my mother's pyjamas. The Gingham Library was a few rooms down from the Smoking Parlour, in between the Game Parlour and the Red Room. Although it seemed silly, the idea that Dante would be in the Copleston Library thinking of me, while I was in my grandfather's library, was the only thing that helped me forget about my parents. The house was quiet and dark, save for the Christmas tree, its lights twinkling in the foyer. As I tiptoed down the hall I could see snow falling past the windows in the moonlight. Portraits of men in three-corner hats and velvet scarves lined the walls, their eyes seeming to follow me as I passed.

But just as I turned the corner, I heard footsteps thumping against the floor. The light in my grandfather's study was still on, beaming under the door. Even though I wasn't at school, I still didn't want to be caught wandering around at night. Just as his doorknob turned, I ran, slipping around the corners in my socks until I found myself in the kitchen.

I decided to get a glass of milk while I was there. So I opened the cupboards, looking for a cup. The kitchen was glistening in the dark, the moonlight reflecting off the long granite countertops, the hanging pots and pans, the knives stuck magnetically to the wall. I had never been in there alone; the kitchen staff was always preparing or cleaning something.

Finally I opened what turned out to be a huge lazy Susan. In the back, I spotted a row of mugs hanging from hooks. Leaning in, I grasped at one, but it was just out of my reach. So I stepped in, plucking the cup from the hook. Down the hall, the grandfather clock chimed midnight. The lazy Susan trembled, and I grasped at the hooks while it rotated. And suddenly I was on the other side of the wall.

An odd sort of room welcomed me with warm, stale air. It was large with angular ceilings and narrow windows that diffracted the moonlight off the walls, giving the room the hazy feeling of an attic. A living room, I thought. One that I had never seen before. One that looked oddly similar to the Second Living Room. I thought back to the tour Dustin had given me on the first day. There was no First Living Room, he had told me. But he was wrong, because I was standing in it.

There were no doors. A staircase carved into the corner led up to the first floor. I walked around, examining the taxidermied animals hung about the room: a raccoon, a badger, a full-sized cougar scowling above the fireplace. In a glass hutch by the windows there was a collection of shovels and odd-looking gardening tools. Surrounding everything were walls and walls of books.

I didn't recognize the authors or titles of any of them. More than half were in Latin or some version of Old or Middle Latin that used an earlier form of the alphabet. The others were antique and leather bound, translated from Greek or French or Italian. They must have been hundreds of years old, I thought, running my hands along their cracked covers until I stopped at a title that caught my eye. I crooked my head to make sure I was reading it correctly. *Seventh Meditation* by René Descartes.

I pulled it out. It was the same book that Miss LaBarge had mentioned in class, the book that had been banned in Europe, that most people didn't even know existed. I opened it. The table of contents read as follows:

I. OF DEATH AND THE SOUL
II. OF THE DEATH OF CHILDREN
III. OF *NON MORTUUS*
IV. OF BURIAL RITUALS
V. OF LATIN AND ITS EXTINCTION
VI. OF IMMORTALITY

In shock, I reread the title of chapter three, "Of *Non Mortuus*". The files, I thought to myself. Those were the words describing Cassandra Millet's status in her file. Through the walls I heard the clock chime a muffled twelve thirty. I gazed around the room, clutching the book to my chest. I had to find a way out. It seemed I had two options: go back through the pantry, or go up. Out of curiosity, I climbed up to the first floor.

It opened into my grandfather's dressing closet. I pushed through his suits until I heard the hangers jangle together. Clasping them still, I froze, waiting for him to burst into the closet, take the book, and punish me. But nothing happened. Stepping carefully over his shoes and horns and polish, I slipped out the door and into his room. His bed was empty. He must still be downstairs, I thought. In the Smoking Parlour or the study, where he often had a nightcap. Letting out a sigh of relief, I escaped into the hallway and ran down the corridor to the east wing.

CHAPTER 13

THE SEVENTH MEDITATION

WHEN I GOT BACK TO MY ROOM I shut the door behind me, turned on the bedside lamp, and sank to the ground. *Seventh Meditation* was a small leather-bound book with unevenly cut pages that had been faded yellow by the sun. It left a dusty residue on my fingers. I opened it, excitement stirring within me. The pages were so stiff I worried they would fall out if I turned them too quickly. Carefully, I flipped to the first section and began to read.

I. OF DEATH AND THE SOUL
In these meditations, I will attempt to consider

the idea of the Dead as Undead. Matters of the Body and Soul are ones that our faithful institutions of government and justice would like to keep hidden. Therefore, in accordance with the idea that knowledge should be accessible to all men, I will divulge in these writings the little-known facts about Life and Death.

I skimmed until I reached the following text:

Humans are made of two things – a *Body* and a *Soul*. Upon death, a person's body dies, after which point his soul is "cleansed" and reborn into a new person. This is why some moments feel as though we've lived them twice; why a person can often have the same essence as someone who died decades before.

The text was peppered with diagrams and sketches – one of the human body; another of the cross section of a human head, inside of which was a drawing of a homunculus. This, presumably, was the soul. I skipped forward to the next section.

II. Of the Death of Children
The matter of Children is one that is particularly troubling to adults. All adults follow the rules

stipulated in Part I of this Meditation. However, there is one exception. When a child dies, his *Soul* leaves his body. Yet, in opposition to our customary education of the biological processes of Life and Death, the child does not die. Instead of "dying", as adult bodies do, the child's body lies dormant for nine days. On the tenth day it rises again without a soul. The child then wanders the world, searching for it. It is my supposition that this is nature's way of giving youth a second chance at life. They are what we call *Non Mortuus,* or the *Undead.*

Non Mortuus. That was the word on Cassandra's file. Did that mean she was Undead? I scanned the page. Beside the text were more sketches, this time of children lying in a field. It looked like they were sleeping, though after reading the text, I knew that they were "dead". I flipped forward.

III. Of *Non Mortuus*
The Undead have no Souls. They cannot be killed by normal means, for they are already dead. Although they are still children, and appear harmless, this is a falsehood. The Undead have no human instincts. They do not eat, they do not sleep, they do not feel. With time, their bodies decay, and they must

constantly seek ways to preserve themselves before their bodies die again and return to the earth.

The observed characteristics of the Undead are those often associated with other dead creatures. Skin that is cold to the touch. A stiffness of the limbs. Breath that contains no human warmth. They have also been identified to have incredible healing powers, their wounds closing as quickly as they are broken. Fluency in Latin and Latinate tongues. A lack of complete sensation and emotion. Yet most notably, they are known to reanimate into the best versions of themselves. Stronger than their human form, or more intelligent, or more beautiful.

My heart began to race as my eyes darted back and forth across the text. I was no longer thinking about Cassandra and Benjamin. *Skin that was cold to the touch. A stiffness of the limbs. Breath that contained no human warmth. Fluency in Latin.*

I read the words over and over, trying to find some other explanation for what I now realized were symptoms. But it all fitted. The cold skin and breath, the way he had healed in a heartbeat. I hadn't been seeing things. It was all true. That's why he never wore a jacket, why he never came to the dining hall, why he never slept. Because he wasn't human.

He was dead. But what did it even mean to be Undead? The word conjured up grotesque images of corpses and vampires and mindless creatures staggering around in a trance. But Dante wasn't any of those. Was he?

Thus, their existence is a tortured and miserable one. They have but one purpose – to seek and obtain their missing Soul. They have twenty-one years to find it, twenty-one being the number demarcating the transformation from child to adult. If by their twenty-first year they do not find their soul, they begin to decompose at an accelerated rate until their bodies are completely destroyed. This, I have observed to be a particularly painful process. However, if they do find the person with their Soul, they reclaim it through the pressing together of mouths, otherwise known as *Basium Mortis*. Through this act the Undead becomes human again, and lives a natural life. The victim dies from a failure of the heart, their corpse aged and withered without its soul.

I reread the last sentence. It described my parents. Benjamin Gallow. And most likely all of the people who had died of heart attacks at Gottfried. This was the Curse. The Undead.

The danger of the Undead lies in this method, for they are also able to take Souls that are not theirs. This temporarily reverses the decaying process; however, it also results in the death of the other. The problem for humans lies in the dire handicap that we are unable to distinguish between the living and the Undead. In my logic, it would thus seem that humans are doomed to fall under the mercy of these unkillable, soulless creatures...

Basium Mortis. The cause of death in Benjamin's file. Did he die because someone took his soul? I turned the page. The pictures were disturbing. They showed children sucking the souls out of other children. Their faces looked hungry and bestial, driven by animal cravings. Though strangely, I thought, it looked like they were kissing. The realization struck me, and I sat up and gasped. *Kissing.* Dante refused to kiss me on the lips. This must be why. A kiss could kill me.

IV. OF BURIAL RITUALS

Ancient civilizations discovered a way to prevent children from turning into the Undead. Before this period, burial rituals were not yet in existence. The dead were left to nature, which was the fate that all of Earth's creatures met when they died. The

Egyptians were among the first to discover that by mummifying their dead and encasing them in pyramids, the children wouldn't rise again.

Later civilizations found that there were three things the Undead could not withstand without decaying: fire, geometric golden ratios and the underground. Since then, each society has discovered new ways of preventing the Undead from rising: by fire – funeral pyres and cremation; by golden ratio – coffins and pyramids; and by the underground – burials and catacombs. Each of these rituals was created for one sole purpose – to let our children rest.

Over time and transgression, the rituals became so ingrained in society that people forgot why they were performed. Soon, everyone – including adults – was buried or cremated, and no one remembered that children *could* rise from the dead.

The words blurred as tears filled my eyes. Raising a trembling hand, I wiped them away with the back of my fist. Images of Dante lying dead in a field flooded my mind as I gazed at the pictures, unable to look away. To illustrate the burial rituals, Descartes had drawn diagrams of each tradition, with steps next to it. One was a six-sided coffin, around which Descartes noted how it had to be made of a hard wood, nailed shut, and buried no less than six feet beneath the earth. This was why Dante didn't go underground. It wasn't a childhood trauma, per se, although dying was traumatizing. He didn't go underground because he couldn't; otherwise he would die for good.

I skimmed through the next few pages, examining the diagrams and rules of the pyramids, of mummification and embalmment. In the margins were all kinds of notes about the kind of gauze that had to be used, the number of layers the mummy had to be wrapped in, and the design of the maze within the pyramids and their geometric orientation. They were all familiar to me from History class, as mummies were of particular interest to Professor Bliss, though I had never considered their purpose.

The next drawing was of a body with coins on its eyes, resting on a funeral pyre. The use of coins, Descartes explained, was a discovery of the Greeks, and were given to the dead so they could pay the boatman on the river Styx to take them to Hades. Below it was a picture of a child with cloth stuffed in his mouth. I stared at it, unable to believe what I was seeing. My parents couldn't have been Undead; they were adults. So why would they have died that way? And what did their deaths have to do with any of this?

V. Of Latin and Its Extinction
Latin is the language the Undead speak. In ancient

times, before the founding of the Roman Empire, before people discovered burial rituals, Latin was only spoken by children. It was the one way to tell who was Undead and who was alive.

In Roman mythology, two children were the original founders of Rome. Their names were Romulus and Remus, and they were brothers. While this is a commonly accepted myth among educated society, what most are not aware of is that Romulus and Remus were Undead, having both drowned in the River Tiber before rising again.

Before the founding of Rome, knowledge of the existence of the Undead was not prevalent. Romulus and Remus gained followers by displaying their incredible abilities in large public gatherings. People were awed at their inhuman healing powers, their inability to be killed by normal means, and their advanced rhetoric and linguistic skills, and believed the children to be sent from the gods to found their city.

However, they quarrelled over who would be king. Romulus slew Remus by burying him alive. As the first king of Rome, Romulus instituted Latin as the primary language, teaching it not only to children, but to adults of the upper class who were involved in governmental matters.

Eventually the clergy adopted Latin. Since Latin came so naturally to the Undead, they believed it had to be a language sent from the gods. Meanwhile, Romulus was trying to find his lost soul, and worried that the other Undead in Rome would accidentally take it. He thus instituted burial rituals and funeral pyres to rid the city of the Undead.

Skimming through the history of Latin through the ages, I skipped ahead to the part on its decline.

With the spread of Protestantism and the reform of the Catholic Church, Latin slowly died out, replaced by the Romance languages. Many people forgot about the Undead and, consequently, the origins of Latin. Thus, it came as a surprise when an entire language ceased to exist. Of course, one realizes that a language can only become extinct when the people who speak it have been exterminated.

Romulus and Remus. The first things that came to mind when I heard those names weren't children, but cats. Siamese cats. The ones roaming about the headmistress's office. It couldn't be a coincidence. The rest sounded vaguely familiar from Latin class, but I hadn't paid enough attention to fully comprehend what Professor Lumbar had meant. Still, Latin wasn't my concern. Cassandra was Undead. Benjamin's soul was taken. Then Cassandra was somehow killed again. Buried. And the school's administration knew about it and was covering it up. Why?

And then there was Dante. My Dante. *Undead* Dante. Slowly, everything began to make sense. I went over everything, every subtle turn of phrase, every inexplicable moment – the séance, the paper cut, the way I felt when he touched me.

He had been on the green the night of the séance because I had accidentally conjured him. He couldn't go in the tunnel with me. His Latin was perfect, but he told me he hadn't studied it before coming here. I thought about what Professor Lumbar had written on the board on the first day of class. *Latin: The Language of the Dead.* "I just woke up one morning and it clicked," Dante had explained that night in the classroom. By that logic, the rest of the Latin club – Gideon, Vivian, Yago and Cassandra – must have all been Undead too.

His skin was always freezing. He didn't use a blanket and he rarely wore a jacket unless he knew I might need it. He kept his windows open even in the winter and seemed impervious to the weather.

And he never slept. He rarely came to the dining hall.

He wouldn't kiss me on the lips. And when he touched me, the world blurred, sounds and smells and tastes collided into an unrecognizable dissonance. Maybe that was why I always felt weak when I was around him: because he was somehow draining the sensation from my body into his.

But if I accepted the fact that my boyfriend was dead, what did that mean? Did these sensations happen to everyone who was around him? Suddenly I felt weak. I crawled into bed, where I stared at the ceiling and thought about death and life and everything in between, until the sun cracked open its eye.

On Christmas morning, Dustin knocked on my door. "Miss Winters," he said cheerfully. "Breakfast."

I didn't move. My parents were dead. My boyfriend was dead. My grandfather had a mysterious hidden room that had books about the walking dead – which is what I knew I would feel like if I attempted to stand up.

"I don't feel well," I said meekly, and rolled over.

"Miss Winters," Dustin said, knocking again. "Are you quite all right?"

"No. Please go away."

He lingered a few seconds longer before I heard the muffled sounds of his footsteps disappearing down the stairs. Not long after, there was another knock. This time, no one waited for me to reply. My grandfather ducked into the room.

"Dustin told me you weren't feeling well," he said, cautiously stepping close to my bed. He set a glass of orange juice on my bedside table. "I've brought you some juice."

"Please go away," I said, my voice trembling.

There was a long silence. I heard my grandfather bend over and pick up *Seventh Meditation*, which I had stupidly left on my bedside table.

He sat on the edge of my bed and placed his hand on the outline of my ankle beneath the blankets. He smelled of cigars and leather. "Death is nothing to be afraid of."

"It's not death I'm afraid of."

"What is it, then?"

"Life," I said, my voice small. The thought of living without my parents was practically unbearable, and Dante was the only person who gave me something to live for. Now that I knew he was dead, it seemed like there was nothing left.

"I haven't been honest with you, Renée. I know this," he said gently. "But if you'll get dressed and come downstairs, I'll explain everything over breakfast."

I blinked back tears. He waited a few seconds longer, but I made no effort to respond. Finally he stood up. I heard the door click shut behind him.

Slowly, I willed myself out of bed and got dressed. I rinsed my face and pulled my hair back into a ponytail. When I glanced at my reflection in the mirror, it was frightening: my eyes swollen, the circles beneath them making my face look hollow.

"Is it true?" I asked, sitting down at the breakfast table.

My grandfather looked up from his coffee and newspaper. Outside it was sunny and snowing, the entire world white and happy, as if the day were mocking me. Beneath the Christmas tree were stacks of presents.

"Is it true that my parents were killed by the Undead?"

My grandfather shuffled around his newspaper and glanced at Dustin, who left for the kitchen. "Yes."

A portrait of Charlemagne standing valiantly over a slaughtered boar hung on the opposite wall. I stared at it in silence as I imagined my parents' last moments. The gauze and coins, which I still couldn't make sense of. And then a faceless child, wild and bestial, sucking the life from their bodies. I closed my eyes as the face transformed into Dante's. Had he killed people? Had he taken innocent lives?

"Who was it?" I demanded, suddenly angry.

My grandfather clasped his hands together and shook his head. "I have spent every day since their deaths trying to figure that out. But sadly, I do not have an answer

382

for you. The Undead are hard to track, especially when they perform random acts of violence, which I suspect was the case with your parents."

A random act of violence? It couldn't be. There had to be a better reason than that. "But what about Benjamin Gallow? He'd died under almost exactly the same conditions."

"Exactly. They were all killed by *Non Mortuus*. It isn't as rare as you think. Why do you think Gottfried exists?"

"So...so everything in the book is true?"

"Most of it. The rest is based on myth and assumption."

"The Undead," I said, trying to get used to the idea. "What exactly are they?"

"Children who died and were not buried."

"So they're like zombies?"

"The common depiction of the zombie does not do them full justice. They have functioning minds, they have thoughts. The only difference is that they don't have souls, which leaves them unable to feel sensation. They can see and hear, but they cannot perceive beauty or sadness or wonder associated with the things they see or the sounds they hear."

"Are you sure?" Dante definitely felt sensation when he was around me. Hadn't he told me that in his room the night after Grub Day?

"Quite positive. It's one of the primary characteristics of the Undead."

"Even when they're around a living person?"

"Yes, even when they're around a living person."

I hesitated. "So anyone can become Undead?"

"Only people who die before the age of twenty-one. You, for example, could become Undead if you died and were not buried or cremated or mummified."

"And then someone else would have my soul?"

"Yes. A child born on the same day that you died."

"And then I would be soulless for twenty-one more years, before I died again?"

"If you weren't buried, yes. Though the myth is that if you somehow found the person with your soul, you could take it back by *Basium Mortis,* or sucking the soul back into the body. Then you would be human again, and live a natural life span."

I imagined Dante taking his soul back from a child, but quickly shook the thought from my head. "Why is it a myth?"

"Because finding one's soul is an almost impossible task. Think of the odds – how many people are born and die each day, all over the world. There hasn't been a single recorded episode of an Undead finding and taking its soul back. It is the great myth of history. That one can cheat death."

I couldn't ignore my grandfather's use of the word *its*. "So why do people think it's *possible*?"

"Because it *is* possible for the Undead to take souls that aren't theirs. It delays the decaying process, giving them a few more years of 'life' before they begin to decline."

"And the human who loses his soul dies?"

My grandfather nodded. "Or, if he isn't discovered and is under the age of twenty-one, he could also become Undead."

"But then couldn't he just take his soul back from the Undead who took it?"

"No, because a taken soul will not occupy the Undead who performs *Basium Mortis* unless it is the original soul of the Undead. Otherwise, it will soon leave the Undead and be reborn anew."

Dustin brought out a plate of poached eggs and Canadian bacon.

"So Gottfried Academy is...is a school for zombies?"

"The Undead," my grandfather corrected. "And no, it isn't. Not exclusively, at least. Though at one point it was."

I waited for my grandfather to continue. He cleared his throat. "It was originally founded to educate the Undead about who they were. As you probably know, Bertrand Gottfried was a doctor who built the school as an infirmary for children. What many do not know is that it was an infirmary for *dead* children.

"He had learned about the existence of the Undead years before founding the infirmary. His idea was to create a hospital that housed Undead children, so he could study them. He was trying to figure out how the bodies of children differed from adults, for only children can reanimate. The seclusion of Attica Falls was one reason why the location was ideal, as was the altitude and climate. At the age of twenty-one 'Undead years', as some call them, the children begin to rapidly decay. Cool temperatures help prevent that process, much like the effect of a refrigerator. The last reason was the lake. Salt is a preservative; each patient was required to take a bath in the lake every morning.

"Now, as you may know, soon after the infirmary was founded there was a reported outbreak of the measles and mumps, which killed over a hundred children. Of course, disease wasn't the real cause of death. Many of Bertrand's patients were due to expire around the same two-year period. Although Bertrand had devised many ways to help prolong the 'life' of the Undead, he had not discovered a way to stop their decay. They all perished. Most of the children didn't have parents or families, so there were no further inquiries." My grandfather held out his coffee cup, and Dustin stepped up to the table and spooned sugar into it.

"When all the children died, Bertrand didn't know

what to do with the bodies. Instead of burying them in plots, he dug a vast underground tomb. Yet these catacombs also served another purpose: if Bertrand encountered an Undead that he wished to put to rest, he could bury them there.

"Unfortunately, Bertrand died not long after the infirmary opened. He was found in the lake. Of course, it wasn't a natural death. One of his patients took his soul.

"After he died, the three founding nurses shut down the infirmary, keeping only the current patients inside. During that time, they went through his office and discovered hundreds of pages of notes and a journal, in which he had documented his findings. His notes have been integral in shaping our understanding of the Undead and how they function. He had also developed plans to turn the infirmary into a school for the Undead. The nurses carried out his wishes and reopened the school as Gottfried Academy. The purpose of the school was to teach the Undead how to live out their 'lives' without searching for their soul or taking the souls of others.

"At first it was only a school for the Undead. The nurses sought to educate them not only in worldly matters, but in matters concerning their situation. Many Undead children were unaware that they were dead. As a result, they suffered from existential crises."

"What do you mean *existential crises*?"

"Imagine waking up one morning and everything is the same, except different. You don't like food any more. You never sleep. You can't hear or see or smell things the way you used to. You feel a constant emptiness within you."

"That's the way I felt when my parents died," I said softly.

My grandfather nodded. "Existential crises happen to everyone. With humans it's emotional rather than biological. This is the real Gottfried curse – the fate the Undead are faced with – and when they are unaware of what is happening to them, they can be very dangerous. Imagine an Undead girl trying to kiss a boy. She would accidentally take his soul and kill him."

Which was why Dante wouldn't kiss me, I thought.

"With the medical and technological advances over time, the Undead became rare, as fewer children died and more of those who did were buried. Slowly, the school began to integrate living children into its student body. Gottfried needed money, and accepting normal students, or what we refer to as 'Plebeians', was a secure way to keep the school running."

Plebeians. I had seen that word before, in Benjamin Gallow's file. "But wasn't it unsafe for them?"

"At first, yes. There were a slew of 'accidents', all caused by the Undead. The school opened and closed, and was soiled by scandals that were artfully covered up by the faculty as natural disasters or epidemics. They only stopped when a new headmaster took over and revolutionized the school, training faculty in defence and burial rituals, designing more proactive coursework, and instituting a stricter code of rules and regulations, which has now become the *Gottfried Academy Code of Discipline*. All of the rules have practical safety applications. For example, the banning of romantic relationships was designed to prevent accidental *Basium Mortis*."

"But it's still unsafe."

"Although the Undead are rather rare these days, there's still a chance of encountering the Undead at any school in the country. Plebeians are far better off encountering them at Gottfried, where there are trained professors and rules. Moreover, the only way to truly teach the Undead not to kill is to expose them to the living, so that they learn to value others not only in theory, but through their friendships. An Undead is far less likely to take the life of a friend than a stranger."

I stared at the food growing cold on my plate and considered Dante. I still couldn't wrap my mind around the idea that he was dead.

"One of the last safety precautions the school took was to dig tunnels that ran through Bertrand Gottfried's original catacombs. As you recall, the Undead cannot go underground. In the event of an attack, professors could direct the Plebeians to the tunnels, where they could seek refuge."

"So all of the professors know about the...the...Undead?" I still had trouble saying the word, as if speaking it out loud made it more real.

"Yes."

"And the...Pleb—"

"Plebeians."

"Right, the Plebeians know about the Undead?"

"No. It has long been Gottfried's policy not to explicitly tell Plebeian students about the existence of the Undead. It was feared that teaching living students about the Undead would create natural segregation and discrimination. The classes at Gottfried address issues that are pertinent to *all* students, not just the Undead."

"But the Undead can tell the difference between the Undead and the living?" I asked, thinking about Cassandra and Benjamin. Had she known that Benjamin was a Plebeian?

"Of course. They were once living themselves; they can recognize the changes one goes through after reanimating because they experienced them first-hand. They also have special classes, in which they are taught about what they are and what it means for them."

Advanced Latin, I thought.

"But more important, they are drawn to life. That is

perhaps their only 'sensation', if you could call it that. So it is a safe assumption that they know the living from the Undead."

"And Gottfried is the only organization in the world that knows about the Undead? No one else knows?"

"There are others. Gottfried is one of three sister schools, each founded by one of the three original nurses who worked with Bertrand. Most of the Undead were listed as disappearances rather than deaths, because the bodies were never found. So when they reanimate and wander home, their loved ones aren't usually aware that they're dead. If they are still in contact with their parents, they might inform them; though more often they prefer to keep their condition to themselves."

"But why? I mean, why is it such a big secret? Why not tell someone? Like the police. Or the government."

My grandfather laughed. "And what would you tell them? Imagine trying to explain the theory of the Undead to someone else. They would think you were insane."

He had a point.

"And even if they believed you, it's difficult to tell the Undead from those who are alive. Can you imagine the kind of damage the police could do if they started blindly arresting children? If the outside world found out, it would be the start of the biggest witch hunt in history."

"How are you so sure? I mean, a long time ago people

did know about the Undead, didn't they? That's how they created all the burial rituals. And then over time we just forgot what they were for."

"Discrimination has always existed, which is exhibited in the fact that they created the rituals in the first place. Romulus killed most of the Undead children in Rome, including his own brother, out of fear."

"So...why did you send me to Gottfried? I'm just a Plebeian, right? What does this have to do with me?"

My grandfather studied me pensively. "Because it is an excellent school. And a safe school. The Undead exist everywhere; at least at Gottfried the professors are aware of their existence and are trained to deal with them. That, and I wished you to know the truth about the world. Aren't you glad you know?"

I shook my head. "I don't know. I mean, yes. And no." Of course I wanted to know the truth. The question was, could I accept it?

That afternoon I went downstairs and knocked on the door to Dustin's quarters. The door opened suddenly. "Miss Winters," he said warmly. "You should have rung the service bell instead of coming all the way down here."

I shrugged. "It's no problem. I don't like using bells anyway."

"What can I do for you?"

"I was wondering if there's a video-rental store around here that's open?"

"There is one but twenty minutes away. Would you like me to take you there?"

"Please."

We drove through the back roads of Massachusetts until we reached a dingy strip mall with a liquor store, a convenience store, a barber shop, an ice-cream parlour and a place that read *KING'S VIDEOS*.

A gawky teenage boy behind the counter eyed us as we came in. I went straight to the horror section in the back.

Without much discrimination, I started pulling movies from the shelves, all about the Undead. *Dawn of the Dead, The Walking Dead, White Zombie, Night of the Living Dead*, and about two dozen others. When I was finished, I brought them to the register. Dustin trailed behind me, carrying the rest.

The boy behind the counter smiled, his teeth crooked and covered with braces. "A zombie freak," he said, giving me a wide grin. "I love this one," he said, holding up a movie with a ghoulish creature on the cover. "It's a classic."

I nodded. "Yeah."

"These are due back in seven days," he said, ringing us up.

"That's fine," Dustin said from behind me. We took the bags and left.

Dustin set up the DVD player in the Red Room, and I arbitrarily picked a movie from the pile and put it in. Images of the Undead flashed in front of my eyes – people rising from the grave, cemeteries overrun by staggering corpses, women screaming as they ran to their houses, chased by zombies; men trapped in their cars, swarmed by the Undead. Over each zombie face I mentally superimposed Dante's, trying to come to terms with what he was.

I didn't leave the Red Room for days. I went from one movie to the next, falling in and out of sleep to the blue light of the screen. Dustin left plates of food outside the door, but I barely touched them. A few times a day my grandfather came in to check on me, hovering awkwardly over the couch before giving up. Every so often I would venture down the hall to get a glass of water from the bathroom. Otherwise, I stayed put. The mansion creaked and groaned as the days grew darker. Gusts of wind rattled the windows. I couldn't eat or sleep. Dante continued to call every night, but I wasn't ready to talk to him. "Tell him I'm busy," I told Dustin when he appeared at the door holding a silver platter with a call note. I couldn't talk to him. Why hadn't he told me? And what was I going to say to him? *Hi, Dante, I know you're the walking dead and that you have a secret desire to kill me. How was your day?*

Night-time was the hardest. I called Annie, but I couldn't tell her about Dante because, where would I begin? So I told her about the mansion and about Eleanor, and she told me about my old friends, who seemed more and more alien to me now. With my parents gone, friends far away, and Dante Undead, I felt so lonely that sometimes I thought I couldn't bear it. I felt betrayed and used and alone – completely and utterly alone. Now that I knew what Dante was, I couldn't fathom how I hadn't seen it before. I wanted to believe that Dante was the kind of boy I'd always dreamed of, the kind of boy who was too perfect to actually exist. And he didn't. Or at least not exactly. Every night I stayed up until the early hours of the morning, curled up on the couch, staring into the darkness until I cried myself into a fitful, haunted sleep.

CHAPTER 14

THE DEAD FOREST

ON THE FIFTH DAY I woke up to two knocks on the door. Wearily, I opened my eyes. In front of me the screen had turned to a scrambled static. Before I could answer, Dustin opened the door, holding a shotgun. I winced at the sudden stream of sunlight. "Miss Winters," he said. "I was wondering if you might accompany me while I hunt for wild game?"

Rubbing my eyes, I gazed from the screen to the gun. It was a bizarre sight, though after watching almost forty hours of horror movies, it didn't seem that weird. I pulled myself off the couch. "Okay."

* * *

"Renée," my grandfather said, delighted to see me at breakfast. "How are you feeling?"

"I could be better."

"I hear there's a boy calling for you," he said over his newspaper.

I shrugged, patting down my hair, which at this point felt like a bird's nest.

"Tell me about him."

"He's no one."

My grandfather gave me a knowing look. "No one indeed. I once heard that from your mother. Two weeks later she had eloped and moved to California, with nothing but your father and the clothes on her back."

I stopped chewing. My parents had eloped? They'd never told me that. "Well, I don't want to talk to him. I've already told Dustin."

"I see," he said, frowning. "Might this have something do with the films you've been watching, and our chat the other night?"

I narrowed my eyes. "No."

Just in time, Dustin walked into the room, armed with the long-barrelled gun, a goose whistle, a bag marked *Shells,* and two brown paper bags.

"Whenever you're ready, Miss Winters."

"I'm ready now," I said, eager to leave the questioning

eyes of my grandfather, who was definitely not going to let Dante go unnoticed.

He clasped his hands over one knee. "What is it today, Dustin?"

"Wild snow geese, sir."

"Excellent. Excellent. Well, have a good time. Try not to shoot any people, now. And if you do, bury them." He winked at me, but I didn't appreciate his humour.

Donning a pair of high rubber boots, a fur-lined parka and earmuffs, I set out with Dustin to the grounds behind the estate. The sky was a cloudless blue, the branches of the evergreens around us heavy with snow. Dustin showed me how to blow the goose whistle, and we followed the sounds of their response calls until we reached a frozen pond.

"Be very still," Dustin said, crouching low while looking through his binoculars at a flock of geese pecking at the snow by the edge of the water. Slowly, he took the duck gun from his shoulder and handed it to me. "Now, all you have to do is aim in their general direction and pull the trigger."

I stared at the gun as if it were a foreign object, not realizing that I was supposed to do the shooting. "I...um... I don't think I can...I mean, I don't really want to kill anything."

"As you wish," he said, handing me his lunch bag. Putting on his goggles, he squinted along the barrel of the gun and aimed it at the pond. And fired.

The birds scattered into the air, flying frantically towards the trees above us. Without flinching, Dustin aimed again, this time almost directly up. There was a squawk, followed by a cloud of feathers. Dustin ripped off his goggles and searched the sky.

"Call!" he shouted.

I looked up. Suddenly I heard something descend through the air. My arms moved without me, and before I knew it, the dead goose dropped into my arms, a flurry of blood and down.

Dustin turned to me, a smile spreading across his face. I screamed and dropped it, shaking the feathers off my hands in a panic.

"An excellent catch, Miss Winters! Excellent!"

"Just Renée," I said, correcting him as I wiped my hands on my jacket. "And nice shot."

"Why, thank you," he said, slinging the bird over his shoulder. "In my time, I was a great skeet proficient."

I nodded, having no clue what he was talking about.

We ate lunch by the pond. Since I didn't want to shoot anything, we ended up sitting by the water, feeding the remaining geese bits of our sandwiches instead.

"Thanks for taking me out here," I said. "It's a nice change of scenery."

"It's my pleasure. I thought you might need a bit of fresh air after all of those films."

I let out a laugh. "Yeah. They were pretty bad." I threw a piece of bread onto the snow.

"Miss Winters—"

"Just Renée," I interjected.

"Very well, then...Renée. I feel compelled to tell you that movies often do not depict reality. The people in your life are still the same people you knew before."

"Except they're not people."

Dustin gazed out over the lake.

"This Mr. Berlin. Has he offended you in some way?"

"He lied to me about who he was. He made me think I was losing my mind and seeing things, when he knew I wasn't."

Dustin frowned and hoisted himself up. "I see. Well, I suppose it's settled, then. Shall we pack up and head back?"

I let my eyes wander over the geese still grazing by my feet, realizing that I didn't want it to be settled. "Yeah, I guess so." And in the dwindling afternoon light we made our way back to the mansion.

"Dustin, did you know about...?" I asked him before we went inside.

"About what?"

"I know you were listening at breakfast. You were there, in the corner. You must know."

"I have been aware of the existence of the Undead

since...since I was your age," he said, opening the door for me. "And yet I still trust your grandfather with your safety."

Wiping my boots on the mat, I stepped inside, peeling off my outerwear piece by piece. Normally, my grandfather worked with talk radio on, but now the house was strangely silent. "Hello?" I called out as Dustin unloaded our gear and brought the goose to the kitchen to be defeathered.

As I took my hat off, my hair wild with static, I noticed a note on the foyer side table. It was on my grandfather's stationery.

R,

Left on business. Dustin will see you back to school.

– BW

January was blustery and bleak. Dustin drove me back to school, where, against his protests, I dragged my suitcase up to my room. The snow moved like sand dunes in the wind, and icicles hung tenuously from the roof, thick and irregular. Everything was white, even the sky, the clouds blurring the horizon into an endless barren landscape.

Even though the investigation about Eleanor was technically still going on, with no leads, no suspects and no evidence, it had degenerated into guesswork and speculation. A few students didn't come back to school

401

because their parents thought it was too dangerous. In response, Gottfried tightened its security by increasing the number of guards both on campus and around the wall, and by enforcing stricter rules for day students entering and exiting the campus.

Although I had no decent theories, my discovery of the Undead made everything more logical. Gideon and the rest of the Latin club had to be Undead. It fitted with their behaviour – and their files. And if Benjamin had died of *Basium Mortis*, that could mean that Cassandra had taken her boyfriend's soul. But who killed Cassandra? And was the same person behind Eleanor's disappearance?

After spending winter break recovering at her mother's house, Eleanor returned to Gottfried. She burst into the room and was about to give me a hug when she stopped as if she had changed her mind, and pulled away before we touched. "Is everything all right?" I asked, giving her a weird look. It wasn't like Eleanor to be stand-offish.

"Yeah," she said. "I just have a cold. I don't want you to catch it."

"We're living in the same room," I said with a laugh. "I'll probably catch it anyway."

For a moment we stood in silence, Eleanor looking uncharacteristically humourless. I didn't know what to say, and small talk had never been my forte. So I just asked her what was on my mind.

"Eleanor, what happened?"

She took off her beret.

"You have to tell me," I said. "I know that look. You're hiding something."

She sighed and sat on her bed. "Okay, so don't get mad at me, but this past semester, I was secretly dating..." She closed her eyes and bit her lip, bracing herself for my reaction... "Brett."

"What?" I said, too loudly. It was so far from what I was expecting that I couldn't help but stare, waiting for her to confirm that I had heard correctly. "Brett Steyers? You and Brett Steyers?"

Eleanor nodded.

"Why didn't you tell me?"

"I don't know. I liked the idea of a secret fling. It was so exciting and romantic to think we could get caught. And then when they found me, I didn't want to tell anyone what really happened because they might suspect him, and it wasn't his fault."

"What do you mean 'what really happened'?"

"On Grub Day I went to the library to study. Later, I snuck out to meet Brett, then tried to sneak back into the dorm through the basement. But just after I stepped inside, someone locked the door behind me. I tried to climb into the chimney to get back to our room, but the flue was closed. I heard four loud bangs, like a hammer on metal, and water came rushing in from somewhere in the ceiling. I tried going to the furnace room to find another way out, but the basement was already filling with water. I screamed and screamed, but the water was too loud for anyone to hear me."

"How did you get out?"

She shrugged. "One day I just woke up and the flue was open, so I climbed out."

"Why didn't you tell anyone?"

"I didn't want them to know about the chimney. It's our only way out. And I didn't want anyone to suspect Brett."

"But what if it *was* Brett?"

Eleanor shook her head. "It wasn't. Because I was coming back from meeting him when it happened. He would have had to be in two places at once to have broken the pipes while I was in there. Besides, why would he want to kill me?"

"So are you guys still...you know?"

Eleanor sighed. "I don't know. I haven't seen him yet," she said, and unzipped her bag.

Sitting on the bed while she unpacked and told me about her winter vacation, I wanted to believe that nothing had changed, that we were back to the first day of school, before the flood, before Dante, before everything got complicated. But it wasn't true. She avoided talking about the flood any further, and remembering what it felt like after my parents died, I didn't ask. Whatever happened in the basement had changed her. It was something about the way she carried herself, the way she now slouched and dragged her feet, the way her smile seemed thinner and crooked. They were subtle differences, barely noticeable to anyone except me. It was as if she had been replaced by a twin, identical, yet essentially different. So instead of talking about what happened, we went to lunch.

"So how was your break?" she asked as we sat in the dining hall. Groups of students gathered in clusters at the tables around us.

More than anything, I wanted to tell her about what I had learned at my grandfather's house. "I was at home and I found this book," I said, trying to figure out how best to explain everything. Where to begin? Should I start with the *Seventh Meditation,* or just skip ahead to what the Undead were and how everything in the book described Dante? "So you know how Dante has all of these inexplicable things about him – like his cold skin and the fact that he never...he never..." My voice trailed off as Eleanor's plate caught my eyes.

"Renée?" she said to me. "Hello? You were saying something?"

"Ate anything," I said blankly. Eleanor's plate was virtually empty. Putting my cup down, I studied her again. Could it be?

"You're not eating anything," I said quietly as I tried to remember how many days Eleanor had been in the basement. Ten?

Eleanor looked at her plate. "I sort of lost my appetite since the flood."

"And you didn't wear a coat when we walked over here."

Eleanor didn't notice until I pointed it out to her. "I guess you're right," she said, looking at the thin sweater covering her arms with surprise. "I didn't even realize. Anyway, what were you saying about Dante and something about a book?"

Should I tell her about it? I wasn't sure that Eleanor even knew what she was yet, and I definitely wasn't the right person to tell her. But I also didn't want to get accidentally killed. "Oh, um, nothing. Nothing."

That night she didn't sleep. She tossed around in bed, tangling herself in the sheets, while I had nightmares of zombies running towards me from every direction, their faces blank and emotionless. Every so often I would wake up in the middle of the night, my pyjamas drenched in sweat. I'd kick off the covers and sit up, unable to stop thinking about all the things my grandfather had told me about Gottfried. And then I would stare at Eleanor and wonder if she was feeling the impulse to take my soul.

Suddenly she stood up and started pacing around the room.

"Are you feeling okay?" I asked, my voice trembling.

Startled, she turned to me. "I don't know. I have to think about it," she murmured as if she were talking in her sleep, the hem of her nightgown fluttering around her legs in the moonlight.

The next morning I woke up early to go to Horticulture. It was our first day back in classes. Eleanor was in bed, curled up, facing the wall. I prodded her gently. "Eleanor, get up. We have Horticulture at six."

Eleanor lay with her back to me. "I'm not going," she said miserably. "I'm not in that class any more."

"What?"

"They switched my schedule. Just go without me."

I waited a moment to see if she would roll over, but she didn't move; and with nothing else to do, I left for class without her.

That morning we gathered by the chapel, until Professor Mumm showed up and led us out the gates of the campus.

"Renée," Brett called out to me as we walked.

I stopped, looking at him in a new light. "Oh hi, Brett."

He jogged up to me, looking like a robust ski instructor in a winter coat and a blue-and-yellow Gottfried scarf, his brown curls emerging from the bottom of a knit hat. "How's it going?"

"It's okay," I said. "You know, I've been better."

"Break wasn't so great?"

I laughed and shook my head. "That's the understatement of the year. But I did watch a lot of movies."

"Trashy horror movies, I bet."

I looked up at him, surprised.

He shrugged, pleased with himself. "You seem like the type."

"What do you mean?"

"Well, you do always seem to find dead things whenever we're in class."

I bit my lip, thinking back to the first day of class, when I found the dead fawn, or later in the semester when I found the carcass of a bird when we were supposed to be collecting baby saplings; or when I found a frozen squirrel when we were supposed to be learning about seasonal mosses. "I guess you're right."

Brett stuffed his hands in his pockets. "It's not a bad thing. Professor Mumm loves you; you're like her prodigy. Maybe it's some sort of special talent."

Letting out a laugh, I said, "Yeah, right. More like a curse. A Gottfried Curse."

I looked at him to see if he recognized the term, but he didn't seem to be familiar with it.

"Anyway, I just wanted to say I'm sorry," Brett said. "About Eleanor."

I smiled, unexpectedly comforted by normal conversation. "Thanks."

"How is she?" His forehead was furrowed with worry.

How to respond? "She's...different. Quieter. I think she's traumatized," I said, which was partially the truth.

"How was her break? Was she at home with her mother? Or was she in the hospital?"

"I think she was with her mom. It sounded like her break wasn't so great. Recovering and all. Why don't you just ask her yourself?"

"Oh, no. I don't think so. Is her brother around a lot?"

Brandon *had* been hanging around Eleanor a lot these days, looking even more stern and angry than normal. And who could blame him? His sister had probably died, and from the scrutinizing look he gave anyone who talked to her, it was clear that he was certain someone was responsible, and was determined to find out who it was and punish them. "He is."

Brett shrugged. "I figured as much. Did she say anything about how it happened?"

I shook my head. "She doesn't know."

We stopped just at the edge of the woods. Professor Mumm cleared her throat. "Today we'll be learning how to read snow. Like soil, the texture and topography of snow

409

and ice can tell us what lies beneath. A dune, a crevasse; whether the snow is powdery or packed, blue or creamy or a brilliant white – each of these characteristics can tell us what's hidden beneath" – she held up an index finger – "if we learn how to read them. Now, what I want you to do is partner up."

Brett elbowed me. "You and me?"

I smiled.

When I got out of class, Dante was leaning on the stone at the entrance to Horace Hall, waiting for me, as beautiful as ever. He looked up at me as I approached, his face young and dark and gallant, his hair pulled back like an Italian model. If I hadn't known everything that he was, I would have fallen in love with him all over again. He was wearing a crisp blue shirt and tie. Only a thin coat, no scarf. Snowflakes collected on his hair. Everything about him reminded me of how different we were.

"Renée," he called out, but I kept walking. "Renée, wait. Why won't you talk to me?" He reached out and grabbed my arm.

Unprepared for the coldness of his skin, I pulled my arm away and stared at him as if he were a stranger. For the briefest moment our eyes met, and a flicker of understanding passed between us before I looked away.

What does it feel like to discover that your boyfriend is Undead? Shocking. Unfair. But mostly disturbing. How was it possible that I had spent so much time with Dante without knowing what he truly was? I couldn't decide which was more disturbing – that he was dying, or that a killer was dormant inside him. Was there a part of him that wanted my soul? I thought back to every time we almost kissed. I shivered at how close he had come to taking my life. Could he do it? I didn't want to ask him or talk about it. What could I possibly say? I was alive, he was dead, and no amount of words would change that.

"Renée, please," he said as I turned to go. "Just listen to me. Talk to me. I've been trying to call—" But I was already gone.

"How was Horticulture?" Eleanor asked while we were sitting in Philosophy, waiting for class to start.

"We had it in the forest," I said.

Eleanor's eyes went wide. "What was it like? What did you do?"

"Snow topography. With partners."

Nathaniel frowned. "What does that have to do with horticulture?" He looked at Eleanor. "So you weren't there?"

I shrugged. "It's pretty useful. You can figure out what

411

the terrain is like below the snow, or if there's stuff buried beneath it, or what the temperature of the ground is."

"They switched me out," Eleanor said. "Now I'm in something called Elementary Advanced Tongues. What does it even mean for a class to be elementary and advanced at the same time?"

"I was in that last year," Nathaniel said, giving her a quizzical look, while I gave him a quizzical look. Was he Undead too? I ran through the criteria in my head, my mouth forming a tiny pink *O* as he spoke. His skin was cold, his senses were terrible, yet he was incredibly smart. "It's Latin. Sort of." He was fluent in Latin.

Eleanor rolled her eyes and collapsed back into her chair. "Great. When they said I didn't have to take Elementary Latin, I thought they were giving me a break after what happened in the basement."

I had been trying to figure out if Eleanor knew she was Undead. So far, the verdict was no.

Nathaniel and I went quiet at her mention of the flood, waiting to see if she would talk about it. I hadn't talked to Nathaniel about it. I thought about telling Miss LaBarge, but assumed that the school knew, especially since they had switched Eleanor's courses. I tried calling my grandfather, but he was away. So instead I tried to stay up as late as I could with Eleanor every night so she would have someone to talk to, hoping that when she did learn

412

what she was, she would confide in me. Plus, it wasn't exactly easy sleeping in a room with someone who I knew had the urge to kill me.

Eleanor looked between us. "What? You'd think a near-death experience would at least exempt me from the most boring class of all time."

Slowly she smiled. I did too, as did Nathaniel, which quickly degenerated into laughter, and for the first time in a long while, even if just for a moment, I felt carefree again.

I didn't see Dante again until last period. When I got to Crude Sciences, he was already sitting at our lab bench, looking statuesque as he leaned back in his chair, his tie and oxford artfully crinkled around the musculature of his neck. In front of him was a tray, upon which a neat row of medical tools was arranged: a scalpel, a pair of tweezers, a needle and hook, and a spindle of string.

Without a word, I sat down next to him, trying with all my will to keep my eyes on the board. Dante turned to me. "Renée, I meant to tell you, but every time I tried, something always interrupt—" Ironically, before he could finish, the bell rang and Professor Starking walked in carrying a large plastic tub. He set it on his desk.

"Life sciences," he said. "Otherwise known as *Scientiae Vitae,* the counterpart to *Disciplina Mortuorum,* or Science of the Dead." He hoisted the tub from his desk and walked down the aisles. Using tongs, he fished around inside until he emerged with a dead frog.

"I tried to stay away from you," Dante said. "The beginning of the year. I kept my distance because I didn't want to put you in danger."

"We can't study life sciences until we study death," Professor Starking said while he walked. "I have given each of you a frog. This is your vessel."

"But I couldn't stay away. I still can't stay away from you. I wanted to tell you, I planned on telling you, but I didn't want to lose you."

I blinked back angry tears as I stared at our frog. It gazed back at me with glassy eyes. It wasn't fair. Maybe it wasn't Dante's fault that he was dead, but it was his fault for involving me when he knew what he was.

"Renée? Say something."

"Who can tell me what some of the characteristics of decay are?" Professor Starking looked around the room.

"Cold skin," I whispered to Dante, looking at him from the periphery as I steadied my voice. "Stiff limbs. No sensation. Disconnected from the rest of the world."

"Living people can have those characteristics too," Dante replied.

"The paper cut? The séance? You knew and you let me second-guess myself all semester."

"I tried to tell you—"

"*You make me feel alive?*" I said, repeating what he had told me that night in Attica Falls. "I thought that was so romantic. I didn't realize you were being literal."

"Why does that have to make it mean less?"

"Have you killed anyone?" I asked quietly.

"No," he said. "Of course not."

"Will you kill anyone?"

"No."

My lip quivered. "Will you die?"

Dante didn't say anything for a long time. "Yes. But one day you will too. It isn't so different."

"Everything is different," I said loudly. In the background, Professor Starking had stopped lecturing and was telling us to quiet down, but I didn't care. "You're... you're..." I looked at the frog. "I don't even know what you are."

The class erupted in murmurs. Professor Starking anxiously tried to calm everyone down and get the class under control.

"I'm still the same person I was before—"

"You're not a person!" I said, my eyes watering as they searched his for an answer that would help me understand what he was. Suddenly the room seemed incredibly silent. The entire class was looking at us.

"I don't know what's going on," Professor Starking said

415

nervously from the front of the class, "but you can figure out your differences in work detail."

We walked in silence to the headmistress's office, me three paces ahead. The secretary asked us to wait outside while she fetched Headmistress Von Laark, so I sat on the far side of the bench, arms crossed.

The office door opened. "Come in," Headmistress Von Laark's voice said soothingly. "Both of you."

When we were seated in front of her, she asked us what happened. After a moment, we both spoke at the same time.

"He provoked me...I was answering a question and he interrupted me," I said.

"I provoked her," Dante said. "It was my fault."

Surprised at his selflessness, I suddenly felt embarrassed for blaming him. But it was his fault, I reassured myself. He *did* provoke me. If he hadn't been dead, and if he hadn't kept it from me, we never would have been in this situation. I crossed my arms, trying to convince myself that I was right, but quickly felt overwhelmed with guilt.

"I see," the headmistress said. "Still, since you disrupted class together, you will *both* have to serve a work detail. Five o'clock tonight. The fourth floor of Horace Hall. Room eight, north wing."

I left without saying a word to Dante because I didn't know what to say. Not wanting to walk in the same direction as him, I went to Horace Hall. I couldn't confide in Eleanor because she already had enough problems of her own, and Nathaniel just wouldn't understand. The bell rang as I entered the building, and I waited for all the students to empty out before I climbed up the stairs to see Miss LaBarge.

The floorboards creaked as I walked down the narrow hallway that led to her office. It was tucked into the corner, a thin strip of light peeking out from beneath the door. I knocked.

Miss LaBarge's voice floated through the wood. "Come in."

She was sitting in an armchair under a yellow cone of light, reading. When she saw me, she smiled and stood up. "Renée," she said, taking off her reading glasses. "What a pleasant surprise."

I wiped my shoes on the doormat and stepped inside. Her office had a warm glow to it, and smelled like cinnamon and burning wood.

"Have a seat."

I took off my scarf and sat in the love seat across from her. A thick hardcover book sat on the ottoman between us, a ribbon resting in its crease.

"What are you reading?"

Miss LaBarge picked it up. "Oh, just some silly stuff. *Beyond Good and Evil,* by a philosopher named Friedrich

Nietzsche. It's about how to decide what's right and what's wrong."

"That doesn't sound silly at all."

She frowned. "Yes, I suppose you're right."

"How *do* you tell the difference?"

She closed the book and put it on the side table. "Sometimes you can't."

"So...say you're dating a boy, and he tells you that he's something, but it turns out that he's actually something else. Is that wrong?"

"Would this supposed boy have a good reason for keeping it a secret?"

I thought about it. Dante probably hadn't told me because he thought it would scare me. And he was right. "I guess so. But it's still lying, isn't it?"

"It is, but if the lie is meant to protect the other person from harm or pain, is it really that bad?"

"But I didn't want to be protected; I wanted to know the truth," I blurted out.

She shrugged. "Sometimes there isn't just one truth. Just because you discovered more about him doesn't mean the person that he was before was a lie. You just had a less complete picture of him."

I wanted to believe that what Dante and I had had before was real; that the things he'd said and done were still genuine even though he was Undead. But even if I could, that reality was slipping through my fingers. Dante had an expiration date, and there was no way I could help him.

"But what if I know we can never be together?"

"Hmm. That's tricky. I think this calls for some tea. Hold on to that thought." She got up and disappeared into the anteroom. I heard water running and then the sound of steam hissing out of a kettle, the clatter of dishes, the delicate clinking of a spoon against porcelain. She returned holding two cups and a teapot. "Chamomile?"

I nodded.

"*Never* only exists in your head. Anything is possible."

"But what if he's too...too different?"

"Do you still have feelings for him? Even after knowing who he is?"

I shook my head. "I don't know." And then I thought about it. "Well, maybe... Yes."

"Then you've answered your question. In love, everyone does things that hurt the other person, so really there is no 'right' and 'wrong'. You just have to decide what you're willing to forgive."

"But what if I know it's not going to last?"

"Then savour every moment."

The pitter-patter of footsteps reverberated from the floor above us. I cradled the cup of tea in my lap. "Have you ever been in love?"

She smiled. "Oh, I'd like to believe that I'm always in love with something. After all, what else is there?"

Professor Urquette was assigned to oversee our work detail. She was our Art and Humanities teacher. Her body was shaped like an eggplant, which she emphasized by always wearing multiple shades of purple and green. Even though she'd never married, she had the *je ne sais quoi* of a jaded divorcée. She hid the baggy skin on her throat beneath crocheted shawls and velvety scarves, and held her pen in the side of her mouth like a long cigarette. Her greying hair was kinky and defied all laws of gravity by puffing upwards, making her seem eight centimetres taller than she was. Every few months she dyed it back to its original colour – red – and when the grey grew in beneath it, her head looked like it was on fire.

I arrived at her office a few minutes before five o'clock. Dante was already there, sitting at the desk by the door. Embarrassed about how I'd behaved earlier, I hesitated before going to the opposite end of the classroom and sitting by the window. Outside it was a beautiful clear day, and I could see Eleanor walking down the path with some girls from our floor. A cool breeze blew in, and I felt the tickling inkling of a sneeze. I tried to hold it in, but it came out suddenly, loud and unflattering. My face grew red and I began to rummage through my backpack for a tissue.

"Bless you," Dante said quietly from across the room.

I looked up at him with surprise. "Thanks."

We sat in silence until the door opened. Professor Urquette bounded into the room, wheezing from walking up the stairs. After dropping her bags on the desk, she collapsed into her chair and let herself catch her breath. Delicately, she patted her hair, making sure it was still in place.

"I understand you were both disrupting a school lecture?"

Neither of us said anything.

"Okay," she said, hoisting herself up. "Normally I wouldn't do this, but the school play is nearly upon us and we need wood to start building the set."

We stared at her blankly.

"Well, gather your things. We're going into the woods."

The forest was on the other side of the wall, the strictly prohibited side. But apparently, even the most stringent rules had exceptions. When we got to the school entrance, Professor Urquette nodded at the guard, who opened the gates.

She brought us to the outskirts of the woods, holding her skirt up as she stepped through the snow in galoshes.

Behind the trees, the White Mountains jutted up from the horizon. After walking a couple of metres, we stopped. Professor Urquette hung her bag on the crook of a tree and bent over. Grunting, she picked up a stick and hoisted herself back up.

"You're looking for sticks, the thicker the better," she said, snapping the twig in half and handing each of us a burlap bag. "Meet me back here in two hours. And don't be late, or you'll be in the woods after dark. I'll be waiting by the entrance. If you need help, just holler." With that, she waddled back to the guard's hut by the gate.

I turned to Dante, wondering if he was angry, if he would forgive me. I tried to think of a way to apologize, but before I could say anything, he looked away and ventured into the woods, leaving me alone. Stung by his coldness, I waited until he was a few paces ahead, then headed through the trees in the opposite direction.

The ground was covered in snow, which I sunk in up to my shins. The oaks were naked, their branches sticking into the sky like fingers. Oddly shaped mushrooms clung to the trunks, creating yellow staircases that spiralled up the bark. Taking giant strides, I walked into the confusing maze that made up the forest.

"You're going the wrong way," Dante called out to me.

"We're picking up sticks. There is no wrong way."

Shaking his head, he changed his course to my direction.

Suddenly, an odd whiteness peeked through the trees. I walked towards it. As I approached, the number of trees diminished until there were barely any. It wasn't until I was standing directly in front of it that I realized that it wasn't a clearing. It was the Dead Forest.

I stopped at its outskirts. The landscape was vast and desolate, the snow peppered with splintered wood. The trees were white, and had no branches or leaves. They littered the horizon like toothpicks. Decaying stumps stood beside them, their bark charred a permanent black.

"The Dead Forest," Dante said beside me, staring out into the abyss of trees. "I knew you were going the wrong way."

"What are you talking about? This place is full of wood."

"It's all rotten," he said. We exchanged an uncomfortable look before I trudged forward.

"So it's true," I said softly, my nose running as I stopped beneath the trunk of a tree that leaned tenuously over the ground like the lip of a bridge.

Dante stepped closer. "That I could hurt you?"

He took another step. "That I would never hurt you?"

Everything was silent except for the hollow echo of the wind. "Yes," he said.

My hair blew around my face in the wind. "That you feel sensation around all humans?" I asked.

He reached out to touch my face, but let his hand hover just centimetres away. "No. Only you."

I let out a breath, unsure of whether or not I should believe him. "That you're dead?"

Dante ran his hand up my back, so gently it could have been the wind.

"The paper cut. The séance. The night in Attica Falls. It's all true?"

"Yes."

My lips trembled as I turned to him, my eyes searching the familiar contours of his face for some sign of death. "Show me."

Suddenly, I heard a crack, and with the full force of gravity, the dead tree above me began to fall. Underneath it, a nest of moths burst out of a hole in the trunk and flapped around me. I screamed and fell into the snow.

It all happened quickly. With inhuman strength, Dante caught the tree before it crushed my body. With two hands, he lifted the trunk as if it were weightless and threw it to the ground. And in no time he was beside me, cradling me in his arms.

I stared at his face in disbelief.

"When we reanimate, we're born into the best version of ourselves," he explained. "The strongest. The smartest. The most beautiful. Whatever your best qualities were when you were alive, those would be augmented."

"Why me?" I said. "Why did you keep calling me? Keep waiting for me?"

"I couldn't help it. I had to see you," he said. "I know my situation is...unusual, but it doesn't change how I feel about you."

When I finally spoke, my voice was so small I could barely hear it. "How do you feel about me?"

Dante took a step closer. "I miss you." He spoke gently, his words delicate, as if he wasn't ready to part with them yet. "I miss everything about you. Your laugh, your voice. The way I never know what you're going to say next. It's like the entire world is dead, and you're the only one living..." His voice trailed off; he seemed embarrassed to have said so much. "I'm sorry if I scared you. I just want you to know that. That I'm sorry. For everything."

I didn't want to blink, didn't want to close my eyes for a minute. I raised my hand and touched his cheek, feeling the coldness of his skin for what seemed like the first time. He smelled like earth, like pine and grass and soil.

"I'm not afraid," I said. "I'm not afraid of you."

"I am," he said, closing his eyes.

And just like that, he became human again.

CHAPTER 15

TRAGEDY IN THE MOUNTAINS

WITH EVERYTHING AROUND ME blurring into confusion, nothing else was certain except this: I was alive. Dante was not.

The rest was speculation, and this is what I pieced together. Cassandra Millet and Benjamin Gallow were in love. Benjamin was a Plebeian, Cassandra Undead. They went to the forest. Cassandra slipped and kissed him. She couldn't control herself, and he died. She left him in the woods. That's what I told Dante after dinner. We were in the library, not studying.

"She told you, and you went and found him. Am I right?"

Dante nodded. "Cassandra came to us after she had accidentally killed Benjamin to ask us what she should do. I told her to turn herself in. When she didn't, I went and found Benjamin myself. Gideon told her to leave Gottfried; disappear for ever. After that, it's mostly speculation, though your theory sounds right. Cassandra disappeared, which makes sense, considering Gideon suggested it, but we all knew that Cassandra would never have just left without saying goodbye. We argued about it, Gideon, Vivian, Yago and I. We knew something was wrong, and Minnie's story led us to consider the possibility that she was dead."

"What was the fight about?"

"Gideon didn't want me to search for Benjamin. He didn't agree with the counsel I gave Cassandra. But after seeing what she was capable of doing to someone she loved, I was afraid of myself. That's why I moved off campus. To protect the school from me."

"Is that why Gideon had the files?"

"I don't know. I've been following him around all year; you know that. But I don't have any evidence that he was involved in Cassandra's disappearance. The files you found in his room sounded promising, but those are gone now."

I took his hand. "You're a good person."

Dante shook me off. "I'm not."

I gave him a level look. "I'm not afraid of death."

But I was afraid of losing the people I loved. And the question still remained: who killed Eleanor and Cassandra?

Dante and I spent time together every evening, his "condition" bringing us closer together than we had been before. I finally felt like there were no secrets between us, and Dante suddenly became comfortably familiar and excitingly unfamiliar, like exploring an old mansion and discovering things that were always there but you never noticed before. I sat through my classes impatiently, counting the minutes until I would see him. The more I learned about the Undead, the more I grew to accept who Dante was, and even envy it. There were a lot of upsides to being Undead. For one, because he was already dead, he couldn't be killed by normal means, which made taking risks a lot easier. He never had to worry about the weather being too cold, and since he never slept, he had endless amounts of time. That's why he was so well read. And best of all, he couldn't feel pain – emotional or physical. Unless I was near him. What I wouldn't give to have that power. If I didn't feel pain then I wouldn't be tormented by the death of my parents, which I still couldn't make sense of.

Later that week when I went downstairs to meet him, I saw the silhouette of a figure standing in the shadows by the stoop. I ran over and wrapped my arms around him, only to discover that it wasn't Dante; it was Brett. He looked just as surprised to see me as I was to see him. "Oh,

I'm sorry. I thought you were someone else," I said, my face turning red.

"That's okay," Brett said, letting out a sigh of relief. "I'm just glad you're not Mrs. Lynch."

I laughed. "Yeah. Okay, well I'm going to go."

Brett nodded and retreated into the shadows.

Dante was waiting around the side of the building. Before I could ask where we were going, he took my hand and led me towards the centre of campus. It was a cold and windless evening. The trees stood around us, barren and lifeless.

"How old are you?" I asked, leaning against the trunk of a giant oak.

Dante played with a lock of my hair. "Seventeen."

I looked up at him. "How old are you really?"

He shoved his hands in his pockets and looked at the sky, counting in his head. "This will be the sixteenth anniversary of my seventeenth birthday."

"And how long have you been at Gottfried?"

Dante laughed. "Just two years. And I'll only stay here two more. Gottfried might be eccentric, but it's still a high school."

Right, I thought, blushing at how silly my question was. Obviously it would look suspicious if all of the Undead stayed here while everyone else was graduating.

"How did you die?"

Dante took my hand and led me into the middle of the green. "I drowned."

I thought about all the times I'd been swimming in the marina. Drowning seemed lonely and alien, like dying in a different world.

"What happened?"

"I told you how we lived in a really remote area of British Columbia?" I nodded and he continued. "One summer, I was out on a walk with my little sister, Cecelia, teaching her how to split wood, when she fell through a partially frozen pond. I jumped in to get her and brought her back to the house, but after a week she couldn't eat and was coughing and shivering uncontrollably. Pneumonia, we thought. Our neighbour was a bush pilot. He offered to fly us to the nearest city.

"We all got into his tiny water plane, and about an hour in, something went wrong. The plane crashed in the ocean, somewhere off the Pacific coast. The whole way down my father was holding us, shouting prayers into the wind. I was seventeen."

My scarf blew loose from my neck, dangling in the wind, but I barely noticed. "Everyone died?"

"I think so. I don't know. I washed ashore somewhere in California. I never saw my parents or sister again."

"I'm sorry," I said quietly. "I'm so sorry."

"It's okay. It was a long time ago."

I turned to him. "If your sister wasn't buried, and she washed ashore like you, she could be out there somewhere too."

"I know. I think about her all the time. But her body might have been destroyed. The plane caught fire when it went down. That much I do remember."

"So, since you weren't buried, you...you...reanimated, and now you don't have a soul?"

"Yes."

"What does it feel like?"

He paused, trying to find the right words. The sky was bruising into night, framed by the silhouettes of the trees lining the path, their brittle skeletons swaying in the wind. "Do you trust me?"

I nodded. Dante led me to the snow by the side of the path.

"Close your eyes," he said.

I closed them, and he tied something around my head. It felt like a scarf. I stood very still. He slipped off my jacket. "What are you doing?"

"I'll give it back."

I began to shiver. After a few minutes my fingers started to go numb in the cold. My nose began to run. My lips felt dry and chapped. Without being able to see the world around me, all the sounds of nature blurred into white noise.

Dante took my hand and led me around the path. I walked with small tenuous steps, stumbling over bumps in the ground and relying on Dante to make sure I didn't fall.

"This is what it feels like on the worst days," he said. "I can't feel anything. I can't smell, I can't taste, I can't hear music – just noise. Even my vision is different. I can see things, but it's like I'm colour-blind. Everything is the same, but somehow muted."

He took the scarf off. I blinked at the brightness of the night as the world slowly came back into focus. "And this is what it's like when I'm around you."

I studied him with a newfound understanding. How could someone live like that? "But it doesn't happen with anyone else? You're sure?"

Dante shook his head. "Do you feel the same way around other people as you do around me?"

I shook my head. "No."

We stopped in front of the Observatory. The door was normally locked after hours, but tonight it was propped open with a book. Dante glanced around, making sure no one was watching, and led me inside, letting the door click shut behind us.

The lab was dark, and I had to feel my way around the room until my eyes adjusted to the light. Above us, the night sky was clear and blue through the glass ceiling.

I looked around, and then at Dante. "It's so different at night."

Dante lifted me onto the countertop, and we lay side by side, staring at the stars through the roof.

"How did you know you were dead?"

"It took me a while to figure it out. I woke up not knowing where I was, with no way of getting home. I wandered around some marina town in California for a few days, trying to figure out what had happened. I asked about my family at the local hospital. They sent me to the police, who told me there had been a crash. I was the only one from my family who had been found. They checked me into the hospital. I stayed for a week. I felt like part of me was missing and I had to go find it. At first I thought that was just my way of grieving the loss of my family, but there were other things. I wasn't hungry, and when I forced myself to eat, I couldn't taste anything. My body temperature was far below normal. A rare circulation condition, the doctors said, but I knew they didn't have a clue. That's when I realized something was wrong.

"So I left. My parents' bodies were found, but my sister was still missing. I had no desire to contact anyone I knew, except for her. In fact, I had no desire at all. Only the feeling of an absent desire. I could remember that once I had felt happy, felt alive, but I couldn't actually feel it again, if that makes sense. I thought finding my sister would help fill that void. So I searched for her. For weeks. Months. Years, I guess. Since I didn't need to eat or sleep, I'd just walk for days at a time. In the meantime, I found work. I enrolled in schools but dropped out when I realized I wasn't interested in what anyone was teaching. Years passed, and I noticed that I wasn't aging – at least not in a normal way. Although my senses were deteriorating, I wasn't growing older. In fact, the rest of my body was abnormally healthy. I didn't know what was happening, so I kept to myself. I didn't want to become a freak show or a science experiment. But I did my own experiments to learn my new limits. It was easy to pick up, like learning not to touch a hot stove. And it was easy to be alone, since I had no urge to date or make friends. I was, in essence, a shell.

"Eventually I went back to the hospital, knowing that there had to be something wrong with me. Outside in the parking lot, there was a flyer stapled to a telephone pole. It read, *For Questions of the Existential Nature*. Below it was an address. At that point I was completely lost. I wrote a letter, talking about all of the inexplicable problems I was having, and sent it to the address. A few weeks later, Professor Lumbar sent me a letter back, asking me to visit the Academy. She said it was a school that specialized in existential questions, and that they might be able to help me with 'my condition'. She didn't explain what that meant. So I went, partly because I wanted help, partly because I was curious. That's how I ended up here."

I turned to him, gazing at his profile as he stared into the sky. "And you're looking for your soul?"

"I'm looking for something. Not my soul, though. I don't want to kill anyone. That's what I've been researching at Gottfried. Another way to live."

"But if you kiss me, you'll kill me?"

"Yes. But I won't kiss you."

"How can you be so sure?"

"Because I can choose. Just like everyone else."

In a way he had a point. I suppose anyone had the capacity to hurt another person; it just depended on the choices they made. How was Dante any different from me in that regard?

He took my hand. "Here," he said, placing it over his chest.

I held it there, but nothing happened.

"Listen to it."

Slowly, I lowered my head to his chest.

At first there was nothing. And then suddenly I could hear his heartbeat. It was like nothing I had heard before: its rhythm was erratic, like the sound of someone running down a flight of stairs.

"Whatever life I have left, it's yours."

* * *

Later that night I snuck into my darkened room through the fireplace and slipped beneath the sheets. Eleanor was curled up in bed, and even though I knew she wasn't sleeping, I still tiptoed so as not to disturb her. I then fell into a peaceful slumber, where I dreamed about Dante holding me in his arms in a field as we gazed at the stars. The grass was prickly beneath my neck, and slowly he turned to me, propping himself up on one elbow. And then he leaned forward, his lips thin and red, so red as they inched closer and closer to mine.

With a start, I opened my eyes.

Eleanor's face was centimetres away from mine, her ringlets grazing my pillow.

"Eleanor?" I asked. With a start, she jumped back. "What are you doing?"

"Renée," she said, surprised. "I was just checking to see if you were awake."

I sat up and backed against the wall, giving her a frightened look. "Are you sure?"

Eleanor nodded. "Yes."

I kicked off the covers and rubbed my eyes.

"Renée, are you scared of death?" She was looking intently at me, but seemed as if her mind were elsewhere.

"No. I think I'm scared of dying, though."

"What do you think it's like?"

"I don't know," I said slowly. "I always imagined it's

436

like falling asleep and never waking up."

She paused. "Renée, there's something I need to tell you."

"Okay," I said.

"I'm...I'm..." She sighed. "I don't know how to explain it. Professor Bliss did such a better job in class."

I straightened out my pyjamas. "You don't have to explain. I know."

Eleanor paused, her forehead wrinkling with surprise. "You do?"

"The Undead."

Upon hearing the word, Eleanor's shoulders slumped. "Yeah. How did you find out?"

"Dante."

Eleanor looked at her feet and then took a step away from my bed. "You must think I'm a monster."

I shook my head, silencing her. Finally I spoke. "What was it like?"

"Being reborn?" She closed her eyes. "It felt like being woken up from a dream. Like the way you feel when you take a nap in the afternoon, and you wake up and you're not sure where you are or what day it is, and the line between yesterday and today and tomorrow is blurry."

She let out a sad laugh, and there was a long silence as we both considered everything that had happened. I imagined Eleanor drowning alone in the basement. It was a harrowing image.

"Life after death. It's got to exist," Eleanor said. I knew she wasn't referring to life literally, but an emotional life after death. She looked at me for an answer, her eyes searching for meaning.

"Yeah, I think it does."

This seemed to put Eleanor at ease. "So what would you do if you only had a few days left to live?"

She waited for me to answer. I considered all the things I wanted to do – backpack through the Himalayas, see the pyramids, take a road trip across America, learn Spanish, live in the city and then in the country, write a novel – the list seemed endless. "I think I would try to spend as much time as I could with the people I cared about."

Eleanor considered it. "Me too."

I curled up beneath the covers. I told her about the files, about Cassandra and how she had accidentally killed Benjamin, and finally about Dante. "What do you think happened to Cassandra? Do you think the *school* buried her, like Minnie said?"

Eleanor looked troubled. "No."

"Yeah," I said quickly, "they wouldn't do that."

We lay there until the early hours of the morning, talking about the things we wanted to do, the places we wanted to go, the kind of people we wanted to be.

* * *

By the middle of March – the ides, as Professor Urquette ominously called them – the weather had warmed and the snow was just beginning to melt. As the water trickled down the sides of the pathways, the campus and all of its secrets were slowly revealed – the yellow grass, soggy and matted down; the benches and statues and fountains that punctuated the natural landscape; and the occasional Frisbee or garden spade or mitten.

I had barely seen Nathaniel since break; he was busy with the school play, in which he had one of the leading roles as Electra. Sometimes I helped him practise his lines after lunch. I never imagined that he'd be interested in acting; it always seemed like numbers were his natural language, not English. But when he took off his glasses and delivered his lines, he transformed into a suave, confident hero, his voice deep and rich and entirely not his own. Otherwise, the only real time we spent together was in class. We had Maths in room π, commonly referred to as "the Pi Room", not to be confused with the dessert section of the dining hall.

Professor Chortle was round and cherubic, with thin lips and rosy cheeks that bespoke an uncorrupted innocence that he could only have obtained by spending all of his formative years indoors, thinking about maths.

Imaginary Numbers, he scrawled on the board.

"Imaginary numbers are numbers that exist in a

different world than ours. As a result, we can only *sense* their existence." All of his lectures had a dreamy quality to them despite their content, making it seem like his natural habitat wasn't here, but in some Renaissance landscape, where he would spend his days sprawled out on the grass, nibbling an apple and pondering the meaning of infinity.

I chewed on my pen. Nathaniel was sitting across from me, his eyes glued to the board.

"For example, when people act older than their age, it usually means they have a lot of imaginary years behind them," the professor explained.

I tore off a corner of my notebook paper.

Do you think Eleanor is okay?

I was pretty sure Nathaniel was Undead, but I hadn't talked to him about it. What would I say? *Are you dead?* But now that Eleanor was Undead too, I couldn't avoid it any longer. I folded up the note and tossed it into his lap when the professor wasn't looking.

Surprised, he looked down at it and turned around to scowl at Yago, who was sitting behind him. Then he brushed the note out of his lap and onto the floor.

I tried to get his attention, but he was too involved in the lecture. I dropped my pencil on the floor, leaned across the aisle, and picked up the note. This time I made sure to write his name on it, and tossed it into his lap again.

Nathaniel was about to turn around again when I caught his eye.

Finally he figured it out. He unfolded the note and then scrawled something back.

I think so? Why wouldn't she be?

I considered how to respond.

She looks exhausted, but she can't sleep or eat. She's cold all the time but barely notices it. She doesn't enjoy doing any of the things she used to do. She talks about death all the time.

Nathaniel stared at what I wrote, clearly surprised that I knew. I waited until he tossed it back and unfolded the paper.

She sounds depressed.

His response was baffling. Nathaniel was Undead; I was almost sure of it. I was also sure that he fully understood what I was telling him. My message wasn't *that* subtle. Yet for some reason he was being obtuse. I wrote back.

I know what you are.

Nathaniel avoided my gaze as he read it.

I don't know what you're talking about.

I shook my head, holding my pencil over the page, unsure of how to proceed. Why was he lying to me?

You don't have to pretend. There's nothing wrong with it. I won't tell anyone.

He wrote a quick note back.

Thanks, but there's nothing to tell. Pretending to do what?

Are you coming to the play tomorrow?

I knew that Nathaniel was insecure, but I never realized he was in such denial. I crumpled the note in my fist and nodded.

The performance was to take place in front of the great oak at sunset. Ever since coming back to Gottfried after winter break, Eleanor hadn't felt comfortable in large crowds. Everyone always pointed and whispered, so instead of going to the play, she went to the library to catch up on her homework. I met up with Dante in front of the dining hall, and we walked over together.

Rows of benches were set up on the edge of the green, which was lit by six massive torches positioned around the lawn in a semicircle. Dante took my hand and pulled me towards the back. We found a spot on the edge of the green under a large maple tree, and sat down. We couldn't see much of the stage because of the benches in front of us, but neither of us minded. Soon the din of the crowd grew hushed, and a line of students, headed by Gideon, filed onto the stage.

I pretended to watch the play, but I was only paying attention to Dante sitting beside me, his shirt grazing my arm. Through the darkened silhouettes of the treetops I could just make out the campus buildings, each engraved and named after a philosopher or headmistress or master: a looming reminder that we were surrounded by the dead.

Dante moved closer until our arms were touching. In the eerie torchlight of the far distance, the chorus recited words about murder and betrayal, enveloping us with voices from the ancient world.

"'Woman,'" Dante whispered in time with the chorus onstage. "'Be sure your heart is brave; you can take much.'"

My head resting in my palm, I looked up at him, perplexed. "Do you have every book memorized?"

"I've been alive for a while," he said. "It's not as difficult as you think."

Taking my hands in his, he pulled me into his lap and wrapped his arms around me. "Two lovers, doomed to death," he said, explaining the play as he nibbled on my ear. "Killed out of jealousy."

"Doomed," I murmured, gazing out into the night.

"'There is a breath about it like an open grave,'" Dante recited in time with the actor playing Agamemnon's lover, Cassandra, on the stage.

I couldn't believe that this was, in many ways, my story too. I closed my eyes, listening to the words, wishing we were somewhere else, anywhere else, as if that would help the fact that Dante was going to die and there was nothing I could do to stop it.

Dante faced me, his eyes sad and watery as they gazed into mine. "'I am going in, and mourning as I go my death and Agamemnon's. Let my life be done.'"

"'Let my life be done,'" I repeated, pressing my forehead to his, our fingers and legs intertwined as if we were two people sharing one body. And together we listened to students recite the lines that Aeschylus had written thousands of years ago, about obsession and desire, about vengeance and curses and lovers, doomed to die side by side.

But our reverie was interrupted by an unnaturally long silence. We turned to the stage, where the boy playing Orestes was standing onstage, blinking blindly into the audience as if he were confused.

All was quiet as everyone watched him. He repeated his line and leaned back, signalling Professor Urquette urgently.

The crowd began to murmur. "Did he forget his lines?" someone said.

I stared at the stage. "This is where Nathaniel is supposed to come in," I said to Dante. "I helped him practise his lines. Where is he?"

Then, from behind the torches, someone pushed a skinny boy out onto the lawn.

"That's not Nathaniel," I said, staring at the pasty redhead.

And it wasn't; it was his understudy, a lanky third year named Kurt Mayburg. He wasn't in costume, and looked wholly unprepared. Orestes repeated his line, and Kurt was just about to give Electra's response when the ground beneath him collapsed. All at once he fell, grasping at the air until he disappeared into the earth.

The audience went silent for a moment, unsure of whether or not it was part of the performance. I arched my neck, trying to see what was happening between all of the heads in front of us. Someone in the front row screamed. The crowd erupted in chaos.

Dante and I stood, trying to see what had happened. Headmistress Von Laark, Professor Bliss, Professor Lumbar and Miss LaBarge were pushing through the throngs of people to the front. They kneeled around the hole in front of the great oak, the headmistress shouting inaudible commands at Professor Bliss, who lowered himself into the hole.

Around us, people were running down the aisles; some were screaming, while others were gathering at the front, trying to see what had happened.

Suddenly a hand shot out from the top of the hole, grasping at the edge of the dirt. Professor Lumbar and Professor Chortle grabbed it and pulled, dragging Professor Bliss out of the hole and onto the soggy grass. He was holding a body.

I clutched my collar. It was Nathaniel; I knew it was, even though he was so covered in dirt, I couldn't see his face. Pushing through people, I forced my way to the front. Dante followed a step behind. Amid the chaos of the crowd I couldn't see anything except for Kurt climbing out of the hole, coughing and shaking dirt from his hair. Everyone else was standing over Nathaniel. Two nurses from the audience had run to his side and were checking his pulse, feeling his chest for a heartbeat, opening and closing his eyelids, shining a tiny flashlight into his pupils. Nathaniel remained unresponsive.

By the time I made it to the front, they were already carrying Nathaniel to the nurses' wing. Mrs. Lynch and a few of the administrators were attempting to keep students away from the hole. "Is he okay?" I kept asking over and over, but no one seemed to know the answer.

Up ahead, I spotted Annette LaBarge. She was standing with the headmistress and Professors Lumbar and Urquette in a secluded area of the lawn. I moved behind the trees until I was within earshot, and listened, with Dante just behind me.

"Did you authorize this?" Professor Lumbar said in a voice so low I thought I might have misheard her.

I looked at Dante. "What does she mean, *authorize* it?"

Dante shook his head and put a finger to his lips.

Maybe she meant authorize the play being performed over the catacombs.

The headmistress looked agitated at the question, and hesitated before answering. "No. And this is not the appropriate place to discuss such matters."

"Students are being attacked, Calysta," Professor Lumbar said firmly. She stood like a stone fortress next to Miss LaBarge's slender body, her hands braced over her enormous hips like a jail warden. "*Appropriate place* doesn't apply any more."

"Edith is right," Miss LaBarge said. "We should send the students home. It isn't safe here. The incident last spring, and then Eleanor Bell, and now this."

"Last spring has nothing to do with this," the headmistress said, gazing at the hole in the ground. "I have it under control."

"Last spring has everything to do with this," Miss LaBarge said. "You can't ignore the facts. Three students are dead. Nathaniel might never fully recover from this. And if we can't find the person behind it, we shouldn't allow students to stay at this school."

When the headmistress finally replied, her voice was sharp and cold. "Enough. You're out of line, Annette. This matter is closed."

They dispersed as the headmistress strode off to Archebald Hall. "Fill that hole," she said to the maintenance workers as she passed them. "It's a safety hazard."

I motioned to Dante and we snuck past Mrs. Lynch, making our way to the edge of the hole. The dirt crumbled as I kneeled down. It was deep and gaping, and opened into some sort of chamber that must have been part of the tunnel system. The catacombs, I thought, staring at the roots of the great oak, which broke through the ceiling of the chamber, their tendrils hanging over the centre of the cavern like a gnarled wooden chandelier.

At the bottom was a giant mound of dirt and sticks and grass where Kurt had fallen. "Someone must have buried Nathaniel alive," I said to Dante. "Just like they did to Cassandra. And then Kurt fell through under the weight of the actors. But who would bury him? And right below the school play?"

"Someone who wanted him found," Dante murmured, deep in thought. "Just like Eleanor. The person who killed Eleanor wanted her to be found too. A flood isn't the easiest way to kill someone, or the most inconspicuous. The person who trapped Eleanor wanted her to become Undead..."

Behind me, Mrs. Lynch was ushering everyone back to the dormitories while the professors convened in a group by the oak to discuss what to do next. Hoisting myself up, I felt something hard in the soil. I pushed the dirt away until I found, buried beneath it, Nathaniel's glasses.

I wiped them off with the bottom of my shirt and joined the crowd. I slowed as we walked past the professors.

"I don't know how this went under the radar," Professor Lumbar said. "The Board of Monitors has been patrolling the grounds at night, and the headmistress wasn't aware of it."

Aware of what? That the Board was patrolling?

"Who was on patrol tonight?" Miss LaBarge asked.

"Brandon Bell," replied Professor Lumbar, her tone ominous, as if the fact that this had occurred while *he* was patrolling made it all the more distressing.

"Do you think a student is behind this?" Professor Urquette asked.

"I don't know. At this point, all we can do is conduct a thorough search, and hope the boy saw his attacker," Professor Lumbar replied.

But I knew they wouldn't find anything, because at Gottfried, as in a Greek tragedy, the violence always seemed to happen offstage.

CHAPTER 16

THE BURIAL OF NATHANIEL WELCH

I COULDN'T SLEEP. AND SINCE Eleanor couldn't either, we kept each other company until the sun rose over the mountains. From the window of our dorm room we watched the professors run back and forth between the nurses' wing and the boys' dormitory, their flashlights bouncing around on the patches of yellow grass like fireflies. I couldn't shake the feeling that I was reliving the past.

When morning broke, I went directly to the nurses' wing. It was on the fourth floor of Archebald Hall. I knocked. Suddenly it cracked open, and I stumbled forward, catching myself in the door frame.

A nurse stuck her head out. "Yes? May I help you?"

She was short and stubby, with thick fingers, a tight bun encased in a hairnet, and a name tag that read *Irmgard*. Dark bags hung under her eyes. She looked like a person who had spent the majority of her life being miserable.

"I'm here to see Nathaniel Welch."

"I'm sorry, but no visitors are allowed in right now." She began to close the door.

"But I'm his friend."

"Mr. Welch is still unstable," she said, her voice stern. "Unless you also have a health problem, I'm afraid it will have to wait until tomorrow."

I put my hand on the door to keep her from closing it.

"Please," I said.

She disappeared inside, and for a moment I thought she might be letting me in. Instead, the door opened and I was met by Headmistress Von Laark. "Renée," she said, her blue eyes studying me. "Are you ill?"

"No," I said, trying to be discreet as I craned my neck to see what was going on behind her. Brandon Bell was sitting in the hallway, flipping through some sort of notebook.

"Then you shouldn't be here. I believe you have Physical Education now, no?"

Defeated, I nodded and stepped back as the door closed in my face.

I jogged across campus, stopping by the dining hall on the way. But when I got there I had no appetite. Instead of eating, I took a salt shaker from one of the tables and shoved it into my pocket.

When I reached the green, the rest of the class was gathered by the lake in front of the Ursa Major statue. The night fog was lifting, and the morning was hazy and cool. An owl hooted in the distance. Everyone was talking about Nathaniel. "It must have been a student," Rebecca said. "Someone who knew him. It's too much of a coincidence that he was buried right below where the play was being performed."

"But why Nathaniel?" asked Greta.

And why Eleanor? I asked myself. What did they have in common? Me, I realized.

Thankfully, before I could dwell on my conclusion, our gym teacher, Miriam Hollis, strode through the trees. She was androgynous and energetic, with a boyish voice that cracked when she was excited. She wore gym shorts all the time, even at night when it was freezing.

"I didn't realize it was already nap time," she said, checking her watch. "All right. Everybody up. And try to look alive."

Our Physical Education classes were less about sports and more about survival. Each class focused around a life-threatening environmental situation that required athletic skills. How to shoot a bird with a slingshot. How to run for an extremely long time if we were being chased. How to build a makeshift shelter if we were trapped outside in a storm, which I personally thought was the most unpleasant lesson so far.

"Swimming! Every year thousands of people die from falling into cold water. Why is this? Because they never learned to master their minds and control their bodies! Therefore, today's objective is to master the art of temperature acclimatization and buoyancy."

I raised my hand, interrupting her. "Ms. Hollis, I don't feel well. May I go to the nurses' wing?"

"Certainly not," she said.

I sighed. It was worth a try.

"Only dead bodies float naturally, and that's because they're incapable of sinking. Hence the term, dead man's float. In order to control your buoyancy and your temperature, you have to train your bodies to be comfortable both above *and* below the water. Our first exercise, therefore, will be to float for thirty seconds without moving any of your limbs."

We lined up along the creaky dock on the near bank of the lake, where the shore dropped off into deep water. It was dark and unnaturally still. While everyone else stripped down to their bathing suits, I slipped to the end of the line and fished through my pocket until I found the salt shaker.

I was determined to see Nathaniel. He must have seen the person who buried him alive; he had to know.

Ms. Hollis marched down the line, barking commands. "Pull your shorts up," she said to Brett. He tugged at them, but she rolled her eyes. "Higher. No one wants to see your genitals." Brett's face went red. A few of the girls giggled. "Rebecca does," Bonnie whispered.

I unscrewed the top of the salt shaker, and when I was sure no one was watching, I poured a mouthful of salt onto my tongue and swallowed.

At first, no one noticed. Emily Wurst was clutching a towel that barely covered her large figure. With one swift movement, Ms. Hollis yanked it off and threw it aside. Some of the boys started to snicker, but stopped when Ms. Hollis spun around and glared at them. I began to sweat. A chill ran under my skin, and I started to shiver uncontrollably. My breaths grew deeper, until I was heaving over the ground.

"Stand up straight," Ms. Hollis said to Neil Simons, who was slouching and scratching at his nose. "And for God's sake, stop picking your nose."

Everyone laughed. The sound of it seemed so loud it was deafening. I covered my ears with my hands.

"Stand up straight," Ms. Hollis repeated to Minnie Roberts, whose gnarled braid seemed to be growing longer. My eyes watered, and I blinked, watching the world slow down.

"Stand up straight," she said to me, her words echoing in my ears as my knees buckled. My legs felt too weak to support me, and as if in slow motion, I tottered and then collapsed with a splash into the water.

The shock of the cold twisted my lungs, squeezing the air out of them. With a gasp, I surfaced and then sank back under, unable to keep myself above water. Unlike the world above, the atmosphere beneath the surface was eerie and muted. Things moved slowly, without sound – the weeds swaying with the waves, the fish meandering between rocks and plants. I tried to will my limbs to move, but they were growing so cold that I could barely feel them.

And then something hit the surface above me. At first all I could see was a blur of white plunging through the water. As the water calmed, a shape began to take form, and before I realized it, Dante was beside me. The sunlight filtered through the surface of the water, and he grabbed my arm. Almost as if he were floating, he pulled me up towards the light.

With another gasp, we surfaced, and I coughed up mouthfuls of water. I wrapped my arms around his neck as he lifted me onto the dock. Everyone gathered around us, but Ms. Hollis herded them away. Dante took a towel from the group and wrapped it around my shoulders. I let my gaze drift up to his, wandering from his trousers matted against his thighs to his shirt and tie, transparent with water. His skin glistened in the sun, and I watched his chest rise and fall, the water from his hair dripping down his neck. Where had he come from? He wasn't in my gym class.

A crowd of people hovered over me, their faces blurring into one.

"Renée," a voice said. "Just hold on."

I nodded and let my eyes flutter closed. I felt two arms scoop me up, and all of a sudden I was being carried across the lawn, through the trees and down the path towards Archebald Hall.

"Renée, are you okay?" Dante asked me when we were out of earshot.

I nodded weakly.

"Can you see me? How many fingers am I holding up?"

I blinked. My hair was matted to my face with water and sweat. All I could see was a blur of colours. Maybe this is what Dante felt like. "I ate salt," I said, my voice weak. "I had to see Nathaniel. It was the only way I could get in."

He wiped the water collecting on my eyebrows. "Shh," he said soothingly. "Don't talk now. Rest."

"Where did you come from?" I said weakly.

"I was walking to the front gate when I saw you from the path," he said. "Then I saw you fall in, so I ran."

I closed my eyes, until all I could see was the outline of Dante's face, white and radiant, like the sun. "Thank you."

Nurse Irmgard frowned when she saw me again, and from the way Dante was talking to her, I could tell she was sceptical of my "illness". But after she pressed the back of her hand to my forehead and felt my pulse, her frown quickly changed to a look of concern.

"What happened to her?" she asked, addressing Dante, who was still holding me in his arms.

Dante glanced at me. "She ate salt," he said.

She gave him a confused look that bordered on frustration. "Why would she do something like that?"

Dante shook his head. "The cafeteria food is pretty bland."

Nurse Irmgard didn't appreciate his humour. She called in another nurse, whom she addressed as Wendy. "Prepare Room Three, and start setting up an IV. Her pulse is at ninety beats per second and she's low on electrolytes."

"She'll be okay, won't she?" Dante asked.

Wendy scurried away, and Nurse Irmgard ignored him and marched down the hall and into an exam room. "Set her down here." Dante placed me gently on the exam table. He lingered as she listened to my heart with her stethoscope, and then took my blood pressure. When she realized he was still there, she shooed him away.

Dante tried to protest. "I'd like to stay, if that's all right."

"Absolutely not." Just before she pushed Dante out of the room, the headmistress entered. The nurse busied herself over a movable table as the headmistress approached us.

"Mr. Berlin," she said, and then noticed me on the bed. "And Miss Winters. Back so soon."

"I fell in the lake," I said weakly.

"She ate salt is what she did," the nurse said impatiently, while she sanitized a needle. "And it's a good thing he told me, otherwise it would have taken a lot longer for me to diagnose and rehydrate her."

"And Mr. Berlin jumped in after her?" the headmistress said pensively.

No one said anything.

"Gallant," she said to Dante, "if not slightly familiar, no? As much as I enjoy seeing you so frequently after these mishaps, perhaps one of these days you will each start to focus on your studies?" She rapped her fingers on the table. Neither Dante nor I responded. And without saying more, the headmistress left.

Nurse Irmgard turned her attention to me. "Just a little prick," she said, and inserted an IV drip into my forearm. "You'll have to stay on this for twenty-four hours in order to replenish all of your water content."

"Okay," I tried to say, though no sound came out. My

458

mouth was dry and frothy. I took one last look at her and let myself drift into sleep.

I woke up after dark to a flickering fluorescent light. The nurses' wing was the only place on campus that was permitted to have artificial lights after sunset. At ten o'clock a nurse checked on me one last time, then retreated to her office for the night. I waited until I heard her door close, and saw the lights switch off, and then pulled the IV out of my arm and stood up. My clothes were piled on the countertop. I rummaged through them until I found my jacket, and took Nathaniel's glasses out of the pocket.

I walked down the hall in my hospital gown, my bare feet slapping softly against the tile floor. Every time I passed a room I peeked through the window in the door. Finally I found Nathaniel's room. Trying to keep quiet, I pushed open the door.

When I stepped inside, I was met with an odour so acrid that I had to steady myself against the wall before continuing forward. The burning hair at the séance had given off a similar smell, though this was stronger and more concentrated. The smell of decay. Was this what happened when an Undead was buried? I opened the windows. A draught floated in, and my hospital gown billowed around me.

Nathaniel was lying in bed. The outline of his frail body jutted out under a thin white sheet. A fly circled above him. I swatted it away. Traces of soil still stained the edges of his face, and his eyes were closed. Without his glasses he looked tired and old – much older than he actually was. The skin on his cheeks sagged, and purple bags hung under his eyes. A folding chair was positioned by his bed, and I sat down in it, watching him shift around in bed, the closest he would ever get to dreaming.

"Renée?" he said in a small voice, squinting at me.

I jumped. I didn't think he was conscious. "It's me."

"What are you doing here?"

"I ate a bottle of salt."

Nathaniel tried to ask a question, but could only mouth it. "*Why?*"

"So I could see you."

"That's a little extreme." His voice cracked. "They're going to let me go in a few days."

I highly doubted that. I wasn't even sure if he could sit up.

He patted around the nightstand for his glasses. "Salt is a preservative, you know."

Typical Nathaniel, lying on what could have been his deathbed, talking about the chemical properties of salt. "I have them," I said, holding up his glasses. "I found them on the lawn."

"Thanks," he said. His fingers trembled as he pushed them onto his nose.

"How are you feeling?"

"I'm fine," he said. "Just tired."

I looked at him in disbelief. He didn't look fine. "Are you sure?"

"Yeah," he said, his voice weak, as if he barely had breath to speak the words. "It's just a little dirt."

I sat back in my chair. So he was still denying the fact that he was Undead. "Nathaniel, you were buried. We both know what that means for you. You don't have to lie. I know what you are and it doesn't matter to me."

I touched his arm, but he pulled away.

"Fine," I conceded. "You're fine."

Neither of us spoke for a few minutes. Eventually I broke the silence. "So what happened?"

"After you showed me the files you found in Gideon's room, I got interested. I wanted to go back and look through them again, but they were already gone. I was sure Gideon had followed you to the library and taken them back. So I snuck into his room to look for them."

"Why didn't you tell me?"

"I don't know. I'm just not like you, Renée. I don't really tell people things."

I fidgeted with the tail of my hospital gown.

Nathaniel lapsed into a fit of coughing. I offered him a glass of water, but he refused. "I'm not that good at snooping, so it took me a while to find anything. But eventually I found the files. And Eleanor's diary."

I shook my head. "What?" I had completely forgotten it had even been stolen.

"I found it in Gideon's room. And inside, there were all these notes in Latin about where she went and what she did and at what time. Parts of her schedule were circled, like he was memorizing her routine."

So it was Gideon who killed Eleanor, I thought, my mind racing. But why? "Why didn't you tell anyone?" I asked, incredulous. "Do you still have it?"

"No. I only found it yesterday. The night before the play. I took it from his room and was running to the headmistress's office to show her, when I ran into Brandon Bell on the green. I figured I might as well just show him, since he was on the Board of Monitors. But when he saw Eleanor's folder and diary, with all the notes in it, he went totally berserk. He started accusing *me* of attacking Eleanor. He kept asking me why I killed her.

"I tried to tell him that she was still alive, but it just made him angrier. Then I told him that it was Gideon who had taken the diary, but he was too angry to listen.

"He brought me to the boys' dormitory and locked me in a broom closet. When he let me out, he was carrying a shovel and a burlap bag. I tried to get away, but he was stronger. He stuffed my mouth, put the sack over my head, and pushed me across the lawn.

"He said, 'I'm going to make an example of you, the same way you made an example of Eleanor. Then you people will finally see what happens when you kill innocent girls.'

"Then Brandon brought me to the green. And you know what happened next."

I was speechless. Brandon buried Nathaniel alive? That meant that Brandon knew about the Undead. He knew that Eleanor was Undead and he knew that Nathaniel was Undead. Either that or it was a huge coincidence that he chose to bury him. "But how? Why? Why would Gideon kill Eleanor? He barely knew her." I almost confused myself saying it.

"I don't know," Nathaniel said meekly. "But Brandon has her diary now, and all of the folders."

That must have been what he was flipping through when I saw him earlier today with the headmistress.

Nathaniel coughed. A deep, hacking cough.

"Are you sure you're okay?"

"I told you, I'm fine. But I'm not sure if you are."

I frowned. "What do you mean?"

"Gideon had your file too. I didn't get a chance to look at it, but it was definitely there."

"Why would he want my file? He has no idea who I am."

"I don't know. But there must be something in there of interest. The real question you should be asking is: do *you* know who you are?"

CHAPTER 17

THE BOARD OF MONITORS

IT WAS NIGHT-TIME WHEN I snuck out of the nurses' wing and back to the girls' dormitory. Dante wasn't anywhere to be seen, and when I got back to my room, Eleanor wasn't there either. Probably in the library, I thought. I shut the door. There was only one other person who could give me answers. I pulled out my suitcase and dug inside until I found a folded piece of paper. Picking up the phone, I dialled the nine-digit number scrawled on the bottom of the note. After three rings, Dustin picked up.

"Winters Residence."

"Is my grandfather there?"

"Miss Winters?" he said, lightening his tone. "Of course. One moment."

I waited until the line clicked. "Renée?" My name sounded strong and definitive in my grandfather's baritone voice.

"What aren't you telling me?" I demanded.

There was a long silence.

"Renée, have you ever felt pulled to someone?"

Immediately Dante came to mind. "Yes."

"I'm not talking about love. I'm talking about something else. Something more magnetic."

"Yes," I said, the word leaving my mouth before I could stop it.

"Good. And do you remember when I told you that the early headmasters built tunnels beneath the campus to keep the Plebeian students safe?"

"Yes."

"They also took another precaution. The Board of Monitors."

"But the Board of Monitors does *nothing*. They don't even help Mrs. Lynch patrol the halls."

"Because patrolling the halls isn't their function."

Confused, I waited for him to continue.

"The Board of Monitors was originally formed as a group of living students who had the gift of sensing death. It is virtually impossible to tell the difference physically

466

between the Undead and the living. Monitors represent a small percentage of the population who can actually make that distinction. It's a skill that often runs in families. Monitors are usually drawn to death even from a young age. At Gottfried, the headmistress and professors are able to identify these students through a series of examinations that take place during the admissions process. They then elect a Board of Monitors, whose role is to help protect both the living and the Undead. When a student is elected to the Board, they are then educated by the headmistress about the details of the Undead; before that, their education is no different than yours.

"However, the role of the Board isn't only to protect students. It is also a way for us to begin training young Monitors for what they may face in the world outside of the Academy. After Gottfried, almost all Monitors go on to continue their work in the greater world. It is understood that Monitors are a rare breed, and trained Monitors are even rarer, and Gottfried is one of the few schools that teach a very specific set of skills to those who are perceptive enough to understand how to use them."

"Do the Undead know about Monitors?"

"They are educated about people with the ability to sense death. They are not, however, educated about the Board of Monitors. That would create an environment of fear and resentment at the Academy."

"And Headmistress Von Laark is a Monitor?"

"Yes."

"And all of the professors?"

"Correct."

I gripped the telephone. "So the headmistress and the Board of Monitors could have killed a student?"

"Only if the student was Undead, and had violated the one rule that both humans and Undead share: do not kill."

I let the receiver drop to my shoulder as Minnie's drawing flashed through my mind. The Board of Monitors had buried Cassandra as punishment for taking Benjamin's soul. Minnie had been right all along.

"So it's okay if the headmistress or the Board of Monitors kills an Undead? That isn't right."

"Which is why Gottfried exists. To teach the Undead not to kill. And to teach the Monitors to use their skills only as a last resort."

But that isn't what happened to Nathaniel, I thought. Brandon Bell was a Monitor. That's how he knew what Eleanor had become. And he exacted punishment on Nathaniel without knowing if he was guilty. "That doesn't seem right," I said.

"Who can really say what's right and wrong?" my grandfather said.

"So it's just the professors and the Board? Or are there others?"

"There are others, though Monitors are extremely rare. Usually only a few are admitted every year. Sometimes only one. And even then, there are levels of talent in Monitors, just like there are stages of being Undead, which is why we administer admissions tests. The level of sensitivity towards death varies. Often a mediocre Monitor will be able to sense a bird carcass hidden in a bush a couple of metres away, which is something that a normal person could probably sense too. But they wouldn't be able to find the dead bird across campus. Only the most talented Monitors are elected to the Board of Monitors, where they are educated and extensively trained. Otherwise, it's like giving a loaded pistol to someone who is unable to shoot properly."

There was a long silence as I considered everything my grandfather had just told me, trying to work it out in my head. "So the Monitors protect *and* kill the Undead?"

"Monitors are hunters. But they're also like judges. They have the heavy responsibility of deciding whether an Undead is harmless or harmful. If the latter, the Monitor puts that person to rest. That's why the Monitors can't be replaced by actual police. Because only a select few have the ability to sense death. You being one of them."

"Me?" I said with wonder. Memories began to crowd my head, memories of all the inexplicable moments in my past; things I had done but couldn't explain, things that had happened to me that didn't make sense and never seemed to happen to other people. Was it possible that the reason behind all of it was that I was a Monitor? Yes, I wanted to say. Yes, I was different. I had always been different.

"Renée, you have all of the traits that are characteristic of a Monitor."

"But I can't be. I mean, I'm just me. Renée. I don't have any special sixth sense."

"You found your parents, dead, in the redwood forest."

"That was luck. I saw their car on the side of the road. It was coincidental."

"When you first came to this house, you played croquet with Dustin and found a dead bird on the edge of the lawn."

"The ball rolled to it. It wasn't me. I'm just bad at croquet..." My voice trailed off as I remembered my first Horticulture class, when I found the dead fawn. Or how I'd found the dead mouse in the library. Or how I always seemed to find myself in the crevices of my room, staring at a dead spider or insect.

"You've always been drawn to death. It's as if you can sense it. There were hints early on. Your mother told me about how, as a child, you would wander around the yard, always returning with some sort of dead insect crushed in your tiny fist. During one of my visits when you were six, you found a mouse caught in a trap behind the refrigerator. It smelled wretched; it must have been decaying for days, but it didn't seem to bother you. You picked it up with your bare hands and presented it to us just before dinner. Your father wanted to throw it out, but you insisted on giving it a proper burial. *Sepultura,* as we call it. You did the same with all of your pets."

"*Sepultura?*" I repeated. The second cause of death in Cassandra's file.

"Interment. The preferred method of putting the Undead to rest, at least in these parts. That's another reason for many of the rules at Gottfried – to protect the Monitors while they do their work. The no lights after curfew rule, for example, was designed for this specific purpose."

I no longer cared about the meaning behind the school rules. "But I didn't know. If I were a Monitor, shouldn't I have known, instinctively?"

"Underclass Monitors, such as yourself, take one training class per year, through which the faculty is able to assess their skill sets. For you, that class is Horticulture."

"Horticulture?" I repeated, going over all of our class exercises. The burials, the soil, the graveyard, the medicinal plants, the snow topography.

"And like yourself, they are not told of the existence of

the Undead, but are left to discover it on their own. The process of discovery is incredibly important, as it distinguishes a truly excellent Monitor from a capable one. Information as shocking and disturbing as the existence of the Undead is not something one can merely be told; it has to be felt thoroughly and utterly. This is why I resisted telling you about it, as much as I wanted to."

"So you think that I'm some sort of...killer?"

"Not a killer, a Monitor."

"Monitors still kill people."

"Monitors only kill things that are already dead. The instinct is genetic. It runs in families. It was your great-great-great-grandfather, Headmaster Theodore Winters, who created the Board of Monitors. He was also the man who planted the great oak. In essence, it's literally our family tree. Every generation of our family has been connected to Gottfried since then; most have served as Monitors, even after graduating from Gottfried. Your mother and father included."

"My parents? But they were teachers."

"How do you think they died? They didn't just happen to stumble across a few Undead children. It's a mystery to others, but it's no mystery to our kind. The cloth. The coins. They're tools – tools to put the Undead to rest. Putting two coins on the eyes of the dead is a burial ritual devised by the Greeks. According to them, the dead would

472

use the coins to pay the boatman to cross the River Styx into Hades. The cloth was used for mummification."

"Are you saying that my parents were Undead?"

"No, no; that is impossible. Remember, only those under the age of twenty-one can become Undead. What I've concluded is that they were on the trail of a feral Undead, seeking to put it to rest. They were unsuccessful, and their target took their souls."

"But why was the cloth in their mouths?"

"To prevent their souls from leaving their bodies just before the Undead performed *Basium Mortis*. Just as mummification keeps the dead body from rising, it can also keep the soul of the living from leaving the body. Your parents put the gauze in their mouths themselves, though perhaps they did not act fast enough."

The information was overwhelming. My parents were killed by an Undead? That alone was difficult to accept, but what was even more troubling was that I thought I'd known everything about them, when really, I knew nothing.

"Why didn't they tell me?"

"Your parents wanted to give you a chance at a normal life. That's why we had a falling out. I disagreed. Not about your having a normal life, but about them hiding your talents from you. You can't run away from who you really are, and you can't change it. And why would you want to?

You have an extraordinary gift. That doesn't mean you have to use it, but the choice should be yours, not your parents'."

I considered everything he had told me. Was that why I felt so strange around Dante? Because I was a Monitor, designed to kill him? "So I'm...I'm supposed to kill the Undead?"

"Not all of them. But some."

"But I don't want to kill anyone," I said, thinking of Dante.

"They are killers. Some of them, at least. They often don't understand the situation that they're in, and depending on their age and how bright they are, many don't even realize they're dead. All they know is that something is different. Food doesn't taste good any more. They can't sense changes in the weather. There's an emptiness that wasn't there before – an emptiness that they're constantly trying to fill. It's instinct. Like an animal looking for food."

"But if it's instinct, then why should we interfere? If it's a part of the cycle of nature, then why can't we just let it run its course?"

"Nature also created us. And first and foremost, nature values life. Without life there would be nothing. What's worth more? A child's life, or the life of the Undead, who already had the chance to live?"

I thought about Dante and the person who had his soul. Who's to say that that person's life was more valuable than his? How could anyone compare the value of two lives?

My grandfather interrupted my thoughts. "Renée, this is what you were born to do. It will always be inside of you, no matter how much you fight it. Any talent can be used for both good and evil. If you think it's unfair, then use your talents to make it fair. Work with what you have."

"Are you saying I'm supposed to train to kill the Undead? Even if I wanted to, which I don't," I stressed, "I wouldn't know how."

"There are a number of options. One way to 'kill' an Undead, so to speak, is to completely destroy its body. Fire, explosion, et cetera. Though I find that method to be a little messy and hard to control. The fire spreads, and suddenly you have the California wildfire situation.

"An alternative method is to capture the Undead and bury or embalm it by force. Your parents were fond of that method. It's far more difficult and dangerous, but they found it the most humane."

I swallowed. I didn't want to do any of that.

"Of course, there is another option."

I twisted the telephone cord around my finger, waiting.

"Teach them how to value the lives of others. The way

that Gottfried does. The way that your parents did, as 'teachers'."

"And you? You're a Monitor too?"

"It's in our blood. In your blood."

"A Monitor," I repeated softly.

The realization came over me quickly, and when it did, I collapsed back into my chair. If Dante found his soul somewhere and tried to take it back, I would have to kill him. And if he didn't, he would gradually waste away. Any way I looked at it, the outcome was the same. I was destined to watch him die.

My grandfather was saying something, but I wasn't listening. Cutting the conversation short, I told him I had to go. And throwing on a coat, I climbed into the chimney.

CHAPTER 18
THE GENTLEMEN'S BALLET

I RAN DOWN THE HALL of the basement and slipped out the fire escape and into the cool New England night. I had to talk to Dante. Once outside, I snuck around the building and was about to run onto the path when someone whispered my name.

"Renée."

I jumped, and then relaxed when I saw Dante waiting for me in the shadows by the stoop.

"I looked for you in the nurses' wing, but you weren't there. Are you okay?"

Putting a finger to my lips, I glanced around and

pulled him behind the building.

I told him everything. Well, almost everything.

"But what I still don't understand is why Gideon killed Eleanor," I said.

Dante thought. "Last spring, when Gideon suspected Cassandra was dead, he was furious. He wanted revenge..."

"So he went and found the files," I murmured, "to see if she had been buried, and if so, to find out who did it."

Dante nodded. "He found something in the files. Some sort of evidence."

My shoulders dropped when I realized it. "Minnie's drawing. Her testimony. She said that Brandon Bell was the one who did it."

"Killing Brandon would have been very difficult, considering he's a Monitor, so Gideon decided to kill his sister," Dante said. "But he didn't just kill her. He purposely turned her into an Undead, the one thing he knew Brandon wouldn't be able to live with."

"Brandon understood what had happened to Eleanor," I continued, "and wanted to punish the person who killed her. He found Nathaniel with Eleanor's diary and the files, and assumed it was him, then buried him to make an example of him to all the other Undead. Revenge," I said. "Just like a Greek tragedy."

"Brandon is losing it," Dante said when I was finished. "He's doling out his own personal justice."

Neither of us spoke for a long time. Finally, I broke the silence.

"We have to tell someone."

Dante surveyed the lawn. "You have to stay here."

I shook my head. "No I don't. Why would I do that?"

"It's not safe."

"But it's safe for you?"

"Renée, I'm already dead. But you...you're mortal. You could get hurt."

I took a breath. "Actually, that's not completely true..."

That's when I told him that I was a Monitor. That practically everyone else in my family had been one too. After I broke the news, I closed my eyes, not wanting to see his reaction. He was silent for a long time. Finally, he bent over and kissed me on the forehead. "I've always liked you the way you are, and still do."

But just as the words left his mouth, a hand grabbed my arm. And it wasn't Dante's.

"Caught in the act."

I gasped. Dante and I turned to see Mrs. Lynch smiling behind us. She was gripping me so tightly that I could feel her fingernails pressing into my skin.

"To the headmistress's office." She could barely contain her excitement.

I shook my head. "No, please, we can expla—"

Dante cut me off, taking my hand. "Mrs. Lynch, I made Renée meet me here. It's my fault—"

"How valiant of you," Mrs. Lynch said. "But I highly doubt that." And with that, she tightened her grip on my arm and dragged us towards the headmistress's office.

Archebald Hall was empty and dimly lit now that it was after hours. All of the secretaries had gone home or retreated to their quarters. I gazed at the portraits hanging on the walls as Mrs. Lynch led us into the office, her heels pressing softly into the carpet. She rapped twice on the door, and the headmistress opened it.

"Caught these two again, outside after curfew," Mrs. Lynch said.

"Thank you, Lynette," the headmistress said, gazing at Dante and me, her eyes placid. "Come in."

She shut the door behind us. "Please, make yourselves comfortable."

The two chairs that were normally in front of her desk were gone. So instead, we stood in the centre of the room while the two Siamese cats circled in and out of Dante's legs.

Headmistress Von Laark sat behind her desk and folded her hands. "It seems as though fate has brought us together tonight. I was planning on summoning you both anyway, but your continuing disregard for the *Code of Discipline* seems to have done my job for me."

I shifted uncomfortably.

"Do either of you know why I wanted to see you?"

"No," we said simultaneously.

She leaned back in her chair.

"Nathaniel didn't kill Eleanor," I blurted out. "It was Gideon DuPont. He killed her to get back at Brandon for burying Cassandra. He was the one who stole Eleanor's diary and wrote all those notes in it. And he took the files."

The headmistress put on the pair of glasses hanging from a chain around her neck. "Really?" she said, seeming genuinely surprised, though not at all disturbed – as if I had just told her an interesting fact about the migration patterns of flamingos. "I'll make sure to let the professors and the Board of Monitors know."

Dante and I exchanged confused looks. Why didn't she seem to care?

She tapped her fingers on the desk. "Normally I don't take an interest in the personal lives of my students. My role at Gottfried and with the student body has always been an academic one. But you two" – she waved a hand between us – "your relationship has captivated me."

"Us?" I said slowly. "Why us?" I didn't understand. Beside me, Dante inched closer until our hands were almost touching.

The headmistress ignored my question. "I have been watching you closely, Mr. Berlin, after what happened last spring. And with a name like Winters, I of course wanted to keep an eye on you, too," she said, looking at me. "So when I discovered that you were romantically involved... well, that was a shock, to say the least. And an interesting turn of events. That's the brilliant part about being the headmistress. You spend the year thinking you're in control of your students, that you have to do everything yourself, and that nothing can possibly surprise you. And then something like this just falls into your lap."

As if called, a cat jumped in the headmistress's lap, and in long, languid strokes, she caressed its back until it began to purr.

"It was also fortunate that both of you have a knack for getting into trouble. Our meetings together allowed me to observe you."

"Observe what?" Dante asked.

Once again, the headmistress brushed off the question. "I wasn't sure of it at first, but now there's no longer even a shadow of a doubt in my mind."

My mind raced through all the times I had been called into the headmistress's office, trying to figure out what she was referring to.

"What is it that you're so interested in?" Dante asked. His voice was calm, which comforted me. If Dante wasn't worried yet, then I didn't have reason to be either.

"Are you familiar with Descartes' *Seventh Meditation*?"

Neither of us said anything.

"A seminal work," Von Laark said, almost to herself. "It was banned, you know. Do you know why?"

"Because it was about the Undead," I blurted out. "And it was supposed to be kept a secret."

The headmistress raised a long, sinewy finger. "Yes. And no.

"In that work, Descartes not only discussed his discovery of the Undead, but the process through which they regain their mortality, a process we have since considered a myth, because in the history of history, no Undead has ever found his rightful soul."

Beneath the folds of my coat, Dante laced his fingers through mine.

"It is the question of a lifetime," the headmistress went on. "What would happen if an Undead finds his soul and reclaims it? Would he become human again? Would he cheat death?"

Dante tightened his grip around my fingers as my heart began to race.

"But before I continue, a few questions."

I looked at Dante, confused, but his attention was set on the headmistress.

"Mr. Berlin, when did you die?"

At first Dante didn't say anything. The headmistress stood up and took a step towards him.

"Your year of death? Surely you remember it."

"Sixteen years ago."

"Be precise."

"August twentieth, 1994."

I was concentrating more on the headmistress than on what Dante was saying, but when I heard the date, I went rigid.

The headmistress turned to me. "Do you recognize the date, Miss Winters?"

Of course I did. August twentieth. It was the day I found my parents dead. The same day that I turned sixteen.

Dante died on the day I was born.

I didn't have to say anything. From the look on my face, Dante knew. Finally I understood the strange connection between us. I thought about how Dante always seemed to have a craving inside him when he was around me, as if he were barely able to control himself. Why we always spoke at the same time and said the same things. Why Dante couldn't touch me without making me numb. Why I felt drained and tired after being with him. Why he could only smell things, feel things, taste things when I was close to him. It was why we had been drawn to one another in the first place, and why, I now realized, it was impossible for us to ever be together.

I had Dante's soul.

"How do you feel when you're around her?" the headmistress asked, her eyes dark fixed intensely on Dante with curiosity. "Do you feel sensation? Do you feel alive?"

But Dante wasn't looking at her; he was looking at me, hoping I would say something that would prove her wrong.

"What I'm about to ask you to do should be painless. Perhaps even enjoyable. For one of you."

She approached me and spoke in a voice that was dark and commanding. "Now, what I want you to do is to give him your soul."

"And why would she do that?" Dante said.

"Because she's in love with you." She turned to me. "Think about your situation," the headmistress said. "He only has a few years left. You alone are in control of his fate."

Nausea curled through my body as I began to realize that she was right. But before I could say anything, Dante's voice cut through the air.

"No. She won't. I won't let her."

I watched his body tighten as he readied to approach the headmistress. She took a step back.

"You can do whatever you want to me," she said quietly, "but it won't make this go away. Renée will always know what she has to do. I'm not forcing her to do anything." She glanced towards the door. "It's unlocked," she said.

Dante gave her a suspicious look, and then took my arm. "Renée, let's go."

But I didn't move.

"Renée, come on."

"No," I said. "Wait. I want to hear what she has to say."

The headmistress smiled. "See? There are things worse than being Undead. Such as watching the person you love die when you knew you could have helped them."

My stomach felt hollow as I imagined my life without Dante.

He pulled my face in his direction. "Renée, no. If you give me your soul, you'll die."

"She won't *die*," the headmistress said. "She'll become Undead. Haven't you ever wondered what it was like? To never feel pain? The pain of your parents' deaths?"

I had wondered what that would be like. I gazed at Dante. His eyes pleaded with me.

The headmistress continued. "The desire to stay alive, regardless of the consequences, is a value of modern society. In the ancient world, the only thing men aspired to was dying an honourable death. Just think of what you could accomplish in death. Not only would you be giving your love his life back, but you would be shedding light on one of the greatest mysteries of all time. The mystery behind death. If you, Renée, can give life to another, what could that mean for the world? The possibilities are endless."

"Renée, you don't have to do this. There are other ways."

The headmistress laughed. "No – no there are not. You will die of decay in five years, and Renée will live a long, lonely life knowing that she could have saved you but didn't."

"What good is saving me? We would only switch roles," Dante argued.

I turned to him. "We would have more time," I said. "Don't you want that?"

Dante looked at his feet, shaking his head. "I want you. Right now. The way you are."

"Don't you understand? You can't have me. We are the end of each other's lives. One of us has to die, and I'd rather face death than live without you."

Dante turned to me and grasped my face in his hands. "Renée, look at me." His voice was pleading. "I had my chance. I lived my life. And now I have you, and that's enough."

The headmistress strode towards me, resting her hand on my shoulder. When she spoke, her voice was lower, deeper, darker. "It's either your life or his," she said.

Dante's eyes searched mine, begging me not to do it. "Let it go."

"I'm not afraid of death," I said, looking at Dante. And

this time I knew it was true. "I'm afraid of life without you."

Before he could respond, there were two knocks on the door. I froze and stared at it as it opened. Mrs. Lynch stepped inside, pulling Gideon by the arm. "Headmistress? I found this one lurking around the girls' dormitory again."

"You!" I shouted, pointing at Gideon. "It was him. He killed Eleanor! He stole the files and Eleanor's diary, and then he trapped her in the basement and broke the pipes."

Confused, Mrs. Lynch pulled out her metre stick, but before she could do anything, Gideon pushed her out of the room and slammed the door. I could hear her protests from the hallway as Gideon bolted it shut.

"Gideon," the headmistress said, her voice wavering. "Unlock that door immediately."

Ignoring her, Gideon took off his dinner jacket and slung it over the doorknob, his eyes set on me.

"Gideon?" the headmistress repeated. "Did you not hear my request?"

He rolled up his sleeves.

"If Renée's claims are true, we can still help you," she said, taking a tenuous step towards him. "You still have options. But you must do as I say."

Dante pushed me behind him as Gideon walked towards us, his eyes dark and wild.

"I warn you: if you touch anyone in this room, you will regret it," Von Laark continued.

Suddenly Gideon turned to her, his voice silencing the room. "Shut up."

Her face ablaze, she snatched a roll of gauze from her desk and approached him. "How dare you," she said. "This is my school and I demand that you follow my orders."

Dante shielded me with his arms as we watched them collide in the middle of the office, the headmistress trying to restrain Gideon as he pushed her back towards the wall. Even though she was a Monitor, she was no match for his strength. Pinning her against the ground, Gideon pressed his lips to hers.

Colour began to flow through his pale skin, like blood pooling beneath the surface. The headmistress struggled, her arms flailing against his back. Muffled cries floated through the room. "No!" I said. "Wait!" But Gideon didn't stop.

Slowly, her arms grew paler, weaker, until they fell limply to her sides. I watched in horror as her legs began to convulse against the floor, relaxing to a twitch until all was still.

Heaving, I covered my mouth with my hands, unable to take my eyes off her feet. I let my shoulders slump, unable to hold them up any longer.

When I looked up, Gideon was approaching me. I backed away from him, pushing myself against the wall. His face was flushed and pulsing as he loosened his tie, the veins in his arms flowing with life.

With a swift movement he lifted me up and lowered his mouth to mine.

"No!" I heard Dante scream as he ran to us and pushed Gideon off me.

With a gasp, I fell back and watched as they struggled, Gideon's strength growing with the soul of the headmistress streaming through him. The Siamese cats crouched and yowled in the corner as Gideon and Dante struggled, knocking over books and papers, breaking the glass of the hutch behind the headmistress's desk, the shovels, which I now realized were Monitor burial tools, clattering to the ground around them. I watched in horror as Dante pushed Gideon onto the desk, breaking the hourglass, the sand and glass spilling across the floor around me.

I screamed, the glass cutting through my skin.

Upon hearing my voice, Dante turned to me. Taking advantage of the lapse, Gideon slipped out of his grasp, picked up his tortoiseshell glasses from the floor, and unbolted the door, disappearing into the hall.

"Are you okay?" Dante asked, kneeling by my side.

I nodded, barely able to speak. "I'm fine."

"Stay here," he said, touching my cheek. "So I know

you'll be safe." And with that, he grabbed a loose shovel that had fallen from the shattered hutch and ran out the door in pursuit of Gideon.

Picking myself up, I followed him.

I caught up to them on the green. They were in front of the great oak, teetering around the gaping hole that Nathaniel had been buried in. Maintenance hadn't filled it in yet, but had sequestered it with caution tape, leaving only one thin rope ladder dangling into the pit. Gideon stepped around the hole and Dante followed, thrusting the shovel at him. Every time Dante swung at Gideon, Gideon seemed to move out of the way at just the right moment – a hop, a swish, an arabesque, in an elaborate gentleman's ballet.

I circled them as Dante raised the shovel over Gideon's head. I closed my eyes, not wanting to see the outcome, even though I knew they were both already dead. But just as Dante brought the shovel down over Gideon's skull, Gideon ducked away and grabbed the shovel from him, splitting it into shards.

The rest happened quickly. Gideon tackled Dante, thrusting him into the dirt by his neck, pushing him dangerously close to the edge of the hole. If Dante fell in, that would be the end. He couldn't go underground, and the hole was at least four metres deep. I wouldn't be able to get him out by myself before Gideon took my soul.

In horror, I watched as Gideon stood over Dante, one hand around his neck. I had to do something. I was a Monitor. I was supposed be able to handle this.

Without thinking, I picked up a broken shard of Dante's shovel and ran up behind them. With all the force I could muster, I thrust it into Gideon's back.

Surprised, he spun around and threw me off, pulling the shard from his back and stalking towards me, his shirt bloodied and ripped. I inched back on the grass as he loomed over me, holding the jagged shovel. Just before I closed my eyes, Dante took him from behind, and Gideon fell on top of me, pushing the wooden shard into my skin. I winced as I tried to pull the handle out of my side while they grappled around me, their bodies nudging the wood shard deeper into my stomach.

Slowly, their grunts seemed to fade as my eyes fluttered. And as I let them close, I heard Dante calling my name, clutching my hand as we both fell through the caution tape into the deep, dusty hole.

With a cry, I pulled the handle of the shovel from my side and opened my eyes. I was lying in a mound of soil and rock in the catacomb beneath the great oak. Across the cavern, I could see Gideon's grass-stained trousers and loafers, limp.

"Dante?" My voice echoed through the darkness as I dug through the dirt and felt his arm beside me. "Dante!"

Brushing the soil off him, I took him in my arms and tried to wake him. "We're underground," I whispered. "What do I do?" He was barely conscious.

Mustering up courage, I wiped the dirt from my face and stood. "Don't worry," I said, trying to pick him up. "I'm going to get us out of here." But as much as I tried, I couldn't lift him. Sinking to the ground, I wrapped my hands around his neck and buried my face in his shirt.

"Dante, please wake up," I pleaded. "I'm not strong enough. I can't carry you out."

As if I had willed it, his lips moved. I watched as they parted slightly, taking in a faint breath. And sitting there beside him, watching him die, I knew what I had to do.

Why is it that you enjoy life the most when you're about to lose it? The only way I could save Dante was to give him my soul. I was going to die. Strangely enough, the realization only made me feel more alive. I took one last look at the world. Somewhere far away, Annie was sitting down for dinner with her family; my grandfather was sipping tea and watching the evening news; and the girls on my floor were finishing up their homework and getting ready to crawl into bed. I felt as if I were worlds away from them. They had time to take it all for granted – all the small pleasures in life that I was already beginning to miss – the first cool breath of autumn, the empty silence you hear just after turning off the television, the smell of chicken roasting in an oven. These things only existed in my mind now, and soon, even that would be gone.

I let my eyes travel across Dante one last time – his nose, his lips, his eyes, now closed. It all seemed familiar yet somehow still unexplored. This is what it meant to feel: realizing that part of the value in life is knowing that everything around you could be taken away. I loved him, I thought, already thinking in past tense. I love him. This would be my goodbye.

I lifted my hand to his cheek, touching his skin for the last time, and I pulled him towards me, until my lips grazed his.

"I love you," I said.

And I gave him a kiss. A real kiss. Because if I had anything left to give, I wanted to give it.

Suddenly I felt his hand on the back of my neck, pulling me towards him with a force I had never experienced before. Unable to help myself, I succumbed to his embrace. The air escaped my lungs. I gasped and grabbed at the grass. And the world as I knew it faded away.

CHAPTER 19

THE UNTIMELY DEATH OF DANTE BERLIN

I COLLAPSED ON THE GRASS. Slowly, I felt all of the warmth in my body leave me, as if it were being pulled from my mouth like a thin thread of air. And as it left me, all of my memories began to unravel. Scenes from a previous life flashed through my mind and then vanished, the people and places distorted and dreamlike. Annie, my parents, California, Wes – I could barely recognize them before they disappeared; their figures fleeting and unreal, as if my entire life before Gottfried had been imagined. I grew weak. My breathing became thin. And then suddenly I woke up.

I was outside the girls' dormitory, lying on the grass by the stoop. It was night-time. Was I dead? I wasn't sure. I stretched and stood up, but I didn't feel the same. It felt like I had been lying there for hours. I was wearing clothing that was strangely familiar, yet not mine – an oxford shirt and a pair of trousers that were worn at the knees. I was about to lean over and examine them when I heard movement around the side of the building, the soft padding of footsteps against the ground. Quickly, I ducked into the shadows and waited.

But the person who emerged wasn't the headmistress or Mrs. Lynch. It was me. I was in my coat, my brown hair dangling freely over my shoulders. I looked pretty, I thought.

Unable to control my mouth, I uttered one word. "Renée."

She turned to me, her look of surprise fading into relief as she put a finger to her lips and pulled me behind the building.

"I looked for you in the nurses' wing, but you weren't there. Are you okay?" The words came out of my mouth before I realized what I was saying. They were the same phrases Dante had said to me earlier that night, before Mrs. Lynch escorted us to the headmistress's office. I tried to stop speaking, but my body was out of my control.

My past self was standing in front of me, saying

something about the Board of Monitors and the headmistress, but I wasn't listening; I already knew what she was going to say. Instead, I stared at her with an affection and longing that I could never have felt towards myself. I wasn't reliving my life; I was reliving Dante's.

"I've always liked you the way you are, and still do." I said to my former self. The scene faded away, and I was transported to a darkened classroom in Horace Hall. I was standing in the shadows, water dripping from my clothes. The old Renée was beside me, her clothes matted to her body.

"Well, as your teacher, I should make you write lines," I found myself saying.

The old Renée gave me a challenging look. A droplet of water inched down her nose. "What do you want me to write?"

I took a step towards her. "*Cupido*," I uttered.

She raised her hand to my face, and I closed my eyes, feeling the softness of her palm. As she passed her hand over me, it awakened senses I hadn't felt in years. My nose, my eyes, my lips, they trembled at her touch.

"Do you feel different when you're around me?" she whispered.

Yes, I thought. Yes.

The room became blurry, and I was transported to the Observatory. It was a different day, an older day, and the

September sun was shining through the glass panes of the ceiling. The door opened, and Nathaniel walked in, a younger version of Renée next to him. Her hair was shorter, and she looked more innocent, her face still sun-kissed from the summer.

I sat down next to her, feeling her presence like a force beside me. I didn't know what to say, so I looked at the board. Something strange was happening to my body. A prickling sensation came over me, and I could actually feel the breeze floating through the window. I could hear the nuances of nature – the leaves of the trees rustling against each other, the delicate sound of sparrows on the branches, all mixing together like some sort of melody. Renée bent over to pull a notebook out of her bag, and I could even make out the smell of her shampoo. Finally she turned to me.

"Why do you keep staring at me?" she muttered under her breath.

Her voice was soft and low, and I was surprised by how forthright she was. How could I not stare at her? Even here, the afternoon sun shone through the glass ceiling, illuminating her face in a warm, rosy light, as if she were an otherworldly being, something sent to me by fate. No, she could never know that I had watched her, wanted her, loved her, from that very moment.

"You have pen on your face. Here." Immediately I regretted saying it.

Her face turned red as she rubbed her face self-consciously. "Oh."

Suddenly the scene fast-forwarded. "So you think I'm charming?" I said, leaning over because I wanted to get closer to Renée. "Is that why *you* keep staring at *me*?"

"Alarming, not charming. And no, I'm just curious."

"Curious?" I said, trying to control my desire to hold her, to kiss her.

Her voice wavered. "Why don't you talk to anyone?"

"I thought that's what we were doing."

She was saying something, but I barely heard her.

Dozens of thoughts ran through my mind. Where did she come from? Where had she been my entire life? What did she like and what did she hate? Would she let me learn? Instead I settled for something more reasonable. "That's exactly what I was thinking."

I traced my fingers around her freckles, wanting to collect them in my palm. She said she was from California.

I held out my hand beneath the desk. "I'm Dante."

She bit her lip, doubting herself. "Renée," she said finally, and slipped her hand into mine. It was small and delicate.

Her body froze as we touched. I felt her warmth creeping into me, giving me life again. Her expression shifted from nervous to confused to bewildered. I pulled my hand away from hers and sat very still, trying to understand what had just happened. Everything blurred to black.

Finally, the world came into focus again, and I was running down a long dirt driveway. I couldn't control my legs and I didn't know where I was. It was a place I had never been to before – a large field with a plywood fence surrounding it. The land was flat on either side and patched with yellow, overgrown grass. To the far left were a barn and a water trough, presumably for horses. Beyond that were other houses, all spread out over acres of land. They looked exactly the same as the house the driveway was leading towards. It was small and square, with a shingled roof and a wrap-around porch littered with old lawn furniture. The rocking chair swayed in the wind.

Suddenly I was standing in the doorway of a bedroom in my house; no – Dante's house. A girl was lying in bed, the frail outline of her legs visible beneath the sheets. I didn't recognize her, but somehow I understood that she was my sister. Dante's sister. The curtains were drawn and the room was dark.

I blinked, and I was in an aeroplane, cradling my sister, Cecelia, in my arms. She was wrapped in a blanket, her eyes tired and barely open, her face red and matted with sweat. "It will be okay," I whispered to her. "We're almost there."

Sitting beside us were a man and a woman who I knew to be my parents even though I couldn't recognize them. The man was wearing a flannel shirt and a pair of worker's trousers stained with grease. He had Dante's eyes. The woman was wrapped in a shawl and leaning over Cecelia, petting her hair. She was crying.

All at once we heard something crack. The erratic swoosh of the propellers as they slowed. And then my father screaming as we plummeted to the ground, "I pray to thee, O true and living God. I believe in thee, O eternal Truth. My hopes are fixed on thee, thou endless Good and Mercy. I love thee with my whole heart above all things, O my kindest Father, my highest Good."

The world became darker, and I was underwater. I knew that this was my last moment on earth. The waves were violent and I was sinking. Salt water stung my eyes and throat as I was flushed under. I tried to swim to the surface, but couldn't. I opened my eyes. Everything around me was a foggy blue. Bubbles rose around me, swirling like schools of fish. I reached out, trying to catch them in my fist, and slowly, everything withered away.

I was pulled out of my reverie by two hands pushing me away. My body convulsed as I felt Dante leave me, his memories spooling out of me like a reel of film. Our lips parted, and I gasped.

CHAPTER 20
RENAISSANCE

TO BE REBORN. I SHOULD have known that it was my destiny. Even the meaning of my name pointed towards it. Renée. Renaissance. The rebirth. With a start, I opened my eyes.

I was being carried down a hallway and out into a blue sunny day, so bright I had to close my eyes. Was I dead? Was Dante dead?

Slowly, I peeked open an eye. I was wearing a hospital gown. Someone was carrying me down the path towards the chapel. Turning my head, I looked up. It was Dante.

"Hi," I said, my voice wavering.

Dante looked down and smiled. "Hi."

I swallowed. "Am I dead?"

Dante took a turn to the left. The path was empty. It must be early, I thought. "No."

"Am I alive?"

Dante sighed. "No."

My eyes widened as I took in my new world. Flowers grew wildly out of the soil, and leaves budded on the trees – the first signs of life after a long, dark winter. "How long—"

I didn't even have to finish my sentence. "Ten days."

"And you? You're—?"

Dante looked away.

I let out a sigh. So the kiss worked. "Where are we going?"

"You'll see."

He looked older now, more masculine. He aged well, I told him, like an expensive cheese.

He laughed. "Did I ever tell you how romantic you are?"

I smiled.

Dante took me to the cemetery behind the chapel, now overgrown with poppies.

"Hold out your hands," he said, lifting my arms until they extended out like wings. He carried me through the field of red, my hands dangling limp on either side. And as the cold of my fingers grazed the tops of the flowers, the petals closed, leaving a trail of green behind us.

I blinked, unable to believe that this was my life. That this was real. That life could be this beautiful.

Setting me down in the middle of the field, we lay side by side, our hands barely touching as we watched the reflection of the clouds in each other's eyes.

"I wish I could wake up to this every day," I said.

"You can't wake up without sleeping."

I looked down, realizing what he meant. It hadn't fully dawned on me yet that I was Undead. Lifting the left side of my gown, I looked at my stomach, where the shards of the shovel had cut into me. To my surprise it had already healed, leaving behind a jagged pink scar. Dante traced it with his finger.

"Your grandfather is coming to pick you up today," he said.

"Does he know?"

Dante shook his head. "It doesn't matter."

"Why not?"

"Renée, this isn't what I want."

"Us?"

Dante gave me a sad smile. "No, this. I brought you here so we could be alone. So we could say goodbye."

"What do you mean, goodbye?"

"Just for the summer. But you have to promise that

when you leave this field, you leave me here."

"You don't mean you're going to kiss me?"

Dante nodded.

"You can't! I won't let you!"

"I know," he said, lacing his fingers through mine as he lowered his lips to mine until they were barely touching. "But you also can't stop me."

I closed my eyes as I felt an explosion of sensation run through my body. My fingers tightened around his.

"Why are you doing this? I want you to be alive."

"Because," he said, tracing a finger along my cheek. "Real love is selfless."

"I miss you already," I whispered, my insides in panic.

Dante plucked a flower and tucked it behind my ear. "I'm with you, always."

And then he leaned over and kissed me.

ACKNOWLEDGEMENTS

Ted Malawer, for making everything happen; Ari Lewin and everyone at Hyperion, for making me a better writer and for turning my manuscript into something more beautiful than I could ever imagine; Donna Bray, for taking a chance on this book and on me.

My Columbia workshops, especially those of Gary Shteyngart, Binnie Kirshenbaum and Nicholas Christopher, for their invaluable feedback on this book. L.J. Moore, for Romulus and Remus and her insights into Latin and Roman history.

Nathaniel, for being a bytz. Brandon, for his perverse zombie knowledge; Katherine and Bec, for keeping me sane; and the rest of my extraordinary friends, for generously lending me their names.

Finally, Kivi, my real-life Dante, for his jokes and his friendship; and my family – Mom, Dad, Paul, kitty senior and kitty junior – for their enthusiasm, humour, and their many "useful" zombie suggestions.

Thank you.

ABOUT THE AUTHOR

YVONNE WOON grew up in Worcester, Massachusetts, USA, in an old stone colonial house surrounded by woods. It was here that she first developed a taste for the macabre, and she has been writing mysteries ever since.

Yvonne attended the prestigious Worcester Academy prep school in Boston, where, like Renée, the length of her skirt was routinely measured. She first began thinking about Latin and the Undead while studying in the library of Columbia University, New York, where she obtained a Masters of Fine Arts in fiction.

Dead Beautiful is her debut novel.

For more breathtaking discoveries, go to
www.deadbeautiful.co.uk

For more intoxicating reads, go to
www.fiction.usborne.com